A Light Emerges

S.J. Cunningham

A Ramsay Castle Mystery, Book 3

A Light Emerges: A Ramsay Castle Mystery, Book 3
by S.J. Cunningham

ISBN 978-1-964369-13-6
Paperback Edition

This edition published by S.J. Cunningham:
www.sjcunningham.net.

"Sweet Scotia! From thee a
light emerges..."
From a lost hymn celebrating the wedding
of Margaret, only daughter of King
Alexander III of Scotland, to King Erik of
Norway (1281)[1]

---

[1] Barrow, G.W.S., "The Kingdom of the Scots: Government, church and society from the eleventh to the fourteenth century 2nd Edition." Edinburgh University Press, July 11, 2003.

Chapter 1

"In just a few days, ye'll be my wife."

Liza Ramsay shut her eyes and leaned back against the broad chest of Lachlan McClaren as his powerful arms snaked around her waist. "I cannae wait," she whispered, mirroring his Scottish brogue.

She tipped her head back to look up at his chiseled face, and he angled his head down, pressing his lips against hers, softly, slowly. Lingering…

"Ach, come on, ye two!" The booming voice of Bruce Baxter interrupted their bond. "I don't need to be seein' the likes o' that this early in the mornin'."

"You're the one who called us down here at this ungodly hour," Liza exclaimed, but she wore a smile. At six in the morning in the summer months in the Lowlands of Scotland, the sun—and Liza—had been up for hours. She hadn't slept well, for mostly delightful reasons. She caught her bottom lip between her teeth, remembering Lachlan's lips on hers.

But there were other reasons sleep eluded her. Those reasons, she didn't want to think about. She hadn't told Lachlan of the disturbing and elusive dreams she'd been having the past few weeks. Instead, she chalked the nightmares up to some secret disquiet about the upcoming wedding. In fact, she couldn't remember most of the images, though she did remember the feeling of being trapped in a time that was not her own. She remembered the terror. And she remembered the loneliness.

She forced those thoughts and emotions aside and returned her attention to Bruce Baxter, the big, burly contractor who had overseen the year-long renovations of the Ramsay Castle, in particular the sanctuary, which over the course of the last few centuries had fallen into disrepair. If Bruce noticed Liza's distraction, he gave no indication. And Liza did her best to mask any outward appearance of worry, lest she quell his enthusiasm.

She granted him an encouraging look.

Given their current warm relationship, it was hard to believe Bruce had once been virulent in his opposition to Liza's inheritance of the castle…and to Liza herself. Since the murder of two billionaires at the castle earlier in the year—along with Liza's own near demise—the local tradesman had warmed significantly toward the American heiress who now claimed ownership of the ancient estate.

"Aye, and it was fer good reason I called ye down here. Because the chapel is now complete, and a whole three days before the ceremony!"

Liza glanced up at Lachlan. "Seventy-two entire hours." She gave him a wry smile.

Lachlan's eyes twinkled. "Right under the wire." Then he murmured in her ear, "I told ye I wouldn't let ye down."

At that moment, Liza couldn't fathom Lachlan ever doing anything to disappoint her.

The sentiment was naïve, of course. Since she'd met Lachlan a year earlier, they'd both done plenty to let each other down. But they'd also saved each other. And every one of those challenges had created the strong bond they shared today, which would carry into their life together as husband and wife.

Bruce shifted from one foot to the other. "Ye can stare at each other any time," he grumbled. "Today is yer first look at the renovations."

Liza pulled away from her soon-to-be husband and approached the doors to the chapel. "I'm ready to be awed, Mr. Baxter."

Bruce made a gruff sound at the back of his throat, but he flashed a rare and tender smile at her. "Lady Ramsay...yer chapel."

He pushed open the doors to the renovated sanctuary.

Liza's hands flew to her mouth.

Through a kaleidoscope of stained glass that extended the entire length of the east wall, the early morning sunlight glittered with thousands of richly colored prisms. Liza followed the sparkling rays to the arched ceiling, where two bronze chandeliers hung elegantly. The walls were adorned with light fixtures that resembled ancient torches.

Liza drifted into the room, running her hands over the smooth mahogany of the pews. She gazed at the antique piano positioned in the corner. Though unassuming, she knew the notes of the instrument—alongside the sound of traditional bagpipes—would fill the room with rich music on her wedding day.

As if she'd traveled a few days into her future, she walked slowly on an elaborate red runner toward the altar at the center of the far wall.

There, Liza would stand with Lachlan, and in front of friends and family, they would pledge their lives to each other.

She'd be lying if she said she felt no anxiety. The strange, dark dreams of another reality were proof of it.

But in *this* reality, standing in this beautiful space, she waited for some sense of unease to creep into her mind. Some lingering doubt as to whether she was making the right decision.

There was nothing but the rush of relief and the knowledge she had found her person—her other half. Her *anam cara*.

She looked up at the light, allowing it to wash over her, and when she turned, Lachlan was staring at her.

"It's perfect," she said.

"Ye're perfect," he murmured back softly.

Before Lachlan could reach for her, Bruce rushed between them. "Do ye love it? I ken ye'd love it. The Fleming Stained Glass employees hae been awaitin' yer reaction. They're as excited as ye are."

With one last glance and smile for Lachlan, Liza turned her attention to Bruce. "You did a fabulous job, Bruce. Callum Ramsay would be pleased. And proud," she added.

At that, Bruce colored. "I'd hae done anythin' for the late Laird Ramsay."

It was hard to believe it'd been a year since Callum had died trying to protect the castle for his long-lost relative Liza.

Liza, Lachlan, and Bruce all seemed to pause together to pay a moment's homage to his memory.

"And now, I'd do anythin' fer ye, Lady Ramsay. Fer both o' ye," he said, gesturing toward Lachlan. "E'en if ye are a McClaren."

"The feelin' is mutual," Lachlan responded.

They'd all come so far over the prior twelve months. When Liza thought about the time that had passed, there was the good—falling in love with Lachlan—and the bad—almost being trapped and murdered in her own home...*twice*.

But it was more than that. She was a different person now.

Still...there was a small part of her that didn't quite

think she deserved the Ramsay Estate.

Of course, she was a Ramsay in name. Her estranged father had died for her opportunity to claim her birthright. It had been bequeathed to her from the late laird of this land.

But there had been others who'd done so much more for this land and this country. At heart, she was a simple American from a rural part of the United States. Though she lived in Scotland full time now, she wasn't truly *of* this land.

Over the stark beauty of the refinished chapel and under a shadow of shame, Liza felt in danger of tears.

Lachlan, with his keen eye, said, "And now, I think it's time we got back to work. There's still a lot to be done before the guests arrive." Liza shot him a secret, grateful look.

Bruce nodded in agreement. "Right ye are. I need tae head into the city today, and tomorrow the tent company will be here tae start settin' up on the lawn. They're goin' tae wrap the entire sycamore in lights—a beacon fer our guests and the whole of Cockpen and Bonnyrigg."

He flashed Liza a quick, brilliant smile before transforming back into his surly self and plodding out of the chapel, leaving Liza and Lachlan alone in the splendid sanctuary.

"The sycamore..." she said to Lachlan. The tree was sacred, not only to the land of the Ramsay Estate, but because of what had happened there.

"It'll be all right," he answered, aware of the direction of her thoughts. "I dinnae think Brodie Graham would hae wanted his place of death tae be a reminder of tragedy forever."

Lachlan was probably right, though her edginess about having a castle full of guests had also re-emerged. While the plan had always been to fill the castle with friends and family to celebrate the wedding, now that the time was here, she wasn't sure she was as ready as she thought she'd been. The ghosts of Aaron Scott and Sergei Popova were never far from her mind, either, though the rest of the world would never know what had happened to those men in her home.

She sucked in a few deep breaths, attempting to quell her nerves. Her mind was racing, and she was manufacturing scenarios for anxiety. She needed to relax. She needed to breathe.

"It's all goin' tae be just fine." Lachlan's voice was soothing and reassuring.

She exhaled and nodded. "It's hard not to remember it all."

"Ah, I ken. But soon we'll have a whole new set of memories fer ye to think about." He pulled her close.

Again, wrapped in Lachlan's embrace, Liza shut her eyes and inhaled the clean scent of him. "Can't we just get married here alone?"

"Aye, we could," his deep voice rumbled into her

ear against his chest. "But dinnae ye want yer gran and pop tae see ye married in the place that's yer birthright?"

She nodded. It had been Christmastime when she'd last seen her grandparents from Pennsylvania. They didn't travel as well as they used to, and she was thankful they were still able to make the trip across the Atlantic.

"And don' ye want all yer friends from the States tae be with ye?"

Liza lifted a shoulder. Since she'd relocated overseas permanently, she'd reconnected with and become closer to friends she'd fallen out of touch with when she'd been engaged to Owen. Thank God he'd cheated on her, she thought. The irony wasn't lost on her. But if the man-child *hadn't* cheated, she might still be festering her life away—friendless, loveless, joyless—in the suburbs of Boston.

"Don' ye want Marion Dean tae officiate the ceremony?"

Liza considered Detective Chief Inspector Marion Dean with her halo of short dark curls and her observant gaze. The woman had saved Liza's life on more than one occasion, and though she'd nearly put Lachlan in prison for life, the two of them had made their peace. Lachlan had agreed eagerly when Liza had suggested Dean act as officiant. She hadn't seen Dean since the detective had left the police force to contract on a full-time basis for billionaire Petrus Bothas, and Liza missed her stern and surly friend.

"Don' ye want everyone tae see what a radiant bride ye'll make?" Lachlan asked quietly. "'Cause I surely do."

At this, she let out a quiet laugh. She wasn't a vain person, but her wedding dress was beautiful—an antique ivory lace gown with a long train. It was the perfect mix of vintage and modern. She couldn't wait for Lachlan to see her in it. "Maybe I do," she admitted.

Lachlan tipped her chin up with the tip of his finger. "I want tae see ye walk down this very aisle and meet me at the altar in front of God and everyone." His voice trembled slightly in its whisper, and he leaned his head down once more to kiss her. "I'm goin' tae be by yer side for the rest of our lives."

"Dinnae the two o' ye hae a bedroom?" Bruce's voice boomed, echoing through the room with its rich acoustics.

"I thought ye went into town," Lachlan shot back.

"I'm headin' that way soon."

Liza noticed the yellowed and brittle item he held in his big hands. "What have you got there?" She took a step forward, and he held it out toward her.

"I'd been meanin' tae give this tae ye. One of the men found it when we were workin' on the chapel last winter. What with the commotion surroundin' that group of fools…" He gave a disgusted look, clearly remembering Bothas, Scott, Rabbie Rose, Daphne St. James, and the other rich men and women who'd caused so much havoc in their lives. "…I'd put it away fer safekeepin' and forgot about it."

Liza craned forward to see it better. "Is it parchment?" She reached out to examine the paper-like item lined with faint, thin handwriting. The surface was dry, soft, and smooth to the touch.

"Looks like vellum," said Lachlan, peering at the document. "Fine rolls, maybe?"

Liza squinted to try to make out the writing. "What are fine rolls?"

"Financial records. Maybe for the Barony of Ramsay to record the payments and debts of its tenants. Its tax records."

"Is there a date recorded?" Liza asked. The material looked and felt sturdy enough, but it was extremely old, and she was afraid it might disintegrate at her touch. "What is the material made from?"

Lachlan took the item from Bruce. "Could hae been made from wood pulp, or cloth, or even calfskin." He bent his head over the tiny symbols. "A date," he exclaimed. "Looks like twelve-ninety-something." He leaned closer. "I cannae make out the last number."

"Is it possible this is original?"

Lachlan shrugged. "The original structure was built in the twelfth century. I'm not sure why these records would hae been hidden in a wall, but given the quality of the parchment, from the look of it, this very well may be authentic."

Liza reached out tentatively. "May I?"

"It's yours."

Liza held the document delicately in her palms and tried to make out some of the letters. She clearly saw the name 'Ramsay', along with the names 'Claray', 'Uilleam', and 'Elesbeth'.

"Elesbeth," she whispered. Her mind frayed at the edges. Her thoughts blurred, and the world became foggy.

She felt a shift in consciousness—a tumble of voices and thoughts, as if she were falling backward into darkness. "Lachlan," she whispered, as a lass cried, *Help me, please…*

"Liza, what's wrong?" Fear colored Lachlan's words, and Liza blinked up into his emerald green eyes.

She tore her gaze away and looked down at the document in her hands, which had begun to shake. "Can you take this?" she whispered to Bruce.

Bruce gently gathered the parchment from her.

"Put it in the desk in the library," Lachlan said.

The entire episode lasted less than a second, but Liza couldn't help but feel as if something significant had occurred.

She had no idea what it might be.

"Did ye get enough sleep last night?" Lachlan asked, leading her out of the chapel into the cool hallway of the castle's first floor and toward the back staircase.

"I was up early," Liza responded, evading the question. She smiled weakly. "And someone had me up late." She didn't mention the dreams. There was no reason for Lachlan to worry.

Lachlan returned the grin. "Can't say I feel bad about keepin' ye awake. But let's get ye back tae bed for a bit. I'll get ye some tea and breakfast after ye sleep."

She didn't argue. She allowed him to guide her through the sitting room, which overlooked the back grounds of the estate leading to the Creagan River, to their apartment at the rear of the ornate main floor. What had once been Laird Callum Ramsay's private living quarters had been renovated to the style of Liza and Lachlan. Lachlan drew the curtains.

Liza didn't bother to undress. She climbed beneath the thick comforter. "Maybe you should join me," she murmured, reaching for her fiancé. She ran her hand down his chest and lingered at the waistband of his jeans.

He caught her wrist in his grasp. "There'll be plenty o' time fer that later, *mo ghaol.*"

"If I were really your love, you'd come to bed with me," she murmured. The truth is, she didn't want to go to sleep alone. But as soon as she'd lain down, she felt herself needing the reassurance of his touch.

"Ye ken ye're my only love," he said, meeting her

gaze. He grazed a hand over her long dark hair fanned across the pillow.

"I know," she said, but something about his words pulled at her.

"I'll be right here if ye need me."

Liza yawned. Maybe a daylight sleep would do her good. Maybe the dreams wouldn't come—with their faraway shadows of dirt, filth, and peril. The sensation of being trapped in a vacuum alone, without hope of escape.

A therapist would probably tell Liza she was experiencing a latent fear of commitment, but Liza knew that wasn't it. She just didn't know what it was.

As forcefully as she'd wanted to fight sleep, her body wasn't cooperating. Within moments, she felt herself falling, falling into blackness.

Chapter 2

Liza slept a deep, dark velvety sleep without dreams. There were no whispers, no cries, no specters or nightmares. And when she finally reentered the world of the living, she felt rested and relieved her sleep was not haunted by her anxieties.

She opened her eyes slowly to find Lachlan reclining in the sitting chair near the end of the bed, a book resting on one palm. She watched him silently for a moment, admiring the fine cut of his jaw. She smiled at the crease of concentration on his brow as he turned a page.

"What are you reading?" she asked. He startled, and she saw the thick black letters of the hardcover's title: *Under the Hammer.*

Lachlan set the book on the nightstand. "Ye're awake," he exclaimed.

"I am now. What time is it?"

"Nearly seven in the evening. Ye slept the whole day away."

Liza shot up in bed. "Why didn't you wake me?"

"Ye were restin' so fast. Ye needed it, *mo luaidh.*"

Despite Liza's irritation, Lachlan's use of his Gaelic endearments always softened her sour mood. Today was no different. Besides, it wasn't Lachlan's responsibility to look after her, even though he often did.

"I asked Sadie to hold our supper."

The curtains in the bedroom were still closed, and Liza rose from the bed to open the heavy fabric. The sky was still light at this latitude, and she looked out over the south grounds toward the Creagan River. Hidden within the trees, the river snaked steadily toward the Firth of Forth.

It was Bruce Baxter who caught her attention on the lawn. His stout arms were crossed tightly over his chest as he supervised a group of people erecting a large white tent. Liza frowned. They had a few days before the wedding, and she thought they might've waited until the next day to erect the tent.

She glanced at the sky, which was darkening with the threat of rain in the distance.

Three men had leaned a ladder against the ancient sycamore tree on the other side of the back lawn. They were wrapping strings of white lights high into its branches and around the tree's broad trunk. Even in the daylight, the lights twinkled.

She shivered with a sense of déjà vu and remembrance. She'd stood in this very window after Lachlan had cut down the body of Brodie Graham from that tree. She hadn't known Brodie well, but he certainly hadn't deserved the fate befallen him simply because he'd been in the wrong place at the wrong time.

"Are ye chilled? Looks like it's dreich." He came up behind her and wrapped his arms around her stomach.

"I don't like the idea of the lights in that tree."

He watched the activity on the lawn with her, and they remained lost in their own set of memories.

As much as Liza had been through, Lachlan had endured more. Even now, his words were filled with a deep wisdom. "But maybe the illumination is a nice way to signal our victory over the past. From tragedy, a light emerges."

"A light emerges," Liza repeated softly, considering the turn of phrase. "I like that."

"Mmm…" The low sound rumbled from his chest and into Liza's body. "I like *you*."

She reached a hand up and cupped his cheek in her palm. "Back at ya."

"Come on," he said, moving away and grabbing her hand instead. "Let's get some supper in ye before ye fade away. And before I'm tempted tae lay ye down on this bed."

Liza could've been tempted, but as if in response to his initial words, her stomach audibly responded, and Lachlan gave her a knowing look.

"Let me just freshen up," she said. Lachlan nodded, abandoning her hand and then the room.

In the washroom, Liza splashed some cold water on

her face and considered her reflection. She looked more rested than she had in days, though she suspected she wouldn't sleep well that night. She pondered all the things she needed to do before the wedding. Things she should've done while she'd been sleeping. A swell of panic rose in her chest as her mind began to spin.

After she'd eaten, she'd retire to the library and send her emails. She'd confirm with her planner the flowers were set to be delivered on time. She'd check in with the caterer to ensure there were no last-minute issues. She'd send friendly texts to her bridesmaids bidding their travel remain uninterrupted.

Her dress was scheduled to be delivered in the morning, and while she was sure she hadn't gained weight, she was concerned she may have lost a few pounds. In which case she'd need to call her tailor and beg for some last-minute alterations.

Liza grasped the edge of the sink as the quick blur of dizziness whirled through her head. She took in a deep, centering breath and slowly let it out.

As she blinked into the mirror, a cool breeze fluttered over her face and wrapped itself around her shoulders, as if combating the unsteadiness. Liza might've thought she'd imagined the cool flutter of air if the edges of her hair hadn't lifted slightly in the reflection.

None of this matters, a voice seemed to say at her ear.

No, not at her ear. The voice was within her and around her.

She whirled about, and though she didn't expect to see a ghost, she cast her gaze about for the source of the whisper.

The figure of a young woman dressed in plain clothing and plaited hair appeared in the doorway to the washroom. Liza let out a screech of surprise.

The woman screeched back.

Her hand on her heart, Liza exhaled. "Sadie, please don't sneak up on people like that."

Her cook and housekeeper appeared more terrified than Liza was. Liza softened.

Sadie Gilbraith had come to the castle the previous year, just prior to the gathering of world moguls and oligarchs. Sadie, too, had seen her fair share of tragedy—and in some cases, discovered the tragedy herself. After signing a non-disclosure agreement, she could've chosen to leave the property and take with her some of the castle's secrets.

And yet, Sadie had stayed on at the Ramsay Estate along with their footman Shaun Fraser. Sadie and Shaun were now engaged to be married next Christmas in the castle.

Sadie's hand was still on her chest. "Mr. McClaren told me tae come check on ye fer supper."

Liza nodded. "I was just about to come down."

"Who were ye talkin' to?"

A frown creased Liza's brow. "I wasn't talking to anyone."

"I heard a voice," said Sadie, who was sensitive to the castle's spirits. "Perhaps someone was talkin' tae *you*."

Liza didn't bother with a response and instead gestured for them to leave the room. Sadie moved ahead of her, and Liza glanced around, half expecting to see the source of the female voice who'd issued her counsel. Or her warning.

Liza shivered as she caught sight of the ancient sycamore tree in the window, its lights twinkling in the sky, a sky which had darkened further, approached by the impending storm.

Liza was glad for Sadie's chatter as they made their way to the castle's remodeled kitchens on the ground floor. "Mr. McClaren told me tae prepare ye somethin' comfortin'. I've got cullen skink fer ye this evening." The thick soup made of smoked haddock, potatoes, and onions had become one of Liza's favorite dishes. Her mouth watered.

Lachlan was waiting for them at the large butcher block counter with two steaming crocks of soup in front of him. He handed Liza a cup of whisky tea. Liza took a seat and accepted the cup gratefully, enjoying the quiet coziness of the kitchen. Although the space had been renovated after the fire and other events which had nearly claimed Liza's life, the designers had maintained the kitchen's ancient charm. It was one of the original rooms built in the twelfth century by Simunus de Ramesia, who'd followed King David the First to Scotland.

In just a few days' time, the kitchen would be bustling with activity as a hired catering staff would prepare their wedding feast. Liza considered how many other wedding feasts had been prepared in this very room.

She glanced over at the original brick fireplace where most of the meals throughout the ages had been prepared, imagining the hearth as it must have been centuries ago—a great sooty cavern alive with glowing flame, blackened pots suspended over the embers, and perhaps a haunch of stag turning slowly on a spit, filling the air with the scent of roasting meat and peat smoke.

She shook herself from her reverie and blew lightly on a spoonful of her soup.

"Did ye have any more disturbin' dreams?"

Lachlan's question was asked quietly, gently. Even so, Liza nearly dropped her spoon. She'd purposely kept the nightmares from Lachlan. He didn't need to worry about her. And he certainly didn't need to worry that she was having doubts about the marriage.

"Ye talk in your sleep," he said without meeting her eyes.

"And what do I say in my sleep?"

"Nothin' I can clearly make out. But ye seemed to be worried about somethin'. Or someone. My name's come up more than once. Along with some others I'm not sure I recognize."

"Like who?" she asked. She was curious now. The dreams, while disturbing, faded quickly after she woke, leaving her with only a vague sense of disquiet, and sometimes terror.

"Someone named Grete."

Liza frowned and shook her head. She knew no one by the name of Grete.

"It's interestin', though. I just this mornin' received a text from my cousin Margaret from Norway. She'll be able to make it to the ceremony after all. We called her Grete when she was a child."

Lachlan had mentioned his younger cousin on his mother's side a time or two since Liza had known him. And since moving to Scotland, Liza had learned of the strong connection between the countries. Over the centuries, many Scottish residents had emigrated to Norway, and vice versa. The nations had enjoyed centuries of cooperation.

Liza was glad Margaret would be able to join them. Lachlan's immediate family had dwindled over the years, and he'd spoken fondly of this woman. But he'd not spoken of her frequently enough that Liza would be dreaming of the stranger.

"When is she arriving?"

"Tomorrow. I know it's a little early, but I didn't think you'd mind."

"Not at all."

Sadie approached with a kettle to refresh their tea. "I've already got the room ready, my lady," she said.

Lachlan smiled, a faraway expression on his face. "Margaret was like a young sister to me when we were kids. We shared a close bond goin' beyond kin. As we got older, we went our separate ways as families tend tae do."

Liza placed her hand on his forearm resting on the countertop. "I agree this is the perfect occasion to reconnect."

"It's funny…she always said this place felt familiar tae her. She swore she'd lived here before."

"In a past life?"

Lachlan shrugged. "Maybe. Stranger things hae happened, I suppose."

"Did she see the ghosts?" asked Sadie, her eyes wide.

"Nah," answered Lachlan. "But she always said she had a vague sense of familiarity. And every once in a while, she'd share a memory of somethin' that didn't happen to her. At least, not in this lifetime."

Sadie leaned against the side of the counter. "Like what?"

"It was a long time ago." But Lachlan pressed his lips together as his brow furrowed in concentration.

"Once she mentioned an evil man who'd tried tae harm her. Another time, she mentioned a man she'd fallen in love with. Anthony? Arran?" He exhaled. "I can't quite remember now. And we were just kids. We thought she was bein' fanciful. But o' course, with all the experiences we've had, there could hae been somethin' to it."

Before Sadie could ask more questions, Bruce came bustling into the room bringing the damp smell of rain with him. He wiped his face. "It's *gaothach*," he exclaimed, seeming pleased about whatever development this might've been.

"I'm still American," she reminded him.

To his credit, he didn't quite scowl. "Pourin' cats and dogs and gustin' up a storm."

This, she understood. "Is the tent going to hold?"

"Aye, it's sturdy. Amazin' what they can build out of some cloth."

She was fairly certain homes had been built of cloth and mud and sticks and hay throughout the ages, so canvas or nylon wasn't quite the marvel he thought it was. But she let him have his moment.

"'Tis braw they were able to erect it today so we can test it fer conditions."

Liza finished her soup as Sadie placed a crock down for Bruce.

"Well, hopefully this weather blows over before Saturday," Liza said. She certainly didn't want the guests outside, even in a sturdy tent, in the middle of a summer storm. For inclement weather, they'd put in place a contingency plan to gather in the main floor of the castle: the ballroom, music room, large dining room, and drawing rooms. It wasn't what Liza had envisioned, but after the last year in the castle, she'd learned to be flexible.

"Are the men still out there?" Lachlan asked.

Bruce took a bite of a hunk of crusty bread. "Just finishin' up. The tree is also nearly done. It'll be a beacon for all tae see."

A light emerges…

Lachlan's earlier words rattled around Liza's thoughts. She didn't like the idea of men out there working on the tree as a storm approached any more than she did the sacrilege of lighting it up given the misfortune that had taken place in its branches.

Turning to Lachlan, she changed the subject. "Do you think Margaret would like to join the wedding party on Friday evening for our facials, manicures, and massages?"

"I think that would be lovely if ye'd be willin'."

"Of course," murmured Liza as a thought—thin as a strand of silk—threaded through her mind. *Grete. Who is Grete?*

She recalled the female voice in her apartment earlier. *None of this matters,* it seemed to whisper again in its lilting Scottish accent.

"She was always a lovely girl," Lachlan was saying. "A bit regal, but not in an arrogant way. Just rather…otherworldly, I guess."

"Otherworldly?"

"Ye know. She was always…different. Ethereal," he said with a snap of his fingers.

"Ye're making her sound like a spirit," said Sadie.

Lachlan chuckled. "She's very much flesh and bone." Then his laughter faded. "But she does have a sort of supernatural aura around her, I suppose."

"Ye've all gone aff yer heids," Bruce grumbled, slurping the remainder of the soup from his crock.

"You don't believe in the spirits?" asked Liza.

"I don' believe in callin' them on purpose. They'll show up when they have somethin' of import tae say tae ye." He shot a pointed look at Sadie, who he thought was a silly lass.

Two hints of pink colored Sadie's cheeks as she turned to busy herself with the kettle at the stove.

Since Liza's thoughts had been headed in the same direction, she changed the topic. "Will Margaret be bringing a guest?"

Lachlan shook his head. "She's comin' alone. I dinnae think there's a significant other. At least not one she mentioned."

"Maybe she'll meet someone at the wedding," said Sadie, forgetting her previous embarrassment. "Wouldn't that be romantic?"

Because of Liza's station as Lady of the Ramsay Estate, along with the position of Lachlan's father as Permanent Secretary to the Scottish Government, not to mention the notoriety surrounding the relationship of Liza and Lachlan, a number of high-profile guests would be in attendance. Liza doubted many of them would be single.

"I do hae someone else who might be attendin'."

Liza sighed quietly, a slight irritation niggling at her. Their guest list had been set for months. It was one thing to add his kin. "Lachlan, of course your cousin is welcome, but we can't keep adding people."

Though her words had been gentle, he gave her a petulant look, and she relented. "Who is it?"

"A friend from uni." His voice was quiet, and Liza stared into the deep brown water of her tea. What had happened to Lachlan when he'd been a student at Stirling all those years ago had been tragic, and it had altered the course of Lachlan's life in unimaginable ways.

"I wasn't aware you'd kept in touch with anyone from that time."

"I haven't," he said, then shrugged. "Not really. But there was a guy—an American—who stuck by me through everythin' with Nicola." Liza noted the hitch in his voice when he said his deceased girlfriend's name. "We'd fallen out of touch, but he reached out just a few weeks ago unexpectedly. I'd mentioned the weddin', and he said he didn't think he'd be able to come. I got another message from him today sayin' his fate had changed."

Liza frowned. "His fate? That's an odd turn of phrase."

"He's a bit of an odd duck."

"What's his name?"

"Tommy MacClure."

"I'll add him to the list for seating," Liza said and leaned over to kiss her soon-to-be husband. "But only because you're cute."

He winked at her, and she added, "MacClure sounds pretty Scottish to me."

"He has some o' the good blood from way back."

"Ach! I nearly forgot," Sadie exclaimed, then disappeared from the room.

Bruce shook his head at the girl's daftness, and Lachlan raised his eyebrows.

But the men did not comment further on Sadie's frivolity. Like Liza, they recognized what the girl had endured at the castle. They were all in this life together. And they were family, like it or not.

Sadie returned with a small envelope in her hands and offered it to Liza. The gold insignia stamped into the creamy paper was immediately recognizable as the Great Seal of the Realm.

With the small group looking on, Liza carefully ran a finger under the sealed lip of the envelope. The letterhead was marked with an ornate letter 'W' capped by a regal-looking crown.

Liza held her breath as she read the short note aloud…

Ms. Ramsay,

I apologize for this highly unusual request and lapse in social etiquette. I've been informed your union with Mr. Lachlan McClaren will take place presently. I am hoping to make a very brief appearance, not only to witness and celebrate your matrimony, but to acknowledge the unfortunate events that took place at your estate earlier in the year…at the hand of one of the Household's former stewards. As a result of my own personal circumstances at the time, I didn't sufficiently extend my sincere regrets for those unfortunate circumstances.

Again, I realize this request may come as a surprise. Therefore, I will hold no ill will should you choose to refuse my query. I kindly ask that you contact my private secretary with your response at your earliest convenience.

The letter included a phone number and email address for the secretary and was signed by the Duke of Rothesay, the Scottish title of the Prince of Wales.

Sadie's hands were pressed into her mouth, her

eyes wide. Lachlan's lips were parted in disbelief. Even Bruce seemed speechless.

Liza's fingers trembled. The 'personal circumstances' to which His Royal Highness referred was the tragic passing of his young wife. She'd been diagnosed with an undisclosed illness around the time the billionaires had wreaked havoc at the Ramsay Estate. The poor princess had died not a month later, and the Royal Family had been in mourning since.

Liza was quite certain the heir to the throne had not made a public appearance since that time. And while their wedding was private, the fact that he should choose their event as his soft foray back into society was as flattering as it was shocking.

After a silence, Lachlan let out a sigh. "I'm not sure we should agree."

Liza furrowed her brow and caught her bottom lip between her teeth. "I don't see how we can't," she answered. "I worry, though, that witnessing a wedding ceremony might be too emotionally taxing on a person who's lost so much, so publicly, in his life."

"Ye're worried about *him*?" The words had no sooner burst from Lachlan's lips than Bruce interrupted, "What about security?"

Liza considered Bruce's question. They had a skeleton security crew and had planned to bolster it with a private outfit. She assumed the prince would bring his own detail, but Liza said, "I'll contact Petrus." The world's richest man would not be attending the event as he was tied up with a new, extremely high-profile project in the United States. But if Liza called with a request, she was certain he'd come through within the hour.

"Of course," Lachlan said, his words dripping with sarcasm. He waved a hand in front of him. "Call up, Petrus, why don' ye?"

Liza drew herself up. "What is your problem?" But she did not have time to stay and listen to his answer. She stood and left the group, murmuring as she went, "It looks as though I have some calls to make." She was glad she'd had that nap.

She tried to avoid once again questioning their decision not to elope to a sunny private beach and celebrate their love without heads of state, society's elite, or royal patronage. Or ghosts…

Liza had just finished the phone call with the Royal Private Secretary, affirming the prince's invitation and presence, when Lachlan entered the library.

The rain slashed against the room's window in gray sheets, and despite the fact it was summertime, Liza had asked Shaun to light a fire in the hearth. The flames danced and crackled cheerfully, keeping the damp chill at bay.

"Ye look troubled," Liza said, a hint of her soon-to-be husband's accent slipping into her speech. Usually when this happened, Lachlan would share a playful word or look.

But this evening, his face was stoic. He remained silent. He sank into the leather armchair, and Liza approached from behind, resting her hands lightly on his shoulders.

"Are you having second thoughts?" she asked lightly.

She expected the denial to be quick and adamant. Instead, it didn't come at all.

Liza's pulse quickened, and she removed her hands from Lachlan's back. When he still didn't speak, she came around to the front of him and perched on the edge of the identical armchair positioned before the fire.

"Lachlan?" she prompted, her voice tight.

"I'm not havin' second thoughts about the marriage," he finally said. "I'm havin' second thoughts about the weddin'."

She swallowed down a sudden swell of shame as anger bloomed in her chest. She attempted to keep her voice even when she said, "Just this morning, you scolded me for suggesting we elope. And I was joking," she added. "It doesn't seem like you're joking right now."

"Well, that was before we had a feckin' king attendin' the ceremony."

"He's not a king."

"That hardly matters, now, does it?" The words exploded from Lachlan's lips, and Liza straightened, raising her chin a notch.

He held out his hands. "I'm sorry…I'm just a wee bit crabbit."

"Telling me you're having second thoughts about the wedding is more than just *crabbit.*"

He ran his hand through his hair and exhaled. "Look," he said, then paused. In the firelight, shadows licked at his handsome face. Despite the warmth, Liza shivered. The shadows distorted his features, making him unrecognizable.

"I don't know how tae explain any o' this tae ye in the right way."

"Just say it." She waited while he collected his thoughts. Liza had also silently questioned their decision to hold the wedding at the castle. And perhaps it was unfair of her, but she'd been relying on Lachlan to quell her nerves and make her feel like they'd made the right decision.

The fact that he, too, was having second thoughts… Well, perhaps they were on the wrong track after all.

Finally, he sucked in a breath. "I feel like I've been waitin' many lifetimes over for ye, lassie. I want the day I finally get to marry ye tae be perfect."

It hadn't been what she'd expected, and it was her turn to be speechless.

He continued, "I've nearly lost ye now twice. Maybe…more than that. I'm–I'm just terrified it might happen again."

"Lost me," Liza exclaimed softly. "I've always been right here."

"Ye're right here *now*. Ye haven't always been."

"Is this about Ki and Petrus and the lot?" she asked, referring to the temptation neither of them had expected or intended earlier that year.

Lachlan shook his head and waved his hand in front of him, dismissing the concern as if it had been a triviality. "This is about more than a silly attraction or a human desire," he said. "And that was nothin' compared to the bond I hae with ye. This is about destiny."

All of the tightness gathered in Liza's chest loosened, and instead shifted to a painful lump of unshed tears in her throat. The air felt heavy with the weight of Lachlan's words.

She wanted to reach for his hands, but his body was still tight and coiled, as if he were ready to battle some unknown intruder.

"I nearly lost ye 'afore. I won't lose ye again." But the words weren't said with tenderness. There was a distinct hint of anger threaded through the declaration.

In the distance, the faint rumble of thunder sounded as an errant flame leapt from the hearth toward her, flashing.

She should have felt comforted by Lachlan's words.

Instead, she was filled with a deep sense of foreboding.

Chapter 3

Long after Lachlan had gone to bed, Liza sat alone in the library, thinking about the conversation.

He was her person—her *anam cara*, as he was wont to say.

But his vehement declaration of devotion to her and their union had taken her aback. Of course she knew he loved her as much as she loved him, but she hadn't heard him speak in such obsessive terms before.

In the past, it had been *she* who'd been focused on their upcoming union. But for much more superficial reasons.

She'd wanted to stand in front of friends and family in her beautiful gown, that they may bear witness to their love for each other.

She realized, to her, the thought of their wedding had very little to do with her commitment to Lachlan.

And that made her feel rather dreadful.

Liza went to the liquor cabinet in the corner of the room and poured a dram of good cognac into a tumbler. She wasn't much of a drinker, but with the rain and the fire and the general moodiness of the night, a strong drink seemed to be in order.

Besides, after her earlier hours-long nap, she still wasn't the least bit tired. Perhaps a small nip would relax her enough to sleep.

She sipped the drink, and her mind strayed to Lachlan's warm body stretched out in their bed.

If she hadn't known better, she would climb into bed and press herself against the hard length of him. Oh, he'd allow her to do that, and he would most definitely respond. But she knew he'd suspect her advances were attempts to assuage his mood even if she insisted her motives were pure.

She downed the small amount of alcohol and poured another tumbler, filling the glass this time. The next swallow—longer and deeper—seemed to seep its sweet numbness through her chest and out through her limbs. A pleasant haziness warmed her cheeks and slowed her rambling thoughts.

She moved around the room, running her fingers over the ancient tomes that filled the floor-to-ceiling shelves. The works of Robert Burns, a first edition *Poetical Works of Sir Walter Scott*, the original Waverly novels, and Boswell's *London Journal*—the collection was priceless and precious.

She glanced over at the locked glass case where the equally priceless complete collection of the Lewis Chessmen gazed up at her with their forlorn expressions.

The cohort of pieces which had, centuries earlier, been carved from walrus ivory and whales' teeth, had been found on one of the outer isles in the nineteenth century. While the pieces had been scattered around Scotland over the centuries, they'd all somehow made their way home to the Ramsay Estate, where they now watched over the library.

Liza stared into the haunted protruding eyes of the king who clasped his sword on his lap. His queen glanced sideways toward him with her wide eyes, her hands affixed to her cheeks.

Scholars who'd studied the pieces marveled at their cartoonish expressions, but the characters didn't seem frivolous to Liza. Instead, they seemed trapped and lost, as if they'd been waiting centuries to be claimed by their rightful owner.

Liza said a prayer for the regal kings and queens, their fierce warriors, and pensive bishops, and gave a quiet thanks to their sculptor who had etched the figures with painstaking detail.

Then she ran her hand over the rough wood grain of the antique desk where her laptop glowed its eerie blue light.

She was about to power down the device and head to the bedroom to try to get some rest, when she noticed the parchment tucked into the top compartment of the desk where presumably Bruce Baxter had placed it earlier in the day.

What had Lachlan called them? The charter rolls?

"Fine rolls," she murmured aloud.

The record of financial transactions of the Ramsay Estate and its surrounding lands.

Liza took a last, long swallow of the amber liquid in her snifter, then set the empty tumbler on the desk. She switched on the lamp with a click, then she carefully lifted the soft material between her fingers, unrolled it, and held the unfolded vellum on her palms. She moved the document under the lamp so she could see the small, faded handwriting more clearly.

Squinting, she picked up her phone and used her flashlight to shine the light across the letters.

The writing itself was very fine. She could clearly make out the top line: '17 Edward I.' Liza frowned. As far as she knew, Scotland had not been under English rule under King Edward the First. At least not for an extended period. She had to admit—most of her knowledge of that time came from a certain historical action film her grandfather had watched when she'd been a child.

The first paragraph was harder to read, though she thought she could make out the words: 'Record assigned to Claray of Ramsay on behalf of husband William of Ramsay, in absentia, the month of July.' Liza struggled to make out the year, but it was impossible.

Liza had never heard the name 'Claray Ramsay'.

The name William Ramsay, however, had appeared multiple times in historical documents kept at the property.

The rest of the entries included various transactions. Liza skimmed the list.

Master Henry de Bray acknowledges he owes Laird William of Ramsay seven shillings. In lieu of payment, he levies his land and chattels.

Alexander de Thaney paid one hundred marks to Lady Claray of Ramsay.

John de Bitterly delivered four bucks from the shire's forest to bailiff and tenant-in-chief Lachlan McClaren in lieu of payment of twenty marks.

Liza stared. *Lachlan McClaren.* Could this be a relative of her Lachlan? She knew his family had lived on this land for years, but she couldn't imagine their involvement extended as far back as the time of King Edward I.

She would ask Lachlan about it in the morning.

She skimmed a few more entries, but mostly they outlined what appeared to be routine financial transactions.

Then another entry caught her eye.

Goerge Baird, by witness of Sir John Comyn of Badenoch and Lady Claray of Ramsay, in-

quired after the hand of Lady Elesbeth Ramsay in marriage. The query was deferred until such time as Laird William Ramsay returned from his service abroad.

This was the second entry Liza had seen to William's absence, and she imagined the deferral of marriage had taken place because Lady Elesbeth was not having her hand given.

"Good for you," she murmured.

The sash of the window rattled when jolted by a swift gust, and Liza glanced up when the dying fire unexpectedly blazed and the lamplight flickered.

Just as quickly as the draught had blown through the room, the air suddenly stilled, as if an unseen hand had soothed a fevered temper.

Liza carefully rolled the parchment and tucked it back into the desk's cubby.

She went to the fireplace and spread the embers out, then slowly placed cooler ashes from the bottom of the hearth over fading flame until the light died.

With the fire gone, gloom settled over the chamber.

Liza's eyes were bleary, and the alcohol seeped into her limbs.

She moved back to the desk to switch off the light. As she reached for the switch, a cold chill touched her neck and snaked its way around her body. Light as a breath at first, the chill quickly became sharp and penetrated to the bone.

Liza's mind raced for a logical explanation for the pall. She turned to the window again. The gale still battered the pane, but Liza crossed the room to secure the ancient latch. Through the glass, she struggled to peer out across the back western side of the grounds, but all she could see was her reflection illuminated against the darkness. Her visage was distorted and grotesque in the wave of vintage glass.

Then, for just a moment, there seemed to be two faces staring back at her.

She whirled around, her heart beating a furious tattoo.

Liza was no stranger to the castle's ghosts. Hadn't the Gray Lady herself led Liza to Callum that fateful evening, ensuring she became the rightful heir to the Ramsay Estate? Hadn't Sir Alexander been the one who'd saved her from sure death in the castle's dungeon? And since those occurrences, there had been whispers and sighs that couldn't be explained away. The faint sound of bagpipes played in empty rooms. The soft rustle of unseen gowns, and the low titters of laughter from invisible mouths.

There had always seemed to be an unspoken agreement between the living and the dead. The two parties did not interact directly unless they needed something from each other. Or *someone*.

Just as those words entered her mind, the whisper

sounded clear as the sharp ringing of a bell through the silence.

Help me.

Liza froze and shifted her gaze slowly, methodically, around the empty room, devoid of any other living being. Yet she knew she wasn't alone.

Help me. Please.

Though disembodied, the voice belonged to a young female. It didn't come from one location, but was formed from the molecules making up the air.

Liza looked toward the window, but all she could see was her ghostly reflection gazing back at her. She stared at the image as if she were looking at the face of another.

The whistling of the wind picked up. It came loud, low, and steady, rising in volume and speed until the air rushed around her and through her. Like the voice, the wind howled from inside the castle.

Help me.

Liza whirled around. The voice was so close, an invisible breath fluttered the hair at her ear. She was filled with a profound tremor of terror.

She needed to get out of that room.

As she rushed toward the door, a tremendous crash sounded from within the bowels of the castle. Liza jumped. Already on the main floor, she only needed to make it down the short hallway to the door to her apartment where Lachlan lay sleeping.

She needed to make it into his arms.

A frantic energy followed her as she fled past the faces of her Ramsay ancestors whose portraits lined the corridor. They stared at her with hard, judging eyes—provoked and disappointed.

She averted her gaze, quickening down the passage toward the great hall. She stepped past the hidden doors that led to ornate rooms, recently refurbished and refreshed.

The spectral presence followed, its plea reverberating within Liza's mind.

Help me. Please.

Liza didn't know what was expected of her, and she didn't care. She reached the solid wooden door of her apartment and flung it open in a surge of panic and strength. She stepped over the threshold, slamming the door shut behind her, sure the sound would wake Lachlan with its force.

There was silence.

No howling wind. No appraising eyes. No eerie voice. No movement.

Liza's heart still crashed in her chest, but around her, the world was still.

For a moment, she rested her head against the cool surface of the ancient door. Gradually, the thudding of her heart slowed, and her extremities tingled while the blood coursing through her veins slowed.

She inhaled and breathed out slowly.

In her relief, she laughed to herself. Surely she'd imagined the entire ordeal. In a lonely moment, with the sound of wind and her anxiety thrown into the mix, she'd spun a ghost story.

The stress of the upcoming wedding—the high-profile guests, the unpredictability of the weather, the uncertainty of Bruce's preparations, Lachlan's uttered reservations... Clearly, the craziness of her current reality was manifesting an inexplicable internal environment.

Liza inhaled deeply and scanned the calm, silent room.

All was well.

Or at least all was *still*.

After exhaling, she returned to her own reality, aware that within a few hours, the first shift of caterers would arrive to begin preparations. Her wedding planner would arrive with her team to decorate the chapel with lace and tulle. They would place a runner between the rows of wooden benches, and they would plan locations for humongous bouquets of Juliet roses, calla lilies, and Scotch thistle.

Tomorrow, her grandparents would board a plane bound for Edinburgh. Her bridesmaids would join them.

It was too late to turn back now. Even if she wanted to.

And Liza did not want to turn back. She wanted to

marry Lachlan, who'd been hers all along.

A sudden indignance filled her. This was *her* castle, and it was *her* day. She did not want the threat of castle spirits—real or imagined—to embed themselves in her mind. And while she longed to climb into her big, warm bed and curl herself against her big, warm Lachlan, she felt an overwhelming urge to confront the castle. She would not be afraid in her own home.

Before she could think herself out of her next decision, she pulled open the door to the apartment and stepped back into the great hall.

Like her living quarters, the passage was dark and still.

She stepped lightly down the corridor, making her way toward the grand staircase where the mural of one of the battles for Scotland marked the entryway to the Ramsay Castle. The painting reminded visitors of the land's historical importance as a stronghold between the Lowlands and Highlands.

The castle's location was strategic and critical throughout the ages, with leaders such as King Edward I, Sir William Wallace, King Henry IV, Oliver Cromwell, and Mary Queen of Scots using the bastion to exert political and military influence during wars for land, power, and independence. The castle had changed hands from Scottish to English rule over the centuries, but the Ramsay Clan had always been bound to Scotia.

Liza was well aware of the significance of her home through the ages, and she did not take this responsibility to history lightly.

She drifted toward the grand staircase in the hush of night, her attention on the fresco and its intricate battle scene, under which a placard read, '*I seize the tales as they pass, and pour them forth in song.*'

As she approached, a flicker of movement caught her attention from the large drawing room to her right. Liza hesitated. Perhaps Sadie or Shaun was still awake. This was unlikely, but not impossible. The familiar stroke of fear tickled her spine and sent a smattering of goosebumps prickling across her skin.

She would *not* be afraid. This was her reality, and her home did not belong to impressions of the past.

Cautiously, she stepped toward the drawing room and pushed open the door.

Antique tapestries depicting scenes of Scottish history lined the shadowed walls. Furniture from throughout the ages sat sentry in their fixed positions. But no human presence inhabited the space.

On a table at the far end of the room, a candle flickered.

Liza stared at the object for a mere beat before she rushed to extinguish the light. After the fire in the castle last year, Liza was cautious of open flame. Sadie knew Liza's aversion, and very rarely lit candles.

Liza bent to blow out the flame, but before the

breath crossed her lips, she heard the whisper.

Help me.

Unlike the frantic rush of words and panicked urgency of the library, this time the voice was quieter and more fragile. It caused Liza's heart to tighten in her chest.

The sound seemed to originate from the left side of the room. In the candlelight, Liza spun around and could just make out the outline of a child on the sofa.

She stared at the shape, trying to discern its tangibility.

The longer Liza stared, the more solid and real the small boy seemed.

"Who are you?" she whispered back.

"Ye ken me," the boy responded in his Scottish lilt. The orb-like eyes sparkled brilliant blue in the light and radiated pain and pleading.

He was younger than Liza by nearly two decades, and though his clothing was simple, there was a nobility to him that was difficult to dismiss.

Liza met those blue eyes, and the connection was strong and fierce.

The boy shifted and morphed as the candlelight danced across his features. As surely as he'd been a male child, the next moment the figure was a fair young woman with fine bone structure and refined clothing.

"Ye can see me," the young woman whispered,

holding out a long, slender hand. In the flickering light, those fingers seemed to grow, but Liza decided it must be the shadows from the candlelight playing tricks on her eyes.

Despite her hesitation, Liza forced herself to remain in place and breathe through her fear. "What do you want?"

The response was a soft, ephemeral thought. "I want ye tae help me."

"How can I do that?"

"Say ye'll help me."

"I don't know how," Liza said, her voice rising from a whisper to a declaration.

"They'd labor tae see me dead."

Liza detected an accent in the uttered words—alongside the Scottish lilt, the hint of a land Liza couldn't identify.

"Who?"

The maiden shook her head and her body shimmered, then faded so Liza could see the fabric of the sofa through her form.

"Say ye'll help me," she repeated.

The candlelight flickered along with the image.

"I don't know what I can do."

"Swear it tae me. I beseech ye. Before they take my life."

There was such anguish and terror in the maiden's voice, Liza couldn't deny her. "I–I promise," she said.

The young woman turned her haunted eyes back to Liza. "Declare ye shall nae depart from me."

Liza herself felt as if she were in a trance. She drifted forward. "I won't. I promise it." She held out her hands as the figure reached for her. "I promise," Liza repeated. And just as her fingers brushed against certain flesh, a draught gusted through the room and extinguished the flame.

Liza blinked and the young woman was gone.

Other than a dim ambient glow from an unknown outdoor source, the room was dark. Liza moved to the tall windows overlooking the east and back grounds.

To her right, the sycamore tree stood illuminated on the lawn. The fairy lights installed earlier that day glittered in the shadow of night. A long strand seemed to sway in the breeze, the string blowing against the ancient split trunk of the tree.

The strand of lights lifted and twirled on a gust of wind, then fell back down against the trunk, as if raised then abandoned by some unseen hand.

Liza thought of her promise to the apparition. The spirit had disappeared and would likely be nothing but a strange and distant memory by the morning. Even so, Liza felt a strong yearning to go outside and secure those lights. Perhaps, she thought inexplicably, that action would satisfy the spirit's pleas.

While she knew it was preposterous, the faint imprint of the specter still detectable in her mind seemed to approve.

The rational part of Liza fought the urge. She told herself she could take care of the light strand in the morning. Or better yet, she could ask Bruce and his crew to fix it.

Then she wondered about the tent, just out of view from the windows in the drawing room.

Though the thunder still rumbled in the distance, the rain had abated. Any urge to sleep had long since fled, and Liza found herself turning from the room, alighting the grand staircase, hurrying through the castle's office and into the hallway past the chapel. She reached the back egress, which led to a small yard that once upon a time had held the kitchen's garden.

A fine mist swirled through the air, as if Liza were walking into a cloud. The atmosphere was electrified with an incoming storm, and the giant sycamore was a beacon as Liza crossed the lawn.

To her right, the large tent appeared to have withstood the earlier winds, though one side of the structure looked slightly canted.

She didn't bother stopping to examine it further before she continued to the tree.

She stopped beneath it and looked up at the untethered strand of twinkling lights. She should have brought something to secure the strand, she realized, but she wasn't about to go ferreting around for a ladder in the darkness. Instead, she stood on her tiptoes and caught hold of the edge of the string with her finger-tips. She pushed her fingers and the strand beneath another wire still fastened to the tree. By the time she'd coaxed the lights into place, she was out of breath from straining and reaching.

She stepped back as a bolt of lightning illuminated the sky. A crash of thunder followed.

Liza realized she should not be in an open field under the highest point on the lawn. She turned from the tree, and a sinister laugh filled the air around her.

Elesbeth, ye daft and witless lass…

While she quite agreed with the sentiment, she realized the thought in her mind wasn't hers. The words hadn't been conceived in her voice, nor was it a turn of phrase she would have used.

The skin tingled at the nape of her neck, and her hair seemed to lift like she'd just scuffed stockinged feet across the carpet.

She glanced around her as the air suddenly became still and the night returned to its calm inky blackness.

Liza took one step before a tremendous crack shook the air and a jolt shot through her body, stunning her from the inside out. From her core came a shock of brilliance traveling out to her hands, feet, and the top of her head.

The heat burned through her skin.

She was electrified. She was energy. She was life. She was light.

Time lost its meaning, and when Liza looked toward the heavens, she rose to the sky. A groan sounded from the belly of the earth, and Liza rode the sound high into the blackness until she was lifted above the clouds to the stars.

"Lachlan," she managed to call out before an invisible force let her drop, and she was falling…falling…

She crashed through the clouds and rain, through space and time, back to earth.

There was no breath in her chest, though she had a sense of the hard, wet ground beneath her and the leaves of the sycamore swaying above her. She shut her eyes, and then there was nothing but a velvety blackness to which Liza succumbed.

Chapter 4

A gentle pressure first graced one cheek, then the other. The touch was tender, and she fancied it to be the gentle hands of a wee bairn rousing her from slumber.

A soft moan escaped her lips as she lay dreaming. She attempted to turn her body, and a sharp pain coursed through her spine and pierced her skull. Her mouth was parched as though stuffed with woolen cloth.

With caution, she extended a hand, perceiving the blades of wet grass beneath her fingers.

She parted her eyelids, anticipating the visage of a child above her. Instead, her gaze met the countenance of Lachlan McClaren.

His hands lingered just above her head, a furrow marring his rugged face. Above him, the once lush leaves of the sycamore stood charred and ravaged, as if the entire tree had succumbed to a fiery blaze.

"My dear Lachlan," she murmured, her hand rising to rest gently upon his cheek. "What has become of our fair tree?"

As her fingers grazed his skin, he flinched as if struck by a blow. His eyes darted about with sudden urgency, and he swallowed hard, his throat bobbing visibly.

"Lachlan?"

"My lady…" His voice faltered. "Are ye well?"

"I'd feel more at ease if ye weren't acting so…strangely."

Her own voice sounded strange to her ears. She touched her temple lightly. Had she taken a blow to the head and found herself bewildered?

All at once, as though whispered by some capricious spirit, a remembrance not her own flitted strange across her mind. She recalled the fall of King Alexander—the sovereign hurled from his mount, leaving the realm rudderless and in sorrow.

How came she to ken such a tale? She scarce knew from where the knowledge sprang, as if it had lain hidden in the shadowed hollows of her mind.

Glancing about, she saw nary a horse and recalled not having ridden in many moons.

She remembered her strong aversion to the stables, how tears and heavy breaths would seize her each time she neared the beasts.

The sight that met her eyes now, however, was unexpected—a throng of cottars toiling earnestly under the first light of day. Two men, garbed in simple léines and tartan trowse, worked the distant fields with sturdy beasts of burden, while a lass fetched water from the chain pump.

Her gaze then settled on two more tending the garden near the castle's watchtower.

She blinked, looking up at the keep's red stone. It struck her as peculiar. Something was amiss.

All was known to her, yet somehow foreign.

"Lady Elesbeth?" Lachlan inquired.

Elesbeth…

She must have softly uttered the name, for Lachlan leaned close, gazing intently at her with a worried expression.

She gazed into the familiar green hue of his eyes.

Her glance wandered down his long, straight nose to his full lips, which had caressed her so tenderly in her imaginings. She found her hand reaching up to grasp Lachlan's blouse, which she realized was no shirt at all, but a long swath of loose cloth gathered about his waist with a piece of twine.

His feet were clad in coarse brown boots, fashioned from the hide of some creature. And his chin, though shaven, bore the shadow of a few days' growth.

He was dressed strangely; yet, this was the man she loved.

"Take me to bed," she murmured.

Lachlan's face turned a shade of rose, and he withdrew from her. "Lady Elesbeth, I beg ye." His whisper was fierce.

Her heart smarted from the spurning, and she blinked at him. As her eyes fell upon his snug breeches, much like those donned by the cottars toiling in the fields, she could clearly perceive his reaction to her touch. This granted her a measure of satisfaction that somewhat soothed the sting of his refusal.

"Elesbeth!"

The lady's voice rang out, shrill and commanding, causing Lachlan to leap away as he sought to conceal the evidence of his ardor.

The woman was garbed in a fine rose-colored silk cyclas atop her chemise. Her fair locks were twisted into coiled braids at her ears, secured by silver crispines, and a wimple was held in place by a delicate barbette beneath her chin.

She strode forth with purpose, and as she drew near, the fierce arch of her brows and the steely line of her jaw compelled the cottars to step aside, though her ire was not directed at them. Even in her anger, she possessed a striking beauty.

"Elesbeth, hae ye lost yer wits?"

Liza's head was befuddled. She had no rightful cause for lying upon the earth or for clasping Lachlan in her arms. The man was known to her as the bailiff, or bailie, of the Ramsay Estate.

And yet, that was not right…

Was it?

Liza turned back to Lachlan. "Ye are not mine betrothed?" she asked, to which Lachlan replied, "Lady Elesbeth, I beseech ye," through teeth clenched tight.

The woman was swift upon them. Liza knew her as Lady Claray of Ramsay, her father's wife and her stepmother.

"My Lady Ramsay," Lachlan murmured, his eyes cast to the ground.

"What does this mean?" she demanded, her haughty gaze fixed upon Lachlan.

"I–I found Lady Elesbeth here. She seems to be…muddled."

Claray fixed a piercing gaze upon Lachlan, as if weighing the truth of his words.

Liza came to the bailie's defense. "He tells the truth. I woke up here, though I know not how I happened to be outdoors in the light of morn."

Claray turned attention to Liza. "Ye look a slorach. Yer hair is unbound, yer léine is sullied, and ye're drenched and covered in mire. As I've oft told yer father, ye'll never secure a husband."

Liza sprang to her feet, her naked soles caked with muck and her kirtle bespattered with filth. "I seek no husband," she said, her voice ringing clear.

Lady Claray opened her lips to answer, but before she uttered a word, Liza pointed to the tree. "The sycamore is ruined."

Claray stared at her, frowning, before her gaze lifted to the charred boughs. She remained unmoved.

"I trust the bailie will see to it."

"I will, Lady Ramsay," answered Lachlan, and Liza knew he would. He tended the lands and beasts of the castle as though they were his own bairns.

Claray turned on Liza. "Ye're a daft lass, full of folly."

Liza ignored her stepmother's words as a chill stole over her skin. This land was half known, half strange to her. It felt as if both home and a dream.

She knew not how she'd come to awaken beneath the ruined tree, nor why her head pounded with memories of distant years both to come and of long ago.

"Ye shall no' roam with the serving folk," Claray snapped. "I hold yer father tae task. He holds some blind fealty to the bailie."

Lachlan gave no sign of offense.

"Ye should be wed and with bairn by now."

"I'm only nineteen summers past," Liza said, her lips tight.

"Aye, nineteen summers," Claray echoed sourly as she seized Liza's arm and nudged her toward the dry moat and drawbridge. "I'd already born yer brother by years at that same age."

Liza looked 'round to gaze at Lachlan, but he'd turned to haste away.

Her breath heaved, and she turned her thoughts instead to young Uilleam, her sweet brother ever lurking in the shadows, lost in this world without their father and elder brother Alexander, who toiled for their country abroad in France.

King Phillip was yet a supporter of the Scottish cause, while England's King Edward remained a foe and a threat to both nations. Though Scotia was without a ruler, there were those still bound to the English king, Edward. Some of these supporters, she suspected, lived in their own midst.

Liza again experienced the strange sensation, as if reborn in her own flesh in a world both familiar and bewitching.

"Must I call the cunning folk?" Claray murmured low, so the servants could not overhear her talk of witches and wise folk. The monks of Watret Abbey would blanch at such whispers. Yet Liza well knew Claray would employ sorcery when it benefited her.

They crossed the bridge over the moat, and Claray changed the course of their discussion.

"There is a supper this eve, and ye must appear bonny." The woman's speech bore a soft lilt of lower birth and humble lineage, though she strove to hide it with her noble station.

After Liza's own mother, Jennet Ramsay, died along with her newly delivered infant—a sister Liza never knew—Liza's father wed Claray for her youth and fair looks, not for her rank.

Liza was a child of only five winters, and this stepmother, scarce more than ten years Liza's senior, had mothered her in all but name.

They trod in silence toward the castle's keep which looked somewhat unfamiliar to her. The rounded drum tower was gone, and the red sandstone looked altered, uncanny to her eye.

From the guard tower, a burly man clad in tight hose and thick cuirass armour covering his breast glanced suspiciously, a smirk twitching at his mouth.

Liza halted, causing Claray's slender form to jerk back.

"Do ye have something tae say tae me?" she demanded of the rough and disagreeable sentinel.

"Elesbeth!" cried Claray, tugging Liza's arm. "Are ye off yer head?" The woman paid no heed to the guard's straight stare, and dragged Liza forward into the courtyard and then to the keep.

When they were safely inside, Claray rounded upon Liza again. "And what do ye think ye were doing with the bailie? I saw how ye looked on him. And I saw ye laid hands upon him. Lachlan McClaren is no match for ye," she hissed. "Should ye cavort with the servant help, I'll hae ye locked up."

A fierce yearning gripped Liza's heart, though she knew Claray's words to be true. Lachlan, with his strong arms and eyes like the forest... She yearned for him beyond reason.

"Goerge Dicson arrives with John Comyn," Claray

announced. "Ye'll sup at their board and table."

Liza frowned.

The name rang some faint bell in her mind, but she cared not a whit for this Dicson fellow. It was Lachlan's face that filled her dreams.

In the passageway, they encountered Wyolet, a chambermaid clad much as Liza in plain léine and kirtle. The maiden's braided hair gleamed fair and yellow, and her eyes were the color of cornflowers, not violets as her name suggested.

She curtseyed low. "My lady," she said, looking at Claray, not Liza.

"Fetch water for Lady Elesbeth's bath," Claray demanded.

Wyolet's glance at Liza was cool as the water of the River Creagan and rife with unspoken spite. But she nodded at Claray and turned to do her mistress's bidding.

Liza stared after the lass before Claray tugged hard on her arm yet again. Liza puzzled at her recognition of the folk around her. She knew them all, though how, she was unaware.

Up the shadowed winding stair they climbed, Claray leading without a word.

On the third floor, they traversed the corridor to a door that creaked open, revealing Liza's empty chamber. Gray morning light showed through the narrow encasement and cast long shadows over the rumpled boxbed.

Claray set rush lights aglow from the dying hearth, coaxing the embers back to flame.

As her stepmother tended to the fire, Liza drifted to her commode dresser made of French oak and walnut. The furniture was wrought with marble and bronze and looked of great worth indeed.

She lifted a small bronze hand mirror and beheld her face: her amber eyes were flecked with gold, leaves were caught in her auburn tresses. She was both herself and a stranger. A dreamer half awake. *Elesbeth*, she thought. The name, too, was both familiar and foreign.

She turned to Claray. The woman's wrath now gone, she may have been like a sister to Liza. "What think ye of marrying for love?" she asked.

Claray, rifling through a wardrobe, made a hard noise. "What has love tae do with anythin'?" She paused, glancing back. "If ye speak o' that bailie, ye're crack-brained."

"I did not say I love him," Liza protested. "Yet he is not a serf but the bailiff by my father's warrant. Is my father not the laird and chief of this land?"

Claray turned to display a silk kirtle upon the bed. "Love comes in many shapes, lass," she said, though her eyes gleamed with something like contempt.

And at that moment, none other than Lachlan appeared, shouldering a great wooden tub lined with linen. His léine stretched over muscled arms.

Claray's nostrils flared with displeasure. "Where is the attendant?" she demanded.

"He is just returnin' from the hunt. He must skin and gut the hare and prepare the venison for tonight's feast," Lachlan said, setting the tub close to the fire. "I will fill the bath for Lady Elesbeth."

Claray snorted but said no more. She waited until Wyolet replaced her at the armoire before she swept from the room.

Liza noticed Lachlan's look at bonny Wyolet before he mumbled about fetching more water. His gaze then met Liza's, and a glow warmed her chest. Could he have crafted a reason to wait upon her?

"Wyolet," Liza said when Lachlan had gone, "do ye know how I came to lie beneath that tree in the darkness? Have I habit to wander during my slumber?"

Wyolet glanced over her shoulder. "Only Uilleam roams in sleep, lost until dawn."

Liza smiled at her brother's name. Uilleam, with bright blue eyes, the color of the sea, and endless curiosity, no mischief meant. He wandered the halls at night, and the castle's laborers would gently guide him back to his bed.

How then had she strayed alone into the castle's yard while all lay safe indoors? Perhaps Uilleam could provide answer to the query. She would seek him out after she'd washed the mire from her skin.

Lachlan returned with two buckets slung upon a

carrying pole. He tipped them into the tub and bowed, two more attendants following close behind with more vessels of heated water.

When the tub was of suitable depth, he said, "I'll fetch more wood fer the fire then," and alighted again from the chamber.

The two women watched him take his leave. Wyolet's lips pinched tight, but she did not speak.

Liza considered her feelings for Lachlan, trying to summon the reason for her desire. She was certain she'd always had eyes for him, though perhaps she'd never dared to speak or act upon those yearnings.

Wyolet kept her gaze cast downwards as Liza disrobed and entered the warm waters. The chambermaid silently gathered Liza's soiled garments and made to depart the chamber.

Due to her position, Liza was sure there were few with whom she could speak freely. "Tell me of Lachlan," Liza called out, before the lass could take her leave.

"What is it ye seek tae ken?"

"How has his kin and clan come here tae these lands?"

After a considerable pause, Wyolet breathed softly. "The Clan McClaren hail from the hills, but his kin dwell now in the shire below. Laird Ramsay trusts him as tenant-in-chief and baron bailie while he and young Alexander sojourn in France." Pride sounded in her tone.

"And is he a kind and decent man?"

Another silence met Liza's ears before Wyolet spoke. "A better and more noble man may ne'er be found in all of Scotia."

Liza's heart grew heavy. "Ye are smitten with him as well." She hazarded a wary glance over the edge of the washtub.

Wyolet's cheeks colored red. "I…" She cast her gaze away. "It seems no' proper to speak on it."

"Truth is seldom proper," Liza whispered so softly the maiden perhaps did not hear her.

Wyolet's slippered feet made scarce a sound as she crossed the threshold.

Liza lay back in the wooden tub, half her body warmed by the waters and the other half touched by the morn chill in the chamber. Again, she had the feeling she'd been reborn, and this day marked the dawn of her life's journey anew. What was she to make of this existence? She knew not, and she longed for a time and a place she could not name.

Moments passed, and Lachlan returned to the chamber bearing an armful of firewood.

His presence without witness was as improper as Wyolet's truth.

Both were mindful of the unseemliness. Yet, if they were happened upon, it would be Lachlan who would face punishment.

When his glance met hers, a bright ember leapt between them, old as the stars.

Memories half-formed danced in Liza's mind, as if she'd loved him through many lives. An ache swelled her heart, burst into her throat, and then sank to hopeless depths.

Their ranks too far differed.

Claray had uttered an unwelcome truth, and Liza knew she must face it.

A movement at the chamber's passage, and Wyolet did again appear. The maiden's gaze burned with silent longing or envy, Liza couldn't tell which.

Liza's spirit yearned to share with Lachlan her visions, and the certainty that in an age far from this one, he might be hers. But such notions were folly, even in her own mind.

She drew a deep breath and summoned strength in her voice. "Leave the kindling, then leave the chamber, bailie," she demanded. A flicker of bewilderment flashed in his ensnared gaze. Liza cast her glance away. When he made no move to follow her command, she pressed on, "Ye're dismissed, then."

With abrupt motions, he placed the firewood hearthside.

She mused he ought to have possessed the wisdom to refrain from approaching her, despite her earlier, heedless dalliance under the ruined tree.

She'd been wounded and bewildered. And though

her blood was noble, she was but a lass, and he owed his loyalty to her father, the laird of the land and chieftain of the clan.

He should know as well as she such a union was nothing but folly.

Liza's heart withered within her, yet she knew it must be so. She could nearly feel the relief radiating from Wyolet across the chamber.

Lachlan McClaren could never belong to the likes of Lady Elesbeth Ramsay, and it filled her with a desperation she knew not what to do with.

Chapter 5

Wyolet's deft fingers plaited Liza's long, dark tresses and secured them in coils just above Liza's ears. Shimmering crispines held her locks in place. Liza did not bother with a cap or barbette, though she would don both later for supper, when she took her place at the head of the board, next to the powerful men of the realm who visited Claray on this summer night.

For now, Liza wore only her long chemise and her plain pinsons.

The léine Wyolet had laid out was of a fine material and would be topped by a bliaut with fitted sleeves, the color of gentle heather. It was an extravagant garment sent for Claray by her father. But since Liza would be the object of display at this repast, Claray had instructed Wyolet to lay it out for Liza, instead. No doubt Claray would be dressed in equal finery for the Scottish Guardian of the Realm, John Comyn, whom Liza hated beyond any reason.

She chanced a look into the mirror which had also been an extravagant gift from her father. She was content with her reflection, though even absent the fine braids and elegant garb, Liza would likely find no difficulty in drawing a fitting husband from a wealthy clan. Not only was her station appealing, but her countenance was still fair, despite her years creeping onward.

Yet the quandary remained—she did not want any of the suitors presented to her.

She dismissed Wyolet, and with a deep sigh, she wandered from her bedchamber to find Uilleam skulking about in the hallway.

The lad had been but a bairn when his father and elder brother journeyed to France near four years past. Though he now stood near the cusp of manhood, Claray declared it far too perilous for her precious son to travel alone. He'd have to bide his time a few more years, should the Ramsay men not have returned by then.

Uilleam had the fair looks of his mother, Claray. Liza favored her own mother, Jennet, who in Liza's faint memory possessed kind, dark eyes and the soft smile of a graceful woman with hair the color of night.

When Claray assumed Jennet's position, the new lady's concern for Liza as a bairn was scarce, though never did she show cruelty. Liza held the belief that Claray labored for the enduring prosperity of the Ramsay Clan, herself included.

"I saw you with him," Uilleam said, giving Liza a start.

"With who?"

"The bailie. Lachlan."

Liza said nothing and continued her way down the passage. Uilleam trotted after her. He was still much more lad than man.

"I favor Lachlan. He allows me to lend a hand with the hobelars." Like the wee ponies bred upon the estate alongside their full-sized kin, Uilleam dashed with swift strides down the passageway before Liza.

When he'd slowed his gallop at the stairway, Liza reached him and said, "What is it ye think ye spied?"

"Ye were touchin' him upon the front grounds as the first light did break." Uilleam offered her a mischievous grin. "The village lads shared tales with me of what transpires between lads and lassies."

Though Liza had been of muddled mind when she'd awakened in the grass, that was scarcely a suitable excuse for her unseemly behavior. Especially in front of her young brother.

"Perhaps ye should keep your imaginings to yerself," she answered lamely.

"Ye only mean I shouldnae tell Claray." He proffered another grin that Liza did not return. "Did the bailie touch ye back?" he continued as they descended the staircase.

"'Tis not fittin' tae speak on such matters," Liza muttered, echoing Wyolet's counsel concerning her own affections for Lachlan.

"Thorfinn MacTiridh told me all about it. A lad inserts his manhood inside an opening—"

"Uilleam!" Liza exclaimed, her cheeks suddenly aflame.

The lad looked swiftly stricken, but quickly recovered and shrugged. "That's just what Thorfinn MacTiridh did relay."

"Well, ye shouldnae be cavortin' with the cottars and villagers."

"What else am I tae do about this barren place?" It was a fair question. With the castle's menfolk away, none remained to keep him company save for the servants and their bairns. And of late, they'd grown wary of having the heir of the laird and lady in their midst. "Mother says it's perilous to stray from the keep with the state of affairs in Scotia."

Liza's brow creased at the whisper of danger. She hadn't paid much heed to the political strife, yet she knew well the land would be without a sovereign until Margaret, Maid of Norway, rightful heir to the throne, reached her years and claimed her place at Edinburgh Castle.

Until the granddaughter of the felled King Alexander ruled, the land was governed in his absence by the Scottish Guardians of the Realm. They maintained a courteous alliance with King Edward I, the one they called Longshanks due to his great height.

While Liza had caught whispers of the discord in

the Highlands, closer to Edinburgh, where the Ramsay Estate lay, there had been no disturbance of the peace.

"Perhaps I can convince Claray of your safety," said Liza, mostly for Uilleam's benefit. Claray wasn't inclined to listen to any musings of Liza, especially when it came to her precious bairn, Uilleam.

But Uilleam scuffed the toe of his common bund shoe on the stones and muttered, "She doesn't think fer herself. She only does what John Comyn, the rotten donkey, says."

John Comyn of Badenoch, one of the realm's Guardians, had been lingering much at the estate in recent months. Liza took care to keep her distance from the towering man, whose eyes bore upon her with a look both disdainful and unseemly. Still, she chided Uilleam for uttering the insult.

"Ye must respect yer elders, lad," she said, though she herself held nothing but scorn for the man.

He was the nephew of John Balliol, whose own father had served as guardian to King Alexander himself.

"I'd like to take a stick to the head of John Comyn," said Uilleam.

Liza recalled the man's cruel eyes. She stopped walking and grasped her brother by the shoulder. "Ye mustn't say such things aloud."

Uilleam's lips turned down in a pout. "But he's an arse."

"That he is. But we will keep that as a secret between the two of us."

The boy continued to pout, and Liza said, "Ye can accompany *me* about the castle."

Though Uilleam grimaced, he also nestled closer to Liza's side.

Should Claray take offense to Uilleam joining with the cottars, perhaps Liza might persuade her stepmother the lad ought to take on more tasks upon the land. He might assist Lachlan in a more official capacity. This would grant Liza a defensible reason to spend time with the bailie…

"Where are ye goin' now?" Uilleam interrupted her musings.

"To see Hexilde."

"Because ye missed breakfast since ye were bathin' with Lachlan."

They reached the main passageway, and Liza said, "I was not bathin' with Lachlan."

"He carried the tub and water in for ye."

Liza continued toward the kitchens without responding. The lad really did need something to keep him occupied.

Though the walls of the castle were swept with a draught, a warmth enveloped them as they stepped into the kitchen upon the floor of the stronghold. A fire blazed fiercely in the grand hearth, and the kitchen folk—both lads and lasses—bustled about the chamber with great fervor.

"Hexilde will only give ye bread and cream now," cautioned Uilleam unnecessarily.

"Then I'll eat only bread and cream."

"Ah, behold who hath chosen to grace us with their presence." Hexilde's voice resounded mightily above the clamor of the chamber. "The fine and bonny Lady Elesbeth." Her tone was filled with a light and mirthful scorn, and Liza couldn't help but smile.

The elder woman's crown of curly white hair lay constrained beneath a white coif, with wispy tendrils escaping their confines like rebellious vines. "And whence, pray tell, were ye this fine morn?"

"She was out with the bailie," offered Uilleam. His round face was the picture of innocence, but his tone held the sure implication of misconduct.

"The bailie," Hexilde said as she kneaded dough with sturdy hands on the flour-dusted board. She raised an eyebrow at Liza.

Liza kept her lips stubbornly closed.

The cook wiped her hands on her apron and fetched a thick slice of bread and a small pot of cream. In a mazer vessel, she served Liza a thick ale brewed from malted oats.

As Liza bent forward to partake of her meal, Hexilde gathered two great pails and foisted them upon Uilleam. "Hurry yerself tae the Creagan Burn and draw some water for the boiling," she commanded.

"Can I have some bread and ale?"

"When ye've finished yer task."

"I'll fetch the water from the chain pump," he proclaimed.

Hexilde, with her formidable presence, positioned herself before the young lad. "Did I not bid ye to hasten to the river, not the pump?"

Her voice warned of no defiance. Uilleam recoiled.

"Aye," he muttered, departing the chamber.

"Claray spoils the lad," said Liza, though she could not fault her stepmother for it. Claray, a young woman, was herself adrift since her husband's departure, and Uilleam was in dire need of the succor. Liza, as well, did likely spoil the boy excessively.

She took a bite of the bread and cream and gnawed thoughtfully.

Hexilde made a noise at the back of her throat. "Not so much since the lady has been makin' eyes at John Comyn of Badenoch."

Liza's chewing abated as Hexilde's meaning struck, and Hexilde bowed her head, belatedly recalling Liza's position. Hexilde had been with Liza's kin since she herself was a bairn, and had seen Liza come into the world. "I pray yer pardon, Lady Elesbeth. I shouldn't be speakin' out of turn."

Liza remembered her stepmother's comments that morning about love coming in different forms and wondered if she'd been referring to the dreadful John Comyn.

Hexilde went back to her breadmaking. "And what's this about ye consortin' with the likes of the bailie, Lachlan?"

"I wasnae consortin' with him," Liza declared. She sipped the hearty ale, savoring the frothy brew. It dawned upon her she hadn't partaken of sustenance since the morn prior, which might lend reason to her muddled mind and unbecoming demeanor. "He chanced upon me beneath the sycamore," she answered, making no mention of the bath.

"The great tree?" Hexilde cried out. "It was smitten by a heavenly bolt! What madness drove ye to wander in the tempest and gale?"

The other kitchen folk continued to bustle about the chamber, preparing the supper that carried the importance Claray had proclaimed. They paid Liza no heed, for they, too, were accustomed to her visits to their rougher world to spend time with Hexilde. "Just some strange night visions, I suppose."

"What of these visions, child?"

Liza paused, pondering how much to reveal to the cook, whom she held in confidence. The dreams made her appear touched by madness. "It seems they've ebbed away now, and I cannae claim to glean much sense from them anyways." She hesitated, then said in her voice soft and hazy, like a light mist at morn, "Is it possible to dream…of what's to come?"

The woman glanced around the kitchen and leaned

closer. "Do ye speak of visions of days lyin' ahead?"

Liza nodded.

"Aye, I've heard it told. When I was a lass, my grandmither told me tales of people who took passage through time. It isn't what we think it is, ye know."

"What then is it?" Liza whispered fiercely.

"There be some cunning folk—witches and wizards—who hold that time disnae flow in a simple line as we reckon it, but rather all things are unfolding at once. Other realms do unfold at the very same moment as this one."

A cold chill wracked Liza's body despite the heat of the kitchen chamber. "The monks at the Watret Abbey would care little fer yer tales," said Liza carefully. She longed to ask many more questions.

Hexilde swiped her flour-dusted hand through the air. "Yonder monks know nothin' but what they can weave into the web of their unseen God. Any event beyond that creed—especially from a woman—they lay at the feet of devils and daemons." She scoffed. "I'll heed them nae a whit."

"Well, if Claray hears the talk, she'll invite Bishop Robert Wishart to perform an exorcism in yer kitchen."

Robert Wishart was the most revered and gracious among the Guardians. Unlike John Comyn, Liza relished the visits of the wise man from Glasgow to the castle. He brought with him words of kindness about

Liza's mother, Jennet, of whom he spoke with great fondness.

"What happened in this night vision o' yers?" Hexilde asked.

Liza furrowed her brows in thought, struggling to remember. "I was surely at the castle. And I was myself, yet not myself. None there called me Elesbeth."

"What did they name ye?"

"Liza." She realized she'd been thinking of herself in the same manner without realizing it.

"Can't say I've heard that appellation afore." Hexilde took her unleavened loaves to a surface at the other end of the long board, covering them with a linen cloth to rest.

When the woman returned, Liza said, "In my dream, I was smitten with Lachlan."

"Ach! Smitten with the bailie!" Hexilde bellowed.

Two servant girls looked over and tittered. Hexilde shooed her hands at them. "Make haste with yer work before I turn ye out." When the scullery maids had hastened away, Hexilde said to Liza, "He's a braw, sturdy lad, but the likes of ye can never be with him."

Liza knew this. But to Hexilde, she confessed, "When I awakened outside, on the cold, wet earth, he was there. As if the hand of fate had ordained him to me."

When Hexilde did not answer at once, Liza's desperation grew, and she spoke aloud what thus far her heart had borne in silence. "I cannae stop thinkin' on him."

Hexilde's stern gaze was her only reply, leaving Liza more wretched than before. "Ye said ye believed in travel through time and distant realms. Why then believe ye not in love?"

"Because 'tis no' love, lassie, but a dream."

Liza cast her gaze downward and watched a wee mouse scuttle across the floor with a crumb of bread. It disappeared into a crack between the stones at the far side of the chamber. The vermin, Liza realized, had more freedom than she.

"Dreams may hold great power, and at times prove true," Hexilde continued. "But this vision is no' real. Ye'd be wise tae remember that."

Liza pushed the last crust of her bread and the dregs of her ale aside, her face reflecting Uilleam's earlier pout.

"Ah, lass," Hexilde chided gently. "Yer feelings for the lad will grow fainter."

"And if they shouldn't?" Liza's voice trembled. She didn't dare say she wished they'd never wane.

"Ye shall be wooed this eve by a nobleman of Berwick-upon-Tweed named Goerge Dicson. He may be the companion ye've been longin' fer."

"I havnae been longing for any husband," Liza protested.

"'Tis a folly," Hexilde declared. "Ye hae much tae

offer a man. A fittin' man," she clarified. "What waste tae die alone in this auld castle without joy or bairn tae leave fer times tae come."

At Liza's sour face, Hexilde's brow darkened as she gestured to the bustling kitchen. "Each o' these wenches would give her right eye to stand in yer place, and ye would spurn yer fortune? Perhaps 'tis ye should be turned out."

Liza lifted her chin. "Believe ye not in a union fer love rather than name or coin or land or power?"

"In this life," Hexilde replied, her voice like cold, sharpened stone, "ye may hae love or ye may inherit station, but rarely both. And station is the nobler o' the two."

Hexilde left her in her seat at the board then. Liza considered the servants who on this day—and perhaps every day—appeared far merrier than Liza could ever recall of herself.

The cook spoke true. Liza was indeed ungrateful and indulged herself too much. If she did not tread carefully, the Lord might strike her down to impart a lesson.

Yet, there must be more to this life…

When Hexilde came again close, Liza said, "Have ye ever yerself known love?"

She was prepared for another lecture, but was surprised when Hexilde's face softened with a faraway look.

"A long while years gone," Hexilde answered. "But 'tis naught but ashes now. It would be fer the good of the land to rid yer head o' clouded fancies and do yer proclaimed duty for the clan and yer kin."

Again, the woman spoke the truth. Liza knew it.

She rose to take her leave, but Hexilde left her with one last counsel. "Ye came tae me seekin' my thoughts, and my thoughts shall ye hae. Let silly Claray array ye in yer finest garments, stain yer lips with berries, and ye catch yerself a wealthy and powerful laird. 'Tis what yer father would yet wish."

Liza spoke no further words. Her answer lay within her heart, and she left the chamber before Hexilde might impart even more counsel for Liza's benefit.

She sought her bedchamber, where she lifted her Psalter from the board at her bedside, and settled to read the sacred psalms that might give her heart comfort.

Even those sacred words awoke earthly longings within her body and her heart.

She closed the book before the Lord's hand might smite her down.

Chapter 6

The great hall thundered with laughter and merriment.

Feasts at Ramsay Castle were a grand gathering, not solely for the household, but also for the clansfolk from the lands. This was owed to the generosity of William Ramsay, chieftain of the clan.

His absence mattered not to the revelers; food and drink flowed in abundance, and they made merry before the high table of Scotia's powerful Guardians.

While the bellies of the revelers were filled with ale and venison, fresh-baked bread and spiced mutton stew, fruit tarts and custard pies, Liza, seated at the head of the board, felt faint of heart, mind, and body. The hall was sweltering, and her bliaut weighed heavily upon her, causing her cheeks to blush crimson.

She took a small sip of the heather ale in front of her, wishing instead she might sip the milder ale or mead of the commoners. The fermented and sharp heather brew caused her tongue to burn and her head to pound.

The discourse among the nobles at the grand head

table was more reserved than that of their rougher kin as they feasted upon the choicest cuts of meat with sturdy eating implements, unlike the common folk who used their hands to stuff full their mouths.

Liza was seated next to Claray, and on her other side was Sir Goerge Dicson, a man nearly a decade her elder. The nobleman was not displeasing to the eye, yet he carried an air of superiority and a haughty tilt to his head. He donned a lengthy tunic shorn from fine linen, decorated with an embroidered cloak clasped by a golden brooch. A gold signet ring, embossed with a noble crest, gleamed upon his finger. He was attired as finely as she imagined Longshanks himself might be.

Even Liza's fine outfit and accessories from France seemed plain by comparison.

As if reading her thoughts, Claray hissed close to her ear, "Do you see what fineries Laird Dicson will offer ye?"

Liza took a draught of her bitter ale. Then she said, "His riches matter not tae me. Maybe *ye* should marry him," she added.

Claray smiled. "Silly hen. I'm married to yer father."

But Liza, and everyone else in the great hall, could see how closely Claray huddled to the side of John Comyn of Badenoch.

John Comyn engaged in earnest discourse with James Stewart, the fifth High Steward of Scotland, while at the board's distant end was seated the benevolent and gracious Robert Wishart, Bishop of Glasgow. Liza longed to be beside the venerable elder, a steadfast ally of her father and the sole Guardian who truly appeared to hold Scotia's welfare in his heart.

Liza searched the raucous chamber for the face of Lachlan, but she couldn't locate him in the throng of faces.

Hexilde had advised Liza's affections for Lachlan would wither away much like the fleeting dream. Even as the vision became harder to recall with the passing hours, however, her feelings for Lachlan flourished anew within her heart.

She felt the unwanted awareness of Goerge Dicson upon her, and she purposely turned her interest to the other side of the board where she seized on stolen phrases from the conversation between John Comyn and James Stewart.

The name 'Margaret' reached her ear on more than one occasion, and Liza knew they spoke of King Alexander's granddaughter, the young maid from Norway and rightful heiress to the Scottish throne.

These Guardians had appointed themselves to govern the realm until the lass reached maturity. She would then journey hither to claim her rightful place as sole sovereign, and the Guardians would be relieved of their duties at her command.

Liza pondered the maiden's true age. Though idle

chatter claimed she was but a bairn, none could rightly declare how many winters had passed since her birth.

James Stewart suddenly raised his voice above the din. "There is the Treaty of Brigham to consider."

John Comyn's retort came sharp, though muted by the angle of his head. As he turned back to his trencher and pierced a hefty piece of meat with his sharp dirk, his voice grew clearer and more foreboding. "I care not what the writ declares, nor should ye. Longshanks merely believes he understands his own actions."

"Once the maid marries Edward of Caernarfon—"

John Comyn shook the board with the strike of his great fist. "Enough," he ordered, and a hush fell over the merriment.

The stunned silence lingered for more than a minute, until John Comyn gave Claray a rough nudge. "Speak to yer folk," he hissed sharply into the hush.

Claray stood as the lady of the land, her voice quivering like a reed in the wind. "Pray, do continue with your merriment," she bade the revelers, who stared at the fiery exchange unfolding before their eyes. "As with ye all," she continued, "we are apt to grow merry with a hearty fare filling our bellies." She mustered a laugh, casting a wary glance downwards at the formidable Guardian.

"And drink on our lips," John Comyn added with a forced smile. He held up his mazer, then gulped down the herbed ale.

A cheer sounded from the crowd, who resumed their laughter and discourse, louder than before.

On Liza's other side, Goerge Dicson leaned close. She could no longer ignore him.

"Lady Elesbeth, my father tells me you're an educated young woman, like your mother." He nodded appreciatively toward Claray who had also retaken her seat. John Comyn's hand rested upon her stepmother's thigh.

"Claray is not my mother."

"She is the Lady of Clan Ramsay." His voice dripped with disdain for Liza.

It was such an obvious statement, Liza didn't bother to address it directly. Instead, she said, "Isn't that why ye're here, courting me? Fer my name?"

His sneering smile grew more disdainful. "These alliances serve the interests of Scotland, and the lands of the Ramsay Estate are fair and bountiful. Laird Ramsay, were he present, would surely give his blessing."

Though the man hailed from Scotland, to Liza's ear, his speech bore the lilt of the English. It was another strike against him.

She took a bite of boiled and herbed potato, though appetite eluded her and a dull ache throbbed behind her eyes.

"As I had commenced to utter a few moments past, ye won't have much need for education as a married woman."

Liza had no intention of marrying this man.

"I expect ye'll be with child shortly. Preferably a son."

It made Liza ill to imagine the act of conception with this bobolyne.

He pressed on. "By your years, many a lass has birthed several bairns." His words bore no flattery. "I must admit, ye are fairer than I'd reckoned. There's that, at least." It did not seem as if he held her beauty in high regard.

Liza cared not. And verily, she did not take kindly to the recitation of her virtues and flaws spoken aloud and straight to her face. "I have many things to do and learn before bairns would be of interest to me." She was not sure if this were at all in truth, but no matter what the man said, she had a strong yearning to answer contrarily.

Before he could correct her again, she said, "Tell me, Lord Dicson, how did you come to be acquainted with the Guardian John Comyn of Badenoch?"

He appeared startled by her query. But perceiving another chance to enlighten Liza, his lips curved into a smile. With a cloth, he wiped his mouth, slick with venison grease, and then spoke. "My father, though ever a champion of Scottish independence and bearing steadfast fealty to King Alexander, sees much merit in fostering amicable ties with our southern neighbors."

Liza knew this meant the English. She straightened, alarmed.

He continued, "I, indeed, hold the same belief as Laird Comyn."

Liza considered this. She finally spoke. "I'm quite sure my own father does not share that persuasion."

"Your father is not here, Lady Elesbeth." This was said in a low whisper at her ear. "And there is a different strategy we might consider for the good of our lands."

"Strategy fer what purpose?"

He opened his mouth, then quickly shut it again, frowning. "I don't expect you to be interested in such matters."

Liza spied a chance and seized it, though it troubled her to conjure the words and the manner.

She smiled with the grace of a gentle lass. "But how will ye expect me to aid ye as life's partner if ye be hesitant to share yer grand wisdom with me?"

The man had seemed indifferent to her beauty, though that he'd spoken of her looks at all meant he'd taken note. She gazed up at him and leaned nearer, her bosom brushing lightly against his forearm.

Despite his finery, he smelled of meat and herbs and stank of something rotten.

While Liza retched, the man appeared well pleased with this change in her demeanor. "I reckon you may be right." He relaxed back into his seat. "Though I do not expect you to grasp much of my stance, I shall explain that it has become increasingly clear a full divide from English concerns might indeed be a harm to Scotia. What we ought to pursue is a cordial alliance with King Edward. Such a union will make both nations stronger."

Though King Alexander himself had maintained a fragile peace with the English king, Liza had often heard her father ponder the frailty of this bond. Is this not why he now sojourned in France? To nurture a Scottish alliance with King Philip of France, the sworn foe of Longshanks?

To Dicson, she said, "Like the one our own king held?"

He gave a dismissive snort. "Alexander was a fool. We're better off he's gone."

Despite Liza's shock, she managed to keep her countenance bland. "I've heard the child-queen Margaret will marry Prince Edward of Caernarfon. Will that not give us the friendly alliance you seek?"

For the first time in their interaction, Goerge Dicson regarded Liza with something other than derision. "That's what they want you to think," he whispered, leaning closer again, this time as if he were sharing a secret. "The bonny prince is weak, and the maid is but a child. Longshanks will use the arrangement to his sole advantage. Instead, we should endeavor to install a leader who can both maintain independence while securing English benefits. The Treaty of Brigham—"

His words were interrupted by the sudden presence

of large, heavy hands on his finely clad shoulders. The ruddy face of John Comyn bent close to the ear of Goerge Dicson, and in turn, close to Liza. She jerked her head away from the Guardian who terrified her so.

"You wouldn't be boring the fine lass Lady Elesbeth with whimsical political opinions, would ye, Laird Dicson?"

A sheen of perspiration moistened Dicson's brow. "Of course not, my laird and liege."

Liza cast her eyes downward, aware of just how much influence John Comyn held, not only at her humble estate, but across the whole of Scotia.

As much as Liza disliked the courtier, she disliked the Guardian even more. "Laird Dicson attempts to enlighten me on Maid Margaret of Norway," she interjected, attempting to defend her suitor against the brute.

John Comyn turned his gaze upon her, causing her to recoil and regret her words. She could not fathom what Claray might find appealing in this man, who stood in stark contrast to her truthful and virtuous father in every conceivable manner.

The man was tall and imposing with a halo of dark curls, graying at the temples. He had likely once been handsome, but his gaze spoke of evil and cruelty.

His teeth bared with his smile. "He shouldnae be telling ye fanciful tales." A crust of ice ran through his exaggerated lilt of the northern lands, and he ran a hard knuckle down her cheek.

Liza clenched her lips together, though she did not flinch.

He turned back to Goerge. "We would not want to share falsehoods about our future queen, now would we?"

"No, my laird." Goerge Dicson's voice barely rose above a tremulous whisper.

Liza cast a glance at Claray, a faint smile dancing on her lips like a wisp of mist.

His harshness brings her joy, Liza realized. So long as it be aimed at others and not upon her own head.

The woman was a fool.

"Upon the utterance of our noble queen's name," John Comyn proclaimed with a voice which once again echoed through the hall, his hands still resting heavily and ominously upon the shoulders of Goerge Dicson. "Tenants, villeins, and laborers," he bellowed, his words cutting through the clamor of the great hall. As the merrymakers gradually stilled and a solemn silence descended upon the assembly, he pressed on. "My kinsmen, ye may wonder why we've been summoned to such a grand feast under the gracious invitation of the esteemed Lady Claray Ramsay."

He clapped his hands together slowly until everyone in the hall participated in the cheers in honor of Liza's stepmother, who beamed. Pleasure colored her bonny cheeks.

John Comyn held his hands up and waited for the room to once again quiet. "We're also here to celebrate a momentous occasion. My friends, Ramsay countrymen—ye are the first to hear this news that may well change the course of our great land of Scotia forever."

A multitude of muted murmurs filled the ensuing pause, and Claray cast her gaze upon the Guardians at the far end of the board. Both seemed either troubled or vexed, yet Liza could not know which.

"My fellow Guardians and I have received tidings from King Erik of Norway that his daughter—the granddaughter of our revered King Alexander and rightful heir to the Scottish throne—is presently making her journey to assume her place at Edinburgh Castle. With the coming of our child queen, Scotland shall once more assert its rightful dominion, ceasing to be a realm adrift in uncertainty."

After another brief moment, a great joyfulness rose forth from the gathered crowd. There sounded shouts and weeping and laughter and wails.

Liza joined in the joyful celebration only superficially. She couldn't help but wonder at the words of Goerge Dicson, who now appeared pale, his gaze darting about the room as if searching for some source of unseen peril.

John Comyn raised his large hands in cheerful union with his fellow countrymen. He then leaned forward and placed his hands again on the shoulders of

Laird Dicson, who startled at the touch. The Guardian said something in his ear that caused the younger man to turn even paler.

Goerge Dicson rose from the table and walked out of the great hall, not sparing a backward glance.

With that movement, Liza noticed the crease on the brow of Claray.

When John Comyn sat again at her side, he whispered, too, in her ear, and she nodded, though the frown did not fade completely.

Despite the departure of her unwanted suitor, an uneasiness filled Liza's heart. Whatever had taken place, Liza was certain she'd never see Laird Goerge Dicson again.

John Comyn snaked a possessive arm around Claray's shoulders, and her stepmother leaned into this other man, who might or might not hold the fate of Scotland in his malicious hands.

Chapter 7

By and by, Bishop Robert Wishart took the seat vacated by Goerge Dicson. "What ails ye, Lady Elesbeth?"

Even to this man whom she trusted, Liza would not be wholly truthful. She offered him a feeble smile. "Nothing, Your Grace."

Robert Wishart, the eldest of the Guardians, had hair as white as fresh snow and blue eyes sharp with a keen brilliance few could match.

He cast his gaze upon the merrymakers, now quaffing their ale with great gusto.

A minstrel had been beckoned, and the hall was alive with dance.

"Perhaps we may share the same vexations," he spoke quietly.

Liza lifted her gaze to meet his. "I'm certain I don't possess yer knowledge."

"Aye. Yet ye have eyes in yer head." He cleared his throat lightly. "And ye possess the intuition of yer father and the mother who bore ye."

Claray had begun making merry with John Comyn,

and Liza gazed upon her as she laughed up into his ruddy face.

"I despise the notion that folk think her tae be my true mother."

"None who matter truly believe such a thing."

"Goerge Dicson seemed tae think it so."

"Laird Goerge Dicson the younger is but a doty-polle," said the bishop with a wry tone.

Liza's eyes opened wide at the wise man's use of the insult. He chuckled at her shocked countenance, and she rested a hand over her mouth to hide her laughter.

When her humor had faded, Robert Wishart said, "I don' believe ye'll be seeing the likes of Goerge Dicson again."

"Where has he gone?"

"Back to the East Marches and his baronies, I'd expect."

Liza recalled John Comyn's sinister gaze and doubted Wishart's assumption. Instead, Liza conjured an image of the man's headless body drifting down the River Creagan; the skull would be fastened to an iron rod—a grim caution to other men to hold their words right.

The bishop's words brought her back to the present. "Yer father, though—he'd want ye to take a suitable husband. He wouldnae want ye rambling about this castle under the heel of Claray."

"There's much my father would *not* want." She sent

a pointed look at her stepmother who was nearly falling into the arms of another man.

"Mayhap. But ye can aid Laird William Ramsay by joining in a sturdy and true union and marriage."

Liza felt free enough to give a dismissive flick of her wrist. "I'm no' interested in an alliance o' that sort."

"What sort does pique yer interest, then?"

Liza opened her lips, then clamped them shut.

The man folded his gnarled hands across his embroidered tunic. His episcopal ring glinted in a room brightly lit with torches and flame. "Ye're too much like yer mother fer yer own good."

"What of my mother?" she asked, trying to keep the eagerness for knowledge at bay.

By the cautious look on the kind Guardian's face, she knew she'd failed. He leaned forward and tore off a piece of dry bread, chewing it thoughtfully. Then he said, "Yer mother was born a MacDuff, kin to the Mormaers of Fife."

Liza scoured her mind for a remembrance of this knowledge. Finding no trace of it, she furrowed her brow.

"Ah, they wouldnae have told ye," Robert Wishart said and looked around the room. "The Earls of Fife were none too pleased with her decision to wed yer father."

Liza followed his gaze to the tenants of the surrounding baronies. "Why, pray tell, not?"

"The Earls of Fife stand as the foremost nobles in the land. The Ramsays, for all their sway, possess neither the same kin nor clout." He leaned in closer. "'Tis a truth the present Lady Ramsay knows well."

Liza pondered the hidden strain of jealousy in her stepmother's voice and interactions with Liza. As a coinless lass from the Highlands, she must have felt truly out of place amidst the nobles. Liza watched her dancing, her head thrown back, and her fair curls escaping her coif, barbette, and wimple.

She looked livelier than Liza could ever recollect.

"Yet," said Robert Wishart, "Claray is keen enough to know the merits of yer lineage. And she means well, in her own fashion."

Any compassion Liza might have harbored for Claray was overshadowed by Liza's own unwavering loyalty to her father. "Even as she frolics with John Comyn in her husband's abode whilst he is away, defendin' the realm?"

"She's blinded by Comyn's self-imposed power, I fear." He leveled a serious look at Liza. "All the more reason fer ye to wed and forge yer own path, Lady Elesbeth."

Liza ignored this. "Why did my true mother join with my father if he was below her station?"

Robert Wishart seemed surprised by the query. "Because she loved him, o' course."

In that precise moment, Liza spied Lachlan loitering near the rear of the hall. His eyes locked with hers, and her heart leapt into her throat. Had he been observing her all the while?

"What if I also mean tae wed fer love?"

"That's a luxury not often afforded to women of your station." The bishop's words echoed the earlier words of Claray and Hexilde.

It was not what Liza sought to hear.

"My mother did it."

"And she graced the grave early."

"Are ye saying she was slain?"

Robert Wishart gently clasped her hand. "I'm telling ye, lass, there be matters beyond yer grasp in this realm. The wisest course is to bow yer head and tread within the confines of yer own knowledge and station." He shifted as though to rise from his place. Before he took his leave, he offered one final counsel. "This life is a harsh enlightenment, my lady. Why burden it further with yer own ill-conceived deeds?"

Liza desired to protest but found herself uncertain of the cause she'd stand for.

Union with a commoner? Her mother had taken a clan chieftain as husband—a man held in high regard across the realm. Even *that* had not found favor with her God, or so the bishop had declared.

She lingered at the board for a while longer, lost in her dire musings. And then, deciding she'd indulged in enough revelry for the eve, she rose to make her departure from the hall.

She observed others absent from the high table as well. Most notably, Claray and John Comyn were nowhere to be seen.

As she wove her way through the crowd and made her way toward the rear stairs oft-used by the household where she was less apt to catch a curious or wandering eye, she spied a gleam from the chancery where the records for the estate and neighboring baronies were kept.

Liza's brow creased. Her father's seneschal, Peter Syward, did not frequent the chancery this late into the night. At least, Liza did not reckon it so.

Since rising from the dampened earth that morn, she'd come to see how blind she'd been to the life surrounding her.

She crept silently through the dim shadows, pressing her form against the hard stone wall, daring a glance into the chamber.

Peter Syward hunched over his spindle-legged desk, the lamp's ragged wick throwing shadows on the stone wall. In his cramped hand he clutched a quill, its nib stained in ink black as night, as he scrawled words across a sheet of yellowed parchment, likely a gift from the Watret Abbey to the Ramsays, traded for a lesser tenant's due.

The man's hand stuttered across the page, and his body radiated a kind of desperate heat; beads of sweat prickled at his scalp.

Liza had never spoken to Peter. She'd seen him about the castle, of course, but they'd had no reason for discourse.

She might have felt the same about Lachlan McClaren just a day past.

She was on the verge of stepping into the chamber when Peter heaved a great sigh and laid his quill upon the ink-blotted desk. He rubbed his weary eyes, then took up the blotter and rocked it over the vellum parchment.

He blinked again at the words before muttering to himself, then tucked the sheet into a grand leather-bound ledger, which he slipped into a drawer at the front of the desk.

Before Liza could make her way into the chamber, he scraped the chair back across the floor and seized the rush candle affixed to the brass holder upon the wall.

Without knowing why, Liza scurried back, hiding herself within a shadowed nook.

The man passed by her without a glance in her direction.

Though there was no harm in wandering about the castle she called home, Liza felt as though she were trespassing, and her heart thundered wildly as she crept into the dim chamber. She approached the desk under the cover of shadow and opened the drawer, casting about for the ledger with her fingers.

A weak light from a passageway sconce gave her just enough radiance to open the thick book and pull out the top parchment, which she rolled and tucked beneath her bliaut into her léine. What possessed her to abscond with the parchment, she had no idea, but it felt urgent in the moment.

As she hurried through the darkened passageways and up the staircase to her chamber, she heard soft whispers coming from the laird's bedchamber, now occupied by only Claray. A feminine laugh sounded, followed by the deep drone of a male voice, much too sonorous to be that of Uilleam.

Then, afeared that the pair might be Lachlan and Wyolet, Liza slowed her pace and dared a peek within.

The pair that met her eyes was no servant couple. The striking face of Claray was upturned toward a man whose back faced the doorway. Liza knew the broad back clad in a black cloak and tartan trowse belonged to John Comyn. Their bodies were closely entwined, and Claray's face was tenderly cradled within his hands. Those hands gradually descended along the woman's neck to the bodice of her chemise, where he slipped his fingers into the fabric. Claray sighed with delight and her body trembled. The man then leaned in to kiss her deeply, turning as he did so, such that the pair were in profile.

His countenance was fierce, as if he meant to devour his prey. In a way, Liza knew it was exactly what he sought. Overcome with repulsion, she was about to turn when the Guardian drew back from the kiss.

"Once the child is away, we shall ascend, my lady. Not only for Scotia, but for our own destiny, *myn leman.*"

Liza stood upright. *What child?*

Claray's voice was breathless as she replied, "There remains the matter of William and Alexander to ponder."

"They shall be well heeded. Fret not, my lady."

"No harm shall come upon them?"

His lips curled into a slow smile. "They shall be none the wiser."

"And the lass?"

"My lady, have faith I shall do what serves us both best. And for Scotia," he added, his hand moving slowly within the weave of her garments.

As she moaned and leaned into him, he continued, "The Ramsay Estate and its baronies are crucial to the independence of this grand nation. When John Balliol is king, all shall fall into place, and ye, Lady Claray, shall have wealth beyond yer wildest dreams, surpassing the Earls of Fife. And when King John Balliol has fulfilled his purpose, our true might shall be revealed. Ye and I shall be the rulers of the realm."

Claray moaned again. "Aye," she breathed as his hand moved swiftly inside her gown.

"Do ye trust me?" he murmured in her ear.

Despite her revulsion, Liza found she could not avert her gaze. She knew of the carnal activities between men and women, yet had never beheld the act itself. She felt her own body respond as blood coursed through her veins, leaving her near as breathless as Claray.

Claray's hands traveled down the front of the Guardian and found their way to the prominent bulge at the juncture of his trowse. He let out a long, primal groan, his movements growing abrupt and urgent as he lifted Claray against him, bearing her away from the door.

Before they might behold her, Liza stepped from the doorway's sill and pondered her next course. It was then she spied Uilleam trodding the corridor toward her. What was he doing, wandering the darkened passages at this unseemly hour?

She raised a finger to her lips, bidding him keep his silence. In the shadows, he heeded not her warning.

When he spied her, he cried, "I've been seeking ye!"

Liza sprang forth to drag him into the nearby garderobe. But before she could clasp the lad, heavy, wrathful footfalls sounded, and she darted into the privy alone, flattening herself against the stone for the second time this very evening.

The lad mistook her haste and pressed onward, and Liza shut her eyes when she heard his strangled cry.

She was sure John Comyn had accosted him. She prayed the evil Guardian would grant the boy a swift birching upon the seat and send him on his way with no further harm.

"What hae ye heard?" demanded the brute.

Uilleam stammered, then blurted, "I–I heard nothing. I swear tae it!"

"Ye speak lies!" roared John Comyn.

The boy shrieked in pain, and Liza stifled her breath, restraining the urge to rush forth and bear the blows in his stead. She convinced herself there lay no honor in both of them suffering; she could comfort Uilleam at a later hour. And surely the man would deal more kindly with a bairn than with a woman of her own age. She shuddered to recall his feral gaze and the hands that had touched Claray. He would not do the same to her.

She vowed to pilfer some sweetmeat from the kitchen and bestow it upon Uilleam as reward for his pain.

Claray's shrill voice sounded through the corridor. "Uilleam, ye should make haste to yer chamber."

"What hae ye heard?" snarled John Comyn again, and again Uilleam cried out.

Liza kept her eyes tightly shut, expecting the lad to betray her presence in the garderobe. Yet he spoke nothing of her.

"I–I thought I heard a sound. Nothing else, I swear

to it," he wheezed, and cried aloud once more.

Claray's voice was closer now. "He swears he's heard nothing," Claray pleaded. "Let him go."

"There must be no loose ends," John Comyn grunted.

"He's but a lad," Claray implored.

"A lad who makes sport of eavesdropping at the privy chambers of elders," said the Guardian.

Liza knew she must step forth. Before she stirred, the Guardian and child passed swiftly.

Uilleam cast her a fleeting glance as they made haste, but John Comyn spied not the garderobe door.

"Where do ye go with him?" cried Claray.

"I shall lock him in his chamber, with a guard, that he meddle no more in the converse of grown folk."

"Harm him not," Claray pleaded.

Before the stir abated, John Comyn let forth a snarling growl not unlike the wanton sounds he had made in lust. His words echoed in the passageway. "Sniveling and whimpering shall but quicken the end in this life."

Liza knew not whether his threat was leveled at Uilleam or Claray. She lingered until the only sound remaining was Claray's faint sobs, then she crept forth and made her way to her chamber.

There, Wyolet—or some other chamber wench— had tidied, strewing fresh linens upon the plump and full mattress. The wooden bath had been stowed, the hearth's flame quenched. A lone rush lamp still burned in its sconce beside the door.

Liza stood in front of her ornate commode for a long while, waiting for battle should John Comyn let himself into her chamber when Uilleam, in his fear, revealed her presence in the corridor.

But John Comyn did not come, and sometime later, Liza removed the stolen parchment from her chemise and laid it out on the marble top of the commode, struggling to read the fine handwriting of Peter Syward.

The document appeared to be an unremarkable accounting of levies and dues from the barony. What drew Liza's gaze was the final entry, likely what Peter had been penning when she'd spied upon him earlier.

Laird Goerge Dicson, by witness of Sir John Comyn of Badenoch and Lady Claray of Ramsay, inquired after the hand of Lady Elesbeth Ramsay in marriage. The query was deferred until such time as Laird William Ramsay returned from his service abroad.

At no point in the eve had Goerge Dicson bespoken her hand, nor had William of Ramsay been named in any word of matrimony. Even had they spoken of such, who would have informed the seneschal and bid him set it down?

Liza coiled the parchment scroll and slipped it into the drawer of her commode, meaning to restore it to its ledger at morning's light. Perchance she'd ask Peter

Syward who had bade him pen the entry.

She turned toward her boxbed, musing how to strip off the weighty bliaut's folds without aid. She had not planned to return at this late hour, after the chamber-maids had lain down for the night, and she would not summon Wyolet. Better to lie full-clothed and hope the morrow mended this day. With a soft sigh, she plucked the crispine from her hair and uncoiled her braids until her auburn waves fell about her shoulders and back like a silk veil.

A movement at the threshold made her wheel round, her eyes wide with dread, hand at her throat. She braced to see John Comyn.

It was Lachlan McClaren who stood there, a bundle of firewood in his arms and a single rushlight in hand.

His voice was low as a whisper. "Pardon, Lady Elesbeth. A chill lingers in the air. I've come to stoke the fire."

Liza could not trust her tongue. Her heart hammered in her breast, and she scarce could swallow. She simply inclined her head, bidding him entrance. He bowed and crossed the chamber, passing near her on his way to the hearth. She watched as he set the wood, struck his rushlight reed, and coaxed the flame to life, blowing gentle breaths until the fire took hold and glowed.

When at last he turned, their eyes met once more. A spark leapt between them, fiercer than the hearth's blaze. He broke his gaze first and moved toward the door. She watched him go.

Before he could cross the sill, she spoke. "Bailie, may I ask a favor?"

"My lady?" he answered.

"Might ye help me with my gown?" She lifted the heavy sleeves bound tight at her wrists.

His mouth opened, then snapped shut as a scowl furrowed his brow. She feared his refusal, yet he exhaled and crossed the chamber, laying his rushlight upon the coffer. He stood so close she felt the warmth of him, the scent of pine and earth, of embers and night air drifting between them.

Uncertain what to do, he simply waited before her, and she cast down her gaze as she stooped to gather the hem of the bliaut and lifted it upward.

Lachlan took the fine cloth from her hands as she raised her arms, so he might slip the garment over her head. As it shifted from her shoulders, her hair fell down her back, hiding the thin chemise beneath.

It was the undergarment she often wore, covered only by a léine. She now stood before Lachlan with nothing but a thin cloth to shield her. She felt as naked as if she wore no gown at all.

As if to occupy himself, he laid the gown with gentle care upon the pallet beside her bed.

"*Tapadh leat.*" She whispered her thanks in the soft Gaelic of her kin.

When Lachlan turned again, she let her gaze rise to meet his. Her lips parted, and he regarded her with such fierce longing she felt herself drawn forward as though by some other will.

Her mind bade her stay her step, yet a deeper voice within her soul urged her on. What harm if she yielded to Lachlan?

She surely knew the answer. He was so far beneath her station that the stain could never be cleansed.

The thought should have made her turn away. Instead, it thrust her forward until she stood within his arms. His body pressed hard against hers and she molded herself to him. He threaded his fingers through her fine hair and raised her face to his.

The kiss was, at first, as gentle as a summer breeze, soft and sweet. The touch of his lips then grew urgent and demanding of that which she yearned to give.

Lachlan's hands roamed beneath her chemise, and Liza arched against his touch, his lips still fast upon hers. With his fingers, he traced her neck and shoulders, her arms and bosom, until he found her breasts. She gave a cry at the pleasure so fierce it nearly brought her to tears.

He rested his brow against hers and searched her soul through their shared gaze. "There shall be no returnin' from this, *m'eudail.*"

Liza recalled the precious endearment from another time. Another place. Perhaps it was this memory that bade her nod, their foreheads still pressed close.

Her whispered "Aye" was the only sound in the realm. Time stood still, and yet a hundred years might have passed. It seemed their souls were wrought in the very stars and bound together for eternity.

At last, he set his jaw. "I'll bear ye tae the mattress now, Lady Elesbeth."

She swallowed. "Will ye…call me Liza?"

He frowned just faintly, then blinked and spoke her name with solemnity. "Liza."

A wave of relief warmed her heart at the sound of her name upon his lips. "Aye," she said. "Fer all that's amiss in this world, this one thing is right."

And so, at last, they were together again.

Chapter 8

The wail resounded through the stone walls, striking Liza's very soul.

She sprang upright in bed, roused from a troubled slumber.

The fall of retreating footsteps followed the sudden, harsh cry.

Liza remained motionless as the early morn's light seeped dimly through the narrow slit of the window. Dying embers cast a feeble glow in the hearth. Beside her, the sturdy, unclad form of Lachlan McClaren stirred. His slumber had surely been deeper than hers. Liza gazed upon him, striving to gather her wits. She felt ensnared between a dream state and wakefulness…yesteryear and the morrow…life and death.

His brow creased. "Did I dream a cry, Lady Elesbeth?"

She pressed a finger to his lips, shaking her head gently, then cast aside the blankets of linen and vair. She reached for her cast-off chemise, and when clothed, she swept her hair back from her face. "Await my return," she murmured, gesturing to the sheltered confines of the boxbed. "Stay still as night."

His eyes laughed at her. She did not smile back.

Should any soul burst in, prying eyes would not swiftly discern Lachlan concealed within the recessed mattress and shadows. And should Wyolet be the one to attend to their indiscretion…

A shock of shame flowed swiftly through her. Lachlan did not belong to her, yet she had partaken of him. Though the eve had been filled with delight, she had to refrain from pondering upon the wronged Wyolet.

She tread softly on bare feet toward the door, eased it open, and peered down the passageway. The cresset lamps affixed to the walls had also burned down, and it took a moment for Liza's eyes to adjust to the shadows.

No movements sounded, and nothing stirred.

She was on the verge of turning back to the chamber when a shape upon the ground near the corridor's end drew her gaze. She strained to discern the pale form, concluding it might be blankets or linen, rashly cast aside by a heedless chambermaid.

A fresh panic surged through her.

What if that unknown maid had entered Liza's chamber and discovered Lachlan while their bodies lay entwined? What if the cry had been at the shock of finding the bailie within the lady's room?

Liza lifted her head. This was a risk she'd chosen to embrace, and she steeled herself for the consequences.

With determination, she moved down the passage

toward the heap of clothing. Her pace slowed as she approached. Aside from the light-colored clothing, Liza noted the veil of gorse-yellow hair spread across the ground. A dainty hand lay palm up on the dark stone.

Liza's breath caught in her throat, scarce believing what her eyes did witness.

She crept closer, her mind convinced the poor soul on the ground had partaken too heavily of the previous night's ale. Then she caught sight of unseeing cornflower blue eyes staring at her from another realm.

"Wyolet," Liza cried and sank to the floor next to the body of the chambermaid. The flesh was cold and unyielding.

Liza snatched her hand away.

"What's happened?" a voice said from behind.

On her knees, Liza looked round at Claray who had appeared in the passage.

"Elesbeth?" Claray asked, a note of surprise strangling her words. "Who is it that lies before ye?" When Liza didn't answer, Claray looked at the form on the ground and let out a cry.

"It's the chambermaid," whispered Liza. "Wyolet."

Claray's hands went to her mouth. "But how? Is she..." The words melted in the air.

Liza turned back to the body which held no essence of the lass they'd known. She then noticed the dark pool spreading across the stones.

"Blood," Liza said, daring to peer closer at the lifeless corpse.

The back of the head seemed to have been struck with such force that the skull was left misshapen.

Claray clasped her slender arms around her waist and leaned forward. "The blood's as black as bile," she whispered, beginning to sway.

Liza barely managed to steady her faltering stepmother, whose face had turned ashen, her life's essence having fled her cheeks.

Footfall sounded from the far end of the corridor. Liza turned and laid eyes upon Lachlan, now fully clad in his léine and trowse.

She attempted to shift her body to conceal the form of Wyolet.

He took notice of Claray held strangely in Liza's arms. Before he could speak, his eyes fell upon the lifeless body sprawled upon the stones.

As the gruesome sight registered, his knees nearly buckled beneath him. He let out a soft, "No…"

"It's Wyolet," Claray cried, unnecessarily. She added, "Bailie, we'll need tae see to it the girl is removed, and the stones are washed before the others awaken. Can ye alert the chamberlain, Donvaldus MacTavish?"

Lachlan remained silent, his entire being focused on the lifeless maiden lying before them. The sorrow etched upon his visage clamored louder than any words could, and Liza could see with clarity that he'd been bound to Wyolet by more than mere bonds of servitude.

Liza did not want to feel glad at the girl's death, and truly she was not. But there was a small, secret, shameful part of her that did not mourn for the lost life.

Lachlan's hands trembled as he reached forward to check for life—a breath or beat of the heart.

None was detected when he shook the body gently. "Wyolet," he whispered. "Ye must wake now. 'Tis morn." His voice quaked with a faint hysteria. "'Tis time tae awake fer the day. There's much tae do."

"The girl is dead," Claray announced with sudden strength. She pushed herself from Liza's arms. "We must haste her body away." She glanced around the passageway, her eyes darting furtively as if searching for someone. Or something.

"Don't be cruel," Liza said.

Claray moved forward so swiftly Liza did not have time to react. The woman grabbed Liza's wrists so her fingernails dug into Liza's skin. "Ye know nothin' of cruelty. Ye'd best keep yer mouth shut and yer head low, lest ye'd like to feel it fer yerself."

Liza's eyes widened. She pulled her arms out of Claray's tight grasp.

Claray turned aside as Lachlan gathered into his arms the lifeless form of Wyolet. He held her in much the same manner as he had cradled Liza's living body but hours before. His face was damp with tears before he turned and started down the passage.

Liza didn't want to let him go. "Lachlan," she called. He turned slowly, and Liza could see that the back of Wyolet's head shone wet with blood and matter. The maiden's face, though, was still beautiful as her lifeless eyes stared up at Lachlan.

Where will ye take her?" Liza asked.

Lachlan didn't answer immediately, and he didn't meet her gaze. "Tae the abbey," he mumbled. "The monks shall see tae her burial rites. I will...alert her mother."

"And her father?"

"He passed of the bloody flux in the cold o' winter. Wyolet was all she had left."

"I am..." Liza halted and swallowed her words. She shifted her gaze. Claray no longer stood in the passageway, yet her absence gave no assurance she wasn't skulking and eavesdropping from some hidden nook.

"I am sorry this has happened," she said, her words but a whisper.

Lachlan's chin quaked as he cast his gaze to the body in his arms. "This wouldnae hae happened if..."

He left the thought unspoken. There was no need to utter it. Had Lachlan not been in Liza's chamber, perhaps he would have instead lain with Wyolet the eve prior.

Liza had a terrible thought. Perhaps Wyolet had spied them together, and the cry Liza had heard was the lass's heart shattering. Perchance, as she did flee, someone mistook her for an intruder.

Perhaps someone had mistaken her for ye, a small voice whispered inside Liza's mind.

Lachlan turned upon his heel and walked away with his burden, while Liza beheld his retreating figure. This was her due penance. To hold affection for a man—to have surrendered herself to him—who could never truly belong to her.

And to bear the burden of his heart's ruin.

Chapter 9

After Lachlan had departed with Wyolet's cold and lifeless body, the chamberlain Donvaldus MacTavish bade three young maidens bearing buckets of water to scour the stones and wash away the girl's spilled humor.

Both the servants and Donvaldus cast wary glances upon Liza, as though she alone had summoned death upon the chambermaid.

Liza cared not. She could barely banish the grisly sight from her mind, and she lingered in the passage, watching the maids' bowed backs as they completed this gruesome task.

Claray did not return, and Liza wondered if the lady had crept back to her bed to lie in John Comyn's arms. The memory of his cruel handling of poor Uilleam but the night before caused an anger to smolder within her. She scanned the corridor's end, expecting her brother to emerge from the staircase and question the turmoil. He remained locked in his chamber. For that she gave silent thanks.

Uilleam was but a child and still ill-suited to the

land's violence. Claray was correct—the lad was not ready to journey to France to join his kin. With the whisperings of unrest, 'twas better for him to stay at the Ramsay Castle, where he was safe, sound, and out of reach of harm.

When the stones had been scrubbed and scalding water sloshed into the passage, Liza at last sought her chamber, despair trailing in her wake. The servants she passed threw suspicious glances at her, pressing themselves against the opposite wall as she neared. If her eyes met theirs, they quickly turned away, as though she were a witch whose presence cast evil upon them.

Within the chamber, the bed lay unmade and her garments unlaid—tasks Wyolet would have tended— while the hearth's embers lay cold and damp. No attendant had been sent by Lachlan to stir the fire, so she shivered in her shift.

She surveyed the rumpled blankets, and at once the vision of Wyolet's pale form fled, replaced by more stirring recollections: Lachlan's mouth upon hers, his hands beneath her shift fondling her tender breasts, drawing sighs from her very soul.

Her breath grew shallow as her thoughts drifted to the wet heat between her thighs, to the fevered strokes that had driven her mad with a feral need to be filled and claimed. Even now her cheeks burned and her body flamed, banishing the chill.

He had guided her hand to the hard pillar of his manhood, and as her fingers closed about it, he drew a sharp breath. Then, with a tenderness that set her soul alight, he entered her. A fierce ache gave way to a radiant bliss as he moved within her—first with slow ardor, then with urgent thrusts. Her body felt immersed with a light not of this world, and when he whispered not "Elesbeth" but "Liza," she shattered like starlight, every fragment aflame with a joy so fierce she swore the heavens bore witness.

Afterward they lay entwined, and she felt the steady beating of his heart against her own, as though they shared a single soul.

"Pardon me, my lady," a soft voice hailed from the doorway. Liza whirled as though her secret bliss had been laid bare.

A young chambermaid stood just inside the door's sill, clutching a bucket of water.

Startled, Liza fixed her with a gaze of surprise and impatience. "What seek ye?" she demanded.

"I was bid to attend, my lady," the girl said. She lifted her chin, and though she cast a wary eye upon Liza, she seemed resolved to embrace bravery. The lass was not as bonny as Wyolet, though she was hearty and hale, with full lips and gray eyes clear as a Highland loch.

"I bid ye enter, then. Ye cannae serve me from the passageway."

The maid stepped in and poured the water into the wash-basin near the commode chest. She then smoothed the linen blankets of the boxbed and laid a soft gray vair upon the mattress. Liza wondered if the lass grew suspicious of the passions that had transpired upon these sheets.

For a heartbeat, she envisioned what might have happened had Wyolet been summoned to serve her that morn. Would Lachlan have fled before the maid's entrance? And had he done so, would his scent have lingered still upon the bed?

A swift pang of guilt was chased by relief that no scandal would arise.

"What's yer name?" Liza asked, watching the girl array her garments.

A pause. "Forsy, my lady."

Liza inclined her head and crossed to the encasement. Though the window was small, the opening granted her sight of the lands beyond. Below, the courtyard lay sodden from recent rain, and ghostly mists drifted over the earth, promising warmth where shadows lingered. A gentle breeze bore the scent of morning fare from the cottars' hearths and the barony's kitchens.

The activity in the outer court and beyond the dry moat was customary—two women bent over the chain pump, and a half-dozen watchmen in hauberks tramped purposefully, back and forth, beyond the watchtower.

When John Comyn and the Guardians made residence within the castle, the watchmen's numbers waxed greatly. The armed sentinels set Liza's heart pounding with unease as they paced the courtyard.

She turned her gaze to the right, where the stables lay dimly in the mist. She could just conjure a groom tending to the steeds and hobelars. Beyond, in the hazy fields, peasant folk bent to their chores.

Her eyes fell upon the blackened tree where Lachlan had found her, and a draught coiled about her shoulders. A flash of memory. Thousands of tiny lights glowing on a trunk and bough she'd spied from this very vista. Liza felt a tug of *cianalas* for a time and place she could not name. She searched her mind for the source of that yearning. She shut her eyes, plunging deep into her spirit for a knowledge that eluded her.

At last, she sighed and let her mind's search fall away.

When she opened her eyes anew upon the grounds, a rider drew out from the stables on a small hobelar—one that Lachlan had acquired from some distant kin.

Liza scarce would have marked the breed of those ponies had not a fierce quarrel erupted between her father and Lady Claray before his departure, years ago. The cause of the strife was half-veiled from her as a bairn, but even then she knew well her father's fondness for buying, breeding, and raising fine horseflesh. Lady Claray, for her part, railed against the purchase of the smaller breed at every turn. Liza had to assume it was because the hobelars were not the typical majestic breeds that Claray favored. Instead, they bore short legs and a stout body and looked quite irregular and ugly.

Though the matter brought Liza neither gain nor grief, she stood staunch by her father's side, defying her stepmother's chiding as a dutiful daughter.

The rider crossed the drawbridge over the dry moat and halted to speak with a watchman. Liza saw it was Lachlan, bearing a great shrouded bundle at his breast.

Wyolet's body, bound for the abbey and the rites of burial.

A sob knotted in Liza's throat. She turned swiftly, finding the maid, Forsy, gazing on her. Liza strove to veil her grief.

"Would ye hae me help ye tae dress, my lady?"

Liza realized she was still in her shift. She eyed the clean chemise and léine laid out near the wardrobe. Forsy seemed to cower away from her. Was the maid afeared for a fate like that of Wyolet's…or was there some ghostly presence about Liza? She herself felt the otherworldly air tenderly touch her cheek.

"Begone," Liza declared, and Forsy offered a small nod and scuttled toward the door. But ere she reached the threshold, Liza's eyes alighted on her commode. She called out, "I have a charge for ye, Forsy."

The girl paused and turned, and Liza lifted the

stolen vellum she'd secreted after supper. "Will ye hide this for me?" she whispered, approaching the lass.

"Why, my lady?"

Liza could not say why the deed need be done, for she did not herself know. Only that it must. "Set it among the men laying stones by the postern gate," she said. The last true word from her father had been a demand that the castle walls be widened, and laborers still bore stone from the quarry near the burn.

Forsy stared at the parchment as though it had been penned by the Devil himself. Liza sighed and fetched a boddle from the commode. The coin was a small silver piece, King David's head stamped upon it. She thrust it into Forsy's palm.

The maid's eyes widened. "I cannae take this from ye, Lady Elesbeth."

"Ye shall," Liza pressed, "and hide the scroll for me. If ye be queried, I'll swear tae it that I gave ye the coin fairly."

At last Forsy met Liza's gaze, snatched both coin and vellum, and fled the chamber without a word. Liza let a soft breath pass her lips. Forsy might be no friend, yet perhaps the coin had forged a bond of sorts. Aside from young Uilleam, whom she held dear, she had none other.

Her eyes drifted to the empty mattress. No sign of last night's warmth remained. Lachlan would not return tae her bed.

Casting off her melancholy, Liza turned to tend to her duties. The grand hall would soon lay host to the morning meal, if it had not already begun. Despite the griefs of the day, hunger gnawed at her belly. She had scarcely touched her supper, her spirit burdened with foreboding.

She washed her face and her body at the basin, then anointed herself with the rosewater Alexander had sent as a gift a year past. She donned her chemise and léine anew, clasped a light linen mantle with a brooch at her breast, and coiled her braids beneath a simple lace crispine.

When she peered into the cloudy mirror, she scarce knew the face that stared back. With a start, she set aside the glass and hurried to the great hall.

Chapter 10

A throng of folk were gathered, supping on ale and pottage. The hearty stew, boiled from the remnants of meat and tatties from the evening's repast, was far heartier than the usual thin broth of root vegetables and cream. Hexilde and her scullery wenches had fashioned the ample mush in trenchers made of stale bread.

Liza took a serving and a mazer of thick, fermented wort, seasoned with herbs and honey. She seated herself at the far end of the head table, distant from John Comyn, who sat near Claray.

Others were gathered there, as well. Bishop Robert Wishart squinted blearily, clutching his mazer, and James Stewart, with his small face like a sly weasel, paid heed only to the Guardian on his right. Their yeomen were also in attendance, a gathering not often frequented by the household staff or the tenants of the neighboring baronies.

Liza had the notion John Comyn fixed her with an inscrutable gaze, and when she bid herself the confidence to return his gaze, she could feel the heated stirring of his hostility.

She met his stare longer than was wise, emboldened by a newfound courage. Perhaps it was Wyolet's passing that had eased her dread of the man. Perhaps it was her newfound dominion over her own body. Yielding herself to Lachlan marked her secretly, yet the knowledge was hers to wield as she saw fit. No longer was her body John Comyn's to offer to his conspirators as a prize of lands and wealth.

A faint, spectral smile of satisfaction danced upon her lips as she gazed upon him. John Comyn's lip curled in a nearly hidden sneer.

Satisfied, Liza broke the stare and settled to savor her pottage. This castle belonged to her father, not to John Comyn. She would not be intimidated by either him or his henchmen.

As she ate, she looked about for Uilleam, who had yet to appear. She reckoned he lingered in his chamber, suffering punishment for eavesdropping.

It was not fair the lad had been delivered a punishment meant for Liza. She would take him a trencher of pottage and a mazer of ale for his troubles. And she would beg Hexilde for a piece of sweetmeat.

Feeling emboldened and contrary, she mused aloud to all in the chamber, "I wonder what's become of Goerge Dicson. Perchance he was not so taken by the Ramsay name as was meant."

"Elesbeth," hissed Claray, a warning in her tone.

Liza felt John Comyn's wrath envelop her, but he answered with measured calm. "Laird Dicson has been summoned back to Berwick to mind urgent matters. He's not a man for silly maidens who'd seek to waste his time."

"And I have not the patience," retorted Liza, "for silly men who'd waste *mine*."

Claray sputtered into her ale, but before she could rebuke her stepdaughter, John Comyn gave Liza a slow, wicked grin. "Ye are clever, that I've seen with mine own two eyes. I've known a few lasses as canny as ye think yerself tae be."

Liza had no idea how Claray suffered such company.

"And what of them, my laird?" piped James Stewart, eager to curry favor with the mightier Guardian.

"Every single one," John Comyn replied, his gaze fixed upon Liza, "met an early death. They may charm with their wiles, but the Lord above gazes not kindly on wenches who deem themselves above their lairds. He shall find means to smite them down in due time."

A chill touched Liza's spine even as fury blazed within her. "Ye would dare speak so in my father's house?" she demanded.

John Comyn burst into a coarse laugh. "Yer father is deserted in France on a vain errand bid by a dead king. Before many moons, all shall see how fruitless his quest be. And no ransom shall free him."

Liza's heart stuttered. His words rang not as idle prophecy, but as grim certainty. She stood to take her leave of the hall, the occupants of which watched this flyting with amusement and curiosity.

Claray laid a pleading hand upon her paramour's arm. "John—" she whispered.

He shrugged her touch aside and rose to block Liza's path. She did not flinch. She stood up to him, small in stature but brimming with defiance.

"Before long," he spat, "ye shall know how little yer name and title may benefit ye, Lady Ramsay."

Liza's eyes narrowed, and she meant her stare to pierce the core of his soul. "Be that a threat, ye craven cur?"

Her words were an insult so insolent that the entire hall fell silent, every mouth paused and every eye turned to the pair. Time seemed to teeter and wobble, but Liza's contemptuous gaze remained resolutely fixed on the dark eyes of the Guardian and into the depths of pure evil.

And yet, ye are still a man, Liza thought. He was made of nothing more than the serf shoveling shitte from the dry moat to make fertilizer. Still, he might reach forth and with nothing but a light clasp of his large hand, throttle her easily. Her stare defied him to try, and the folk about them seemed to be holding their breath for just that.

A rumble of laughter arose from his chest, at first a

soft chuckle that seized upon itself and increased in mirth, then a roar of merriment which scorned Liza.

James Stewart followed suit, then the yeoman at the high board. And each cottar, castle servant, and maid within earshot. Perhaps their mirth sprang from the easing of tension, like a swift flood of relief. But their humor was directed at Liza.

Only Lady Claray and Bishop Robert Wishart declined to smile. They sat in silent gaze at the table.

Liza's cheeks burned with shame, yet she fled not the hall. Over the merriment, she declared to John Comyn, "I fear ye have laid threats upon the wrong soul."

"We shall see who has provoked the wrath of the wrong man." His lips twisted to an expression of pure malevolence. "And I trust ye'll mind who wields the power in this life." He leaned low and whispered, "Ask the chambermaid."

With those words, Liza recoiled. She could not fathom his meaning, though the hint was enough to make her believe him the slayer of Wyolet.

But...why?

A dread blossomed within her, and now she did flee the hall, passing Lachlan, back from his sojourn to the abbey, as she ran. He spared her nothing but a cold glance as he entered the chamber. Her heart almost broke in two.

She put it out of her head. There was another she

must find. Uilleam had not appeared. And John Comyn's words had caused her to fear anew for her brother.

She ran through the passage and up the stairs, heeding not the startled stares of the servants.

When she reached the third-floor corridor—where her brother's bedchamber lay in the northeast tower—a watchman with a strong build and a cruel eye barred her path. "None may enter," he declared, planting his legs wide and holding a cutlass blade at his side. His fist tightened around the hilt.

"By whose command?" she demanded, though her heart beat fast.

"By command of Lady Claray Ramsay, lassie."

Liza's cheeks flamed. Though this was one of John Comyn's men, he well knew Liza's rank within these walls. To call her 'lassie' was a grievous slight. With difficulty, she quelled her ire. "The lad is my brother," she said in measured tones. "I come by Lady Claray's bidding to fetch him and break his fast."

The sentinel stood his ground. "Ye won't pass unless Guardian John Comyn himself accompanies ye tae grant the order."

"Yet ye declared Lady Claray issuer of the decree."

"Aye, she did as much, giving voice to John Comyn. It is from my laird's own lips I take my bidding."

Liza stepped a pace forward, and the watchman

tightened his grip on the blade, widening his stance. "Dinnae make me hurt a lassie," he snarled low, lips twisting in malice.

Liza knew he'd take grim pleasure in inflicting pain upon a 'lassie', and she halted before attempting to force her way past the door. Feigning retreat, when he eased his posture, she sought to slip swiftly around him, using his cumbersome hauberk and his bulk against him.

The man, despite his girth, proved swifter than he seemed. He caught Liza about the waist with one arm and crushed her close, squeezing so she could scarce draw breath.

He chuckled softly in her ear, and the stench of rot on his breath made her stomach churn.

She writhed, striving to wrench free, but he only tightened his hold and pressed the sword's spear-point against the tender skin of her throat.

"I see no other soul but ye in this corridor, Lady Elesbeth. It would be but a simple matter to press ye against the stones," he hissed. She could feel against her the hard evidence of the violence he might inflict upon her between his legs.

Liza had kept herself from the rough men within the castle, and they all showed respect for her station as daughter of William of Ramsay. But this varlet cared not for her rank or her father's name, especially in his absence. And following John Comyn's words but an hour past, Liza knew no honor would stay him, even if her father were to stand before them.

Fury flared within her. She drew a deep breath and spat upon the watchman's cheek.

He reeled back, loosening his grip, but Liza was not quick enough to slip free. In the same heartbeat, he slammed her hard against the cold wall, and the blade's sharp tip cut her throat, making her bite down hard to stifle her cry as warm blood welled and trickled from the surface wound.

He dragged his weapon down her throat and into her chemise, tearing the linen and baring the top of her breast. Liza parted her lips to scream, but his greasy hand clamped about her jaw.

"Dinnae even think o' raisin' a cry," he whispered.

He drew his swollen tongue across her cheek, then pressed his foul mouth to hers, thrusting his slimy tongue between her teeth. She gagged, then opened her lips, allowing entry to the assault. When he thrust his tongue deeper into her mouth, she clamped her jaw, biting down hard.

His blood flooded her mouth in coppery waves.

The watchman howled in pain and staggered back. Liza collapsed to the flagstones, breath stolen from her lungs. Blood spurted from his mouth, running down his chin. "Ye rotten whore," he roared, words thick with anguish. "I'll see ye dead." He leveled the blade at her. Liza's heart seized. She had no strength to rise and nowhere to flee.

From the far end of the passage came a clear voice. "What think ye ye're doin'?"

The watchman whirled, and Liza scrambled up. She would have fled the other way, but Lachlan came dashing hard upon them, and she held fast.

"What's the meanin' o' this?" he demanded as he reached them.

"The harpy bit me," the watchman spat. "Place her in a witch's bridle, I say."

Lachlan's gaze swept from the bruised varlet to Liza, then he interposed his bulk between her and the watchman. He avoided her eyes, though his glance was tender as it alighted on her body. He marked the blood upon her throat and her torn bodice. Rage flamed upon his face. "Are ye…well?" he asked in a low, steady voice that quavered about the edges.

She nodded. "He didnae…touch me," she murmured.

Lachlan set his jaw and looked aside.

He faced the watchman, who outweighed him but was neither so young nor so powerful. The man was still holding his bleeding mouth.

In a blink, Lachlan pressed the guard against the cold wall, hand upon his windpipe, squeezing until the man's eyes bulged. "The lady o' the castle stands outside yer bounds. Do ye ken that?"

The watchman's face turned a shade the color of

the gloaming sky. A croaking sound escaped through his bloodied mouth, and Lachlan eased just a fraction.

"I've…rights to defend myself," the man gasped.

Lachlan's grip tightened again, and the rogue's face colored like a bleak storm moving across the lands. "I–I know it," he choked out.

For a moment longer Lachlan held him, his green eyes flashing.

Liza opened her mouth to urge restraint. One dead soul was enough for the day, though this brute deserved nothing but a dishonorable death. Before she could speak, Lachlan let him loose.

The man coughed, clutching his throat and sputtering as he slid down the wall.

"I'll see the lady to her chambers," said Lachlan, turning back. "If I spy ye again near her, I'll finish my task."

He took Liza's arm and led her off. Liza cast a glance behind at the watchman, who dared not scowl but wore a mask of fury, shame, and panic that made her lips curve with wicked delight.

Her mirth was but brief. "He's got Uilleam locked in his chamber," she told Lachlan. "He'll let not a soul inside—not even to bring him food."

"The Guardians will be gone before long. Leave it be."

"But the bairn has not eaten since yesterday."

"Dinnae tempt the Devil's men."

"Uilleam's punished for my sake."

Lachlan's mouth was a grim slash upon his face. No word crossed his lips until they'd passed the third-floor bedchambers and stood in the dim stairwell. Then he spoke. "Lady Elesbeth, these men be dangerous. They dinnae care who ye be, nor of yer father's name. Heed my warnin' and keep your distance."

He spoke truth, and her own thoughts led her to the same dread conclusion. 'Twas not fair. "Why should I fear fer my life in my own castle?"

"Ye'd be wise tae ask Lady Claray that." He shook his head. "But the men are here, and there's little we can do."

"I'll send word tae my father," she said. "The monks of Watret Abbey can surely bear the message swiftly."

Lachlan's head dropped. "There be darker matters at hand. I've heard whispers."

"What matters?"

"Matters o' the realm."

"Ye speak of the Maid of Norway? Is her passage in danger?" She minded the words of John Comyn the eve prior.

"Dinnae be prattlin' on o' such tales." His voice was hard, and he glanced about for lurking servants.

Liza's eyes flared. "Is that how ye think of me? A silly lass ramblin' over superstitions?"

In that moment, Lachlan seemed to recall his station. He dipped his chin low. "Of course not, my lady."

They stood mute. Liza felt the sharp sting of frustration—of Wyolet's death, of Lachlan's rank, of their impossible plight. She drew a breath. "I..." She steadied her voice. "I dinnae care of our stations. I dinnae care that I am the lady of this castle and ye but my father's man." She stepped forward and laid a trembling hand upon his rough jaw.

He did not pull away.

Her thumb brushed his lower lip, and his mouth parted, if but a fraction. She felt him soften beneath her touch, sensed his heart stir. A lone flame flickered in a wall sconce, casting shifting shadows upon his face.

His jaw then clenched and the tenderness fled. He seized her wrist in a fierce grasp and flung her hand aside. "We are no' meant for each other, Lady Elesbeth. Wyolet and I should hae been the pair, free tae build our lives upon the land, tae watch our bairn grow. But now she's gone, and 'tis on my doin'."

Shame burned upon Liza's face.

Lachlan's voice softened. "And if I were tae be with ye," he added, shame in his eyes, "I'd risk another death."

Tears stung Liza's eyes. "Do ye ken who slew Wyolet?"

"We shouldnae speak o' this," he murmured. "'Tis dangerous, and I'll never hae the blood o' two women on my hands."

He turned and walked down the stone steps, leaving her alone in the gloom.

He spoke the truth—a union between them was folly. But never had she yearned more.

Liza withdrew to her chamber to nurse her wounded pride. There she lingered, lost in the passage of time, pondering the day's happenings. She mulled over the clash with the Guardian and her perilous encounter with his sentinel. Her thoughts lingered on the shattered form of Wyolet and Liza's own unwitting hand in the demise of an innocent soul.

But most of all, her mind lingered on Lachlan. She lamented her helplessness. With a heavy heart, she cast herself upon the bed, drowning in her sorrow. Deep within, she knew her despair was for naught.

She must rise above this hopelessness and press forward with her life, regardless of how aimless it appeared.

Her heart swelled with determination. Hexilde had spoken true—the noblest way to honor her father and the Ramsay lineage was to seek a worthy husband. One who matched her stature and held her in respect as a woman.

She held no eagerness for the quest, but surely there dwelt a kindly man who would treat her with fairness and allow her to spend her days in tranquility. Her mind's resolve was firm, though her heart did heave fiercely against this course. Angry tears spilled down her cheeks at her plight.

It may have been minutes or hours before she was roused by a second scream that split the air. And if the first that morn had chilled her blood, this cry pierced her very soul.

A dread seized her, and she fled down the stairs toward the clamor at the castle's rear, pressing through the throng in the courtyard. Before she could force her way through the gathered crowd, Hexilde grasped her arm. "No, my lady," she said. The cook's voice was breathless and her face grim.

"What is it?" Liza demanded.

"'Tis not for ye tae see, my child."

Liza recoiled as the foreboding filled her soul. She longed to hide from the world. But she could not. She must know of this happening, even if it caused her life to alter.

"He has leapt from a great height!" she heard someone cry. "I did see it with mine own eyes," uttered another voice.

Liza wrenched free from Hexilde's grasp and the woman did bellow, "Ye cannae go out there!"

But Liza was free, and the crowd parted as she appeared.

Liza beheld the form on the cold flagstones. Another broken body, lifeless eyes fixed upon the gray heavens.

An inhuman scream tore from Liza's throat.

Her brother lay dead before her.

A fine mist had begun to fall, as though Heaven wept its holy anointment and blessing upon Uilleam.

Chapter 11

A full fortnight hence, the passage from Watret Abbey to the Ramsay kirkyard by the wee stone chapel near the River Creagan felt the longest in Liza's life. The days between had been a mire of tears and sorrow. Liza found herself desolate, unable to partake of food or solace. Her dreams had been filled with fevered visions of dread and destruction.

Now her body was heavy as she and Claray trod in black crape hoods, their heavy veils trailing as they followed the menfolk, Lachlan among them, bearing the small wooden casket upon their shoulders.

Liza could not fathom that Uilleam's body lay within. The box surely could not contain her brother's mischievous grin, his sulky sighs, his sudden laughter. It could not hold his heart.

She turned her gaze away before the ache of Uilleam's absence made her chest burst with sorrow. Her attention shifted to Claray, who leaned heavily upon the arm of Bishop Robert Wishart. The kindly Guardian had led the rite at the abbey, with the folk of the baronies gathered in solemnity. A smaller group of cottars and staff followed them to the graveyard, where Liza was aware of their soft whispers. And their pity.

She did not want their pity. She took a breath and lifted her chin high.

Every few steps, Claray let out a dreadful, mournful wail, and the old Guardian patted her arm, muttering words in a foreign tongue. Claray would then fall into a dazed silence, calmed by either the Guardian's words or the small draught of 'the great rest', a potion of opium, henbane, and mandrake given by a kind villager. Liza suspected the villager to be one of the cunning folk.

In the mournful days between Uilleam's passing and the burial, Liza clung to the hope her father might yet arrive. The abbey monks had kept her brother's body for as long as they dared. Neither Laird William Ramsay nor Sir Alexander had made their presence or their voice known. Though word of her brother's passing had been sent to France, she knew not if her father had received the missive. John Comyn had pledged to send swift tidings with his own men.

And absent a laird or lady to provide voice to the decision, it had been Liza who'd commanded the burial to proceed, her heart unwilling to linger in the void any longer.

She cast her gaze about, hidden beneath her veil.

Where was John Comyn in this time of grief and sorrow? He was absent from Claray's side. Though his absence brought relief, at least to Liza, she couldn't help but muse upon it.

In recent days, the weather had shifted from chill dampness to bright warmth. During the long procession, the sun warmed her through her dark léine and cloak. Her gaze settled upon Lachlan's back, damp with the sweat from the day's swelter.

The bailie regarded her with a distracted compassion, nothing more. And she to him returned the same. This was the second coffin he'd borne in but a sevennight's span, and his grief surely neared her own.

Liza had abandoned hope of anything but a cool nod in passing from Lachlan, though the secret knowledge of their shared intimacy still flushed her cheeks and set her limbs tingling.

She'd made a second promise to herself during her grief. There would be no kindly husband. No other would claim her heart. Lachlan would be the sole man she'd cherish with her body. The decision, she knew, was right. And she would take her loneliness as punishment for the pain she'd caused with her careless actions.

As though he felt her gaze upon him, Lachlan turned. Liza swiftly looked away.

Throughout the somber march, she recited a prayer. *May Uilleam's soul in stillness abide, held in love on every side. May he rest in Thy gentle arms, O Lord, and may our hearts be bound in peace.*

Upon finally reaching the wee kirkyard nestled among the trees, Bishop Wishart commenced his final blessing, and Claray sank to her knees as the casket descended into the sweet, damp earth.

Liza, too, shed her tears, but in silence, her cheeks damp and the warmth of her sorrow tracing down her neck.

The Guardian recited the *Officium Pro Defunctis* in his deep, tremulous voice.

> "*O Domine, libera animam meam, misericors*
>   *Dominus, et iustus: et Deus noster miseretur.*
> *Custodiens parvulos Dominus: humiliatus sum, et*
>   *liberavit me.*
> *Convertere anima mea in requiem tuam: quia*
>   *Dominus benefecit tibi.*
> *Quia eripuit animam meam de morte: oculos meos a*
>   *lacrymis, pedes meos a lapsu.*"

As the words swept over her, Liza endeavored to envision Uilleam in a realm of beauty and peace, yet her mind was haunted by his shattered form, his limbs askew in an unnatural heap. Crimson tainting the earth beneath him, and his eyes, unseeing, fixed upon the bleak heavens above.

> "*Et tu puer, propheta Altissimi vocaberis: praeibis*
>   *enim ante faciem Domini, parare vias eius.*
> *Ad dandam scientiam salutis plebi eius: in*

remissionem peccatorum eorum.

Per viscera misericordiae Dei nostri: in quibus visitavit nos oriens ex alto.

Illuminare his, qui in tenebris et in umbra mortis sedent: ad dirigendos pedes nostros in viam pacis."

Liza felt a gentle graze upon her hand, a whisper of fingers brushing her skin.

Startled, she withdrew her hand swiftly and cast a glance beside her.

The touch was nothing but the sway of a wayward thistle. She rubbed her wrist, and despite the warmth of the day, a shiver coursed through her.

She surveyed those around her, but the eyes of the folk gathered were fixed either upon the man of God or on Claray, whose wailing nearly drowned out his solemn words. The only one she found beholding her was Lachlan. When her gaze met his, she turned away quickly, believing he could discern her eyes through the veil's cloth.

Once the soil was cast, the crowd retreated to the castle, greeted by the vassals, farmers, and cottars from the lands about. The household was assembled, and a grand feast awaited them.

Claray had been carried to her chamber, having fainted during the solitary march back to the castle's keep. It was Lachlan who cradled Claray like a bairn in his arms and made away with her wailing form.

Liza assumed her place beside Bishop Robert Wishart at the high board at the front of the great hall. She presided as the Lady of Ramsay Castle over the feast, though her heart yearned only to retire to her chamber and shroud her eyes with the soft vair blanket.

After the repast was done and the guests had taken their leave, Liza found she could not further endure the haunted glances of the serving folk who eyed her as though she were a spirit herself. Nor, she found, did she seek to be alone with her thoughts—and her ghosts—within her chamber.

Despite her weariness, she feared sleep would not come.

In the noonday heat, she slipped unseen into the castle's garden.

Beneath the sun, two scullery maidens plucked parsley, marjoram, violet blooms, and summer savory at a leisurely pace. They were dawdling outside the sweltering confines of the kitchen. Hexilde would surely fetch them before long. The maidens did not cast an eye toward Liza, who remained still and hidden against the cool stone wall.

"I heard he cast himself over the battlements," said the fair, bonny maid, her cheeks rosy and plump.

"Ooh," answered the other, plain of feature but sweet of voice. "D'ye think he'd do't? He seemed not the sort. And with his father and brother sojournin' abroad and in right peril, he might've been laird one day."

Liza's heart seized. They spoke of Uilleam.

"He was daft in the head, so I've heard it said," added the bonny wench. "For a laddie of twelve, he clung tae his mother and Lady Elesbeth as ivy to an old yew. Laird he ne'er would've been."

The plain maid chewed a sprig of savory and mused, "Mayhap he tumbled by accident."

Both lifted their eyes to the castle's soaring walls. Liza forced her gaze to the ground, unwilling to ponder the height or the dread Uilleam's last thoughts might have known.

A young chamberlain of perhaps sixteen winters, cheeks ruddy, entered by the gate and pinched the bonny maid's arm. She squealed, then clapped her hand over her mouth. "Malcolm, dinnae!" she chided, glancing about the garden.

Liza crouched behind a row of yew, her heart pounding should they spy her.

"What are ye doin' with yerselves out here?" Malcolm asked, leaning back against the garden's fortification.

"Lady Hexilde's granted us a respite," replied the bonny maid. "She says 'tis a day of mourning, and supper will be meagre after the midday feast."

"Aye, 'tis true." Malcolm's voice was heavy and low.

"Think ye he cast himself off the battlement, then?" pressed the plain maid, her voice soft as air, but her musings grave and dark.

Malcolm stiffened, uneasy at her bluntness, while both maidens stared at him, awaiting his answer. They were unbothered by the ghoulish idle talk.

The lad finally shrugged. "Dinnae ken what was goin' through his skull. But he was an all right sort o' lad. He used to come 'round to play with my brother from time tae time."

"Was he kind, then?"

"Aye, seemed so. I didnae spend much time with him, but as I mentioned, he appeared decent enough. My father put an end to his comin', though."

"Because he was touched in the mind?"

"Nay, he was not at all."

"Then why did yer father forbid it?"

The lad's voice hushed, and Liza leaned in closer to catch the words.

"My father holds Laird Ramsay in regard, but he speaks no good of Lady Claray, and he disnae trust John Comyn." He paused, then pressed on. "He says somethin's afoot."

"Like what?" the plain lass said with a loud, eager whisper.

"Dinnae ken what it be. I dinnae think my father knows, either. But he reckons John Comyn is here fer a purpose."

"To do the deed o' darkness with Lady Claray," the bonny lass said, and the other girl tittered.

"Wyolet claimed she'd seen him with his hand beneath her skirts."

The trio's laughter subsided before they fell silent, likely thinking of the fate of Wyolet.

Liza's face burned. *What did they think about her?* she wondered.

She need not have pondered long.

"Lachlan did strive to shield Uilleam, I've heard it told," Malcolm spoke. "He couldnae guard the lad nor Wyolet from peril."

The bonny lass chimed in, "I've heard it told Lachlan was with Lady Elesbeth when Wyolet met her fate." A pause followed. "In her bed," she clarified.

"Nay," murmured the other maiden in a low voice. "Lachlan did hold Wyolet in his heart."

"He broke Wyolet's heart by lying with Elesbeth. Forsy saw them, she did. And I reckon Lady Elesbeth be a witch."

Liza's cheeks burned as the three servants lapsed into another quiet pause, pondering her mystical powers.

Malcolm appeared in her sight as he circled the outer garden wall, while the lasses tarried, their herbs forgotten.

The lad was the first to shatter the brief silence. "I'm not one to spread idle chatter," he said, "But there was talk of a quarrel between Lady Elesbeth and one of John Comyn's watchmen the day Uilleam perished."

"A quarrel of what?"

Malcolm shrugged. "I ken not its purpose, though it took place outside Uilleam's chambers. And jesting aside, all within the castle walls ken the Guardian Comyn spends his nights in the laird's chambers. He does not sleep there alone."

"What has that to do with Uilleam?" The plain maiden's voice rose and fell like a song.

"What if John Comyn seeks to claim the castle and the lands?" The query was met with silence, then Malcolm let out a weary sigh, continuing, "With Chief William and Alexander still away from Scotia and yet absent from Uilleam's burial, mayhap their absence speaks of their demise. John Comyn would then need only Uilleam out of the way to seize his holdings."

"There's Lady Elesbeth to consider."

"Not if John Comyn provides Lady Claray with a male heir of his own seed."

Liza nearly let out a cry from her hidden nook. She could not bear it. Not if it meant her father and now both her brothers were gone to the grave. Even if the male line were extinguished, John Comyn could not simply sire a male heir with Claray and claim his dominion.

The blood of the Ramsay Clan coursed through her veins.

The fair maid spoke the same thought aloud, then added, "Lady Elesbeth—she was dabblin' in witchery when Lachlan found her in the mist. She called upon the Devil to scorch the tree."

The notion was folly, yet the other lass was gullible. Liza could discern the awe in the maiden's voice when she asked, "Why would she do such a thing?"

"Tae claim the castle for herself and tae lie with the bailie. And look what's come to pass—Wyolet lies dead, and Lady Claray is driven mad with sorrow."

"But Uilleam was her brother."

"Wouldnae matter to a witch."

Malcolm turned out to be the voice of reason, but there was a noticeable quaver in his voice. "That's daft talk."

He opened his lips to speak again, but Hexilde bustled into the garden. The cook first spied Liza and gaped as though to speak, but given her position lurking behind the hawthorn hedge, thought better of it. Hexilde knit her brows and set her ample form between Liza and the trio of servants before she clapped her palms together.

"Caristìona! Rhona!" she thundered.

The maidens yelped in unison.

"Get yerselves inside!"

They snatched up their half-filled baskets of herbs

and fled within, never daring a glance in Liza's direction.

Malcolm had slunk back toward the gate, and Hexilde called after him, "Master Malcolm, ye hae no leave tae prattle with the wenches. I hae a mind tae tell the bailie of yer idle chatter."

Unlike the scullery maids, Malcolm glanced over his shoulder. When his eyes fell upon the veiled Liza, he turned as pale as a corpse and made off around the castle's keep.

Once he was gone, Hexilde wheeled upon Liza. "Ye shouldnae be wanderin' around, my lady. The serving folk—they whisper of matters…best unheard by noble ears."

Liza scorned their chatter. Let them name her a witch. But her thoughts dwelt upon their musings on Uilleam's death.

"He wouldnae have cast himself down," she murmured.

Hexilde folded her arms over her breast.

Liza's voice faltered, "The alternative is more dire." For it spoke of the evil that had befallen her brother. And perhaps that evil had been her own doing.

Hexilde cast her gaze over the deserted garden, and her tone dropped to an urgent hush. "Listen tae me, my lady. Strange and fateful days lie before us. I feel them in my very bones. With Laird Ramsay gone, Sir Alexander vanished with him, and Master Uilleam laid in the earth, the fortune of Clan Ramsay rests upon yer blood alone."

"Claray—" Liza began.

Hexilde halted Liza's speech, sweeping a broad arm between them. "Claray lies in her bed, numb with opium. I have lived long, and ken that a weak lady such as she will not find swift reprieve from her bairn's passin'."

Liza frowned beneath her veil. Claray was still yet the Lady of the Land.

Hexilde looked around again. "John Comyn has more than designs on the Ramsay lands," the woman said. "But I fear his plans here have been interrupted." She wet her lips with her tongue. "Ye've got a tall order in front of ye, child. Ye must take charge of the castle and the lands, but ye must also watch yer back."

"I pose no threat tae the man," Liza declared. If only she truly had been born a witch.

Hexilde reached out suddenly and grasped Liza's arms with a firm grip. "Elesbeth." Her voice was beseeching. Liza pulled away. Hexilde slackened her grip, but did not release her hold. She swallowed and spoke gently.

"Liza…"

Liza was startled by the sound of the secret name that resonated within her soul, but Hexilde's eyes were bright and intense, having seen much of the world— and maybe other worlds, as well.

The woman continued. "After Master Uilleam's passing, I fear Wyolet's death was no accident." When Liza still did not speak, Hexilde said, "That eternal sleep may hae been meant fer ye."

A memory of Wyolet's shattered skull and the thick black pool of blood struck Liza with a surge of terror.

"And what am I tae do about that?" she whispered.

"All I can say is the fate of this land rests in yer hands. Ye've been spared once, maybe for a divine purpose. Because the Guardians—especially John Comyn—have plans fer Scotia. But those plans will benefit no one but himself."

The Guardian John Comyn was a vile being. And though the workers inside the castle walls might believe her evil, Liza was not a sorceress. How could she possibly battle against such a man? Especially one who may have succeeded in slaying two of those closest to her?

Hexilde offered no words of comfort. The woman gave her a meaningful stare before ushering her back into the castle. She shooed Liza out of the kitchen before the scullery maids could resume their chatter.

Though burdened, Liza managed to keep her head high as she traveled through the passageways to her chamber. She did not cmeet the eyes of any of the servants, but her senses were heightened, and she watched warily every movement they made.

Instead of movements that threatened, the servants

backed away in fear.

Ye are a witch, she reminded herself. The thought was a solace, despite the falsehood.

A familiar voice met her ear. In the chancery occupied by the seneschal, the steward and Lachlan McClaren spoke in raised tones about the price of a fresh herd of hobelars.

"The estate disnae need more of the useless light ponies," Peter Syward argued. "I'll not permit release o' the funds."

"Ye dinnae hae the right to withhold the coin. Chief William Ramsay himself tasked me with the responsibility for the estate's management."

"And he's charged *me* with the estate's silver. With the current state of affairs, lackin' as we are a laird, and now bereft of a lady, I'm takin' the reins of the coin and the *cáin*," the seneschal declared, speaking of the dues paid by the peasantry.

"I cannae defend this land without the provisions I require," Lachlan yelled.

Syward's reply was smug. "I fail to see how a band of tiny horses will aid ye with yer defenses."

Liza halted outside the chamber, her presence cloaked in shadows. In their fiery discourse, the men did not notice her in her dark attire. She stirred, and with that motion, their gazes lifted from the desk, both bereft of words.

"Lady Claray is unfit at present," she uttered, her

voice gaining strength with each word. She drew courage from Hexilde's caution. "It seems I be the rightful heir of the estate. Would ye agree?" She intended it as a sincere query, expecting either a confirmation or denial. Instead, both men bowed their heads. "Aye, my lady," they murmured in unison, conceding.

Liza did not speak. This melding of lady and sorceress might prove quite beneficial, indeed.

Lachlan lifted his eyes and met her gaze through the veil. Even through the cloth, the ember burned between them. She ignored the temptation and returned her mind to the matter at hand.

Like Peter Syward, Liza knew not what Lachlan might realize with more of the small ponies, but she proclaimed, "By decree and in the name of Clan Ramsay, the coin for purchase of the herd of hobelars shall be confirmed."

Peter Syward hesitated and swallowed whatever words lingered on his tongue. He nodded once and mumbled again in a strained voice, "Aye, my lady."

Lachlan's lips curled in the faintest of smiles. Her lips returned the expression.

She knew not who she might trust in this new role she was set to take on—Lachlan included. Yet her father had placed his faith in the bailie, and Liza had welcomed him into her bedchamber. It may have been folly, but it was a bond—a mighty one, indeed. It was more than she shared with any other upon this land. Lachlan would serve as her bailiff, and she would stand as his lady. The choice was made.

And with fortune's favor, that would suffice.

Chapter 12

Over the following cycles of the moon, Lady Claray Ramsay came to wander the cold passages of the castle day and night. Her fair tresses unkempt, her bonny stare now wild and distant, she muttered to herself and at times split the air with cries for her lost bairn. When the servants found her, they would softly shepherd her back to her chamber, lay her upon the bed, and grant her a dram of 'the great rest'. Under its spell, she lay quiet at last, staring at the rafters as if her spirit roamed some realm unseen by mortal kin.

From secret whispers and stolen words not meant for her ears, Liza discovered John Comyn had returned to Lochindorb Castle in Badenoch. And none raised voice when Liza, in due time, assumed the day-to-day charge of the realm's affairs.

Though tongues still wagged that she was a witch, that very fear—if not respect—kept vassal and cottar alike in obedience. Liza found the dread to her great advantage.

Her chief delight was poring over the rolls of the castle—marking down each debt unpaid, each levy rendered by the barons' men and the peasantry. She knew Peter Syward took no small displeasure at her meddling, not on account of witchcraft, yet because she was but a woman. As the days unfurled, his bearing shifted from displeasure, to vexation, to fierce hostility.

Despite his grumblings, her stewardship prospered the stronghold.

It was in the month of September, two moons after the deaths of Uilleam and Wyolet, that Lachlan came upon Liza seated at the high board in the great hall. Before her stood Donvaldus MacTavish, the head chamberlain, delivering his account of the castle's servants in preparation for winter's harsh arrival.

"My lady," spoke Lachlan, entering the chamber. Both Liza and the chamberlain lifted their gazes, and the bailiff gave a stiff bow.

"Hold yer tongue, bailie," said Donvaldus. "Lady Ramsay tends to matters of household at present."

A flush crossed Liza's cheek. She might be younger than the men, though she chafed to be spoken for. And Donvaldus bore her no less loathing than Peter Syward. He plainly wished for the return of Lady Claray, who had never once pressed him on his steward's tasks.

He was within his right to silence the bailie, and Liza, mindful of whispered tales of her secret union with Lachlan, let his rebuke stand.

She bent once more over the parchment, marking

the rates for liveries and victuals.

"It is of great consequence, my lady," Lachlan pressed, stepping squarely before her.

Donvaldus exhaled sharply. "Now is not the time fer ye to speak, bailie." He rose half from his seat, voice stiff and frosty.

Liza raised her gaze to Lachlan. She had cast aside the black mourning veil, but still clad herself in garments of dark color, yet grieving her fallen brother. Her heart ached for dear Uilleam.

In Lachlan's stare, she discerned a look she could not quite place. A portent or a disquiet. It was plain he wished not to converse before Donvaldus.

Liza raised a hand to the chamberlain. "We shall continue this after midday," she declared.

With a dismissive huff that Liza chose to ignore, the man scraped his chair roughly back on the stone floor and strode from the chamber.

Once she was alone with Lachlan at the head of the room, Liza gestured toward the vacant stool. Lachlan shook his head. "Ye're needed at the Watret Abbey."

She bristled at the bailie's unkind tone. And she knew not why she'd be called away. She had no desire to yield to his abrupt command. "Why, pray tell, would I be summoned there?"

Lachlan cast his gaze about the room. They were alone. "My lady, I beseech ye. Come with me." He extended a hand, and Liza stared at it. Surely, he did not presume she should clasp his hand in hers?

Despite her softening, she let out an unladylike snort and offered him a gaze chilled by ice. "What mean ye by this, bailie?" She knew well their stations prevented their union, but his boldness where interested eyes might witness them was unwise and left Liza laid bare.

His countenance again hardened, and he made a noise deep in his throat. "There is a matter demanding yer immediate attention."

"I hae many pressing matters in front of me." She gestured toward the parchments on the board.

A muscle twitched next to his mouth. "Ye are summoned at the behest of the monks."

"And can ye not tend to the matter without my presence?"

"The abbey courier did in secret come here and plead fer yer presence." Liza gaped, and Lachlan added, "The query is made by the abbot himself."

This declaration caused Liza to blink up at him. Liza had scarce seen the abbot with her own eyes. The man of God, appointed by the Pope himself, bid his prior and cellarer to tend the daily functions within the abbey walls. Liza had heard it said the abbot often traveled the land to forge bonds with the other baronies, which rendered him akin to a politician in Liza's eyes.

Something cold chilled her bones. There'd be

scarce matters that would call for her urgent heed from a source on high. She thought of the health and well-being of her father and brother, still in apparent banishment across the sea. Had this summons something to do with her kin?

With resignation, she rose. Lachlan's discontent with Liza was clear, and she half expected him to storm from the chamber before her. He allowed her to pass by with a bow of his head.

As they strode together, they passed by the watchtower where two guards stood ramrod straight in their leather armour. The Watret Abbey lay a short distance from the castle grounds, and the journey was but a delightful stroll on a day as fine as this. Yet Lachlan made his way to a pair of steeds.

Liza's steps faltered. She was neither a swift nor capable rider. The horses made her nose tickle and her eyes weep. And if she tarried in the stable, her breath became heavy and labored. She was sure Lachlan knew this. He had not prepared the small hobelars for the journey, but had fetched his favored beasts—more akin to beloved pets.

He climbed atop his tall chestnut horse, Gwrol, and when she made no movement to mount the smaller mare beside him, Lachlan said, "We must make haste."

Liza was about to protest when Claray appeared upon the drawbridge. "John, is that ye?" she called, shading her eyes against the harsh light of day and casting her gaze toward Lachlan. "John, come tae my chamber! Lie with me again!"

One of the sentinels had moved to intercept her, but the frail and slight woman escaped from his grip.

"John!" she cried out, straining as if she might sprint to Lachlan.

"For the love of the saints," Liza muttered, struggling to mount the mare, who neighed softly under Liza's weight. Liza adjusted herself with a touch of unease. "I'll trail behind ye," she declared, in deference to Lachlan's abilities as a masterful horseman.

"Nay, I'll ride behind lest ye fall from Luar, and she escapes yer clumsy burden."

Liza squinted at him, seeking any sign of jest, but his visage was earnest.

"John, come tae bed!" Claray cried out again, freeing herself from the grip of the guard who had been overly soft with the frantic lady. Her sullied and yellowed chemise flapped about her slender frame in the late summer breeze as she made haste toward them.

Liza gave Luar a sharp nudge with the heel of her slipper, and the beast tossed its head and let out a startled whinny before galloping forth. With a cry, Liza clung on, and this time, Lachlan laughed before overtaking the pair.

Riding alongside, he reached over and seized the reins, pulling back gently.

The beast Gwrol sensed his master's intentions and

followed Lachlan's command while Luar slowed to a gentle trot in response to Lachlan's skilled movements.

Liza's breath gasped, though her heart eased.

Lachlan offered her a reassuring smile. "Are ye well?"

She offered a nod, and they journeyed in silence for a time. This was the first they'd been truly alone since that night in her chamber. Even then, it seemed they had been watched.

In the bonny heather fields on the sojourn from the castle to the abbey, Liza and Lachlan were the only souls within sight. She often sensed deep kinship with Lachlan, even when he was far away. It felt as though she knew him well from some other realm or age. Her thoughts summoned visions of shared mirth and gentle touch. It made no sense, yet it was as true as life itself. It was as real as the feeling of the warm sun upon her skin, and the gentle breeze that danced through the locks escaping her coiled tresses and simple crispine.

She struggled to find familiar words to fill the silence between them. Some acknowledgment of their shared union.

"Ye can call me Elesbeth when none are near," she hazarded softly.

He offered no reply, and she dared a glance his way. He was looking straight ahead, but sensing her gaze, he straightened upon his steed.

"Ye ken I cannae do that, my lady."

"Ye can do whatever ye desire, I should think."

"Ye mean tae say, I must do whatever *ye* decree." His voice held a hard edge. He dulled it swiftly. "Amongst the servants and peasantry, there remains talk of our bond. Best not to stoke their idle gossip."

They also whispered of Liza's witchery—her enchantments against Claray and her scheming to rise to power. "I heed not the chatter of servants," she declared with scorn.

"Yet I am one of those servants, and it bears meaning fer me. It shall bear heeding fer ye, as well. Even if ye claim it is beyond yer notice."

Liza longed to argue, though she knew Lachlan spoke truth.

She gazed upon the vast fields of lavender unfurling before them. Her nostrils twitched, and she sought to stifle the sneeze. It erupted with force. Four more violent expulsions of air swiftly followed like a tempest. She had no kerchief, and she swiped at her red running nose, careful not to touch her eyes, which had begun to burn and itch.

Lachlan cast her an apologetic look.

The abbey was not much further. She could see its tall steeple rising over the trees.

"Ye haven't told me why we're ridin' to see the monks," she said with a sniffle. "What is this cause fer urgency?" She'd convinced herself the message had little to do with her father. That missive would be delivered directly to her. It would not require her to journey in grief.

Lachlan hesitated. "I received word from a courier that a…shipment had been delivered."

Liza's apprehension shifted quickly to delight. "From father?" she asked. A thought struck her. "Has he returned?" Before Lachlan could answer, a renewed sense of dread seized her. "Is he hurt? Is it Alexander?"

Lachlan held up a hand. "Slow yer words and yer thoughts, my lady." A smile crept upon his lips at her heedless queries. Liza relaxed. She returned his smile, their gazes locking.

The familiar flash of memory—his mouth upon her lips, his hands upon her breasts, his body pressed against, then into, hers.

The emotions were too intense for the experience to have been bound to a mere moment. She refused to believe their love would never again manifest.

Lachlan broke the gaze first, his voice coldly devoid of emotion when he spoke. "I've no word from Chief Ramsay nor Laird Alexander."

Liza's fear returned. Neither her father nor brother had sent word after Uilleam's death. There had been no shipment of finery from them for months, and Liza had begun to suspect she may well be an orphan.

She would grasp hope until tidings were delivered otherwise, heartened by the fact John Comyn had made no appearance since the day Uilleam was lost to her.

"Then I must demand tae know what I'm riding toward."

"I only hae a vague notion myself," Lachlan answered. "We'll be there in due time."

Liza exhaled with vexation. His scarce response indicated he had no intention of offering more explanation. It seemed as if the title Lady of Clan Ramsay only held weight when it pleased him. She knew well such an observation, spoken aloud, would yield no fruitful outcome.

The rest of their journey passed in silence, and when they approached the adorned entrance of the Watret Abbey, two monks in their long dark frocks and shorn heads made haste to meet them.

The abbey had been wrought with the same red limestone as the Ramsay Castle centuries earlier. King David had offered generous coin in erecting the altar to the Lord to serve the baronies west of Edinburgh.

The abbey was both kirk and chapel, though the monks performed their duties as men of God, teachers, scribes, and purveyors of goods. The keep to the left of the chapel served as a school. A dwelling for the abbey's inhabitants lay on the sanctuary's other side.

The Ramsay family had wrought its own kirk next to the graveyard, and Liza attended the abbey only for noble weddings and funerals. If she were to marry, the rites would be read in the sanctuary, with its gleaming wooden altar, adorned lancet stained-glass windows, and vaulted rafters held up by carved corbels.

Liza gazed up at the fine architecture while a young boy, dressed in a woolen cowl, collected Lachlan's horse once he'd dismounted. Lachlan reached up and aided Liza in her dismount. She endeavored to ignore the heat of his touch on her hand and the intimacy of his arms around her waist as he settled her on solid earth.

Liza smoothed her léine and noticed two men of God standing patiently at the door of the abbey. "What is the meaning of this? Where is the abbot?" she demanded.

"Gratitude to you, Lady Elesbeth, for making passage to our home," said the more solemn of the two in an English tongue. "We've heard whispers Lady Ramsay is not in good health." He paid no heed to her query about the abbey's head.

Liza, with keen awareness, understood the comment questioned her authority, even though Lachlan had surely spoken of her stepmother's ailment. They sought to hear it from her own lips. "I have assumed the role of Lady of the Ramsay Estate in the absence of my father and brother."

The monk, with a pause, said nothing more and inclined his head slightly. "If ye'll follow me, please."

He turned, and the second monk beckoned them onward.

Though Liza stepped forth, Lachlan wavered. Liza

grasped his hand and drew him beside her so they walked together. She did not relish the thought of wandering the dark, perfumed hallways of the abbey unaccompanied by a friendly presence. She knew not why they had been beckoned, and she was afraid.

If the second monk noticed, he gave no sign, and they moved through the chambers of the building, which reeked of herbs and incense, dust and timber. Liza's reaction to the steed lingered, and she sneezed yet again. Or perhaps it was to the musty scent and dust within the aged dwelling.

They ventured through dim corridors until they reached a passage leading to the dormitories, where Liza stopped. Surely this was not a place meant for guests. The monk hazarded a look at her and bid her journey forward. With an uneasy gaze at Lachlan, Liza continued down the row of closed narrow doors, the wood of which did gleam with fresh polish. Their footfalls echoed through the quiet passageway. Near the corridor's end, the monk opened one of the polished doors, holding it ajar for Liza to enter. Lachlan followed and lingered behind Liza in the shadows.

She dared a glance within the darkened chamber and was taken aback by the sight of an old woman— her long white tresses cascading down her back in tangled strands—perched upon a small stool beside a narrow mattress where a shadowed figure lay. The old woman's lips moved as she recited what seemed like an incantation in hushed tones. She tended to the figure with a cloth in hand.

The crone turned her gaze upon Liza. In the wavering candlelight, her eyes shone a deep dark blue, akin to the sea Liza often imagined.

A force passed between them, leaving Liza ensnared by the bond. She barely dared inhale—so robust the connection, yet so fragile the tenuous thread to the present moment seemed in that breath.

The old woman returned her gaze to the straw mattress, breaking the bond.

Liza breathed in sharply.

The monk entered and stood behind the woman. He paid her no heed. Instead, he motioned toward the form on the bed.

"She arrived at our doorstep early this morn, sent by Bishop Robert Wishart. Gravely ill she may be, yet we hold hope for her survival."

The crone spoke then, her voice unexpectedly pleasing, like that of a lass younger than Liza. "The life force and might is strong within her. She shall endure."

Liza leaned forward and peered forth, striving to glimpse the figure more clearly. "Who is she, pray tell?"

"Certainty eludes us," the monk declared.

"Surely Guardian Wishart must know if he sent her hither."

The monk held his silence, and the woman declared, "Her name holds no weight if she's been brought to fulfill a higher calling."

Liza would have contended the girl's identity might then matter all the more.

The candle's flame swiftly flourished, casting its glow upon the form's visage, and Liza was taken aback to behold a maiden, perhaps a year younger than Liza herself. She was bonny and fair of face. Even in her ailment, her countenance bore a regal grace, though a gentle frown did lie upon her temple as if the lass were troubled, even in repose.

A sudden blast of wind coursed through the chamber, causing the candle's flame to dance and sway. A coldness chilled Liza's form.

The crone cast her gaze back at Liza and smiled. In the flickering glow of the flames, the aged visage seemed to alter. At once, she was no longer a crone but a maiden with smooth skin and fair golden tresses.

"Ye bring with ye spirits and enchantment, my sister," the transformed maiden spoke. "And the holy specters seek somethin' o' ye." She turned her look to the lass on the mattress. "Both o' ye," she softly muttered.

A moment later, the draught stilled, the flame steadied, and the woman next to the bed was again a crone.

"What is it I can possibly do?" asked Liza.

It was the monk who next spoke. "Once she is

stronger, she cannot stay in the abbey."

The inference hung in the air. "Ye want me tae conceal her in the Ramsay Castle?"

Though the air lay still, an unseen force, charged with peril and promise, throbbed and vibrated. Liza knew the answer to her query, though no other soul cared to speak.

"She shall be fit tae journey the brief stretch in a cycle of the moon," the crone muttered.

"Under the cloak of night?" Lachlan inquired, peering keenly at the young lass's visage as though he might perceive some familiar form.

"Aye, that may be prudent," the monk replied.

The room's occupants acted as if the decision to house the girl had thus been wrought.

"And should I choose tae defy this act?" Liza questioned. As she cast her gaze down upon the fair face of the girl, a wave of compassion swept through her heart.

"She will surely perish without yer pity," said the woman.

Another lengthy silence lingered between them, thick as the stone walls of the chamber. Many a word went unsaid, not merely the name of the lass. How had she come to rest here under such concealed conditions? And why did the very air hang heavy with the specter of danger?

Liza had already come to terms with the unavoidable nature of her choice, though she begrudged the predicament in which she found herself. "I shall take responsibility for the lass within the walls of the Ramsay keep," she declared. "And I wish to summon Robert Wishart, with all due haste."

"I dinnae think—" Lachlan began, but the monk interjected, "We can discreetly arrange to carry your request to Glasgow, though it may be some time before the Guardian can traverse the land."

Lachlan's frown was deep, but he did not argue further. A hush fell over the room; the only sound was the deep steady breathing of the young girl.

Liza broke the quiet. "What are we tae call her?"

Another silence, this one uneasy.

The crone said, "She will give ye the answer tae that question."

But the air was filled with a meaning that remained unspoken. This girl was surely known to them all.

On the journey's return, she and Lachlan exchanged but few words, shadows cast by their visit to the Watret Abbey still lingering. The journey proved taxing for Liza, her breath growing heavy even amidst the crisp air as she traveled on the back of Luar. When they reached the stables, she swore an oath to never again mount a steed.

Lachlan helped her down upon the earth. Liza half-expected a word or token of farewell, a lingering look before they parted, yet he turned aside, his manner guarded and grave.

Liza felt adrift, the ground beneath her seeming less certain than before.

As Lachlan busied himself at the stables, Liza made her way alone to the gatehouse.

She crossed the drawbridge over the dry moat, where she spied the cottars and vassals gathered in clusters upon the grounds, their speech urgent and motions frantic. Even as she entered the keep, Liza's presence went unheeded—a rare occurrence and one she often desired. She now found the scarcity of attention unsettling.

Seeking Forsy to bid the maid to prepare a chamber for their incoming guest, Liza stumbled upon Hexilde, her face flushed and tears brimming in her eyes.

"My lady, the tidings are grievous, are they not?" Hexilde inquired, misreading the redness in Liza's eyes and her blocked nose as signs of sorrow and lament.

"I've been…away from the grounds," Liza replied. "What has transpired?"

Hexilde gaped to speak, but sobs claimed her, rendering her words nothing but muddled murmurs.

Liza's thoughts turned once more to her father and brother.

Is this the hour I learn I stand alone in this world? she pondered, feeling life itself ebb from her form. The foreboding she'd sensed before Uilleam's passing would this day unveil itself as truth.

It was then the seneschal, Peter Syward, passed by, his visage, too, ashen.

"Seneschal," Liza called. The man halted, bowing his head in an uncommon show of respect.

Her heart sank further within her breast, grief threatening to sweep her away. "It is true, then?" she murmured, her voice barely a wisp upon the air.

"I'm afraid so, my lady."

Liza nearly collapsed, and Peter caught her before she could meet the hard earth.

She'd believed herself braced for the sorrow and torment. Alone she had felt, in this time and place, even before Uilleam's passing. Since Lachlan had found her under the now-ruined sycamore, she'd felt but a spirit in her own existence. Now, she found herself forsaken by nearly all who bound her to her own self. She was adrift.

"Seneschal!" Lachlan's voice cleaved the heavy sorrow that hung in the air, and a stillness fell upon the folk of the keep.

The bailie strode forth as Peter Syward clutched Liza closer to him.

"Remove yer hands from the lady of this castle," he commanded, and in his urgency, Peter released her. For the second time in mere moments, Liza teetered on the brink of collapse. Lachlan seized her, lifting her into his embrace.

"What be the meaning of this?" he demanded of Peter Syward.

"The lady… Sh–She's just received the tidings," Peter sputtered. "She is in shock like the others."

"What be these tidings?"

In Lachlan's firm grasp, Liza struggled to voice her sorrow. All she could muster was to press her face against his broad chest and weep.

Hexilde, having gathered her composure, spoke with a mournful tone. "Our bairn queen, the Maid o' Norway," she lamented. "She's gone—claimed by sickness on her voyage to Alba. The poor lass. And now we are a land without the hope of our true sovereign." She released another mournful cry.

Liza's sobs stilled and she pulled her face away from Lachlan's chest. She scrambled from his arms and leaned in front of Hexilde.

"What did ye say?" she asked, but Hexilde waved a hand in front of her.

The seneschal had recovered enough to be affronted by the bailie's treatment. "Ye heard her," he said, straightening his clothing and puffing out his chest.

"My father and brother are yet alive?" Liza demanded.

Peter Syward sniffed. "Haven't heard news to the contrary."

Liza's hand went to her throat, and she laughed.

Both Hexilde and the seneschal regarded her as if she were mad.

"This is a tragedy fer Scotia, and ye're reaction is merriment?" Hexilde asked. "Have ye no heart, child?"

Liza regained her composure. "Aye, indeed," she uttered, her mirth now vanished. "I–I merely thought…" She shook her head. "It matters not. Truly, this be a tragedy. Pray, tell me what transpired?"

Hexilde pondered Liza's apology, at last accepting her earnest demeanor. "Aye, the maiden has departed this world. Her remains were borne to the Isle of Orkney."

"Was it sickness?" Liza inquired.

"This be the tidings from the Guardians of the Realm."

Liza turned pale. A new foreboding entered her breast.

"Which Guardian brought forth this news?" Liza queried, endeavoring to keep the tremor from her words.

Hexilde retorted, "It matters not." Peter replied in unison, "The word has been declared from John Comyn of Badenoch and James Stewart."

"What of Robert Wishart?" Lachlan asked.

"The Guardians of the Realm are one voice," answered Hexilde.

Liza's thoughts dwelt upon the lass presently under care at Watret Abbey, sent quietly by Robert Wishart.

Liza had been told the young queen was but a bairn. The maiden resting in the abbey was closer to womanhood than childhood.

"What age be she?"

Hexilde gazed upon Liza as though she were addled. "The queen? What be the matter o' it?"

Liza bided her time, until at last Hexilde replied, "Some say she was but a bairn, while others claim she was of age to rule. We shall ne'er truly ken." Her lament began anew and her cries echoed throughout the keep as she walked away, her shoulders hunched forward, quaking with grief.

Peter Syward, too, took his leave, casting a wary glance at the pair before he returned to his chamber.

When she was again alone with Lachlan, Liza said, "We must tell no one of the maiden at the abbey."

"We ken not her true identity, fer certain," declared Lachlan. Doubt clung to his words.

"All the more cause to keep her hidden," replied Liza.

"What shall we tell the staff of our coming guest?"

Liza pondered this query. "We shall spread tidings she be kin o' mine from my mother's clan."

"Lady Claray shall surely recognize her own kin."

"Not Claray," Liza countered, her voice sharp as a blade. "*My* mother, Jennet of Fife. A MacDuff."

Lachlan opened his mouth to speak, then closed it. For a fleeting moment, the sharing of this newfound knowledge of her noble bloodline brought her a flicker of joy. He had not known she was born of the highest-ranking native noble clan in all of Scotia.

She grasped it might drive a deeper chasm between them. Her connection to the Earls of Fife bestowed upon her a rank most esteemed in all the realm, save for the royal house itself.

Liza continued hurriedly, "We shall weave a tale she's the illegitimate bairn of my uncle. The scandal shall deter any prying eyes, yet her noble blood shall keep her safe."

"And if she be who we suspect… What shall we name her?"

"Grete is not an uncommon name," Liza murmured. "Though none would ever suspect a queen to bear such a diminutive."

"Grete," Lachlan whispered, and the very utterance of the name seemed to weave the tale into being.

Their eyes locked with resolve, both fully aware of the heavy secret that bound them in solitude.

If that secret indeed be true…

Chapter 13

There were advantages to her standing as mistress of Clan Ramsay. Though Liza oft felt herself but a young maid, in the enduring absence of Claray, the servants had come to show her a grudging respect that had never been granted afore.

Liza need only voice her desires, and her wishes were swiftly fulfilled. Postures straightened as she passed, and the stolen glances and murmurs dwindled, though she noted occasional glances exchanged when Lachlan was near.

Soon, Liza embraced this newfound behavior and her position therein. She found she cared not for the opinions of men like Peter Syward and Donvaldus MacTavish. Neither of them desired to bow before a woman, yet it didn't matter. She had taken her place as head of the household.

She had bid Forsy to prepare Uilleam's chamber for their forthcoming guest, though it pained her for her brother's space to be occupied by another. While other chambers lay empty within the castle, Liza suspected the sudden presence of a strange maiden might invite unwanted attention. The tale she'd crafted for the lass, along with the threat of ghosts, spirits, and superstitions, would hopefully deter any probing queries or meddlings about the visitor.

Besides that, Liza hoped the spirit of her gentle brother might watch over the fair and lovely Grete. If his presence in death should make itself known, perhaps it would provide their guest with some solace.

Though Forsy heeded her duties without question, Liza bestowed no trust upon the chambermaid. Memories of Wyolet lingered freshly in the wench's mind, and it had been Forsy who'd sown the seeds of scandal, whispering tales of a dalliance between Liza and Lachlan among the servants.

Liza maintained her distance from Lachlan within the castle's confines, yet when the harvest season waned and a biting chill crept through the air, young Malcolm the chamberlain sought her presence following the evening repast.

"My lady," he said as he approached, his gaze steadfastly cast upon the ground, for he knew well she'd heard his discourse with the scullery maids in the garden following Uilleam's death.

"Aye," Liza declared, with little warmth. "I reckon a servant ought to show respect to the lady o' the house." The lad bowed with due reverence. Liza let him remain in his humble stance for a time before she bestowed upon him a touch of mercy. "Ye may speak."

"The bailie, Lachlan McClaren, wishes to have a word with ye."

Liza masked her surprise at the summons. Did she fancy the lad's stress upon Lachlan's name? Most likely, the tale of her ill nature and Lachlan's bidding would be recounted amongst the servants. Their imagined chatter did rankle.

"He may approach me in the great hall."

"He's requested ye seek him near the stables," Malcolm replied.

Liza straightened, a realization dawning upon her—this eve was the time their guest would arrive.

She drew herself taller. "Ye may tell him the message has been delivered."

Malcolm halted, perhaps awaiting assurance she would honor Lachlan's request. When it became clear Liza would utter no further words, he inclined his head. "Aye, my lady."

He took his leave, and Liza beheld him traverse the length of the chamber before departing. She followed a distance behind, noting his diversion toward the kitchen, where he engaged in a few moments of flirtation and chatter with the scullery maids, ultimately exiting by the main door. Liza then observed the lad make his way across the grounds, heading toward the stables where Lachlan awaited.

She bided her time for nearly an hour before she made her exit through the rear passage of the castle, her heart thudding heavily within her breast.

Though daylight still glowed in the sky, a chill lingered upon the air, whispering of the winter to come. The green leaves of the trees near the Creagan Burn had turned a vibrant hue, as if warming themselves for the transformation that lie ahead. Liza drew her léine and mantle tighter about her form. Her long hair was coiled in braids at her ears, and she chided herself for not covering her head in more than a crispine as she passed a man who was gathering his tools following the day's toil. He flicked his gaze toward her, and upon discerning her face, his eyes widened with astonishment. He offered a swift and deep nod before hastily scuttling away.

As she traversed the grounds, the savory aroma of the peasants' evening fires wafted through the air, enticing her nostrils with the scent of roasting meats and vegetables. Though their meals were likely not as grand as those prepared by Hexilde, Liza had dined alone at her board. A pang of envy stirred within her for the thatched huts of the workers, filled with the jubilant sounds of children, voices, and laughter.

Liza felt the ache of longing for her father and brother. She ached for Uilleam. A piece of her heart even yearned for Claray, who still dallied in her chamber or drifted about without regard for Liza. Or for any other.

When Liza reached the stables, she found that

Lachlan stood alone within, no trace of Malcolm in sight. At the door, Liza lingered, watching him murmur soft words to a hobelar as he smoothed its dun coat. The gentle care in his touch seemed at odds with the corded muscles that strained beneath his léine.

As ever, at the sight of Lachlan, memories of their hours in her chamber rose unbidden. This time, another vision flickered beside it. She recalled him bearing her forth from some black pit, cradling her tenderly and whispering her name. She blinked, again both the lady of this land and a different soul—one who had wandered far beyond these glens.

Through every realm, she had loved only Lachlan.

A breeze rose, scattering fallen leaves about her feet. The little pony lifted its head and whinnied. Lachlan turned as if startled by a spirit.

"Lady Ramsay," he breathed, recovering swiftly. "I didnae ken ye stood there."

"I should have given warning," she replied with a half-bow.

He smiled. "Aye, 'tis fair enough. Though it was I who forced ye to meet me amid the horses."

Around them the beasts—great and small—breathed, nickered, and shifted their hooves upon the earth. Their steady sounds were a soft comfort.

Her gaze drifted to a fresh pile of straw, and again the other memory seized her... Lachlan's face close, his eyes aflame with joy and desire. Her lips meeting his in a slow, knowing kiss that deepened until his tongue sought hers and his hands roamed her body.

Perhaps her longing showed in her eyes, for Lachlan's gaze darkened as though he shared that secret reverie.

He straightened his shoulders. "Word has come from the brethren at the abbey."

Liza shifted the direction of her forbidden thoughts, recalling the abbey's maiden in graceful repose. "The lass is hale again?" Liza asked lowly, mindful of their covert designs and the dread the maid might perish—or worse, some ruffian might be sent to finish the unfulfilled deed.

"Aye, well enough for the journey," he answered gravely. "The monks ken too well she must not be found hidden beneath their roof."

"And what of Robert Wishart?"

"No reply has been received."

They lingered in silence, neither uttering the obvious truth. It would be little better for the secret lass to be discovered under the protection of Clan Ramsay, yet they had the fortune of a tale more plausible than that of the monks.

"Uilleam's chamber is ready. I shall attend to the lass myself upon yer return."

They had resolved Lachlan would venture forth alone under the shroud of night to fetch their guest. Come the morn, there would be inquiries regarding her sudden arrival. Without the glaring gaze of day, the scrutiny might be lessened and the whispers fewer.

Liza would have the chance to mold and shape the narrative of Grete of Fife.

"I will take this hobelar," Lachlan declared. "The smaller steed will draw less notice in the dark, and we'll be but a fleeting shadow traversing the land."

A weighty silence settled between them.

"Ye'll exercise caution then," she urged, and Lachlan nodded.

"Aye."

"I'll leave a light aglow outside the chamber, and kindle a fire within."

After a moment's pause, Lachlan turned to the dun horse and began to lead it forth. As he passed, Liza laid a hand upon his arm. She knew the action unwise. She could not seem to stop the movement. He halted, gazing down at the contact. She felt the warmth of his being. She inhaled the scent of him—of the wilds, of earth and beasts. He bore the fragrance of home. She shifted her hand from his arm to his face, her palm resting on his rugged cheek.

"Lady Elesbeth," he spoke softly, and she knew he was about to utter words of their parting.

She wished not to hear it. Not this night. Not in the face of secret and peril. Before he could react, she drew his face toward her and pressed her lips to his.

She was the one to deepen the kiss, gently tracing

her tongue against his while his mouth stayed soft but still. She leaned into the warmth and steadfast might of his unyielding form, knowing well he would soon cast her aside. Still, her heart yearned for his touch, if only fleeting.

Just as she prepared for his rebuff, he yielded to her embrace.

The pony gave a small whinny as Lachlan stepped aside, taking Liza into his arms. He bore her to the fresh mound of straw, and without breaking their kiss, he lifted her chemise, the evening air biting against her bare skin.

His fingers traced a fiery path up her thighs until they reached the place where her yearning had gathered. He touched her in that hidden spot. Liza cried out, her longing stifled by Lachlan's lips. She pressed her form fervently against his hand, and his movements matched her fervor. Her cries grew louder, and his fingers slipped upon and into her. All sense of time and space vanished. There was only Liza and Lachlan, their breaths and bodies entwined.

"Liza," he murmured in her ear, cradling her head against him with his free hand. Her lips burned against his neck, and she nestled her face into his skin while his fingers took her ever higher.

At last, with a blinding burst of light and frenzy, she reached the peak of her pleasure, and rapture crashed over her like the relentless waves of the sea.

Ecstasy washed over her, again and again, wetting Lachlan's fingers, until they slowed.

Finally, they ceased.

Liza reentered into her senses from her place of bliss. The horses nickered and snorted, heedless of Liza's tempest. She reached for the firm length of Lachlan. She longed to hold him, to feel him bare against her. But he caught her wrist in his grasp, holding her back.

His voice was rugged as he spoke. "No, my lady. I can offer ye this…relief, but I can give ye no more."

"*Relief.*" The word was uttered lightly. An echo.

"For yer yearning." He withdrew his hand from between her legs and discreetly removed her dampness upon the straw. Then he moved away from her.

"A service, then," she said. A scorching sense of shame and humiliation overtook her desire.

"If ye'd like."

Liza snatched her léine about her waist. Tugging herself from the yielding straw proved no small task, and she tumbled into the mire before setting herself upright.

Lachlan's back was turned as he tended the horse.

"Do ye do this then for all the maidens?" she asked, her voice edged with spite as she glared at his back.

"I serve at the pleasure o' Clan Ramsay," he replied dryly.

Her cheeks burned. "I can find another to serve me, bailie."

"Perhaps ye should," he answered, without turning to her. "A husband tae grant yer every fancy. A nobleman tae garb ye in silks and jewels."

"I need no husband tae clothe me in finery."

"Ah, because o' yer name and station, ye can do that alone," he conceded. "Forgive me. Ye need but a body then."

Liza was left speechless. He had doubled her shame. "That's not my desire."

At last, he turned. "Then what is it ye would ask of *me*, Lady Ramsay? What can I—but a simple servant— possibly give tae a high-bred woman such as yerself?"

Tears welled in her eyes. She brushed them fiercely aside.

He stood indifferent to her distress. "Would ye have me slide my rod within ye?" he asked in a low tone. Despite her mortification, her body stirred at his bluntness. "Would ye have me sow bairns in yer noble womb? One? Two? Three?"

Her lips parted, wordless. In her mind's eye she saw two wee ones: a flaxen-haired lad clambering at her skirt; an infant suckling at her breast. Lachlan's steady gaze upon her as she nursed.

She hungered for no greater bliss.

"Or would ye leave the comforts o' the castle and dwell in my hovel and live yer life as a servant?"

Had she not just envisioned such a life? Hearth-warmth, children's laughter… so far from stony halls, yet rich in quiet joy. The indulgences of the castle mattered not.

His words rang true. Such a life was for him, and another—some gentle Wyolet perhaps—not for her.

Her tears fell unchecked.

Eventually, Lachlan's broad shoulders drooped, and he extended his hands. "I've pledged tae aid ye with the maiden, Grete," he declared. "It's the proper course, though I shall not be entangled in any foolish dream of yers, Liza. It is unjust to the pair of us."

At the sound of her true name, she lifted her head, startled through her tears. "Ye called me Liza," she whispered.

He frowned. "I didnae call ye that."

She raised a hand to her brow. Perhaps she'd been mistaken. Yet he spoke true of one matter—her demands of him were not fair. Lachlan deserved his joy, and it could not be with her.

"I must make my way to the abbey." His voice fell gentle as a breeze.

Liza gave a nod, allowing him and his pony to pass without uttering another word.

Chapter 14

Liza had not entered Uilleam's chamber since before the lad's sudden passing. She surveyed the simple space which was plain of furnishing: an oaken boxbed, a humble chest of drawers, and an armoire far less ornate than that in Liza's sitting.

A bright fire crackled in the hearth. Liza sat upon a low stool beside it, awaiting their visitor.

Forsy had been bidden to bear in a trencher of coarse bread and steaming broth with a flagon of ale once Lachlan returned. To her honor, the chambermaid inquired not a single query and fulfilled all tasks with nary a word spoken.

In the warmth, Liza almost nodded off until a subtle stir in the passage beyond caused her to half rise, certain at last Lachlan had come. But the figure at the threshold was lone, gaunt, and pale. It glided like a wraith.

"Forsy?" Liza called, striving to lend her voice some strength.

A soft murmur answered. Despite her heart's fierce beating, Liza rose and stepped into the corridor. Claray stood there, her face drawn, her thin fingers at her throat, her eyes focused upon Liza.

"Uilleam," Claray whispered. "Ye're here."

"It's Elesbeth," she replied gently to her stepmother, who seemed in the grip of the great rest. Liza glanced back into the chamber's warmth and laid hold of Claray's arm. "Let me guide ye back to yer own chamber," she bade, her voice firm yet kindly.

Claray tugged away. "I would see my Uilleam."

"Uilleam abides elsewhere, in a safer place."

But Claray, roused by wild longing, slipped from her grip and darted behind Liza into the chamber, casting frantic glances about.

"Uilleam is not here," Liza said softly from the threshold.

Lucidity flickered in Claray's gaze, which had shifted from hope to heartbreak. "Why is the hearth alight if Uilleam be buried and cold within the lonely ground?"

"We await a visitor," Liza answered, choosing her words.

"A visitor?" Claray echoed.

"Grete of the Clan MacDuff," said Liza to Claray. "The maiden is a kinswoman of my mother Jennet." It was the first time she'd uttered the falsehood, and it slid from her tongue with ease.

Liza's thoughts drifted to John Comyn, as absent in body these past months as Claray in mind. She knew the Guardian would surely return when it served his ends. She recalled his dark words against the child queen Margaret, Maid of Norway, vowing she should never rise upon the throne. It was a grave folly to grant the maiden harbor here, Liza mused, albeit too late. Should the Guardian return and his suspicions be stirred, the tale of the lass of noble blood, born of shame and out of wedlock, would stand no chance against his knowledge of folk and clans.

It was all Liza possessed.

"A MacDuff," Claray said. Her voice resumed its slurred and dreamy quality. "A daughter of Donnchadh?"

Liza didn't know the answer to this query. She nodded. "Of sorts. But…" She cautioned after a pause, "…this bairn has been kept secret." She trusted Claray would understand her meaning.

"Secret," she echoed. Then whispered, a note of pleasure in her tone, "A *secret*."

Liza drew near to her stepmother and clasped her small, cold hands in her own. "Can ye hold a secret?"

Claray gazed into Liza's eyes, yet Liza could not decipher the woman's unreadable expression. Then Claray withdrew from Liza's grasp and drifted away, gazing into the hearth, ablaze and warm.

"How came she to be here, then?"

"My…father hae sent word she would arrive."

"William?" Claray's eyes widened. "Ye've heard

from William?"

Liza tarried before responding, "He's sent word."

"It's not true then," she murmured.

"Of what do ye speak?"

"The Guardians declared him dead. John Comyn professed I'd lost everyone."

A fresh wave of despair settled in Liza's breast, followed by a deep ire. She knew not if what the Guardian spoke was truth or falsehood. She knew not if she'd ever see her father or her brother again.

She despised John Comyn of Badenoch, and if it were the last thing she did, she would vanquish him.

"Ye have not lost everyone," Liza declared fiercely to Claray. "Ye still have me."

Claray seemed not to hear her. She cast one last glance around the room, and whispered "Uilleam," as if the whole of the discourse with Liza had not transpired. Then she glided from the bedchamber, ghostlike in her white chemise, illuminated in her withdrawal by the dim candlelight along the passageway.

Liza turned back to the fire, which no longer roared but crackled merrily in its stone recess. As she gazed into the flame, she became more and more uncertain if she could continue the charade of this life. She couldn't quite explain her haziness, but she was pondering more than just the falsehood of their guest.

Liza's true self eluded her. All that remained was an

indistinct character—a shell of a woman inhabited by a soul from another realm.

When had she become a woman who would risk everything to lie with a stableman? Who would give up her title and position for a *nighean*—a young woman—she'd never met?

Liza let out a long breath and lowered herself back to the stool in front of the flames, waiting.

Another hour passed before Liza was roused by footsteps shuffling heavily across the stones. She rose and stood next to the hearth, twisting her hands together.

When Lachlan entered, he carried the cumbersome burden of a shrouded figure. He spared Liza no glance as he moved to the bed and laid the weight onto the mattress along with a leather pouch that he tucked beside her. "She had but few belongings," he said.

Liza peered at the maiden. The blanket had slid down to reveal a very slight, very pretty, very pale face, with eyes closed and long lashes extending nearly to her cheeks.

"She will survive?" Liza whispered so as not to disturb her.

"Aye, though she remains frail. The monks reckon she was fed some vile herb, and the terror of whatever plight befell her may have cast her into a deep slumber."

Liza knew many deadly herbs and tart berries,

easily found, could cause a racing heart, delirium, and demise. She shuddered to think of the other terrible deeds that may have befallen such a bonny lass upon her journey. Especially had she been marked for death.

She peered more closely at the figure, who did not seem to be exhibiting any terrible symptoms.

"They've been prayin' o'er her, and the cunning folk have cast their charms, if ye believe such folly." It was clear Lachlan held no faith in miracles, regardless of their origin. "The worst of it is behind her, yet she has still not stirred. There may be unseen harm."

Liza beheld the girl's chest rising and falling steadily. Her lips, though pale, still bore a hint of color.

Lachlan stood near, and Liza was acutely aware of his presence beside her. She shifted away and, seeking to break the silence, said, "Claray did inquire after our guest." She gestured about the chamber. "She took issue with the use of Uilleam's chambers."

"And what did ye tell her?"

"The tale of the MacDuffs of Fife."

Lachlan nodded but offered no further reply.

"John Comyn has relayed tae Claray that my father and brother are now dead."

These words drew Lachlan's gaze at last. He opened his mouth to respond, then clamped it shut. A muscle at the side of his face twitched. The bailiff held Chief William Ramsay in the highest esteem, as did her father Lachlan. It was the very reason Lachlan was named bailiff in his stead. Lachlan would feel nearly as troubled as Liza herself at the grim possibility of William's demise.

"John Comyn be a knave. His words might not be true," he at length managed to say.

John Comyn was also a brute. "Perhaps not."

The maiden in the bed stirred and emitted a soft sound, drawing their attention back to her form. The soft down mattress was of finer quality and comfort than the meager cloth coverings of the monks' narrow beds. Liza fancied that after the harsh voyage across the sea and land, this mattress might be the first semblance of comfort the lass had encountered since her long journey began many long months earlier.

The fire's flame cast an eerie glow upon her countenance, rendering her both magical and sinister.

"How old is she?" Liza whispered.

Lachlan held out his hands. "Her father delayed her passage tae Alba until he'd deemed her old enough tae make her own decisions and see tae her own protection."

There had been tales the queen was naught but a wee lass. Liza pondered if King Erik of Norway had indeed sent her forth as a bairn, perhaps the Guardians might have shown her mercy. A young woman with a mind of her own, defying their commands, would not sit well with them. They'd find little trust in a woman who bore the fate of the realm and their riches in her tender hands. And though she was betrothed to the English King Edward's heir, the bonny Prince Edward of Caernarfon, it would be far simpler for the Guardians if the Maid of Norway never existed at all.

Liza felt the quickening of protectiveness. She had not been able to save Uilleam, but she would not let this girl meet the same fate at some perilous hand.

Forsy entered the room carrying a flat slab of wood holding bread and thick cream, a thin pottage made of vegetables, and a drink of prunella which Hexilde made from wild plums for anyone ailing in the household. She set the slab atop the chest and peered curiously at the bed. "What shall we call her?"

Liza tarried but a breath. "She is called Grete. She hails from Fife, and her kin have sent her to bide here with her own folk."

"She's a Ramsay, then."

Liza recounted Grete's crafted tale. The saga of the MacDuffs, and the need for a haven for this descendant of the Mormaers of Fife. With each telling, Liza's voice grew firmer and the tale rang truer.

Lachlan had gone to the hearth to tend the fire, and Forsy's gaze followed his every move. His ears were beyond the reach of the chambermaid's softened voice when she whispered, "Another fair and bonny lass to cast her eye upon the bailie, I reckon."

Liza was taken aback for a moment. She took a deep breath before she straightened herself. "That's not a proper thing to say to the lady of this keep."

Forsy kept her eyes on Lachlan, shunning Liza's fiery glare. "Until she's gone, Claray remains the lady of this hold." The maid's voice quavered. "Wyolet was the lass meant to wed the bailie. Till ye took him from her. And then ye took her from him."

Words eluded Liza, so startled was she by the lass's bold accusation. To her face, no less.

"What is it ye charge me with, Forsy?"

"M–My charges shouldnae matter to one with an innocent heart and mind," Forsy stammered, yet she seemed resolute enough to voice her thoughts.

Liza's cheeks flamed as if she'd been struck. "Yer task here is done," she declared, her voice quivering as she dismissed the maid. "Yer services be no longer needed in this chamber." She hadn't realized her voice was raised until Lachlan's gaze fell upon them.

"Is all well?"

"Aye, sir," Forsy replied, acknowledging his higher station, though not that of Liza. She blinked up at him with wide eyes. "I was merely lettin' Lady Elesbeth ken the staff was eager for another young lass to tend to." Her tone was meek and innocent. Lachlan glanced between them both.

But Liza held her tongue, as Forsy must have sensed she would. Countering the lass would mean exposing the maid's words concerning Wyolet. Liza would not be so cruel to Lachlan. More than that,

Forsy's words mirrored Lachlan's own from the stables.

He ought to have wed a lass like Wyolet, if not Wyolet herself.

Forsy bowed her head. "I'll be takin' my leave now." Liza noted the lass's fleeting glance toward Lachlan before she departed the room, her soft slippers barely whispering on the stone.

"Do ye think she suspects anything?" Lachlan asked, his eyes shifting to Grete's resting form in Uilleam's bed.

Liza shook her head. "Nay," she spoke aloud. For Forsy was not thinking of the maiden in the bed, but of her own designs upon the bailie.

They stood in silence a moment longer, gazing upon Grete, before Lachlan said, "She needs rest. When she wakes, she'll need sustenance." He hesitated.

"I'll stay with her," Liza answered. "She's my kin, after all. And it shall look suspicious if ye're loiterin' about."

He looked toward the threshold. "I'm not sure it's safe."

Liza wasn't sure anything was safe anymore.

Lachlan exhaled. "I'll have a watchman posted fer protection. No one will want peril tae befall a descendant of the Mormaers of Fife."

Liza gave a nod. Forsy's words lingered in her mind, and the presence of Lachlan troubled her spirit. Her safety was of little concern to her at that moment.

She turned back to Grete as Lachlan took his leave.

Throughout the long night, she kept vigil by the bedside until the fire dwindled and the sky outside the window took on a soft gray hue.

Liza tilted her chin upward, gazing at the vaulted ceiling of the chilled chamber. She drew a mantle over her léine and wrapped her arms tightly around herself.

At some point, she succumbed to a fitful slumber. In her dreams, she plunged through a deep, dark void, startling herself awake. Roused so violently, she blinked and stretched her stiffened limbs, sore from perching on the hard stool.

Upon casting her eyes on Grete, she found the lass observing her.

"Ye're awake," she exclaimed, her heart quickening.

The lass offered no reply, but her blue eyes widened slightly in acknowledgment.

Liza stood and took up the bowl of warm prunella. "Ye must be parched." She extended the vessel like a sacred offering. Grete fixed her gaze upon the vessel, then looked to Liza without any movement forth.

"Who are you?" The words were melodic and pleasing, though not of this land. And though her tone was soft, the voice carried an undeniable strength and challenge.

It reminded Liza of…someone. The flashes of another life had become less common, but at the girl's question, Liza had a brief sensation of another time.

As swiftly as the feeling arose, it faded, and Liza returned to the present moment. She leaned forward. "My name is Elesbeth of Ramsay," she murmured. "And ye are Grete of the Clan MacDuff, descendant of the Mormaers of Fife. Ye are the unclaimed kin of my mother Jennet of Ramsay who passed many years ago. I'm also ye're kin, and ye've been sent here after yer own mother recently passed."

A strain, fragile as a spider's thread, lingered between them as the lass held her tongue for a great while. She blinked, myriad emotions flickering across her fair countenance.

Finally, the lass wet her lips. "Grete," she repeated softly.

Liza nodded.

"I only wish to return home." The whisper was so plaintive and filled with longing, it stirred a kindred emotion deep within Liza.

Tears welled in Liza's eyes, and she blinked them back. "Aye, I ken ye do. But ye cannae, yet." Her whisper was fierce. "It's too perilous, I reckon."

Grete turned her gaze away. "They will slay me for certain." Her words rose with an inflection at the end of her sentences.

If this maiden were indeed who Liza believed her to be, she envisioned her perilous voyage across the tempestuous North Sea.

Liza clasped one of Grete's cold hands in her warm grasp. She yearned to shield this tormented soul. "Ye'll be safe here. I'll keep ye safe."

A renewed resolve surged from deep within her. The emotion was larger than herself and greater than the potential truth of Grete's identity. It was even grander than the glory of great Scotia. An overwhelming sense of destiny transcending space and time forged Liza's promise.

Unaware of Liza's solemn silent vow, Grete's eyes roved around the chamber, visible now in the soft light of morn.

Liza followed Grete's gaze, striving to see the space through the lonely visitor's eyes. It was cold and austere, but a few of Uilleam's playthings still occupied the room. A wooden hobby horse rested against the stone wall, and toy soldiers and knights carved from stone lay scattered on his simple carved chest.

"We can make this space yers," Liza assured the lass.

Grete gazed up at the rafters. "It shall never be mine."

Liza was uncertain if Grete spoke of the chamber or something else. She again offered the vessel of plum nectar. "Try tae wet yer lips," she urged.

The lass accepted the vessel and obeyed her bidding. Liza then spread the cream upon the bread. Grete shook her head in refusal.

"Just a wee bit," Liza coaxed. "Ye must gather yer strength if ye wish to return home."

Despite the lass's look of despair and uncertainty, she took a nibble.

A rustling at the door startled Grete. It was only a young lad bearing a bundle of kindling. The lad kept his gaze downcast, attending to his task. Though he was beyond hearing, Liza whispered, "Ye must hold yer tongue until we can sharpen yer speech tae that o' this land." Grete swallowed the bread in silence. "The MacDuffs are noble, yet their voices ring raw and echo with the shores of the east of Scotia, not the inlets and fjords o' the northern way."

When the lad had departed and the fire blazed anew in the hearth, Grete asked, "Do you know who I am? Who I truly am?"

Liza softly caressed Grete's wrist. "I can well surmise. I bid ye not affirm my notions. The less I ken of ye, the better it shall be fer us both."

"'Tis the truth," Grete agreed. "You do not wish to know what I have endured because of my name." She trembled, her eyes growing distant.

Liza perceived that Grete's travails upon her journey may have been far graver than a mere attempted slaying, and she reached forward to enfold Grete in her arms. "We're sisters now," Liza affirmed. "And I'll shield ye from peril. No matter what."

Chapter 15

Throughout two cycles of the moon, Liza spent much of her time with Grete. The lass's limbs remained heavy and she seemed to struggle to rise from her bed, though Liza suspected much of the ailment lay within Grete's mind.

To deter prying eyes from the chamber, Liza bribed a guard with silver to patrol the passageway. The young guard was loyal to Liza's father and held fond memories of Uilleam. He performed his duty well.

When Liza arranged for the wooden bathing tub to be brought before the hearth, Grete insisted Liza leave her be while she washed and tended to her attire. The maiden's yearning for solitude had more to do with a maiden's mere sense of modesty, and Liza grew more and more suspicious of what had transpired on Grete's journey to the Isle of Orkney.

Save for the bathing, however, Liza was Grete's constant companion, and a blessing to this time alone was the chance to work on Grete's northern accent. Though Grete's body was still frail, Liza managed to school the maiden in the tongue of Eastern Scotia and the brogue the MacDuffs would have used. She was also able to provide Grete with what she prayed was sufficient knowledge of her supposed kin.

She repeated the tale so often, Liza nearly believed it herself. "Yer mother was a bonny lass who raised ye in the Castle of Clan MacDuff until she fell ill. Upon her passing, ye were sent away by yer true father, Duncan, Earl of Fife, at the behest of his wife, Joan de Clare, and transported to Watret Abbey where Lachlan was alerted to yer presence."

Upon the first telling of this tale, Grete had said, "Who is Lachlan?"

Liza bristled. "'Tis no matter," she said, and told the tale anew.

"What if folk should inquire after my mother?"

Liza shook her head. "Yer mother is of little note, but tell yer questioner she was a chambermaid at the castle, and ye know only of circumstances before ye were cast forth."

"Must I then say Duncan, Earl of Fife, is my father?"

"It is tae be intimated," Liza replied. "Should any inquire with the Clan MacDuff concerning an outcast bairn, they will deny the claim, which only lends credence tae yer tale. And truly, as daughter to Jennet, sister of Duncan, I had no choice but to take ye in. Fer ye bear my own noble blood in yer veins."

Grete sighed. Understanding her peril, she assented. Still, each time her feigned father was named, sorrow would fill Grete's face. If she were indeed the maid Liza suspected, Grete surely pined for her true father, who believed her dead across the cold North Sea.

In those waning months, as daylight dwindled and jeelit winds swept across the land, Liza spoke seldom with Lachlan, and when the occasion arose, they discussed only Grete.

Lachlan did his duty, weaving Grete's borrowed history among the castle folk, and Liza learned the tale had taken root. All believed the strange maiden found in Uilleam's chamber to be kindred to Lady Elesbeth's lost mother, Jennet, countess of Clan MacDuff.

Meanwhile, the realm of Scotia lay in darkest mourning for the Maid of Norway, perished en route to the Isles of Orkney, leaving the land without a sovereign and the Guardians at bitter odds for the crown.

When word came of the maid's doom, Liza had awaited John Comyn's naming as heir, but the chief claimants proved John Balliol and Robert Bruce, Lord of Annandale. For this, Liza did give thanks. Nothing but woe would befall their country should a man like Comyn sit on the throne.

The winter solstice drew nigh and the household prepared for Yule. Liza's heart stayed upon Grete's presence, which lent her some comfort, though it had been near a twelvemonth since she'd last heard tidings of her father or brother.

The mood of the castle lightened as Donvaldus MacTavish supervised the hanging of strings of pine branches that filled the hallways with an earthy pleasant scent. Monks from the abbey visited during the dinner hour and regaled those in the great hall with traditional chants of hope and gratitude.

The scullery maids giggled as they served suppers, and the men of the barony and household teased and pinched good-naturedly.

Liza suspected an influx of bairns would be birthed near the next fall harvest.

She did her best to ignore her own longing for a child—the time for which was quickly passing her by—and tried to feel grateful for her station in life. She knew her circumstances were far more satisfactory than most of the country's inhabitants, but she couldn't help descending into periods of melancholy. And at times, she couldn't even identify from where her melancholy stemmed.

Two weeks before the Yule celebration, during a lonely supper in the great hall, surrounded by noise, warmth, and merriment, Liza overheard the seneschal, Peter Syward, discussing the matter of their new king with an unknown man wearing fine clothing and sheepskin boots. For many reasons, including her distrust of the Guardians and her protection of Grete,

Liza joined their conversation to the obvious impatience of both men.

"I know of Robert Bruce, Lord of Annandale, but tell me more of this John Balliol," she said. "What makes him fit to rule our great land?"

The men exchanged a glance; Liza paid no mind to their stiff postures.

"And who would you be?" the man in the fine clothing demanded before Peter could warn him of Liza's identity.

"I am the lady of this castle," she responded evenly. Over the months since Ullieam's death, Liza had become less defensive of her position. With Claray still mostly confined to her chambers, Liza was all that was left of the Ramsay family.

She noted the man's English accent, long upturned nose, and thick midsection. He may not have been noble, but he certainly held an elevated stature. What on earth was he doing there, and why hadn't she been told? Her skin prickled with both wrath and foreboding.

Peter cleared his throat. "Sir Reginald, this is Lady Elesbeth Ramsay, daughter of Sir William Ramsay."

Something unspoken was exchanged between the two men. Without introducing his guest, Peter turned his attention to Liza and said in a slow, patient voice, "Lady Elesbeth, Lord Balliol, through his mother, is great-great-great-grandson of His Highness David the

First and one generation closer to the throne than his rival by proximity of blood." He may well have been speaking to a child.

The blood rose in her cheeks, but she kept her wits about her. "His rival," she repeated. "You speak of Robert Bruce?" She recalled the charismatic Bruce dining in this very hall with her father. A hearty man he was, with a loud voice, ready laugh, and kind eye. She felt sure if Robert Bruce were to be crowned, he'd be quick to summon her father back from his extended exile in France and might also be persuaded to discuss the current conundrum with Grete. "I feel certain he would be the wiser of the two choices." If proposed very carefully, perhaps they could reach a solution best for not only Grete, but for all of Scotia…

The Englishman interrupted the surreptitious plans wending their way through her mind. "Preposterous," he spat and spared her a contemptuous look. "Bruce will not protect our interests with Longshanks. He wants only power."

Liza drew herself up. "I should think Bruce wants independence," she corrected.

"And what know you of thinking?" the man demanded. "You are but a lassie pretending to rule an inconsequential barony." He guffawed wickedly. "You know nothing of the ways of the world." He leaned close, and despite his station in life, his breath reeked of foul meat and rotten teeth. "But I'll wager you're good for something."

Since assuming the role of lady of the castle, not one person had dared address her in an overtly insolent manner. Liza was so shocked, she didn't react before the man's hand found her breast over her léine.

Peter's face reddened, but he didn't utter a sound.

When Liza had recovered her wits, she swatted the man's filthy paw away. "Out with ye," she ordered, and though her words were not loud, her meaning was clear. "I dinnae care what business ye may have in this castle. Ye are not to return here. I'll give the order myself."

The man chuckled, though he did not move to touch her again. "I'm here by the order of Longshanks himself. Your demands are meaningless."

Longshanks, Liza thought with a start. The King of England had sent this man to her barony? For what purpose?

Liza was about to demand an answer from Peter Syward when another presence appeared in a flash. A *sgian dubh* appeared at the man's exposed throat, the small black dagger held by the hand of Lachlan McClaren.

"Lady Ramsay will not be disrespected in her own dwelling." Lachlan's words seethed from his lips. "If ye dinnae vacate not only the castle, but the barony, immediately, I will slit yer throat and feed yer body to the boar."

The inhabitants of the great hall who'd witnessed Lachlan's passage across the floor stopped their actions and chatter to observe this interaction with horror, curiosity, and glee.

Whatever the man's purpose, it would come to no good for the household to witness the murder of a messenger of the court of England.

Liza placed a hand on Lachlan's outstretched arm. If indeed King Edward had sent this man to the Ramsay Estate for some reason, Liza wanted to know his purpose. She cared little for his treatment of her.

"Bailiff," she said softly, "Let us understand the reason fer his visit."

Lachlan's pressure increased on the man's neck, and a small welling of blood appeared. "The devil with his visit."

The man's eyes had widened, the arrogance fled from his expression. "My name is Reginald Crawford from Berwick-upon-Tweed, a known and loyal servant of the King of England. Should I die at the hand of a member of the household of Clan Ramsay, consequences would be dire for you and all who live here." The words were strong, but the voice was breathless.

A pause followed. In those seconds, time stood still.

Liza's mind began feverishly working and remembering.

There had been tales of skirmishes and invasions even before word of the Maid of Norway's death had spread across the land. While Margaret's hand in marriage had been promised to Longshank's son, Edward of Caernarfon, Longshanks himself had been pushing north and testing Scotland's borders for many years, even when King Alexander had ruled fairly and well.

Before her father's exile, Liza had heard him, as clan chieftain, discuss the position of the Ramsay Castle as a gateway to the Highlands—an attractive position for an English sovereign intent on waging war.

She would not be the soul to give this man reason to take her land. Nor would her bailiff.

"Bailie, enough!" Liza's raised voice rang through the hall. "Release this man immediately."

Lachlan pressed his dagger further into the man's neck, then dropped his arm.

Reginald Crawford placed his hand to his wound, smearing blood on his woolen cloak.

The danger halted, and Liza stepped forward to place herself between the two men. Lachlan's scowl was deep, but the intruder slowly smiled, revealing crooked, yellowed teeth. "A wise choice, lass, to control your brute. Though the memories of the English are long." He cast a fleeting gaze upon Lachlan, then turned his eyes once more to Liza. "And I'll remember the feel of your duckies between my fingers."

Liza felt Lachlan flinch. She held up a hand to him.

Reginald Crawford let out a derisive snort. "I've

beheld all I require of the Ramsay lands and their folk. I shall carry word back to my lord and sovereign." Turning his gaze to Peter Syward, he declared, "You can be sure you've not heard the last from us regarding the matter of the sheriffdom."

Liza looked to Peter who colored again. He didn't dare meet her gaze.

Sheriffdoms had been implemented as an exercise of control by the English king to limit the authority of the lordships and provide Longshanks proxy control over Scottish lands. Not only would the position of the Ramsay barony have been desirable to Edward, but so too would the absence of the laird and true lady. A lass such as Elesbeth Ramsay would be easily enough controlled.

Liza flushed.

She could not allow the castle to be overtaken. Especially not with Grete tucked away within the walls. If the maiden's identity were to be discovered, death would come, and not painlessly. Their tormentors would first make use of the rack or a cucking tool. There would be torture and there would be agony. Liza and Grete would be publicly accused of lying and witchcraft. Their murders would be celebrated.

Liza didn't speak as Reginald took his leave, and she didn't say a word when Peter Syward also slunk from the room.

Her thoughts galloped wildly as she pondered her

scant choices, scarcely taking notice when Forsy hurried into the hall. Liza was on the verge of addressing Lachlan regarding the matter, when Forsy pressed herself against Lachlan's side. "*Mo ghràdh,*" she exclaimed, and the tender term of affection rendered Liza's mind still as stone and her blood chill as the northern winds. "Are ye all right?" Forsy's long fingers clutched Lachlan's hand.

Lachlan straightened. He didn't push the girl away. "All is well," he said, sheathing the *sgian dubh.*

"Ye mustn't get yerself wounded. Ye're tae be my husband, and I'd not hae my betrothed dead afore the weddin'."

Liza's world began to whirl about her. She drew in a breath, hoping she'd misheard the chambermaid. She'd considered Forsy nothing but an insignificant young lass, pale and frail. Spiteful, though benign. It was true—Forsy was not much younger than Liza and indeed of marriageable age. Liza steadied herself, but her head did pound and her extremities felt cold. She couldn't bring herself to look at Lachlan. He remained silent.

She did not address the girl or her words. "Bailie," she managed, then swallowed in an attempt to strengthen her voice and her resolve. "It will become necessary to discuss these recent events and their consequences for the land."

Forsy smiled up at Liza. "Our betrothal will have

no consequence to our positions within the castle," she said. Then she placed a hand to her stomach. "A wee babe may bring a spot of joy tae these dank hallways."

At this, Liza swayed, and Lachlan snatched his hand away from Forsy's to steady Liza.

Liza pulled away quickly, as if Lachlan's touch scorched.

He said quickly, "Forsy, ye are no' with bairn."

"Not yet, but I hope tae be soon after the weddin' with its blessing."

At this, Liza hazarded a look at Lachlan. His eyes were downcast and his mouth slack, but he did nothing to deny this claim.

The chambermaid tangled her thin arms around Lachlan's strong-muscled one, again forcing her hand into his. She turned her steady gaze to Liza. "I mourn Wyolet each day," she said. "But I ken she would hae wanted Lachlan tae be happy. I can make him happy."

Her intent was unmistakable. It was Liza who could not bring joy to Lachlan. And Liza understood the lass spoke true. A bond of love between Liza and Lachlan could never be forged. If, by wedding Forsy, Lachlan might find a measure of joy in this woeful world, Liza could never withhold it from him.

Happiness was not her fate in this existence. Nor was happiness hers to give.

She managed a genuine smile for Forsy. "I'm sure yer bairn will be beautiful," she whispered and managed to flee before the tears flowed freely.

Chapter 16

Liza was standing in the passageway, exhaling heavily and attempting to collect herself, when Hexilde approached with a vessel of frumenty pottage and a slab of bread.

"Fer the girl," Hexilde said when Liza stared at the food.

Liza blinked herself back into the present moment. *Grete.*

"I'd meant to warn ye about Forsy."

Liza drew in a tremulous breath.

"She be a more fitting match for him, Lady Elesbeth." Hexilde spoke with a gentle yet unwavering tone. "Ye must consider yer own standing. Should William and Alexander not make their way back..." Her voice faded, leaving the unspoken words hanging in the air. "...ye surely dinnae wish for the Ramsay name to perish with ye."

Liza had no wish for such a consequence. Yet greater urgencies lay before her. Moreover, she had no yearning to converse upon her sentiments for the bailie with Hexilde.

To cast aside thoughts of Lachlan and Forsy from her mind was a task most arduous, though it was a necessity. Dwelling upon their union would avail her nothing. She carried upon her soul graver concerns. Concerns that bore meaning to more than just herself.

"Have ye heard word of the Guardians?"

"Aye, the men are now brawlin' amongst themselves, since the Maid o' Norway—God rest her soul—has passed. I'm grateful John Comyn seems to have given up his pursuit of Lady Claray. It's wise to keep one's head down with the strife brewin' between Balliol and Bruce." She shook her head. "Longshanks will do all he can to seize our lands. The lass's untimely death has played right into his hands." Her voice rose, as if accusing Longshanks himself of orchestrating the Maid of Norway's demise.

"Aye, but the lass was meant to wed his son, Edward of Caernarfon," said Liza. At the very least, Grete had escaped that fate, Liza mused with a somber heart. It was said that the heir to the English throne was a most ill-tempered knave.

"Pshaw." The sound emanated from the back of Hexilde's throat. She looked around before leaning forward. Her breath wafted of ale and pungent herbs. "That one lies with men, so I've heard."

Liza blinked, as the cook's words slowly bloomed. "The son and heir of Longshanks?" She found herself at a loss, uncertain how to handle this newfound tidbit.

Hexilde nodded, and the skin on her chin wobbled with the movement. "If the tales are true, the dandy would no' hae planted his seed within Margaret's belly. And if the maid had had any fire in her, she'd hae run right over her weak husband, and his father, too. As bairn and kin of King Alexander, I hae no doubt she would hae done exactly that."

Liza squinted her eyes, striving to grasp the woman's intent. "What be yer purpose in voicing such scandalous prattle?"

The woman put a hand to her throat and looked about her again. "I'm no' implyin' anythin' mind ye…" Her words trailed off before she continued in a softer voice. "If Longshanks sought dominion o'er Scotia, it would be far swifter and more certain to seize the land by his own might, rather than through a false union between his foppish son and a lassie queen, heiress of his erstwhile foe." She lifted her bushy gray brows. "One cannae help but ponder the fortuitousness of the maid's untimely passing."

Liza pondered this, as well as the strife between Balliol and Bruce. She recalled the words of John Comyn from that ill-starred eve last midsummer, when he spoke of securing his lands in England. It was the night he'd ousted Laird Goerge Dicson for his rashly uttered thoughts and unspoken allegiance to England.

"And where does the Bishop of Glasgow stand?" Liza mused out loud, referring to Robert Wishart.

Hexilde's brow furrowed deeply, her eyebrows nearly meeting. "Robert Wishart, aye, he stands ever as the voice o' reason and steadfast support fer the cause o' the nation. He stands with Robert the Bruce, who carries the true freedom o' the land in his heart," she solemnly shared. She shook her head with disdain. "They've already taken to callin' Balliol by the name 'Toom Tabard'. 'Empty Coat', that means," she explained. "In truth, an actual empty coat would be far better, I reckon. Fer it'll be Longshanks himself who rules these lands if Balliol takes the throne."

Liza didn't speak. What kind of game were these men playing?

Shaking her head slowly, Hexilde said, "I fear a war is brewin'."

With those ominously spoken words, Peter Syward crossed the passage toward the chancery. He didn't look in the direction of the women. Though the man named Crawford—whose aim was to install a sheriffdom at the Ramsay Castle—had been turned out, it was Peter Syward who'd hosted their foe so very agreeably.

Liza felt a sense of deep impending doom. Not only was her independence at risk, her lands at risk, and her heart at risk, she was harboring the heir to the Scottish throne in her dead brother's chambers. And that heir was very much alive.

She must speak with the Bishop of Glasgow without alerting anyone else in the castle. And she feared the only person in the land she could trust was Lachlan.

"Is the girl gettin' stronger, then?" Hexilde asked, changing the course of the conversation. "Grete," she added with an arch of her brow.

Did Liza imagine the suspicion that touched the girl's name?

She lingered long before she answered, for it was wiser to craft her tale well than to arouse doubt with a rash and heedless reply. "Aye, the lass mends with each passing day. It was a great blow to her, first losin' her mother, then finding herself cast out so sudden from the sole dwelling she'd ever known. Tae find out the mormaer himself is her true father..." Her words drifted into silence, and she cast a furtive glance at Hexilde, who gnawed thoughtfully upon the inside of her cheek.

"I don' suppose we'll hear a word from the Mac-Duffs," the woman said carefully.

"Nay. I suppose not."

"It's a shame. Poor little lassie. Despite her blood-line, her legitimacy will prevent her from marryin' noble stock. Ye're kind tae take her in."

"She's my kin."

"So I've heard."

Had Liza conjured another hint of doubt in Hexilde's voice? She found the canny woman's brow again arched high. "She's come to us at a most unusual time, hasn't she? Delivered to the abbey from the sea?"

A chill enveloped Liza.

Perhaps it was the weary look upon Liza's countenance that led the cook to close her eyes and let forth a deep sigh.

"I shall no' inquire it o' ye, Lady Elesbeth. But heed my words—should it come tae be ken the Maid o' Norway is concealed somewhere, hale and hearty, not only would her life be imperiled, but so too the lives and welfare of all those around her. Any who might dare to shelter such a secret would no' only be flirtin' with death, but invitin' the most dreadful and excruciating torments. As would any others who might ken of it."

Liza pressed her lips tight. Her voice was but a whisper as she inquired, "And what would ye counsel such a soul to do?"

"Aid the lass in her journey back to her native land." She seized Liza's arm with a swift motion. "At once."

Liza's eyes opened wide. She summoned forth what she hoped might seem an easy smile. In truth, the expression felt more akin to a grimace. "As fate should have it, we need not trouble ourselves with such matters." She steadied the quaver in her voice.

Hexilde appeared unconvinced, her visage pale and round as the cold moon. Liza summoned a bright laugh to dispel the unease, her voice quivering ever so slightly as she spoke.

"Hexilde, ye look as if ye've laid eyes upon a specter."

"If ye're dabblin' in some mischief, lass, I fear we might all become phantoms o' this keep."

Liza was at a loss for an answer.

Hexilde handed over the tray. "Ye best be carryin' the victuals to Grete now. The lass will need her vigor for the life that awaits her." With one last meaningful look at Liza, Hexilde turned and sloped back to the kitchen.

Liza felt her heart thundering within her chest. She was indeed treading a perilous path.

Chapter 17

After the Yule festivity, throughout the Daft Days following and nearing Hogmanay, the final eve of the old year, Lachlan appeared at the threshold of Liza's bedchamber as she prepared herself for the morn. He entered behind a young attendant who bore an armful of firewood into the frosty chamber, and he tarried while the servant kindled a blaze in the hearth.

Liza, who had been weaving her tresses into intricate plaits, slowed her actions before the mirrored glass atop her commode. In Lachlan's presence, the air thickened, and her fumbling fingers could not continue their task, even as the chill in the frigid chamber began to yield to the fire's roaring warmth.

For the past sennight, thick snow had blanketed the land without cease, and though the spirit was merry and the feasts were bounteous during Yuletide, Liza fretted that the stores of victuals for the cottars and the beasts of the barony might not hold out once the revelry had passed.

When the attendant scuttled from the room, Lachlan lingered. "My lady," he muttered, his gaze fixed firmly upon the ground, though she was modestly clad in her léine and mantle.

Liza recalled a prior occasion when Lachlan had graced her chambers. Her attire had been far less then. She pondered whether those memories lingered in Lachlan's mind, as well. Or perhaps he was remembering what had happened immediately following their coupling, when Wyolet's screams had pierced the quiet stillness of morn.

And now he belonged to Forsy.

She drew herself up and said cooly, "What is it, bailie?"

"I've done yer bidding, and hae just received word from the Watret Abbey that Sir Robert Wishart arrived late last eve."

Relief and astonishment coursed through Liza. She had sought audience with the Guardian for many months, and still he had not heeded her call. She had feared the holy man would turn her away once more and had not dared to hope he would grace them with his presence during Yule.

"Pray, escort him to the keep. He may reside here through the Daft Days and join us in revelry at the Ne'erday feast," she commanded, speaking of the forthcoming New Year's banquet and merriment.

"He's requested yer presence at the abbey, my lady."

Liza peered through the window at the relentless

veil of white descending from the dreich heavens. "How shall we journey in this *cathadh*? Surely the steeds shall lose the path."

"Luar be a right clever beast. She'll carry ye to where ye need be."

Liza noted the singular manner of his speech and clamped her lips tight.

"I'll send a stable lad with ye," Lachlan murmured.

She dared not request his companionship, and were the conditions less dire, she'd not even think of it. Yet she could not hazard becoming lost in such a tempest. What fate would befall Grete then?

"I need *you* by my side, Lachlan."

The clench of his jaw brought her sorrow. She knew well that he would rather face any task than accompany her on this venture.

Swallowing, she murmured, "If it be Forsy, I can—"

"Ye'll speak naught of this tae her." The words erupted fiercely. Then—she knew not if for her benefit or because of his betrothed—he said more gently, "Forsy must remain untainted by this common folly."

"Common folly," Liza repeated his words. "Ye think we had a choice in this matter?"

Lachlan held his hands in front of him then let them drop. "Why do ye think the Bishop of Glasgow disnae want tae come here? Our land has been exposed, Lady Elesbeth. The presence of that English knave a fortnight ago proves it. We're all in peril."

"I ken ye wish to shield yer love." The final word emerged like a curse—gruff and unseemly. "I had no choice. I must guard my realm and my *queen*."

Lachlan gazed into the fire. "Forsy is no' my beloved," he at last declared.

"What then is yer purpose with her?" It mattered not to Liza's affairs, and she ought not seek the answer, yet she could not restrain herself from voicing the query.

"I seek tae craft a life since my true love is denied tae me."

Liza's cheeks flushed with warmth. "Am I yer true love then?"

"That I can ne'er proclaim." His voice was barely more than a breath. "Ye'll always be the lady of this land, and I'll always be the serf."

"That does not mean ye must marry Forsy."

"I wish tae leave somethin' behind—tae carry my name and memory onward. I do no' possess an estate and legacy like yers."

Her mind raced, and not for the first time she pondered the potential consequences if she were to bear his child. It was impossible. They could not wed—no reputable man of God would think to perform the ceremony. And even if they weres to defy laws, neither the union nor the bairn would be acknowledged.

An illegitimate child was no solution. As an unwed woman—no matter her station—she'd be cast out by society and law. Besmirched. Despoiled. Shunned. The Ramsay name would be sullied. Her father would be disgraced.

She blinked hard as she nodded, understanding even as the knowledge tore at her heart.

"I'll go with ye," he said, his voice tender. "Ye're right about the danger, and if somethin' happened tae ye…" His words trailed off, and Liza waited for him to finish the thought.

He did not.

"I'll ready the horses."

Liza was swaddled in two tartan cloaks, with a woolen cloth wound around her face. She still felt chilled to her marrow when Luar and Gwrol finally bore Liza and Lachlan to the door of the abbey. The only boon of the heavy snowfall was that the biting chill had quelled Liza's sneezing and watering eyes. A young monk clad in a long dark cowl hurried forth to secure the horses, while Lachlan helped Liza down and guided her to the door. The abbot himself—a holy man by the name of Renier—stood waiting at the threshold.

"Your Reverence," Liza uttered, her head bowed low.

The abbot tarried in his response. His dust-colored hair was shorn in a tonsure, a symbol of the crown of thorns worn by Christ, yet there was no kindly look upon the man's sharp expression. His thick brows were drawn over a long, pointed nose, and his receding chin was accentuated by the severe frown of his thin lips. He beckoned them into the dim passage. The door slammed heavily behind them.

The same scents from before met Liza, though now mingled with the unmistakable aroma of smoke and hearty game. Her stomach responded audibly, for she had not taken time to break her fast. The abbot offered them neither food nor drink.

Instead, he said with only a slight northern lilt to his voice, "Lady Elesbeth, the Bishop of Glasgow has come at your behest."

He seemed to be awaiting some response, so Liza said, "And I thank him greatly for his troubles."

"During times such as these, any journey is quite dangerous."

"We just traversed the snow-covered land ourselves, abbot." Lachlan's voice was low but firm.

"Weather is not that of which I speak," he lamented with a heavy sigh. "Lady Elesbeth, I know well why ye've come and why ye've called upon Bishop Wishart. Yer role is to guard Ramsay Castle and its folk during these trying times. And troubling times they are, indeed."

Before Liza could utter a word, the abbot turned and guided them down a passage toward the nave. Liza and Lachlan followed behind, and Liza was surprised at the speed with which the abbot moved through the passageways.

Before they entered the grand vaulted chamber, he veered left near the dormitories where they'd first encountered Grete months earlier. They trailed behind him through another passageway, and soon they stepped across a threshold into the cloisters. The air within the lengthy corridor was sharp and biting, and though wooden shutters were fastened against the cold, the wind crept through the doors with a ghostly persistence. Beneath the windows, straw was strewn upon the stone benches, where sat several monks clad in long brown tunics. Their eyes were closed, and they paid no mind to Liza and Lachlan as they made their way past.

At the cloister's end, the abbot guided them down a flight of stone stairs, descending into the depths beneath the abbey. The air grew even more frigid below the surface, and Liza drew her plaid tightly about her shoulders as her teeth clattered in the chill. Lachlan drew nearer to her, as if to lend her warmth from his own body.

At the passage's end, they emerged into a diminutive chamber with low-vaulted ceilings, where a lone figure sat with its back to them before a small fire flickering in a miniature hearth. Upon his turning, Liza recognized the man as the Guardian, Robert Wishart.

He seemed older and frailer than when she'd last laid eyes upon him.

"My Elesbeth," he said, lifting a hand to his mouth as a cough wracked his chest from its depths. "Forgive me." His breath wheezed from his lungs. "Illness has seized me and willnae release its grip."

Liza observed his rheumy eyes and frail form. "I had heard nothing o' yer ailment, my laird," she replied, her words filled with apology.

He waved away her concern. "Come. Sit with me before this fire."

A lone wooden stool sat beside his. Liza cast a glance back at Lachlan, who beckoned her forward. With some reluctance, she settled herself next to the aged man. The fire's warmth thawed her chilled skin, and the relief was so sweet she scarce noted her companions' departure from the small chamber.

She leaned forward, perilously close to the flames. Once the heat had suffused her, she reclined back. The man regarded her intently.

"How long have ye been ailing?" she inquired.

"It came upon me just before Samhain, the harvest moon," he noted.

"After the maid was delivered."

"Aye. I sought to come sooner." He raised a hand, its skin dry and translucent, and coughed into it. When the fit abated, he continued. "The conditions for travel have turned dire in the land."

"Ye speak not of yer malady nor the weather," she remarked.

"Ye are correct, my child."

They both stared into the flames. "What am I tae do with her?" she asked quietly.

He tarried in the heaviness that settled upon them before he spoke. "I've heard the tale ye've woven. Cunning, indeed. Duncan, Earl o' Fife, has so firmly denied the claim, his wife, Joan de Clare, reckons it must hold truth. The account has spread as gospel throughout the realm, and yer Grete is said to be the bastard bairn of yer mother's brother. And yer kin. This strife and scandal conveniently keeps Duncan away from the affairs of the day. Well done, Elesbeth."

While she was thankful her tale would keep Grete safe—at least for a time—she didn't care much about the effect of her fabrication.

"What happened tae her on that ship?" she asked quietly.

Robert Wishart's pleased countenance waned. "I fear I dinnae know the particulars."

"Ye dinnae know who desired her demise?"

He parted his lips but sealed them once more. "Almost all sought her end," he murmured. "Her father, King Erik, was wise tae keep her at his side fer as long as he could."

"Why could they not let her abide with her father forever and seek their lust for power in some other fashion?"

The man shrugged a feeble shoulder beneath his mantle. "She was bound by the Treaty of Brigham. And even had the Treaty not existed…she would still claim the crown as Alexander's granddaughter. Such a thing couldnae stand."

"According to John Comyn," Liza said bitterly.

"Or Balliol. Or Stewart. Or Bruce. Or even Longshanks himself for that matter."

Liza remembered her conversation with Hexilde. "Was King Alexander slain, too?"

The Guardian leaned forward. "There are those who believe it. There are those who believe Alexander's inability to bear a living son by his wives was also plotted."

From the meaning in his words, Liza knew it to be true.

"And Uilleam?" she asked quietly about her brother, who was of little import compared to the lofty matters of the Crown. Uilleam was significant to *her*.

"I cannot tell ye, child." The Guardian's voice was solemn.

A deep sense of rage filled Liza, though she wasn't sure if Robert Wishart meant he couldn't tell her because it would place her in danger, or if he simply didn't know. In either case, *she* knew it to be true. Her brother had been slain.

"And what of me?" she cried. "What am I tae do with the girl when her very life places us all in such grave peril?"

His eyes blazed as they turned on her. "Ye're to keep her safe," he answered, a renewed fervor in his voice. "Ye're tae help her."

Liza was seized by a sudden recollection. *Help me*, a ghostly presence had beseeched. The memory sent a tremor through her body.

The Guardian paid no heed. "Haven't ye asked yourself why *ye're* here? Why ye were found under that tree?"

Liza found herself briefly dazed. Each morn, she arose with the remembrance of that fateful day lingering in her mind. As she lay upon the cold ground, her eyes fluttered open to meet the gaze of Lachlan, a soul she recognized from a distant place and time.

Following that day, it had taken her time to grow accustomed to her dwelling at Ramsay Castle, though she was well aware of her name, Elesbeth Ramsay, and her rightful place among her kin. The memories of her early years lingered like a distant mist—dreamlike and unreachable. But what would Robert Wishart know of that morn?

"You were sent here for this very purpose, Liza. To save the queen."

It became very warm in the chamber. Her cheeks flamed, and perspiration beaded on her brow. She wanted to flee, but when she turned, she could see the door was shut and there appeared to be no knob on the inside of the chamber. "'Tis madness," she whispered.

"Upon waking, did ye possess knowledge of yer identity or the purpose of yer presence in this realm?"

She unfurled the layer of plaid from her shoulders. "I'd been walkin' in my sleep," she said. "There's a simple explanation fer it. And I remember..." She waved her hand in front of her. "...I remember my father and brother Alexander." Her voice was triumphant.

"And yet, they're not here. So how can you be sure it's them ye remember?"

Liza blinked. He was right, she supposed. Her memories could be a figment of her imagination. Nothing but a daydream.

"I remember Uilleam and Claray," she argued. "And Hexilde. I ken things about all o' them."

Though it had taken time for the memories of them to catch up to her. And even then, the memories were faint, like the washed-out colors of the sky at gloaming.

"Lachlan," she uttered. "I know Lachlan." Truth be told, her memory of Lachlan loomed larger from another realm and age. She could scarcely explain it, but Lachlan she felt in the marrow of her bones and the depths of her soul. Their connection defied the bounds of this earthly life.

She found Robert Wishart smiling at her, as if he knew her secret. He reached out and patted her hand. The contact made her startle.

"It's okay, my dear. Ye're doing fine."

Tears welled in her eyes. She felt as though her deeds were of no avail. Charged with the governance of a clan and a barony, and now to be told she was not of this time? It was madness, every bit of it.

"When will my father and brother return?" she asked, her voice filled with misery. She held no hope the man would tell her they still lived.

"Presently," he said.

"They're alive?"

"Oh, aye. The Ramsay Clan will survive the wars."

"The wars," she repeated slowly. "Are we at war?"

"We've been fighting for quite some time. The war for independence. Margaret should have been the light to emerge, under the Treaty of Birgham. She would have been the conjoining of the nations. I have no doubt she would have been successful in that mission." He wet his dry lips with his tongue. "Ye must keep her light shining, Liza."

Liza. He'd used that other name more than once. The name she called herself in her head. The appellation intimate to her and her alone. Robert Wishart could not have known that name.

In the pause that followed, the only sounds were the crackling of the fire and the soft rush of the flame as the inferno fed upon itself.

The Guardian shifted and made a sound at the back of his throat. "After Ne'erday, King Edward has requested to take part in the feudal court held at Berwick-upon-Tweed to name the next king of Scotland."

"Balliol or Bruce," Liza said softly.

He clasped his wizened hands together. "With a Balliol rule, we grant the power of England over our lands. We hand Edward the keys to the Kingdom of Alba."

"And with a Bruce rule?"

"We preserve our freedom. But make no mistake— that freedom will come at a cost. Longshanks will not loosen his hold easily. Nor will the other Guardians who have interests with Edward. He'll become a hammer upon this great land."

Liza thought of the craggy landscapes and tranquil vistas—the grand mountains and mist-shrouded lochs of her birthplace. Though the Guardian had intimated Liza belonged not to this era, she was undoubtedly of this place. Her spirit was enmeshed with the land, with its untamed wildness and calming serenity.

Any anger she'd felt drained from her, weariness weighing her bones. She leaned forward, her head in her hands. "And how am I tae keep Grete safe in the face of such danger?"

"Ye'll find a way," the Guardian said. "But careful to watch your own back. The fate of Uilleam and Wyolet could befall ye, as well."

"By whose hand might violence befall me?" she

whispered.

Robert Wishart opened his mouth, but before he could answer, he began to cough. This time, the fit didn't stop. His eyes bulged and watered, and his chest wracked noisily.

Startled, Liza sprang to her feet and made haste to the chamber's sole exit. Lacking a handle, she found herself unable to open the door.

The Guardian doubled over on his stool, the fit becoming worse.

She pounded on the thick wood. "Lachlan!" she cried. "Abbot!"

After what felt like an age, she discerned the scuffle of feet upon the stone beyond. When the door burst open, Liza leapt aside in time to evade it crushing her against the chamber wall. The abbot strode into the room, his visage aflame with concern. He hastened to the Guardian and knelt before him, bellowing to some unseen presence outside the chamber in a tongue Liza could not comprehend. The wheezing had turned into desperate gasps for breath, and Liza's hands flew to cover her mouth. Guardian Robert Wishart, Bishop of Glasgow, might not survive this chamber. Her first response came from a well of humanity...and then from a place of self-preservation. Who would shield her from the ambitions of the other Guardians should he pass?

Hands gripped her shoulders, pulling her back

from the chamber's threshold. She resisted until she heard the urgent whisper of Lachlan. "My lady, ye must allow them their sacred duties."

Two monks in their somber tunics swept past them at the doorway, bearing vessels of steaming concoctions.

"Call upon the Cailleach," commanded the abbot, as he carefully poured the steaming draught down the Guardian's throat.

Another monk dashed from the chamber, heedless of all else, his leather-soled slippers skittering across the rugged stone floor.

"We must depart," Lachlan urged once more, but Liza stood firm in the corner, steadfast and unmoving.

Robert Wishart must not perish. Without his protection, Liza dreaded she and Grete would not endure the Daft Days nor see the turning of the year.

Chapter 18

Liza felt the presence of the crone before she appeared. A sudden energy surged through her, raising her hair and causing her skin to prickle with awareness. Along with this energy came a sense of clarity—all would be well.

When the old woman emerged at the end of the passageway, Liza understood the energy emanated from *her*, the same ancient hag who'd tended to Grete when Liza first encountered the lass within these walls. The one who had effortlessly transformed from crone to maiden and back again, as if it were nothing but a fleeting notion.

Though the attention of the inhabitants of Watret Abbey was fixed on the Guardian Robert Wishart, the crone's gaze remained locked upon Liza as she traversed the passage.

She seemed to both shuffle and glide down the corridor like a wraith. Liza had only seen the crone seated beside Grete's sickbed. Now, the woman's long white locks cascaded freely about her shoulders, tendrils lifting and falling around her weathered face, her dark, all-seeing eyes piercing the very fabric of Liza's soul. Her black woolen cloak billowed about her, as though an unseen tempest followed in her wake.

Liza was both captivated and filled with dread.

"Cailleach," the abbot summoned from over Liza's shoulder, while the monks flitted about in hushed reverence. "In here."

The woman named Cailleach halted before Liza. She bore the scent of scorched earth and rotting leaves, of rain upon heated stone, and the icy waters of the Creagan Burn in the heart of winter. She carried the essence of the wind and the sun, the harvest, and the fragrant heather.

Liza felt herself drawn into the scents, as if she would meld with them.

The crone placed a cold, craggy hand upon her smooth cheek, and a burst of energy and color jolted through her.

Flashes of light and space and time...

In that moment, she lived lifetimes and worlds, experienced intense joy and passionate suffering. For one instant, she contained the entire universe. She *was* the universe.

And beside her was Lachlan. They were one. And they were constant.

Cailleach withdrew her hand, and as swiftly as the tremor had shaken her, it ceased.

Bereft of the crone's touch, Liza found herself returned to the low chamber beneath the abbey's floor. She was but a glimmer in the present moment, which throbbed around her as if it, too, possessed life, and she was merely a fragment of this spark of existence. She flickered like the flame of a candle until the moment steadied, and the happenings of the scene about her returned.

Liza blinked, yet none seemed to have taken note of her fleeting departure from reality.

Despite her dread and bewilderment, Liza spoke with urgency. "Ye must save him."

Cailleach turned her gaze upon Robert Wishart, the Bishop of Glasgow. She strode toward the men gathered by the warmth of the hearth.

Liza watched as Cailleach closed her eyes, raised her hands skyward, and murmured words in a tongue unknown to mortal ears. She lowered her hands, placing them gently upon the Guardian's weathered cheeks, as she had done to Liza moments before.

The man's labored breaths and desperate gasps ceased instantly. Soon, he slumped upon the stool, weary yet drawing breath in even, robust gasps.

Liza understood she was witnessing a witch perform an act both magical and sacred. She felt the same mystical, sacred power coursing through her own being.

When the chamber had stilled, the abbot arose. This man of the Lord inclined his head to this woman of enchantment. "Thanks be to ye, Cailleach."

With nothing more said, the ancient one turned and glided from the chamber. As she passed Liza, her words, soft as a whisper and intimate as a thought, reached her ears. "It is ye're task now, my bairn."

And then she was away.

Liza did not speak to Lachlan of the events that had unfolded within the abbey's chamber. They departed swiftly after being assured the Bishop of Glasgow would endure his malady, at least for the present hour. The abbot offered them scant farewell as the steeds were led forth.

The chill of the air was the only thing that kept Liza from succumbing to sleep upon their return to the castle. She was weary and famished, having yet to break her fast. Her head throbbed, though whether from hunger or the strange encounter, she could not be certain.

As the castle loomed into view, Liza straightened her posture, and both Luar and Gwrol hastened their pace. As they approached, Liza perceived a disturbance in the air. The drawbridge had been raised.

"What's the meaning of this?" Lachlan inquired, as if Liza had commanded the defense.

Liza rode ahead of him toward the unfamiliar sentinels standing guard at the castle's threshold. They were formidable men—leering and fierce in their heavy leather mail. They unsheathed their broadsword swords, the blades glimmering even in the muted light as the snow swirled about them.

Before Liza could announce her presence, one of the men demanded as if he ruled the land, "What business have ye here?"

"I am the lady of this castle. I have issued no command for the bridge to be raised. Lower it forthwith." She refrained from inquiring as to their identities. She would show no weakness with her questions.

"Lady Claray Ramsay is the true lady of this barony," the second man spat with a sneer.

Liza cast a glance at Lachlan, whose fists were clenched upon Gwrol's reins. He remained silent.

"I am Lady Elesbeth Ramsay," Liza proclaimed, her voice not as steadfast as it had been. "This is my father's land."

The two men exchanged a glance then looked to the gatehouse, where a familiar guard's face peered down. Liza didn't know his name. Her father would have.

He nodded down at them, bestowing her with legitimacy.

The men looked back at her and then to Lachlan. "What are ye doin' out in the cold and snow?"

Liza hadn't expected this question to be asked of

her. She hesitated.

"I'd received word of an ill young lad from the burgh of Cockpen whose last wish was tae meet the laird o' the land," said Lachlan. "'Tis his last day on this earth, and Lady Ramsay was good enough tae come and bring a small purse of coin fer his family afore the sorrowful Ne'erday."

Liza blinked and stared straight ahead. The guards looked at each other, but the tale must have seemed truthful, for the larger of the two lifted his hand. After a moment, the thick ropes attached to the windlass heaved, as the wooden bridge was lowered across the dry moat.

They passed by the guards without a word, and when they'd entered the bailey courtyard, Lachlan said, "I'll settle the horses. Ye go straight tae yer chamber."

Liza nodded and allowed him to help her from Luar. Her bones were nearly frozen, and she walked with difficulty.

Though a chill draught crept through the keep's walls, the warmth of the fires seeped into her bones. The scent of roast venison and spices hung heavy in the air, and the echoes of voices reached her ears from the great hall.

While the Daft Days were still being celebrated, no grand feast had been set for this day. Certainly not a closed feast with the castle barred from the outer lands. She knew well she ought to heed Lachlan's counsel to keep to her chamber, though curiosity tugged at her. Perhaps it was more than mere curiosity—the lure of the fire and the aroma of food bid her draw forth.

She tread quietly down the passageway and peered into the great hall. The castle folk were gathered within, and a bard with a cithara stood at the fore of the hall before the long head board, laden with platters of meat, vegetables, and vessels of ale.

The onlookers at the head table included John Comyn of Badenoch, Lady Claray, James Stewart, the fifth High Steward of Scotland, and two men unknown to her, to whom John Comyn seemed to defer.

A stir behind her made her start. The head chamberlain flashed a sly grin as she turned swiftly.

"Lady Elesbeth," he said, casting an appraising glance over her. "I'd bid thee join the repast, yet ye look a fright."

She ignored the slur. "What's the meaning of this?" she demanded, gesturing toward the gathering as the bard began to pluck the strings of his instrument.

Donvaldus MacTavish shrugged. "'Tis the Daft Days, after all."

"But what is John Comyn doin' here? And what of Lady Claray? She's barely left her room since summertime. Who are those other men?"

"Fer someone who pretends tae be the lady of this castle, yer queries are many." He laughed, clearly enjoying her ignorance. She glowered at him. "Lady

Claray has been healed by John Comyn's presence, it seems."

Liza suspected the man had fed her a tincture or potion designed to give the illusion of wholeness. "Why is he here?" she asked again, her voice firm.

Donvaldus feigned surprise. "Why to celebrate Hogmanay before they head out after Ne'erday fer the Great Cause, of course."

At her silence, the man made a tsking noise with his tongue. "Lady Elesbeth, certainly a woman as worldly as ye know o' the Great Cause?"

Liza bit back a retort. It was true she'd learned more of politics in the last year than she had in her previous years, but whatever this Great Cause happened to be had eluded her.

Donvaldus was more than happy to educate her. "With no ruler, John Comyn feared Alba would descend into war and fall by its own hand. In his wisdom, he's initiated the Great Cause to decide the next king of Scotland. He will travel to Berwick Castle where King Edward will adjudicate between John Balliol and Robert the Bruce, the fifth Lord of Annandale." At this, Donvaldus tipped his head toward the raucous chamber.

Liza's eyes grew wide with alarm. Robert Wishart had forewarned her of this gathering at Berwick-upon-Tweed. "Robert the Bruce and John Balliol are here now?" She peered into the room to get a better look at the unfamiliar men at the head table.

"John Balliol, aye. But Robert the Bruce is no' here." Donvaldus gave her a quizzical look. His lips twisted into a smile. "My lady, do ye really not recognize King Edward of England?"

Liza blanched and snatched her head away from the door, lest the man see her. "The man they call the Hammer of the Scots is in my castle?" Now more than ever, she wished her father were there. Then again, if her father had been home, Longshanks would not have made it across the threshold.

"Ah, but Lady Elesbeth, 'tis no' yer castle. 'Tis *hers.*" He gestured toward Lady Claray who beamed at the head of the table. She was thin and frail, but as she tittered demurely while the men talked and laughed over the music of the bard, an outsider would have never guessed she'd spent half the year either in bed or wandering the halls like an apparition.

The movement of someone moving down the passageway caused Liza to jump, and she was relieved to see Lachlan. He cast a scornful gaze upon Donvaldus and bestowed upon him no further heed.

"Lady Ramsay, I didn't expect tae find ye in the hall," he said evenly, but Liza understood the true meaning behind his words. She was to have returned to her chamber to rest.

"It seems we have guests." She gestured toward the room, and Lachlan looked inside. It was clear he recognized all those at the head table. The raised drawbridge did now make sense.

"I'd fancy nothing more than to revel in the folly o' the likes o' ye both, but as chief chamberlain, and at the behest o' the laird and lady within, I've duties tae fulfill."

Donvaldus had nearly stepped over the threshold to the chamber before he spun around. "And were I in yer place, my lady, I'd guard my bonny wee neck."

Chapter 19

Liza dashed through the winding passageways and up the stone stairs. In her haste, she saw or heard no one, and when she arrived, the guard was absent from his post outside Uilleam's chamber. Her heart drummed a foreboding beat within her chest.

Please let Grete be safe, she silently beseeched a deity in which her faith wavered. She assured herself the men in the grand hall had scarce a chance of knowing the lass's true identity. How could they be aware of such a thing? Yet Bishop Robert Wishart knew. And if he knew, there was a chance others might, as well. Should that be the case, every man in the hall below would have slit the poor girl's throat without hesitation. Someone had already tried to take her life once.

Bursting into the chamber, Liza spied the fire crackling and a form lying still upon the bed.

"Grete?" she murmured, her steps cautious.

As she reached the bedside, Liza extended a hand to touch the lass's shoulder, giving it a gentle nudge. Grete inhaled sharply with a loud, sudden gasp, causing Liza to startle and jump back, almost tumbling onto the cold stones. She managed to steady herself before falling.

"What are you about?" Grete demanded.

"I–I was merely checkin' on ye," Liza stammered in reply.

"I was fast asleep." Grete's eyes became hazy and unfocused. "I had a dream of home, and I did not wish to wake."

Liza herself had often dreamed of faraway and strange lands she cared not to leave.

Grete wrapped the woolen blanket back around her shoulders as if she meant to sleep again.

"Ye must rise," Liza declared, startling even herself. She understood that if their guests were to believe the tale of Grete's presence at the castle, she could not be hidden away in Uilleam's chamber. Hexilde had already aired her doubts concerning the lass's true identity. Surely, the head cook wasn't the sole inhabitant of the keep who'd conjured some fancied link between Grete and the Maid of Norway.

"I do not care to rise," Grete muttered, her voice muffled against the mattress.

"Ye haven't a choice." Liza tugged the blanket from the lass's form.

Grete glowered at her. "Forsy is bringing me my morn meal," she retorted. "I'll be supping in my bed." She wrested the blanket back.

Liza placed her hands on her hips as Grete curled herself into a snug cocoon. Liza gazed at the fire, crackling merrily in the hearth, pondering the situation. She did not wish to vex Grete, yet the lass needed to grasp the gravity of the matter.

"Grete," she said softly, her voice gentle. "There's somethin' I need to ask ye." Grete made an unintelligible sound. "Do ye ken the name John Comyn of Badenoch?"

Grete unrolled herself from her blanket so Liza could see her face. "No," she answered. "Who is he?"

"What about John Balliol?"

Grete gave a small shake of her head.

"James Stewart?"

At that utterance, the girl's face grew pale and her eyes wide. "He was…" Her unfinished thought was but a whisper.

Liza moved to Grete and sat down on the mattress next to her. "He was what?" she prompted gently.

"He was the one who took me from the ship on the northern isle." Liza could barely hear the girl's soft words.

"I had been ill and weak," she continued, "and the men on the ship had…" She shut her eyes and shook her head.

Liza laid a hand on the girl's arm. "It's okay," she said. "Ye don' need tae speak of it."

"When I was carried off, they took me to a stone

chamber. I barely remember…"

The girl had begun to weep softly, and Liza made a soft shushing sound. But Grete continued. "I heard the men speaking, and I heard that name. Laird Stewart, a Guardian of the Realm," she whispered. "He gave the order to leave me for dead…to seal the chamber. They didn't think I could hear. They thought I was nearly dead already."

"Did he see ye?" Liza asked. "Yer face?"

Grete shook her head. "I don't remember him coming into the chamber, only standing outside, bellowing. I remember his high voice, and I remember his name."

Grete had begun to tremble, and Liza gathered her into her arms. "It's okay," she said. "Ye weren't sealed into the tomb."

"I was, though," Grete proclaimed. "They did heap the stones upon the threshold until the chamber was dark as pitch. The scent of earth filled the air, making breathing a struggle. I know not how long I lay in that darkness. I–I thought I'd perished. Then came the light, and after that, my memory falters. Until I found myself here."

Liza recalled the lass, unknowing and restless, confined within the narrow chamber at the abbey. Her thoughts turned to the woman, Cailleach, who had seen to Robert Wishart. A shiver ran through her. They'd believed the lass poisoned, though perhaps she'd been given some potion to rob her memory…

Liza's voice turned brisk as she finally spoke. "None of that matters now. Ye must become Grete o' the Clan MacDuff. Present yerself as such, and ye must do it this night, as they gather to mark Hogmanay."

"What if they know who I am?" Grete's voice quivered.

Liza shared her dread, lacking a sure answer for the lass, who was to be regarded as her kin. Though Robert Wishart had assured Liza her tale was believed far and wide, she could not know if James Stewart had set eyes upon Grete.

If he'd seen Grete's face, their only hope was that her weakened state and her soiled garments had rendered her unrecognizable.

She said as much to Grete, then added, "'Tis our only hope."

"I might remain concealed here in this chamber." Grete's suggestion was tinged with anticipation, but Liza shook her head.

She pondered upon Claray, whose senses had been restored, though likely only for a spell. The foolish woman would surely recount the tale of Grete's arrival to John Comyn, and the Lord only knew who had filled Claray's mind with what tales. Though Donvaldus MacTavish and Peter Syward had not seemed to outwardly question Grete's presence at the Ramsay Castle, there was no telling the counter tales they might be weaving.

Liza cast her gaze upon Grete, who'd gained flesh during her time of healing. Her cheeks were full and rosy. Though the maiden claimed she could not leave the chamber save for need of the garderobe, Liza had not pressed her to do so, but now it was of utmost necessity.

"Tonight, ye become Grete o' the Clan MacDuff. I've some garments ye can wear," Liza said, thinking of the fine attire sent from across the sea. Grete was but a summer removed in years from Liza, yet not much slighter. With a léine and fine bliaut, and her long golden locks braided and fashioned into a ramshorn at her ears, the lass would be unrecognizable even to those few in the castle who had glimpsed her.

"Elesbeth." Grete clutched Liza's hand. "I fear if ye bid me show my face, this may be my last eve upon this earth." Her plea was earnest.

Liza nearly yielded. She could not vow to Grete her safety. Yet her heart told her this was the sole path. The instinct was so powerful she could not disregard it. "I've taken ye in and become yer guardian. Now, I ask ye to place yer trust in me," Liza declared.

At this, Grete thrust out her lower lip, looking much like a petulant bairn, though she was near the threshold of womanhood. Truly, had the Treaty of Brigham been honored, Grete would have already been wed to Edward of Caernarfon.

Liza shivered at the thought. Aloud, she said, "I'll

have a bath prepared for ye. This night, ye'll make yer first appearance. Ye'll dine at the head table next to the king of England and the would-be king of Scotland. Exactly where ye belong."

Liza felt John Comyn's gaze bore into her as she walked in her finest clothing toward the head table. The Hogmanay celebration had taken place all through the day, and most of the revelers had overindulged in their cups, so the atmosphere had gone from well beyond merry to boisterous and wild. John Comyn, though, appeared to be clear-headed and focused only on her.

Liza walked arm in arm with Grete, who resisted a half pace behind her; Liza nearly pulled the younger woman along.

Bathed and costumed in Liza's finery, her fine pale hair coiled around her ears, Grete had transformed into a bonny lass, and most pleasing to the eye. Liza noticed more than one leering male gaze upon her. But it was John Comyn's steady stare that made her inwardly tremble. John Balliol and James Stewart paid the pair no attention as they drank from their vessels of mead in great gulps. But the King of England noticed the Guardian's relentless gaze, and he turned his attention to Liza and Grete approaching. Around a mouthful of venison, he said, "And who might we have here?"

The royal visitor was a man of grand stature, Liza observed. Even while seated, he loomed above his companions. Though he bore not a weighty crown, his brow was adorned by a modest golden circlet resting upon his dark, wavy locks laced with strands of silver. His immense size brought to mind the reason for the name 'Longshanks', a moniker he'd earned due to his towering height. Liza detected no ill intent from the nobleman, only a watchful curiosity and an amused suspicion.

John Comyn stood, attracting the attention of Claray at his side, who turned her dazed attention in Liza's direction.

"Mine liege lord," Comyn announced in his booming voice, causing a hush to fall over the hall's inhabitants. "The mistress Elesbeth of the Ramsay Castle approaches."

At his words, the remainder of the head board stared in Liza's direction. She stopped her progress, and Grete tucked herself beside her companion.

King Edward finished chewing and brushed his mouth against his sleeve. "The daughter of Lord William and Lady Jennet of Fife," he remarked, a hint of mirth in his tone. He clicked his tongue. "Her passing was indeed a grievous misfortune."

Claray gaped as if to protest, but John Comyn silenced her with a hand on her arm. He said aloud, "And behind Elesbeth, I presume, is the young maiden that shares Jennet's blood. The bastardly borne offspring of Duncan, Earl of Fife."

The king's laughter rang out. His hair danced around his massive shoulders as he shook his head. "The MacDuffs certainly are a fertile clan. Interesting, though, the girl would find her way hither, is it not?"

Liza paused, her face frozen in place. In the quiet that followed, she felt as if all eyes were trained on her. She cleared her throat, and said in a voice stronger than she felt, "Grete is my sister. I would nae turn her away."

"How very noble of you." The king's words were drawn out and grim. "You seem to be precisely like your father in that regard. In all his righteous arrogance, the man never encountered a virtuous cause to which he could deny patronage."

A smirk spread across John Comyn's face, and Claray emitted a small snort from between her closed lips before placing her thin, wasted hand to her mouth.

"My father is a great man," Liza responded, unable to hold her tongue or her anger.

"Indeed," the king repeated, abrupt and dry. He waved a hand. "No matter. Today is a day of celebration, for more reasons than one. Come and join us at the table." He gestured an attendant to bring more food and drink, then he shuffled up on his bench so there was space between his place setting and that of John Comyn. "I'd like the girl—Grete—to take her place next to me."

"Elesbeth," Grete whispered fiercely from behind Liza. She averted her face from the noblemen. "I cannot be seated alone next to him." The distinctive lilt of the Norse realm gave her voice a musical quality, and Liza's pulse thrummed.

Her response was a soft murmur, the words often repeated to Grete over the cycles of the moon since the girl's arrival. "Ye are Grete of the Clan MacDuff, descendant of the Mormaers of Fife. I am of yer blood, and this is yer home now."

"What if he knows?" she gulped. "And the other man beside him…" Her speech halted abruptly as her gaze fell upon the Guardian James Stewart. "He will know me," she whispered.

Liza mourned for whatever ill fate had befallen Grete upon her journey. Yet there was no time for lamentation for either herself or her sister. They must be strong. "Ye are my sister-bairn. My *piuthar*," Liza said, using the traditional word for 'sister'. "There is nothing else for him tae ken."

She squeezed Grete's small, cold hand as they were separated, and Liza realized she'd offered Grete nothing but a tale. Grete was not her sister, and Liza had no idea how much Longshanks might know or suspect. She wished her arrogance would not have overtaken her.

A righteous arrogance, Longshanks had said of her father. Had she, indeed, been afflicted with a similar tendency?

At the board, Liza was shoved between Claray and John Balliol, who regarded her not at all. He seemed unconcerned by her presence or the presence of Grete. And from what she could tell, *he* suspected no threat from the girl. Or perhaps Balliol was a superior performer, like the bard who recited unheeded words from the side of the chamber. In any case, it wasn't the would-be Scottish king she was worried about. It was the English royalty seated next to the one true heir to the Scottish throne. Liza tried to look around Claray and John Comyn to regard Grete, but the Guardian's bulk blocked her view.

Claray caught Liza's eye. Her stepmother's expression was simultaneously shrewd and vacuous, and Liza wasn't sure what to say. *Was* there anything to say to one who'd floated around the halls as a ghost for half the year?

Claray spoke first. "Isn't it so good tae hae John of Comyn back in our presence?"

There was no irony in her stepmother's voice. And when Liza remained silent on the matter, Claray continued, "When Uilleam left us and John departed so quickly after, I'd nearly lost my will tae live. Alone in this cold castle…" Her words trailed off as she rubbed her hands up and down her arms as if to ward off the chill. In truth, the room was warm from the fire, the bodies, the merriment, and the food.

"Ye're not alone, though," said Liza. "And my father will be returnin'." She wanted to remind Claray she still had a husband.

A small, sad smile curved Claray's lips. "I've no one but John Comyn." She glanced at the man with a grateful look, but he was turned away, leaning far too close to Grete for Liza's comfort. The woman's movements became quick and abrupt, like the brisk picking of a cithara's strings. "And I am the lady of this castle," she said. The tendons in her thin neck grew taut. "Ye are but a girl."

Liza knew the words had been planted by the Guardian. She reminded Claray carefully, "Ye were unwell."

"Ye tried tae snare me in my chamber." Her eyes narrowed, catlike. "But ye couldnae keep me hidden forever, could ye?"

Liza turned away from her stepmother's bright, mad gaze.

"The girl—she's come to ruin us all, ye ken. She's been sent here tae make us wait fer our doom." Claray's voice was a fierce whisper, and Liza's blood turned to ice in her body. What lies—or truths—had John Comyn been planting in the ruptured mind of his mistress?

Liza's hand shook as she reached for a slice of bread from a slab upon the table. In her panic, the food tasted of nothing more than dust, but she forced herself to chew the mealy dough.

She drank a sip of the strong heather ale and swallowed hard before she spoke. "Ye speak of Grete as if she's a demon or fiend. The girl is but an innocent, born of ill-starred circumstance."

Liza caught a glimpse of Grete through the bodies between them. Her face was pale, but she seemed to answer clearly when questioned. Liza was both relieved and alarmed at the girl's transformation. Grete might indeed have been regarded as a queen. Were these men clever enough to recognize the innate grace and natural bearing of royalty?

"Grete," Claray said in her frenzied voice. "I'm no' talkin' about Grete, and I ken none by that name."

Liza turned her attention from the girl to her stepmother, frowning. "Then of whom do ye speak?"

"The other lass. The one the cunning folk warned me of."

"There is no other lass here, Claray." If Liza had felt any relief, it was short-lived.

"Aye, but there is." Claray leaned closer as if she were sharing a secret. "'Tis the other one from the storm." Her breath wafted mead, stewed venison, and something metallic and sharp. "The witch lass. The one that calls herself Liza."

Chapter 20

A clatter from the other side of the room caused a momentary pause in the merriment. A male reveler called out, "The lass has dropped the ale!" in a bibulous garble of words. A howl of laughter followed by a woman's merry screech caused the crowd to grow even more riotous.

But Liza could barely hear the noise over the roar of blood pounding in her ears. She wanted to believe she'd misheard Claray's words, but despite the din, she knew she'd heard her clearly.

Claray had said 'Liza'.

It was possible Liza had shared with Claray her strange vision after she'd awoken under the devastated sycamore tree so long ago, but that would not explain the woman's reaction or her reference to the cunning folk.

Liza's stomach lurched. She feared the scant amount of food she'd eaten might come back up.

In the glow of the flickering sconces and the crackling fires, shadows danced upon the countenances of the room's merrymakers, and Liza's head spun while her sight wavered. Perhaps it was the shock of the morn, the dearth of sustenance, the dread and the ire, or all these woes combined. Liza felt herself grow weak and faint.

It was John Balliol who noticed first. "This one is unwell," he called out as she listed against him.

Liza saw Grete's face in front of her own. Liza reached up and touched the girl's smooth cheek. "Thank heavens ye're unscathed," she murmured.

The girl's hair was uncovered, and the soft fine locks had begun to unravel from their plaits. Liza moved her fingers from Grete's face to her unruly tresses. "This does no' befit a queen."

Grete's eyes grew wide. "She's delirious and must rest in her own chamber."

Liza was vaguely aware of faces frowning down at her. The visage of John Comyn and the one she recognized as Longshanks, the King of England. Grete's hands pulled her away from the shoulder of John Balliol.

Liza opened her mouth, but Grete spoke before she could utter another word. "I will accompany her to her chamber."

"Nonsense," King Edward spat. "There are attendants for that." He reached a hand up as if to gesture to someone. "My dearest, Grete of Fife…I have many more questions for you."

"The Ramsay women are a most feeble bunch,"

said John Comyn, laughing.

Claray laughed with him—a high, wild sound. She seemed not to understand the man's humor was directed at her.

The spell of unsteadiness began to pass, and Liza had a sense of coming back into her body. She pushed herself upright, seeing Forsy coming toward the head table, presumably to help her away.

"I–I need Grete to come with me." This was an announcement, not a question, but King Edward frowned and shook his large square head. "Nonsense. The girl will stay with me." He tipped his head toward Forsy. "You there, maidservant. Accompany the castle's mistress from the hall."

"No," Liza yelled.

The king's brows shot up in shock before a cloud of fury darkened his expression.

John Comyn, sensing some unknown peril, sprung to his feet. "My lord, the mistress is out o' her head. Do not take offense." In his haste to assuage the king's anger, the Guardian's words sounded condescending.

Edward turned his wrath upon the Guardian. "And who are you to tell me to what slight I shall take offense?"

The hall's clamor quieted as the rows of revelers sensed discord among the nobles. Whether they quieted from fright or curiosity, Liza was not sure.

"I–I simply meant to say—"

"You seem to think I should care what you meant to say," King Edward interrupted. "Comyn, you must understand. You are but a pawn to me in my quest for peace. It is the only thing I desire between our two nations, and I will accomplish my purpose with or without you." He looked around. "And I will accomplish it with or without the cooperation of the Ramsay Clan." Turning his attention to the would-be Scottish sovereign, he continued, "I will even accomplish it without the service of John Balliol, despite his lineage to King David the First."

The king reached down for his vessel and took a great draught of ale.

Liza had never seen John Comyn look anything but superior and arrogant, but during this moment, she saw uncertainty in his eyes.

Grete must have seen it, too, because she left Liza's side to go to the king where she placed a tentative hand upon his sleeve. "My laird," she said, her eyes downcast. "Might ye find it in yer kind heart to allow me to accompany my sister tae her chamber? She's done so much fer me—a poor, bastard child, cast from her home." Grete's brogue may have fooled any member of the Clan MacDuff, and she let out a small sob as a tear rolled down her cheek.

Liza bit the inside of her cheek to hide a smile. She wasn't sure if the king was moved by Grete as a child or a woman, but the fury fled from his face. "Go, swete herte. But come back to me. As I said, I have more to discuss with you regarding your lineage and your travels to the Ramsay Castle."

"Of course, my laird," she said quietly, and with the hall watching, she grasped Liza's arm, and the two women hurried from the room.

When they were alone in the stairwell, Liza whispered, "What did ye say tae him, ye wily wee wench?"

Grete lifted the léine given to her by Liza. The garment was too long for her smaller stature and dragged as she climbed the darkened stairs, lit only by cresset lamps affixed to the walls.

"He asked me questions, and I answered them to the best of my ability. I don't know if he believed the answers."

"He seemed charmed by ye, that's somethin'."

"I wasn't tryin' to charm him." Grete sounded indignant. "I was tryin' to get him to leave me alone."

"Do ye think he suspected anythin'?"

"Not until ye nearly gave me away." She looked back at Liza with a stern look on her fine features. Liza lowered her eyes.

"I wasn't in my right mind," she murmured. "Claray had just said somethin' dreadful."

When they reached the top floor, Grete and Liza surveilled the passageway, finding it empty.

Grete turned to her. "What did she say?"

"She made mention of somethin' she could not

have known. Someone's been fillin' her daft head with tales, and those tales are meant tae meddle with the likes of us."

Grete blinked at her, and Liza held her breath, waiting for more questions about Claray's comments. But Grete asked instead, "Is it John Comyn of Badenoch who's been telling her tales?"

Liza nodded because he was the most likely suspect. Though it could have been others in the castle. Peter Syward or Donvaldus MacTavish, certainly. Even Forsy could have had a hand in the rumors. Or one of the younger maids or attendants. There was no shortage of servants who resented Liza's swift rise in standing. Or her perceived role in the death of Wyolet.

"Is that why you nearly fainted?" Grete asked.

Liza lifted a shoulder as they entered her chamber, but the importance of the conversation fled as she noted the intense chill. Liza had spent the day preparing Grete for the evening celebration, and her hearth held nothing but ashes. She looked around for some wood, but there was none to be had. Every one of the attendants was at the Hogmanay celebration.

Now that Claray was up and about, Liza was no longer the lady of the castle, and the servants were all too aware of Liza's sudden return to relative obscurity. Liza's anger had no place, but she wasn't able to keep the ire from her heart.

It had become clear she couldn't count on aid from

anyone—not Robert Wishart, not her father, not even Lachlan who now belonged to Forsy. And she certainly was missing Uilleam who had needed her as both a sister and a mother figure. She realized just how much she'd needed him, too.

"You can rest with me this night." Grete slipped her hand into Liza's, and a fresh sadness caused Liza's throat to close painfully.

"I'm meant tae be tendin' to *ye*, Grete."

"It's my duty to settle the favor."

Liza blinked away tears as they exited the chamber and made their way down the passage to the far staircase, climbing to the top floor.

Inside Grete's chamber, the fire burned low in the hearth. A fresh bundle of logs was stacked in the chimney corner, and Grete placed new wood carefully within the flames, using an iron to stoke the blaze higher.

"Did ye tend tae yer own fire in Norway?" Liza asked. It was the first time she'd asked directly about Grete's old life.

The younger woman stared into the light. A shower of sparks sprayed from a log that shifted in the inferno.

"We had attendants at our home in Bergen."

As Liza warmed herself next to Grete, she asked no more questions. For all of Liza's losses, at least she hadn't been taken from her home. She had this castle, at least.

But Grete continued, her voice slipping back into the deep melodic cadence of her homeland. "My grandmother, Ingeborg, was my constant companion when I was a young child. After my mother died, Ingeborg taught me to do many things for myself. She said it was dangerous for a queen to rely on only attendants. 'You must learn to rely on yourself,' she always said." Grete shrugged. "She was right. You can't depend on those who claim to have your best interest at heart."

The flames danced and flickered their long shadows about the room. "What about yer mother?" Liza asked softly.

"I have no memory of her. She died shortly after my birth." Grete let out a long exhale. "My father doted on me, but I know he wished for a boy." Grete laughed. "Had I been born a male, I'd likely have been installed as heir in Scotland by now."

Liza doubted that very much. The powers who had not wanted Margaret, the royal maiden, to be queen would have been unmoved by the child's sex, Liza thought. A male heir may have threatened them even more than a young girl had.

Grete continued, "This Great Cause of which they speak—the right and true answer would have been to allow me to take my rightful place at the throne. The place my grandfather, King Alexander, had intended for me."

It was the first time Grete had directly acknowledged her lineage, and there was both pride and resentment in her words.

"Now, there's nothing I can do but live out an invented life with a false family. I cannot even tell my father I am safe as he mourns a corpse that does not exist."

"Do ye even want to be queen?" Liza thought it sounded like a terrible, tiresome, and perilous burden.

"It's not a question of what I want. It's a question of my birthright and my duty. My mother should have been queen, and that privilege was stolen from her by illness. The same has been taken from me by the pride and arrogance of another." Grete moved to the commode and began loosening the plaits of her long hair. "I'm grateful for the people who saved me from death, and I'm grateful to you for giving me care and shelter. But this will never be my true home, and I've lost my rightful place forever."

Liza blinked into the flames. She knew exactly how Grete felt. While the Ramsay Castle was surely her home, there was a mournful quality to her existence. She wanted to believe it was the loss she'd experienced, but the deepest part of herself knew the discomfit went beyond death. Liza found she was weary to her bones. She wanted to climb into her bed and sleep the time, and her life, away.

Without further talk, Liza unfastened her hair from

the prison of its barbette and slipped off her linen mantle and léine until she was only in her chemise.

Though the fire warmed the chamber, a chill touched Liza's skin, and she nestled herself into Grete's bed, tucking the woolen blanket beneath her chin. Weariness overtook her, and she was asleep before Grete climbed onto the mattress beside her. In the haze of sleep, she felt Grete's small hand clasp hers, and she slept soundly with her sister by her side.

Liza jolted awake, her skin prickling as an icy draught drifted across her face like a ghostly caress. A dim haunting glow of dying embers cast an eerie light, and the bed beside her was empty.

"Grete?" she whispered into the darkness.

Silence answered.

Liza sat up, listening for any sound at all.

A faint skittering and scratching reached her ears; the pitter-patter of tiny vermin.

"Grete," she murmured once more, though she was alone in the chamber.

Had the castle not been brimming with inhabitants eager to see the girl meet her demise upon discovery of her true lineage, Liza would not find herself in such an anxious state. But the castle's watchmen were stationed to protect King Edward, the would-be king John

Balliol, and the Guardians of the Realm with their attendants. To demand protection for a stray bairn of questionable birth would surely have stirred suspicion. And so Grete and Liza were forced to fend for themselves.

Liza rose from the bed, draping a mantle over her shoulders. In the shadows she found a candle and kindled its wick from the fire's waning embers. She slipped silently from the chamber and into the empty passage. The stone felt like ice against the soles of her bare feet.

She dared not call out, uncertain where their guests had settled for the night. It was a dangerous thing for Grete to roam the corridors, even if the strange men were unaware of her true identity. Any young lass ought to be safely shielded in her chamber amidst the shadowy secrecy of the night.

Liza descended the stone steps, her purpose and quest as murky as the dark itself. Perhaps Grete had ventured to the kitchens in pursuit of a morsel to sate her hunger. Though a feast had been laid before them during the evening's Hogmanay celebration, neither Grete nor Liza had indulged.

Liza descended to the second floor and was on the verge of venturing further when a scurrying sound met her ears. The sound bore more weight than that of mere vermin, and as Liza crept into the passageway, a low moan, like the murmur of ancient spirits, echoed from the direction of Liza's chamber.

Her heart hammering, Liza moved toward the clamor when a shadowy figure emerged before her, nearly sending her sprawling upon the stones. Liza kept her footing, though the candle tumbled from her hands, its flame extinguished, casting her into complete darkness.

The figure seized her wrist and drew her back. "We must make great haste," the feminine voice murmured, guiding Liza into the dim stairwell.

"Grete," Liza exclaimed, so startled and relieved she forgot to quiet her words.

Grete hushed her sharply, hauling her upwards with a steady grip. Liza's toes struck against the rough stone stairs as they ascended, and she stumbled, her shins bearing the brunt. When they reached the passageway, they hurried in silence. Upon reaching Grete's chamber, the girl pulled Liza toward the mattress where they collapsed and lay motionless.

Liza's heart thundered madly in her ears.

After a considerable stretch of time, Liza asked softly, "Where were ye, Grete?"

Grete drew a breath. "I–I had made my way tae the garderobe, when a disturbance reached my ears. I wanted tae return tae the chamber, but a force seemed tae steer me elsewhere. I took my candle and descended the stairs, uncertain of my path. It was yer own chamber where I found myself. I must have sensed someone in danger. Perhaps I thought it was ye.”

“I hadnae departed from the mattress,” Liza said. “Ye would have spied me in the passageway.”

Grete didn’t answer.

“Did ye see someone else?”

“I’m not sure what I saw. It was so dark…” Her words trailed off.

“But ye saw *somethin’* in my chamber?”

“Aye,” Grete said softly. “Somethin’ caught my arm, but then…”

Liza waited until Grete had gathered her words.

She continued. “I heard a gentle voice—a soft wail. Whatever seized me released its grasp. There came a rushing and a dull thump, and I made haste toward the passageway before the thing could snatch me again.”

“Was it a man who grasped ye?”

“I cannae be certain. It happened swiftly, and my notions were not sure.”

Liza’s mind whirled. Perhaps someone had spied Grete and, suspecting her true heritage, seized the chance to rid themselves of the trouble she posed. The deed had unfolded in Liza’s chamber; mayhap Liza had been the intended prey of the capture.

“The king and his attendants intend to depart to-morrow to reach Berwick Castle after Ne’erday. Upon their departure, we shall set a watchman at yer door.” In the morn, Liza would find Lachlan and recount the night’s happenings. Perhaps he might overhear some whispers that would guide them to the truth.

"Fer now," she said aloud to Grete, "we're safe. Let's attempt to rest while we're together and secure."

Grete nestled close to Liza's side, but Liza fixed her rigid gaze upon the chamber door, where her eyes deceived her, conjuring foes and fiends intent on capturing them in shadows.

Her eyes grew heavy, and though she fought it, slumber overcame her. Even in her dreams, she was haunted by visions of dread creatures who pursued her and stole Grete away. How long her slumber endured, she knew not, before the clamor of raised voices echoed through the corridor. Liza opened her eyes to find morn had crept in through the window.

The flames had long since dwindled. No attendant appeared to rekindle the hearth.

Liza resolved to see to it herself. The deed might offer an excuse to cross paths with Lachlan and speak of the night's happenings. The notion of sharing a fleeting moment with him sparked a thrill of eagerness and hope in her heart.

As if sensing the musings of Liza's mind, Forsy appeared at the threshold. The girl carried no kindling. Her eyes were as round as the full moon, and her face was as pale. Liza sat up, and Grete stirred beside her. She might have delivered a scolding to the chamber-maid, yet the girl's visage bore such a haunted stare, it sent a shiver down Liza's spine.

"What hae ye done?" Forsy's voice trembled in fear.

Grete sat upright, her long tresses tangled about her face. "What's happened?" she murmured, her words muddled with the haze of sleep.

Forsy thrust a finger toward Liza. "Surely it was ye, afore ye concealed yerself with yer misbegotten sister."

"Of what folly do ye speak?"

The clamor of voices continued, and heavy footfalls thudded in the passageway. The weight of dread crept into Liza's breast. These weren't typical sounds of the morn, even with a castle filled with guests. No, Liza thought. Some misfortune had occurred.

"We all should hae spied the wickedness after Wyolet's slayin'," Forsy spat.

"Who is Wyolet?" inquired Grete, her voice and wits now sharp. "And what fate did she meet?"

"Lady Elesbeth can recount that tale. For when Lady Elesbeth finds somethin' amiss, she disnae hesitate to dispose of it, be it object or mortal soul."

Liza fixed her gaze upon the maid. "Forsy, I implore ye, speak to us of the calamity ye perceive to hae transpired."

"Ye... Ye would have me utter it?"

"Utter what?"

"Ye... Ye took the life of Lady Claray. Yer very own stepmother. Within her very dwellin'. And in yer very own chamber."

Liza opened her mouth to protest, then snapped it

shut again. *Her own chamber?* "What are ye sayin'?" she whispered.

"Ye murdered her, just as ye done to Wyolet." Her hands rested on her stomach. "Am I tae be next?"

Chapter 21

The bellow of a watchman echoed through the stone corridors.

"Every soul to the great hall!"

At the summons, Forsy fled, leaving Liza and Grete to exchange wide-eyed stares, their faces as pale as the snow-covered hills.

"Murder," Liza breathed, her voice barely a whisper. "In mine own chamber?" Her mind raced back to the unexpected and lively presence of Claray in the hall but hours earlier. She could not fathom a soul who might gain from Claray's death. Save perhaps herself.

Grete shook her head. "Ye could not have slain any soul. You were with me the whole night."

"Not in its entirety."

Grete held her tongue for a span before speaking again. Her voice was soft. "It was I who wandered within your chamber."

Liza knew Grete was considering the consequences to herself, given her tenuous position within the household. Liza rushed to reassure her. "And ye weren't alone, Grete. Ye were assaulted."

Despite her fortified words, Liza's blood pooled cold in her veins. She believed Grete, but whoever else had entered that chamber under the cloak of night could have mistaken Lady Claray Ramsay for Liza or Grete.

Forsy had uttered nothing but weird words, mused Liza. Words spun by a lass who felt her standing imperiled by the castle mistress—both by Liza's position over the land and in her sway over the man Forsy adored. Liza would give no heed to these fanciful tales until they were proven true.

A towering watchman, clad in leather armour and grasping a broadsword in his colossal hands, cast his shadow over the threshold of Grete's chamber.

"To the great hall, one and all," he thundered, his eyes unmoved by the presence of two lasses.

They hurriedly slid their feet into the slippers they'd left in the darkness of night and wrapped their mantles around their shoulders to ward off the chill of early morn.

As they encountered others in the passageways, suspicious gazes fell upon them both, and whispers of the attendants followed them through the stairwells. Grete and Liza threaded their arms together. Truly, Forsy was not the only soul to think Liza had partaken in some wicked deed. She remembered the eyes that had fallen upon her when Wyolet met her death in midsummer. Uilleam's passing had tempered those wary stares with a measure of sympathy. Three expired martyrs within the castle walls, however, were sufficient to direct the accusing stares of the castle toward the most obvious suspect. And to those souls, that suspect was Liza.

Liza and Grete shuffled into the great hall with the others and took a place toward the front of the room and to the side, out of direct sight of King Edward and the Guardians, who were huddled together at the head of the chamber.

The king towered above the other men as he spoke to them, giving him the air of authority. She wished she could hear the words they uttered, for the import of the discourse shrouded them like a fine mist.

The only other man Liza had ever seen who was taller than Longshanks was her father, William Ramsay. He would not have abided the King of England—the very foe to the freedom of Alba—in their midst. And yet, in Laird Ramsay's absence, the faces of the barony turned to this enemy king as if he were their savior.

Tears welled in Liza's eyes, and a great sorrow weighed heavy upon her heart. She would trade near all she possessed for her father to stride into the chamber at this very moment. She feared for the country she loved, and the realm she held dear.

Liza glared at the sight of John Comyn next to Longshanks. The Guardian's complexion was ruddy and his eyes blazing as if two embers burned from his soul. Whatever words the king had uttered, Comyn most assuredly did not agree with them. Speaking angry words, his long arms flailed as he gestured toward the threshold.

John Balliol stood silently and rather apart from the other men, his expression unreadable and disinterested. *This is the man who would be their sovereign?* Liza thought. He was but a pawn—useless and insubstantial.

When the second Guardian, James Stewart, attempted to speak, Longshanks held up a hand to silence him.

"I don't spy Claray," Grete whispered at her side. Liza turned from the lairds at the front of the chamber to spy her stepmother. She could not catch sight of her, and a fear wracked her body.

Liza surveilled the faces for Lachlan. She sought the compassion of an understanding soul. Yet…what if Lachlan harbored his own fears for the peril of Forsy—his betrothed—at the hand of Liza? The protection Liza yearned for from him might not exist. The very idea shattered her heart.

She spied him among the crowd and watched him secretly, Forsy at his side gripping his arm as though her very life depended on it. Their faces were fixed upon the men at the head of the chamber, unaware of Liza's gaze. But while Forsy's eyes were wide with dread, Lachlan seemed to regard the men with a simmering anger. A muscle twitched in his jaw, and his hand was tightly clenched at his side. Liza longed to go to him and declare her innocence. She would caress his brow, clasp his hand, and they would steal away across the threshold to another place. Another time. So intense was her desire, Lachlan suddenly turned to her. Their gazes locked, and an unspoken connection kindled. An ember that burned fierce and bright. Liza wished she could fathom its true meaning, for as warm as the connection burned, she sensed no solace.

Before she could dwell upon the bond, King Edward lifted his arms and a watchman called out over the din, "Hark! Were King Edward to speak!"

A hush readily fell over the assembly. Every face was turned toward the King of England.

"We gather on this woeful day," rang his deep voice, "bidden by grim tidings."

The room was silent. Liza and Grete gripped each other tightly, daring not exchange a glance.

"Last night, in the dark hours, was slain our Lady Claray of Ramsay—the noble keeper of these lands."

At those words, the voices of the assembly erupted in a chorus of gasps, wails, and lamentations. Liza's heart leapt into her throat as Grete's fingers pressed fiercely into her flesh. She felt as if the blood had fled her veins.

Liza could not fix her gaze upon any single face

within the hall as she cast her eyes about. The men amidst the gathering clung to their anguished women-folk, and a profound disquiet crept through the chamber. No one rearded her. She cast her gaze back to the front of the room where she looked into the eyes of John Comyn. The Guardian's stony gaze was upon her, and it pierced her soul with an unyielding intensity. Liza trembled.

The watchman called over the lamentations, "Hear ye, hear ye! One and all!"

John Comyn's gaze stayed fixed on Liza, and she stared at the stony floor.

Longshanks' voice rang out again. "It was a young chamberlain who found her at dawn." He shook his large head, unadorned in the soft light of the morn. "Think how she must have lain, butchered so cruelly."

Liza hazarded another glance in Lachlan's direction. His eyes were shut as he held Forsy's trembling body against his.

"Since the Ramsay barony now stands without a ruler," King Edward continued, "By my authority, I decree the land and its fortress shall be held by the King's sheriff. In a fortnight he shall arrive to take possession of the castle and all its domain."

A murmur rose, but Liza would not hold her tongue. "No!" she cried.

Beside her, Grete whispered, "Elesbeth, quit yer words."

Liza ignored her, though her heart hammered in her chest. The Ramsay lands would not be established as a garrison for the purposes of English interest. "Our lady—ill since Uilleam's death—was deposed, and we need neither English sheriff nor royal hand to govern our people or our lands!"

John Comyn's arm jerked forth; his finger shook as he pointed at Liza. "Cunning harlot," he spat. "Lady Claray was found in yer own chamber. It was ye who spilled her blood."

Another gasp arose from the gathered throng as wary eyes fixated upon Liza.

"Nay," Liza cried out. "I would ne'er bring harm upon Claray."

"For the dominion o' yer father's lands, ye surely would!" an unseen male voice from amidst the assembly declared.

"The lass likely slew her brother Uilleam fer her own ends, too!" another voice accused.

"No," Liza protested again fervently. "Uilleam was mine own kin."

The crowd's murmuring swelled, growing more wrathful.

Longshanks raised his arms as if he would speak, but Grete's voice called out over the din, "She was with me all night."

Something in the lass's voice caused a hush to fall over the clamoring of the crowd.

Then a man's voice broke in, sharp as a flint. "Is that so?" It was the seneschal Peter Syward who spoke from the front of the gathered assembly. "Then how came I upon her, candle in hand, pacing the corridor outside her own chamber while the rest of the castle lay in slumber?"

Liza's silence sounded more fiercely than any uproar or lament by the gathered assembly. She dared not utter another word, fearing Grete might be further caught in the seneschal's accusation. Liza did not know what Peter Syward had witnessed, or if he'd mistaken Grete for Liza herself.

It was also within the realm of possibility something untoward had transpired in that cold, dark chamber when Grete had been present. Perhaps whatever malice Grete had confronted in the shadows had concluded in the loss of a life by Grete's hand. After all the trials she'd endured, Liza knew not what the lass was capable of.

"It was not I who slew our lady," Liza whispered, voice small yet steady and clear in the chamber's hush. "My father and brother will return, and I will gain nothing from the death of Claray."

From the crowd called the voice of Forsy, tears streaking her cheeks and coloring her words. "She slew sweet Wyolet to claim my Lachlan fer her own, then struck down her brother to stand heir of Ramsay!" Her cry trembled with grief and rage. "Ne'er hae I beheld such wickedness. Ne'er hae I seen such a witch."

The charge—that ominous spoken word—ascended above the assembly and hovered portentously over the souls gathered, foreboding and black. For a moment, it wavered there, and the air was thick with some unuttered expectancy. Then the cursed accusation descended with force, and as it did, a clamorous outcry erupted. "Witch! A witch amongst us!"

Another voice, shrill with fury, penetrated the furor. "And the other witch, too, she who calls herself Grete—a demon sent by Hell's own legion!"

John Comyn joined in, his voice echoing above the chamber, "Witches, surely! Servants of the Devil himself in our midst!"

Liza and Grete stood alone, their fate as uncertain as flickering flames.

The crowd drew in upon them. Liza opened her mouth to protest, but her throat closed, and her vision darkened as the gathering seemed to come closer and closer. Beside her, Grete let out a soft cry and held tight to Liza. The voices joined and converged—some unholy, strident chorus upon them. They backed against the cold, stone wall of the chamber. Liza knew this would surely be the end. Struck down on Ne'erday, and lost forever.

"Hold!" thundered Longshanks, his voice carrying over the fervor. The horde abruptly stopped. "Such charges of sorcery demand inquiry, and time we have not!"

It was the first Liza detected anger, rather than amusement, fueling the words of the nobleman. The encroaching men and women turned toward the front of the room, though their pause seemed to be taken reluctantly.

King Edward turned toward John Comyn. "You would halt the Great Cause for such a trifling matter as the death of a maiden?" The disdainful flick of his wrist bespoke how little he regarded the passing of Claray. "The Ramsay lands are a crucial stronghold," he pressed on, "and I shall not allow it to be consumed by suspicion and vengeance for an unjust cause."

John Comyn bowed his head, seeming small and meek and subdued. In Liza's eyes, he was but a craven. Had he truly loved Claray, he would have defended her honor. The Guardian yielded to the dominion of another realm without a single word of dissent.

Longshanks shifted his level gaze to the gathered throng. "The maiden Elesbeth Ramsay is merely a lass, not a witch. Should she have slain the lady of this land, her charge shall be resolved through the establishment of a sheriffdom upon those very lands. Yet it shall not be resolved this day—not by my decree nor by the hands of these gathered masses."

The voice of England's King Edward I—Longshanks, the Hammer of the Scots—thundered through the room. And though he was not the right and true sovereign of those assembled at the Ramsay

Castle, he was the authority they recognized in that fateful hour.

Another murmur of acquiescence satisfied him, and he turned to the lords at his side. "We must depart for Berwick Castle, there to gather counsel for the Great Cause." His gesture to the crowd was sweeping and final. "With an English sheriff's hand laid upon this shire, any lurking threat shall be laid to rest." He pointed toward Peter Syward. "You, Seneschal. In the absence of a sheriff's rule over these lands, I bestow upon you the authority of this barony."

Peter Syward.

Liza blinked. She parted her lips to protest, but Grete's quiet murmur, "Do not utter a word," caused her to hold her tongue.

Indeed, silence was wise. Longshanks went on, "And no harm shall befall Lady Elesbeth and her companion Grete of the Clan MacDuff, bairn of Duncan, Mormaer of Fife, for he has served me well."

Chapter 22

Over the course of a fortnight, Liza and Grete found refuge within the confines of their chambers, seldom venturing beyond the sanctuary of their fortified hold. News from Liza's lands came scarce and muted, and life moved unabated at the Ramsay barony.

Young attendants, fresh to their duties, tended to them with scant offerings of victuals and firewood, while watchmen stood vigil outside their chambers, ensuring none among the multitude ignored the edict of Longshanks.

Peter Syward, to his slight credit, ensured their continued existence, albeit his contempt was palpable in the meager and poor fare provided, and the naivety of the attendants assigned to their care.

Upon the cycle of three moons, a new king of Scotland was proclaimed at Berwick, owing to King Edward's interferences. John Balliol triumphed over Robert Bruce, Lord of Annandale, to be anointed the ruler of the realm.

Yet Margaret, Maid of Norway, had not come to

her final rest upon the Isle of Orkney, as those arrogant men reckoned. Nay, she was hidden away within a humble chamber at Ramsay Castle, which, by a cruel turn of fortune, had fallen under the dominion of the English.

Margaret's heart festered with anger at her captivity, her stolen birthright, and the bitter truth that her current protection was delivered by a connection to a feigned illegitimate father who had betrayed his kin to serve Longshanks, their sworn adversary.

The sheriff ordered to the Ramsay lands was a corpulent man named Walter Hastings—some undeserving vassal of Edward, rewarded for an act of fealty, no doubt. As vast in girth as he was, Liza found him equally lacking in vigor. His sole passion appeared to be the kitchen. As much as he was enamored with the larder brimming with victuals and ale, so too was he smitten by Hexilde, and she seemingly by him.

These tidings Liza heard from the young maidservant who had assumed Forsy's duties. Liza held a distaste for idle prattle, yet having barely ventured beyond the safety of her chamber, she found herself reliant upon chattering tongues to stay informed.

During one of Liza's furtive ventures to the kitchen, it came to light that Walter Hastings had claimed his dominion by appointing Peter Syward as escheator for the barony—a station of high esteem, charged with the gathering of debts and their delivery unto the Crown.

Peter, it appeared, took to his new station with great fervor, extending his duties beyond the confines of the barony and wielding his power over both the shires and Watret Abbey, much to the chagrin of the abbot and his prior.

"It keeps the lad out of my own affairs," mused Walter Hastings to Hexilde, as he gnawed on a pheasant's leg.

Liza had entered the warmth of the kitchen quietly, scarcely noticed, save by Hexilde.

When Hexilde turned from Hastings, the man pinched the head cook's ample bottom, and Hexilde cried out in surprise. But from the coloring of Hexilde's cheeks, Liza suspected the cook was not altogether displeased with the attention.

"Best ye be heedful of the monks at the abbey, and Abbot Renier," Hexilde scolded, setting a vessel of honeyed mead before the sheriff. "His power stretches far across the land and extends even into the Highlands and the Islands. Mayhap across the sea."

Hastings snorted. "He has not so much authority as King Edward."

"Longshanks is not the King of Scotia," Hexilde reminded him. "He's appointed John Balliol to that role, as ye should well recall."

Hexilde, aware of Liza's presence, ladled a bowl brimming with hearty venison porridge and handed it to her. Hastings paid Liza no mind. She wondered if he knew who she truly was.

The whispers about Liza and Grete, and the chatter of their witchery, waned as the months wore on. The folk—both lairds and humble cottars—were captivated by the tidings of the land. They pledged their new-found loyalty to Balliol, and bore silently their disquiet at Longshanks' continued and unwelcome interest in the rule of Scotland. It seemed even those who swore fealty to the King of England were caught unawares by his unabated interference in the matters of Scotland.

Yet because of Hastings, while other Scottish households had found themselves bound to English demands for food, coin, and supplies—perhaps a repayment from John Balliol to King Edward for his meddling on Balliol's behalf at Berwick—the Ramsay Estate had been spared such burdens. They dined often and well.

"Balliol be a craven," Hastings declared to Hexilde. "He lacks the mettle to govern this realm."

"'Tis why King Edward placed him upon the throne," answered Hexilde.

Hastings quaffed deeply from his horn of mead. "For that very cause," he agreed, laughing.

Liza slinked into the shadows with her bowl of pottage as the sheriff's words settled in her mind. Longshanks had set Balliol to rule not for his worthiness, but for his lack thereof, just as Hexilde had warned months ago. This meant England could easily subjugate Scottish lands and impose dominion over their noble nation.

Robert the Bruce would never have allowed such folly to transpire.

"Ah, back to it, then. I must find my deputy," Hastings proclaimed after he'd quaffed the last of his mead and pheasant. "Delicious as ever." He cast a grin at Hexilde. "Perchance after the evening's repast, you'll do me the honor of your company."

"I'm uncertain if such a course would be fitting, Sheriff. What if our deeds were to be uncovered?"

"'Tis a fortuitous twist of fate that you be acquainted with the highest authority in the realm." He tipped his head at Hexilde who tittered like a lass.

His sturdy leather brogues scraped upon the stone as he took his leave through the kitchen's threshold.

"What do ye think ye're doin'?" Liza asked as she stepped from the shadows.

Hexilde gave a nonchalant shrug. "Someone must look after the interests o' the Ramsays. Surely, it cannae be ye. Nor the lass Grete."

Liza found herself with no words to counter.

"I've a thing Hastings desires." She proceeded to clear away the remnants of food and mead from the table. "I may as well make use of my advantage."

"He's a vassal of Edward, our own enemy."

Hexilde let out a scornful huff. "Surely, ye dinnae believe ye ken in who to place yer trust? The Guardians have shown their fealty unto only themselves. Ye heard the sheriff speak—King John shall no' be our shield. It comes as no surprise to me, having met the man. What is prudent for us now is to seize the moment as it presents itself."

Liza narrowed her eyes. "Ye like him!" she cried. "Nay, ye're in love with him!" Hexilde turned away, but she did not counter Liza's words. Liza shook her head with a grave expression. "Heed my words," she declared. "Walter Hastings be no ally to the Ramsays."

"And who stands as a true ally? Both Claray and Uilleam lie slain by the hand of some unknown foe. William and Alexander show no haste in their return. Ye stand compromised. And as for Grete…" Hexilde moved in close to Liza, her voice a whisper. "…I ken what ye claim she be, but I harbor my own doubts." She gave Liza a meaningful look that caused Liza to turn away from the old woman. Hexilde continued, "And should those doubts prove true, we must do all in our power to keep such knowledge confined within these castle walls."

Before Hexilde could turn her back, Liza demanded, "Shall we carry on as though all this is commonplace? As though it be fittin' to live under the yoke of English rule, and the Ramsays mere vassals of the King of England and not loyal subjects of Alba?"

Hexilde whirled around. "I hae no better idea. And unless someone conjures a more fittin' proposal, I advise ye to count yer blessings. Ye, my dear lass, might hae met the executioner's ax for dabblin' in witchery, were it no' for Longshanks savin' ye." She half turned, then faced Liza once more. "And who do ye reckon has kept Walter Hastings at bay from ye and Grete?"

Liza knew it was Hexilde herself who'd swayed the sheriff to tend to other, more carnal, matters. Liza was truly thankful for Hexilde's aid. However, a more permanent remedy to their plight must be found. The remedy would not be found on this day.

Chastened, Liza departed from the kitchens and meandered through the corridors in search of Grete. Though the air still bore a chill, the harshest of winter's conditions had left them as Beltane and the beginning of the summer months neared.

While the days drifted by, even with the stifling conditions both within the castle walls and beyond, Grete had flourished, becoming more robust and lovely in her cultivated anger. Tall and fair, she bore the likeness of her Norwegian ancestors from her father's lineage. She moved with a noble stride, and Liza had observed the gazes of the men, as well as the reverence she commanded from the common folk and the gentry alike. But Grete did not care for the attention, and instead sought after news of the political state wherever she could find it. She was especially interested in word of John Balliol's rule of the nation independent of King Edward's grip, and she had become more and more vexed at rumors of Edward's continued encroachment upon Scottish lands.

One day, Liza discovered Grete near the castle's gate, wrapped in a thick mantle to fend off the brisk early spring winds, speaking earnestly with a courier who had journeyed from the abbey bearing supplies. The courier hurried away upon Liza's approach, and Grete appeared angered by the interruption until she saw it was Liza who'd broken the attention of the young lad.

Her countenance brightened, and she clasped Liza's hands in her own. "Sister, I hae received tidings Balliol shall journey to the Highlands in the summer months to enforce unity amongst the northern clans. Such efforts ought to further the Scottish cause and affirm his dominion o'er his subjects there." Grete's voice had acquired the cadence of her new lands, and the melodic accent of her native soil had mostly faded away.

Liza paused, uncertain if she should reveal the words she'd overheard between Hexilde and the sheriff. She relented. Grete's noble blood granted her the right to know of the happenings across Alba. With a measure of reluctance, Liza recounted Walter Hastings' speech along with Hexilde's parting words to Liza.

Grete's expression grew dark, and she was silent for

a time. In the hush, Liza heard the call of a stableman, then the whinny of a horse near the stables. It made her think of Lachlan, of whom she'd seen little over the long winter months. The intense urgency she'd once felt for him had transformed into a dull ache in her breast. While it was not as desperate, it was permanent and painful. And it had not lessened with his absence.

"Ye mean tae say Balliol has been set up as a pretender king, all for Edward's encroachments upon my grandfather's lands?" Grete demanded.

Grete didn't notice the wandering of Liza's thoughts, and when the fair lass turned back to the matter of politics, Liza found herself perplexed before she realized what Grete had uttered aloud, for all to hear.

"Hush," Liza answered, looking around the empty gate. "Do ye mean tae give away yer true identity? That will mean death fer us both."

"Am I then tae waste away in this English-ruled castle while Edward lays waste to my lands?"

Liza halted, gathering her wits before speaking. "Yer claim tae these lands was forfeited on the Isle of Orkney," Liza murmured. "Perhaps there will be an uprising against Longshanks' encroachment by the men of Robert the Bruce. Until then, we must bide our time."

Grete opened her mouth to protest Liza's declaration, but snapped it shut at the presence of approaching voices. From the walls of the castle, as if out of a dream, appeared Lachlan with Forsy at his side. Their betrothal had been pledged, and Liza tried to quell any ill will toward the lass. Upon beholding the couple abruptly, her heart wrenched painfully within her breast.

Forsy's expression turned ashen at the sight of Liza and Grete, as if she'd seen the Devil himself. Liza could not discern if Forsy's belief in their sorcery was true or a cunning ruse meant to disgrace them both. She grasped at Lachlan's arm as if to spirit him away, but Lachlan held his ground.

"Lady Grete… Lady Elesbeth," he said as they approached. Did Liza imagine the gentle lilt in his voice as he spoke her name? "I trust ye be farin' well?" he continued.

There was a lengthy silence, and Lachlan's piercing dark eyes met Liza's. It seemed she had lost the ability to speak. Grete glanced between them and gave Liza a gentle nudge to prompt her response.

"Aye, bailie," Liza finally managed. "And how hae ye fared throughout the lang winter months?"

Before Lachlan could form a reply, Forsy interjected, "We're tae be wed in the summer, as soon as Lachlan raises a dwelling for us upon the lands."

At this, Liza's brows arched in surprise. "A dwelling? Upon the lands?"

"Aye, before he departed, yer father granted me a

parcel o' land by the river."

Though Lachlan's claim was not impossible, a wariness in his words made Liza doubt their truth. He surely would have spoken of this to her sooner.

She frowned, and he added, "I can show ye the deed."

Liza gave a small shake of her head, though she pondered where this plot of land might be. Her thoughts drifted to Forsy in the homestead, caring for a brood of bairns, and another fierce pang of envy coursed through her veins.

"It matters no' tae me," Liza answered, willing her voice free from care. She gestured toward the face of the castle. "These lands belong tae Longshanks now anyway."

Something passed over Lachlan's face. A dark anger, perchance. And some other look Liza couldn't identify. "Dinnae say that, Lady Elesbeth," he whispered. His voice sounded nearly as vexed as Grete's.

"And why not? Walter Hastings said the same this morn. John Balliol is nothing but a puppet king, set in place as a proxy for Edward himself." The fury of both Grete and Lachlan had kindled her desperation. "Uilleam is gone, and I shall likely ne'er lay eyes on my father and brother Alexander again." She lifted her arms then dropped them limply by her side. "We have nothin' left to put our trust in."

Lachlan shook himself from Forsy's hold, heedless

of her objections. He drew near to Liza, clasping her cheeks with his calloused hands. "Ye must not forsake hope, my lass. Not yet."

"Lachlan!" Forsy's voice echoed with a heightened cry.

His gaze swiftly shifted to his betrothed before he returned his attentiveness to Liza. "There be plans," he murmured away from Forsy's hearing, yet within Grete's.

Grete did not hide her interest. "What plans do ye speak of?"

"It is too soon to speak of them."

Grete stepped forward. "I wish to ken, and I wish to join this worthy cause."

Lachlan shook his head. "It's far too dangerous."

Grete's blue eyes flashed fire and ice. She grasped tightly at Lachlan's arm. "I was violated, starved, poisoned, and left for dead upon the Isle of Orkney. Either God or the Devil himself deemed it fit to save me. Speak no' to me of danger. I am ready to fight for this land that is my birthright."

Forsy stepped forward, interrupting the discourse. "Lachlan, we must take leave," she implored. The lass trembled as she drew near to Liza and Grete, fearing their witchlike natures might besmirch her soul. Lachlan permitted himself to be guided away, offering no reply to Grete, whose prior wrath seemed to have transformed into a fervent zeal for action.

The pair watched them go, and when they were nearly out of sight, Grete murmured, "I must know if a rebellion be planned." She clutched her cloak tightly around her throat as she made her way to the gate of the castle.

"Grete," Liza called after her, hastening her pace. "Lachlan speaks the truth—a rebellion would be perilous, and it's my duty tae keep ye safe." Robert Wishart had decreed it so.

Grete spun around. "We'd both be struck down if not fer Longshanks' meddling." She nearly spat on the ground. "And for what purpose do we waste away here?" she cried. "I shall no' be coddled like a fragile trinket—a child—useless within these walls. I've squandered enough precious time confined tae my bed. I meant what I said, Elesbeth. I was spared on that isle for some reason. I now realize, I would have no qualm with death if it meant my life was given for my land, in the name of my grandfather."

Liza found herself at a loss for words. She didn't pursue further discourse as the girl departed into the depths of the keep. Instead, Liza stood alone for some time, regarding her castle and her lands. A strange guardsman glanced at her with interest as he strode by, prompting Liza to lower her gaze. She felt as though she'd wandered astray without ever departing home.

And there was no guide to lead her into the danger that might lie ahead.

Chapter 23

Grete vanished, though not in the literal sense. She remained present, though she was far from the lass Liza had first met at Watret Abbey near a year past. Indeed, she was far from the lass she'd been during spring's re-greening.

As the summer months passed, the Maid of Norway transformed into a different soul. She cast aside her womanly ways and garments in favor of trowse and a short léine. Liza thought she'd even caught a glimpse of a bollock knife tucked beneath her attire. Though Grete's fair locks remained lengthy, she wove her tresses in tight coils upon her head. She was yet beautiful, but the castle's attendants dared not draw near her, for her fierce gaze and frosty manner did bid them pause. At the very least, the whispers of her being a sorceress had ceased.

Peter Syward was occupied with his duties as escheator for the Crown, leaving scant time to spare for either Liza or Grete. Liza was glad for his absence, and vowed if her father were to return, her first act would be to rid the land of the man.

Following the Ne'erday melee, Donvaldus had largely kept his distance from Liza, though he deemed it proper to comment to Liza on the altered appearance of Grete, a remark that took Liza aback.

"Yer ill-begotten sister seems tae hae found herself a new hobby and new acquaintances," he remarked as Liza was collecting a bucket of water from the chain pump in the courtyard.

Liza did not care for the chamberlain's opinion and kept her silence. In truth, Liza took no liking to Grete's newfound appearance nor her ragtag band of companions, which included the unruly young farmers and cottars from the barony and the surrounding shires. They crept about beyond the gaze of English guards and loyal watchmen of the English Crown, towering figures clad in leather and hauberk chainmail, with broadswords at their sides.

Grete had declared she would not heed Liza's cautions, yet Liza kept a vigilant eye upon her as best she could. She'd caught no whisper of any brewing rebellion and, besides, felt sure Lachlan would send word if Grete faced peril.

Lachlan himself stayed to his own affairs, likely laboring on the dwelling for the lass meant to be his wife. Though the summer solstice approached, Liza had received no tidings of his impending union to Forsy, which kept her in a state of heightened anticipation.

Liza tugged upon the chain until the stone disks rose, pouring water into her vessel atop the contraption.

"Did ye hear my words, daft wench?" Donvaldus inquired sharply. Merely a year past, the man would never have dared to address her with such insolence. Not afore he had won the favor of Walter Hastings and sworn his loyalty to the Crown of England.

"Aye, I heard ye fine," Liza answered.

"Yer sister has raised suspicions."

At this, Liza's shoulders drew up. "The suspicions of who?"

"Disnae matter of who."

"Then why bring forth the matter?" She had little time for Donvaldus. Surely he had more pressing matters to attend. "She's done nothing tae cast doubt." Liza wiped her perspiring brow and readied herself to bring forth another vessel of water from the chain pump.

"'Tis no' her deeds," the chamberlain went on. "'Tis her appearance."

Liza was certain the man would have words about Grete's mannish attire. Instead, he continued, "I'm old enough tae remember yer mother, Jennet of Ramsay, before she perished. Grete looks nothing like the Mormaers of Fife, nor any of the Clan MacDuff. Their people are dark and broad. They hae course tresses like yers, not fine hair like Grete." Though Liza's focus on her endeavor wavered, she maintained her concentration and continued tugging at the chain. "With her hair coiled and her dressed like a lad, she appears most familiar, indeed. The likeness to King Alexander in his youth is uncanny." Liza's hand slipped on the metal, causing it to bite painfully into her flesh. If Donvaldus noticed her folly, he showed no sign. "He was a stalwart and loyal king. I even bent my knee before him when I was but a bairn."

Liza blinked down the well's depth into the blackness. She must warn Grete, though she didn't know what good it would bring. If Donvaldus deemed it wise to divulge this information, other tongues were likely already wagging. She could feel the chamberlain's eyes upon her, and she endeavored to keep her expression pleasant and fair.

"I hae just received word Longshanks himself will make his way to our estate with two of his loyal subjects—John de Warrene and Hugh de Cressingham. Methinks he will be greatly keen tae hear of this Scottish royal likeness."

"Hae ye nothin' better tae set yer mind to than chatterin' on like an auld woman?" Liza asked.

The insult did nothing to dissuade him from his talk. "I remember well when Grete appeared. 'Twas about the same time the bairn queen perished, was it not?"

Liza heaved a weary sigh, deeming it wisest to pay

no heed to his prattle. "Fer what purpose would the English king be travelin' to our land?"

"Surely ye're not so sheltered ye have nae heard tidings of a revolution supportin' Robert the Bruce, the rival of King John."

Liza had caught wind of those whispers, and some of those words from Grete herself. What they bore upon the Ramsay lands, she could not comprehend. Though Longshanks graced their midst the past winter, it was John Comyn who had heralded his visit. Now that Claray was laid to rest beneath the ground, John Comyn appeared to hold no further designs upon their lands or existence. With the established sheriffdom over the Ramsay Estate, it was Walter Hastings and his men charged with securing the province. Should any soul upon this land or within this household partake in a rebellion… Liza trembled inwardly, recalling Lachlan's passionate whispers to her as Beltane approached. It would not be Grete alone who might encounter danger.

"When shall this visit take place?"

"What matter be that to ye?" Donvaldus' gaze sharpened, and Liza sensed the danger of stepping into a snare.

With a measured effort, she completed her task of drawing water from the well, choosing silence over speech. As she made her way from him, his low, rumbling laugh followed her.

Donvaldus MacTavish, in his position as chamberlain, oversaw the staff and attendants of the castle. Having ingratiated himself with both Walter Hastings and Peter Syward, his fealty was without question. It was clear both she and Grete were under many watchful eyes, and she would need to find a cautious way to alert her sister.

She bided her time until the day waned before she sought Grete, that she might put some distance between herself and the chamberlain's suspicious words. The hours dragged on throughout the day, and Liza toiled at her daily chores. She felt ever a foreboding that caused her heart to thrum steadily. Surely a shift in the winds was upon them.

At gloaming, Liza stole through the castle's silent and empty passages. In the pleasant weather of summer, the castle's attendants mostly toiled outdoors, in the courtyard and the ward, finding reasons to labor in the mild evening air. But when Liza reached Grete's chamber, it stood empty. Liza left the chamber and found the young maid Mariot, who waited on Grete, walking in the corridor.

"Mariot, hae ye spied my sister?" Liza asked.

The lass would scarcely meet Liza's gaze. "Nay, my lady," Mariot whispered. "I have seen neither hide nor hair of her this day."

Liza's brow furrowed, yet she spoke no more, fearing the maid might carry her questions to Donvaldus. Instead, Liza thanked the young girl and slipped into the courtyard, where many of the barony's folk had made excuse to breathe the mild air of twilight.

Past the falconer she strode, while he bent over his great fowl, scarcely aware of her passing. She thought to ask if he'd seen Lachlan, as he was bailie over both hawk and hound, but she relented. She would search for him where he would often be found—beside his steeds and hobelar ponies.

Toward the stables she hurried, noting with some wonder how the number of hobelars had multiplied these twelve months past. They were small creatures and good for neither plough nor war. Peter Syward, in his role as seneschal, had questioned their keep during the last summer season while Liza had acted as lady of the barony. Now, Liza admitted his doubts were not unwarranted. As she crossed into the stall-yard, her nostrils twitched in warning—an ailment she knew all too well.

Lachlan was not among the horses. Instead, she came upon a young groomsman brushing a dun hobelar.

"Lad, hae ye seen the bailie this day?" she asked.

He spared her a brief glance—no fear upon his face, only disinterest. "He was here at midday, my lady, but since then I have not noticed his comings or goings."

"And did he speak of his plans for the day?"

The lad's brow rose, as if Liza's question was a daft one. "A man of his station speaks little of his errands, my lady."

Liza felt chastened by the lad's answer and turned to go. Then she hazarded one more daft query. "Hae ye heard word of his weddin' to Forsy?"

The youth set aside his brush and took up the rake, turning his back upon her. "Not a word from him, nor from any other lad here."

Secrets in the barony were prompt to leak. Still, she felt a twinge of foolishness for her prying. She assumed the lad would speak no more, when he hurled the rake aside and turned to face her.

"Forsy bides with her mother down by the westerly fields," he said, chin lifted toward the outskirts. "I've heard he's building them a dwelling by the burn."

"Aye?" Liza murmured.

The lad shrugged, then added, "D'ye care to brush one o' the ponies, my lady?"

At the mere thought of their coarse hair, her chest tightened and her nose twitched. "I thank ye, but it will bring on my wheezin'."

He frowned but nodded. "Suit yerself. Yer sister likes 'em well enough."

"My sister?"

"Aye, Grete. She's yer sister, isn't she?"

"When did ye see her?"

"About an hour since. She came in with some fel-low I didnae ken."

Liza frowned. "One of the lads from the shire," she grumbled.

The groom leaned forward, shaking his head and keen at last. "Not a cottar," he whispered. "More like a northerner. He wasnae from these lands."

"A Highlander?" Liza guessed.

He nodded eagerly. "Aye, his hair was long as a bard's and his léine and trowse were caked with mire, as though he'd lain in forest or cave." The boy gestured toward his arms. "His arms were like boulders."

"What was he lookin' for?"

He shrugged. "He eyed the ponies as if they were valuables, though he stroked none as yer sister did. Yet, he seemed right pleased."

A sudden sneeze shook Liza, and her nostrils quiv-ered. "Which way did they go when they departed?"

The groom considered this. "Toward the river, but by the long path. 'Round the fields."

Liza sneezed again. Feeling her lungs were about to seize and burst with each breath, she thanked the lad and took her leave.

What, then, had Grete entangled herself in?

Liza cinched her léine about her waist and strode across the grounds by that same long way around, mindful of her wheezing breaths, still determined to follow where her sister's path might lead.

Chapter 24

Along the River Creagan, Liza trod a narrow path until she came upon an unnatural corridor where the summer foliage lay trampled flat. The light had grown dim, and dimmer still under the shade of the forest. She nearly stumbled over a protruding root before regaining her balance.

"For heaven's sake," she muttered, her voice echoing softly in the woods. "This be a fool's errand."

She was about to turn back, when, in the clearing ahead, she spied a small and rough dwelling of red stone, cut from the sandstone upon the Creagan's steep bank. Liza studied it. As a bairn, she'd often played make-believe by the riverbank. Never had she seen this dwelling afore. From the rocks piled high beside the structure, she reckoned the lodging to be newly wrought.

She watched and waited. Was it the soft flicker of a flame from inside she spied? The breeze seemed to bring to her a low murmur of voices. Could this be Lachlan's dwelling he'd built for his bride? The thought nearly made her turn on her heel. Instead, she stepped out of the shadows and crept forward.

As she reached the low door, a shadow darted from the side. Liza startled as a man sprang forth, his expression grim. Liza had scant time to call out before he pushed a cold blade against her throat.

"Stand, witch," he hissed, "or I'll draw blood from yer pretty throat."

Liza froze as he'd commanded; her heart pounded wildly.

Before the man could make good on his threat, Lachlan vaulted from within the dwelling and caught the hilt of the knife in the man's palm.

"Ease yer hand," he growled, and with a twist, he wrenched the blade aside.

The man glowered. "I've caught us a witch."

"This is no witch," Lachlan declared as Liza gently placed her hand upon the fine prick of blood at her neck.

Another man stormed forth from the dwelling. "Are ye off yer head?" he whispered furiously. "Ye're fixin' tae get us slain. Come within with that clamor."

Liza resisted, but it was Lachlan who hauled her inside the stony chamber.

Inside stood another man, and a slender lad sat cross-legged upon the packed earth floor. As they entered, hands strayed to daggers sheathed at their sides. The lad rose in one smooth motion.

Liza was shocked to find the lad was Grete herself.

Her hair was shorn from her head.

Liza gaped at her. "Grete…what's the meaning o' this?"

When Grete didn't answer, Liza's gaze swept to the others.

They were hardened men, grimy and spent, though pride still burned in the lift of their chins. The one who had pressed the knife against her throat spat upon the earthen floor. Another, his long dark locks tangled and wild, cast a scornful glance between Liza and Lachlan. The third—a striking man with fair hair like fiery ember and eyes as stormy as a tempest—observed her intently.

An uneasy tension brewed in the air.

Lachlan broke the silence. "No threat comes from this lady."

"Aye?" snarled the dark, wild man. "She pranced tae the door's threshold. Who's tae stop another from makin' entrance?"

The one with hair of fire dusted dirt from his trowse. "Peace, William. This wench is not who we seek."

The man who'd pierced Liza's throat stood firm at the threshold, casting a menacing glare. He spoke not a word, and Liza felt certain he took grim delight in the sight of her blood.

"Sister," Grete finally spoke, "what seek ye here?"

"I should ask ye the same," Liza cried. She dismissed the others with a gesture of her hand. "I care not fer these strangers, but I care fer ye, and I fear ye are in peril."

"I am with Lachlan."

It pained Liza that those words brought her no comfort.

Lachlan stepped forward. "Lady Elesbeth," he said softly. "These men are here at my bidding. William Wallace of Ayrshire, Andrew Moray of Pettie, and Thomas MacClure of Dumfries."

At these names, Liza's brow lifted, a tingle stirring within her memory. "I ken the Wallace name, though how escapes me," she said.

Lachlan turned to the men. "This is Lady Elesbeth Ramsay, daughter of Laird William and Sister of Laird Alexander. Her mother was Lady Jennett of the Clan MacDuff, sister to the Mormaer of Fife."

A shift took place in the man called William Wallace. "This is the Lady Elesbeth?" he asked Lachlan. Lachlan nodded. "Is there no sentinel upon her?" As if not expecting an answer, he turned to Liza. "Why are ye roamin' about alone in the dark of eventide?"

Liza straightened. "I can tend to my own affairs," she declared.

William Wallace shook his head with a mirthless chuckle. "The lasses of this clan are truly a breed apart," he remarked, gesturing between Grete and Liza.

Andrew Moray stepped forth, paying no attention

to the gruffer William. He clasped Liza's hand in his own and bowed solemnly. "We bring a message for ye," he intoned. Though his speech bore the lilt of the Highlands, his voice was soft, and Liza felt an immediate bond with him. She glanced at Grete, who regarded the man as though he cradled her very heart within his gaze.

"Yer father and brother bid ye fond tidings, Lady Elesbeth. We've word from France, where he dwells in exile, still under the protection of King Phillip."

The words hung in the air, just out of Liza's comprehension, before they floated down and understanding dawned.

Her world began to spin; her knees gave way and tears sprang forth. "My father...my brother... Ye've spied them? With yer own eyes?" she whispered, voice brittle with relief.

Andrew Moray hastened to steady her. "My men hae encountered them, aye."

The silent sobs that wracked Liza's body came unbidden. Grete stepped forward to smooth Liza's hair back from her cheek. But it was Lachlan who gathered her into his arms and guided her to a pallet in the room's corner. The soft glow of a low fire danced from the hearth on rough walls and rougher blankets.

When Liza's cries of relief and joy had stilled, she rose erect. Surely these strange men, with their unwashed hair and bodies, and easy use of weapons, had not happened upon this place to tell Liza only of her father. Otherwise, Lachlan and Grete—dressed as a lad—would not be gathered with these men of questionable nature.

And with the violent reaction of Thomas Mac-Clure, she'd interrupted some meeting.

She sniffed and gathered her wits. "Tell me, then…what business brings you to my father's land?"

Silence fell. The men exchanged glances. Thomas spat once more.

William Wallace stepped forward. "We plan for Robert Bruce's rising against the English yoke."

Liza took note of the resolute countenances, most notably Grete's. She released a laugh, hoping the words spoken were but a jest. Her laughter was met with hard silence.

Liza's next words were spoken without mirth, and with steel behind them. "Ye'll bring ruin on us all. Walter Hastings, the liege of Longshanks, holds this land. The sheriff may be corpulent and lazy, but he is not unwise. His spies flock the barony. A breath of revolt, and every Ramsay hearth will be burned tae ash."

At this, Thomas MacClure returned her laughter. Wallace held up a hand. "Lady Elesbeth, by yer blood ye must be true tae Bruce. And only upon yer pledge, would we have ye privy to our counsel." He was asking her to swear fealty to Robert the Bruce. Yet her only loyalty was to Margaret, Maid of Norway.

Liza cast her gaze between the men and Grete, whose dress as a lad took on a darker meaning in the face of such information. The girl—the rightful heir to the throne of Scotia—was planning to fight.

Liza couldn't bring herself to blame Lachlan. She turned to William Wallace, the wild-eyed hardened warrior. "Ye'd have me inscribe our names with the very blood from our veins?"

Lachlan moved to her side. "Elesbeth…" He halted, then said quietly, so the others could not hear, "Liza." Liza's pulse quickened at the sound of that strange and familiar name on his tongue. "We'll speak more in private—here's no place fer an argument."

But when he moved to guide Liza away, Thomas blocked his passage. "I doubt her honor."

It was the more thoughtful Andrew Moray who came to Liza's defense. "If Lachlan and Grete trust her, so, too, do we."

Thomas grumbled with a narrowed eye, but he stepped aside so they could pass. Lachlan guided her entry into another small chamber, apart from his companions.

The dwelling was humble, its close walls echoing the low mutter of the companions' voices. The chamber, cramped with kirtles and a pallet laid upon earthen floor, held a closeness and air of secrecy.

Lachlan gestured for Liza to rest upon the mattress,

and when she did, he took a seat very near to her.

She ought not ponder Forsy in a moment such as this, yet her mind wandered to the wedding bed of Lachlan, nonetheless. She took comfort in the notion that perhaps she had rested upon this marriage bed before Forsy.

Lachlan spoke first, breaking the flow of her thoughts. "Ye may hae heard of William Wallace and Andrew Moray."

It was more a statement than a query, and Liza lifted her shoulder. "I hae heard their names whispered alongside that of Robert the Bruce."

He gave a nod of his head. "Since King John was anointed sovereign, it's been made plain his charge shall forever be marred by the meddling of Edward. The people have taken to calling our king 'Toom Tabard'."

Liza had heard as much from both Walter Hastings and Hexilde, long ago.

"It should hae been Robert the Bruce who was crowned king at Berwick Castle during the Great Cause," he declared.

"It should hae been Margaret Maid of Norway named queen," she retorted fiercely. Lachlan was silent, and in this hush, a troubling notion crept into her thoughts, prompting her to lower her voice. "Do those wild men ken Grete's true identity?"

"Nay," Lachlan responded swiftly and earnestly.

"My condition of her involvement in these matters was her anonymity. I told her if she ever dared speak of her true name, I would see her aboard a ship back to Norway."

That was the wisest counsel Liza had encountered in all her days. She turned to Lachlan. "Why have we not done so? With the turmoil, hardly a soul would notice us whisking the lass back to her own land."

Lachlan snorted. "Ye'll need more than luck tae get the stubborn lass tae yield willingly. Grete's sole purpose is tae avenge her grandfather, King Alexander, and defend her homeland. She gives nary a thought fer the title."

Liza cared not what Grete desired for her homeland or her fallen forebear. *Liza's* sole purpose was Grete's safety. She would dispatch a message through a reliable courier at Watret Abbey to Robert Wishart…

As though Lachlan could peer into her very thoughts, he declared, "Dinnae be hatchin' any grand schemes. No' a courier within the abbey can be trusted now. The cloister's been made into an English garrison. Should ye attempt to send a missive, ye'll likely doom her to death. Along with yerself."

Liza frowned and grumbled, "Better tae risk her death than send her forth tae it in battle." Then she sighed deeply. Lachlan was right. She wouldn't risk their safety so boldly.

"William Wallace is my distant kin. He has sworn

his loyalty and life to Robert the Bruce. For the past year, he has been a fugitive, sowing chaos across the land among the English, who now ken his name well."

"And what of Andrew Moray?"

"Moray hails from the clan of the same name from the province of Pettie in the Highlands. He is an esquire skilled in the art of horsemanship and mastery of arms. Wallace stands as a champion of the common folk, yet Moray stands on the threshold of nobility, a leader among men. Should the banners of rebellion rise to triumph, it be Moray who'll guide us to victory."

Liza pondered Moray's thoughtful stare and gentle touch. She also took note of Grete's quite evident response to the lad. "And what of Grete's part in this disordered company and their ill-starred venture?" she inquired of Lachlan.

At this, Lachlan's gaze wandered. "Wallace and Moray have been amongst us a fortnight. In that span, Grete has shown her loyalty. She means to take up arms."

"She is a lass."

"Aye, and she is willful and bears a wit beyond measure, much like her grandfather. Andrew Moray sees worth in her swiftness, her fleetness of foot, and the fire in her spirit."

"She cannot do battle as the right and true queen of this land."

"Ye'd be the one to tell him that?"

Liza struggled with the dilemma. She would think on it, and swiftly. In the meantime, she asked, "And the other man—Thomas MacClure?"

Lachlan's face contorted. "The MacClures are a fearsome clan—thieves and murderers. Yet, Thomas seeks to wield his grim talents for the cause of righteousness. He's loyal to Moray and Wallace, and quick to strike—ye'll not find a more steadfast guardian."

Liza said nothing else. Lachlan knew her hesitation.

"Grete serves as scout and is swift with her blade. Her speed and cunning may well decide our fortune."

Liza drew a trembling breath. "And what is their plan fer battle? Do they plan tae fight on our ground?" She imagined the dwellings reduced to ash. The bodies of her countrymen slain in her gentle fields.

Lachlan shook his head. "Longshanks makes his way north."

Liza had heard as much from Donvaldus.

"He heads to Stirling Castle."

Liza had never set foot upon the site, though she'd heard tales of the Scottish stronghold by the River Forth. As she came to know now, the stronghold lay under the rule of English forces.

Lachlan did not speak further, and understanding dawned over her. "Surely, ye cannae mean tae assail the garrison." Her voice was naught but a whisper.

"We hae the men, and we hae a plan."

"Ye'll get yerself slain, that be certain."

He cast his eyes downward at his hands, avoiding her gaze. Liza's eyes followed, recalling the times his hands had touched her skin. Never again would she feel his touch, for he was pledged to another.

And should he fall in battle … The thought of losing him from this mortal realm was a burden she could scarce endure.

She grew desperate. "I shall ride and tend tae ye and Grete upon the battlefield."

"My lady, ye cannae endure but a few moments astride a horse. A journey of two days with a throng of men on such beasts may finish ye before the battle even begins. Ye'll be of no aid to Grete upon the field."

Liza knew this to be true. Yet, there must be something she could do. Robert Wishart had said she'd been sent here to save Grete. She would surely fail at this task. And what be it all for?

Lachlan's gaze found hers, and his look was tender. "We must all make our passage into the murky realm of death."

She shook her head, ready to utter words, but he stilled her with a gentle touch upon her cheek. "I'd sooner lose ye to death and find ye in another realm than stand by yer side and not be able to reach ye for the sake of our stations."

Her chest tightened. "What o' Forsy?"

He shrugged. "She's a bonny lass, but she's no' you, Liza."

Her breath caught in her throat. "Why do ye call me Liza?" she murmured.

He leaned closer. "Is it not yer true name?"

She gave a nod, and his head moved forward until his lips touched hers in a tender kiss. As he pulled away, he said, "I love only ye. I think I'll love only ye for eternity."

A tear slid down her cheek. Tear-stained, she drew herself up, her expression steely.

The English yoke bound her neck as it did her newfound kin.

"Then may God grant the will and protection tae do what's right," she said.

Lachlan smiled.

And so, in that red-walled croft beside the River Creagan, Liza took up her part in the plot of war against the English king. And she vowed her blade, her word, and her heart as a shield against the coming storm.

Chapter 25

The following two months were fraught with tension. Though Liza did not partake in the battle preparations, she played the role of sentinel, watchful for any lurking danger, and conveyed messages and tidings through Grete to Lachlan, Thomas, MacClure, Andrew Moray, and William Wallace.

Grete had taken to spending fewer hours within the castle walls, and her absence did not go unnoticed by the maidens and servants alike. It was the keen gaze of Hexilde that troubled Liza the most.

"I've seen little of yer kin o'er the past weeks," the cook said one warm afternoon after Liza had finished her meal in the great hall. "What's the lass up to?"

Liza was ready with an answer. "Aye, she said she's been feelin' trapped within the walls. She's missin' the sea and the wide-open spaces o' her true home in Fife."

"Is that so?" Hexilde said as she cleared an armful of wooden platters and vessels from one of the long tables.

Liza stood to depart, but Hexilde remarked, "The last I beheld her, she'd taken to wearing her léine short as a lad, and her hair was shorn tae her scalp. The maiden does no' appear so noble now."

Liza had naught to reply to Hexilde's query, and inwardly she cursed Grete. She'd warned her that her dress endangered her quest. Grete, however, had become more bold as the days wore on.

"And Donvaldus claims tae hae seen her with a man with tresses of fire near the stables. Ye wouldnae ken anythin' of that?"

Surely Hexilde spoke of Andrew Moray. The softspoken warrior seemed to have captured the heart of Grete, and she his. Liza must warn Grete that Moray had been spotted by Donvaldus or one of his spies.

"Eh?" Hexilde prompted when Liza did not speak.

"Perhaps it was one of the grooms from the barony," Liza answered. "Grete has taken tae spending her hours with the ponies."

"Pshaw," Hexilde said with a sweep of her generous arm. "Those silly ponies are useless."

Liza had been of a mind to agree with the notion until she'd unearthed the true intent behind the wee horses brought forth from the lands of Ireland. The stout and sturdy legs of the beasts rendered them fit for fording streams and traversing the steep slopes of the craggy Highlands, where Wallace and Moray planned to venture after seizing Stirling Castle.

Liza hurried to take her leave, but Hexilde blocked her way. "Ye can trust me. Ye ken that, child."

Liza dared not place her trust in any soul. Not with such great stakes at hand. Furthermore, Liza observed that Hexilde no longer lay solitary in her slumber. Her nights were now spent in the chamber of Walter Hastings—the very quarters that once belonged to the laird and lady of the castle.

Liza offered a weak smile in response. "I ken," she lied.

"Ye're witherin' yerself." The woman cast a pointed look at Liza's frail form. "Our fare is bounteous here, thanks to Walter. And the skies be kind. Ye ought to be growin' hale and hearty."

There were many a cause for Liza's waning flesh, not least among them being the dread that Grete might be discovered. Furthermore, her thoughts often wandered back to Lachlan's foreboding words spoken in the humble river cottage.

I'd sooner lose ye to death and find ye in another realm than stand by yer side and not be able to reach ye for the sake of our stations.

Aloud, she said, "I'm but lamentin' the absence of my kin. It's been near a year since Uilleam's mishap. Now Claray is departed, and it seems that my father and brother shall no' return."

"Ah, I thought ye might be lamentin' the bailie, Lachlan."

Liza gave a small shake of her head.

"Just as well." Hexilde leaned forward with a secretive air. "Walter has said the bailie may be plottin' somethin'."

Liza's heart faltered. "Plottin'?"

"Aye, Peter Syward has given the sheriff word of an uprising in the coming weeks. I dinnae believe it," said Hexilde. "Only a fool would plot against the army of Edward. The bailie is no fool. Nor would he hae any men."

"And where might this uprising be takin' place?"

"Stirling Castle," Hexilde said with a chuckle. "It's a mad notion, it is."

"Peter does not favor the bailie," said Liza, striving to keep the tremor of unease from her voice. "He's envious of my father's good grace."

"No need tae feel envy o' that now," Hexilde proclaimed. Then, upon realizing her words, softened her demeanor. "It's just that, as escheator, Peter holds a far superior station tae that o' bailie."

Liza didn't trouble herself with Hexilde's implication. She knew her father to be alive. Much more likely was the notion that Peter had caught wind of the scheme of the men by the river. And if that be the case, the men who fought for noble cause were in danger, as was their quest.

Liza would be the one to bear this news. She darted around Hexilde, who called, "Where are ye off tae?"

But Liza did not answer. She found her way to the entrance and hurried over the threshold, past the watchmen with their suspicious gazes. Slowing her pace, she found her way to the stables where Grete stood stroking one of the small herd with a dappled gray coat, a faraway expression on her regal face.

Though Grete was dressed as a lad, her fine features made it impossible to mistake her for the rougher sex. To be certain, Grete was every bit a woman. And a strong one at that. Liza had half expected to find Andrew Moray by Grete's side, but was relieved to find her alone.

Liza shifted at the threshold, and Grete startled, her hand flying to her throat. "Elesbeth," she exclaimed. "Sister, ye must not creep up so stealthily."

Liza murmured her regrets. Her thoughts lingered upon Grete's distant gaze, pondering the paths of her mind and the yearnings of her heart. "It's a leesome day. Walk through the fields with me," she suggested.

For once, Grete did not protest.

They linked arms as they walked through the fields, and Liza felt a calmness settle into her heart. Such tranquility had been scarce indeed for many a moon.

Perhaps that was the reason the stillness was sullied by a sense of dread.

When they were far from the peril of prying ears, Grete said, "What tidings hae ye, sister?" Grete's eyes burned upon Liza's face, as if she'd delight in the whispers of war from the castle and its inhabitants.

Liza let out a weary breath and cast her gaze upon

the barley fields, the golden heads dancing in the gentle, warm pirl. The same breeze tousled the stray dark locks slipping from Liza's loosely braided tresses. Since the English sheriff had taken up his residence, Liza had forsaken the custom of covering her head, often leaving her hair unfettered like a mere common lass.

Grete prompted Liza for her response, and Liza said, "Aye, there's whisper of treachery at the hand of the bailie."

"Lachlan," Grete murmured, and her visage was reflective. "Who speaks of his treachery?"

"Peter Syward has relayed the prattle to the sheriff himself."

"What knowledge has he?"

Liza cast a wary glance behind them toward the distant castle. From this expanse, she could see no movement or souls. The imposing keep rose from the land like a watchtower. A deep well of emotion ascended from somewhere within Liza's being. This land was her home, and she loved it fiercely. Its peril filled her with sorrow.

To Grete, with her contrasting eagerness, Liza said, "I asked but a few questions so as not to arouse suspicion."

"And neither Peter Syward nor the sheriff ken of William and Andrew?" Grete spoke Andrew's name as if it were a sacred utterance.

"I think not."

Grete nodded, and a laugh escaped her lips. "Then our scheme progresses as planned."

Liza blinked at her sister with her unbound glee as they strode onward through the peaceful fields. "What scheme do ye speak of?"

"We must draw Edward's men tae the spot," her sister replied. "They must know just the proper measure o' our plan tae provoke their reaction and compel their hand."

Liza halted her steps, and Grete's body faltered with the sudden movement.

"What folly be this?" Liza demanded.

Grete looked upon Liza as if she were daft. "How else shall we reclaim the stronghold that be the Castle Stirling? My grandfather's keep," she added with emphasis.

"It would be wise tae make yer charge under the cover of darkness," Liza cried in response. "By surprise, where ye might have a fightin' chance to remain among the living."

"What glory be in that?"

"Glory?" Liza could scarce believe her ears. "The cause be tae fight fer Scotia, not fer sure death."

"The cause be tae show the English they cannot vanquish the Scots. We will not yield without a contest." At Liza's incredulity, Grete cast Liza a look full of pity, as if she were gazing upon a naïve bairn.

"'Tis our purpose Edward and his horde shall know the site of our onslaught and attack," she proclaimed in a measured and deliberate tone.

Liza stood bewildered, disbelief plain upon her face. "But ye hae no army," she said. "Ye hae no men tae ride under yer banner."

"Ye've not been privy to our councils," Grete answered. "There is indeed an army. Andrew hath mustered men from every corner of Scotia for this righteous cause. Even from provinces ye've never heard named. Men from the north—they come tae fight fer their kin, tae fight fer their land, tae fight fer Robert the Bruce."

Liza pressed her hands to her temples, scarce believing the words from Grete's lips. "What hope hae ye against the might o' England? Their legion is vast as the sea. Your motley crew can scarce stand against their numbers."

"Maybe not in multitude," Grete replied softly, "but in purpose and in heart."

"Purpose and heart win no' wars when the enemy outmans ye two to one." Liza's voice was a curse. A plea. No good would come of this foolishness.

Grete shook her head. "Ye know naught of the depth o' our resolve." Before Liza could answer, she continued, "And Andrew possesses a cunning ploy."

Liza's lips trembled. She'd grown weary of the lofty plans that risked the lives of those she held dear.

"Speak, then," she said, though dread gnawed at her heart.

"At Sterling Castle, the River Forth sweeps by on a great bend. A narrow wooden span crosses its flow. If a small band of our men can lure the English across, we may hem them in at the bend and, with cunning rather than force, crush their multitudes in the river's crook."

Never having set foot in these lands, Liza found it hard to envision the ruse. "Aye, ye weave fanciful words," said Liza, "but the ploy reeks of hopeful folly." She gave a soft snort and turned away. Grete stiffened and did not speak.

They strode in silence for a time.

In the far-off distance, the birds called to one another, heedless of the strife between their human kin. A hawk soared high above. It swiftly wheeled, then plunged earthward, perhaps having glimpsed some quarry within the grasses. Liza put her thoughts of heart and kin aside, her gaze captured by the noble bird. Grete's stern countenance then captured Liza's gaze, and Liza turned her notice to her professed sister.

"Do ye believe I am unaware of the peril we face?" Grete asked, her voice soft.

"Ye surely behave as such."

"Would ye hae me behave as a timid wee mouse, afeared o' my own shadow and cowerin' in a chamber that be not mine own?"

Liza gave a slight shake of her head. She and Grete

had traded the same words many times. Never would they find accord on how the other reacted to the present state of the realm and their own barony. Grete believed Liza shielded her eyes and ears from the danger, shunning the truth. Liza reckoned Grete acted hastily, charging heedlessly into danger and forsaking sound judgment.

Liza had no desire for another quarrel akin to the last.

"Do ye believe I am ignorant of what fate befell me on that accursed vessel?"

At Grete's mention of her journey to Scotia, Liza paused. It was a matter Grete evaded, but for a few occasions.

"Do ye know what those men—those *beasts*—did tae me?"

Liza did not know, but she could guess.

"They pounded their fists upon me." Grete gritted her teeth, her words forced through a jaw tightly set. "They thrust their vile, naked bodies against mine, and the others howled while they took their turn, rutting like beasts within me."

Liza parted her lips to offer words of solace, but Grete raised her hands to halt her. "They meant to leave me dead, that I should never live to speak of their evil. And who sits in power now but allies of the very fiends who pledged to oversee my safe passage. The Guardians as ye've called them, were never my protectors. They never meant fer me to take my rightful place upon the throne."

Liza could not refute Grete's convictions. Though not all the Guardians were wicked, they'd become blinded by power and hubris.

"I will not spend my days in despair. This was my grandfather's land, and should have been my mother's—then mine by right. Now what I seek is both vengeance for myself and salvation for Scotia." Liza met her gaze but said nothing. Any words in response to Grete's pain seemed hopeless and offensive. Grete added quietly, "I do not expect ye to grasp it all."

"And yet," Liza breathed, "I do fathom some of it, if not all. Someone slew my brother—someone within mine own chambers. Those same brutes—perhaps o' the same ilk as yers—drove my father and my brother into exile. They may hae even murdered my stepmother. Perhaps it was me they sought to defeat."

A spark of tenderness crossed Grete's stern visage.

"I am not against what ye do or what ye plan," Liza whispered. "I only dread ye should fall. So much blood has flowed already…"

Grete swallowed hard and caught Liza's hands within hers. "I cannot promise there shall be no more. But I vow it will not be in vain."

Before Liza could utter another word, a curious whistle echoed from the trees. Though it had the semblance of a bird, Liza had never encountered a fowl with such a sharp and piercing cry. Grete's head turned swiftly to the sound. "'Tis Andrew who calls," she murmured. "I must away."

"Ye've fallen in love with him," Liza remarked.

Grete halted. "Love," she pondered slowly, a smile on her lips. "Is that what this is?" Though Grete's years were few, she'd witnessed much in her days. And she was well within the age of wedlock.

"I reckon it is."

Grete tilted her head. "He fights with his heart, and his heart is true. He sees the light within me, and I within him. Though peril surrounds us, I feel secure with him."

Liza thought of Lachlan. "'Tis love," she said, her words laced with sorrow for her own love that would remain out of reach.

Grete did not notice Liza's pain, and moved as if to take her leave.

"Sister," Liza called, and Grete turned back. "If ye love him, ye'll not reveal yer true identity. Ye may think yer sharin' yer truth, but yer real station will drive a wedge between ye. He'll be compelled tae place ye on a throne in his mind."

Grete seemed to consider this, though she said nothing else and fled swiftly.

Liza sighed and made her way toward her castle in the distance. If only the realm be at peace and the land quiet. Perhaps Grete would know love, as would Liza herself.

It was not meant to be, she feared. Not in this lifetime.

Chapter 26

Upon the passing of the moons, tidings of strife and unrest waxed heavy upon the realm. Sheriff Walter Hastings, once a slumbering warder putting forth little effort for anything beyond his meals, found himself thrust into the rank of vigilant sentinel of the Ramsay Castle and its lands.

Skirmishes flared in field and forest as factions of Scotsmen marauding on behalf of their lands and for Robert the Bruce swept down upon the shires. Without thought, they burned precious crops and fell upon unsuspecting folk in their slumber.

Liza heard the whispered concern, which had wended its way through the keep's attendants. The sheriff had sent swift entreaties to Longshanks, demanding reinforcements. An answer had not yet arrived. Hastings gnawed his fist with the weight of an anticipated attack. Wallace and Moray took these tidings as a grand jest, and bade Thomas MacClure to spread word across the land of an uprising soon to touch the Ramsay barony and the surrounding realms and shires. Thomas enlisted a band of knaves to ride with him under the cloak of night to feign an impending assault. The rogues would mount their steeds and away ride, swift as the wind, bringing confusion to the watchmen but causing no other harm.

Beset by fretful worry, Walter Hastings soon withdrew to the great kitchen of his embattled castle, seeking to still his growing fears and comfort his unease with bread, stew, venison, and ample mead. It was here, during the gloaming hour, that Liza happened upon the sheriff with his advisors, Peter Syward and Donvaldus MacTavish, as she sought entrance to the kitchen. The men stood at a table near the kitchen's threshold speaking in low tones. So engrossed were they in their words, they did not notice Liza's presence and swift withdrawal to the wall beyond the chamber. Liza swept her gaze around and saw no one else haunted the passage, so she pressed her back against the cold stone and listened.

"I hae heard many whispers of strange riders in the Lowlands," said the voice belonging to Donvaldus, the chamberlain. "Yet no soul seems tae ken their semblance or has laid eyes upon these brigands. Perhaps they are but a tale spun to sow discord among the supporters of the English cause."

Liza then recognized the high nasal tone of Peter Syward. By the Lord himself, how she hated the man. "I, too, hae heard the tales and hae met trustful souls who swear the hordes be of flesh and bone. They bring with them scores of beastly warriors meant to pillage our homes and steal our women. They be no phantoms."

"Trustful souls," scoffed Donvaldus. "As escheator, ye be there to take their coin, supplies, and animals. The countrymen would trust ye with nothin' of theirs."

"They be very open and trustworthy if I leave some of the coin in exchange for tidings," countered Peter, and Donvaldus snorted again.

After a short halt in the words, Liza leaned her head round the side of the stone to spy Walter Hastings's corpulent silhouette. The flesh beneath the man's chin wobbled as he shook his enormous head. "And how shall we know the presence of these bandits and rogues, if they walk hidden among us?"

"They come not disguised as friends," Syward warned. "Their purpose be fer battle alone. We will ken them when we spy them."

Liza's heart quickened in her breast. Many a time she'd pondered if William Wallace or Andrew Moray trod boldly across the land, passing as unseen strangers. They'd lived in the dwelling by the River Creagan now for many months. Surely in all this time, they had occasion to be among the people of the Ramsay lands.

Perhaps Peter Syward, who was misguided in his arrogance, did not recognize the danger that lay under his very nose. That, or Wallace, Moray, and MacClure would be exposed through some fateful meeting with an ill-chosen soul.

Liza harbored suspicions that Lachlan commanded fealty from his cottars and clansmen, and few would breach his trust. However, for an additional coin, a scrap of sustenance, or a vessel of ale, many a man and woman might falter and align themselves with the English cause, just as Peter Syward had himself discovered.

"They plot to reclaim Stirling Castle," Syward went on, voice grim. "And tidings are they muster men enough for the siege."

"They may have swords or dirks to wield," the sheriff muttered, "yet they shall not trouble English garrisons and our armies. We outnumber them by steed, men, and weapon. They fight for glory, though glory does not fill coffers or bellies."

Donvaldus laid a hand upon the table. "The Ramsay lands hold grain stores and salted meat," noted the chamberlain. "Our walls and provisions alone might tempt them."

"Aye, 'tis a concerning truth, indeed," the sheriff said. As if to fortify himself and save some of the kitchen's sustenance, he took only a bit of the fat leg of mutton that had been laid out on a platter before him.

Liza suspected the loss of his bountiful food and ale troubled him more than the strife of war itself.

"We ought to find solace in the presence of troops

stationed at Watret Abbey, which King Edward has claimed upon hearing of Stirling's intended mark," Peter Syward said in response to the plight of Walter Hastings.

His words brought Liza no solace. Her spirits sank at this information, and her thoughts were on the gentle monks likely cast forth from their cloister. What had become of the abbot, she wondered. The man of the cloth had been none too pleased with Liza's visit amid winter's bitter hold to the wizened Guardian Robert Wishart.

And what had become of the aged bishop and Guardian, who had shielded the clergy from the machinations and political folly of the times? No word of the man had reached her ears for many a month, and she dreaded his ailment had taken him. Or else something more sinister.

Surely the passing of such a protector would have been proclaimed across the land.

In the kitchen, the chamberlain spoke next. "And what of King John?" asked Donvaldus. "Had he no role at all in these proceedings? Surely, his interest would lie in the protection of his kinsmen."

The sheriff snorted. "Toom Tabard has been deposed at Edinburgh and borne captive to the Tower in London. The fate of John Balliol—the puppet king— hangs in the balance."

"Edinburgh, too, has fallen to the English?" Donvaldus asked.

Liza discerned a subtle strain of unease in his speech, despite his purported support of the English rule. Liza's breath caught in her breast. If no king ruled, might they all be but English subjects and unaware of their liege?

The sheriff showed no sign he'd noticed the chamberlain's worry, though confirmation of Donvaldus' question was ambiguous.

Liza, lost in reverie and unease, nearly slipped away from the troubling conversation. Peter Syward's low words stilled her steps.

"A rumor stirs which few dare speak," he said. "And it could alter the course of Scotia forever."

"I've had quite my fill of grand and baseless claims and rumors," said Walter Hastings.

"Be this claim baseless, it be dangerous all the same." Peter's voice had lowered to a pitch that caused Liza to inch forward to hear his words.

"What of it?"

"There is talk the maiden queen may be among mortal souls somewhere upon the land of Scotia."

A long silence.

This was followed by a hearty laugh from the sheriff and an uneasy chuckle from Donvaldus, whose humor, Liza knew, was feigned.

The sheriff seemed certain in his denial of the claim. "'Twas none other than the Guardian James

Stewart who set the girl to rest in her grave upon the Isle of Orkney, and the tales of others bear witness to his word. The bairn-queen Margaret, Maid of Norway, surely lies dead."

Syward pressed on. "Some claim she was never interred at all…or that she rose again from that sacred tomb."

"Like the Christ of the Christians?" scoffed Walter Hastings. "I be a man of God, yet I believe neither in holy rattle nor rustic chatter."

"I make no claim of truth," the escheator replied, defensive. "Merely the whisper I have heard. Margaret, Maid of Norway, still draws breath from this realm."

A hush fell. Liza feared the relentless pounding of her heart might draw the ears of the men.

Hastings spoke again, his words less sure this time. "If she be alive, she'd not rest in silence. She would assert her rightful placement upon the throne."

"And likely be burned at the stake fer her claims," countered Donvaldus. "Nay, the lass would be but lyin' in wait fer the time tae make herself known."

"Likely," said Peter Syward slowly, "followin' the disposal of King John of Balliol."

Donvaldus made a noise of agreement. "And likely when her countrymen are preparin' tae take Stirling Castle. It be a grand and exemplary gesture, even should it fail."

"Enough of this," interjected the sheriff. "I've had

my fill of prattle. I shall send official word to Edward warning him of the talk. 'Tis all we can do."

"John of Comyn has been tasked with uncoverin' the truth," announced Peter.

Another halt in the conversation caused Liza to again peer 'round the threshold to find the men making motions as if to take leave of the chamber. Donvaldus stepped toward the door. Liza fled, fleet of foot, down the castle's corridors as though flames pursued her. She resolved to take her fresh tidings to Lachlan, who was, at this late hour, no doubt in his small dwelling at the banks of the river.

Without a moment's hesitation, and heedless of the English guards at the keep, she fled toward the riverbank, though the light be fading. It was only when she found herself halfway to her destination across the lands that the peril she brought upon her kin struck her mind. She may be pursued.

Liza retraced her steps, weaving through the forest until the light waned further and the roots clutched at her slippers and her ankles. When she was certain she be not shadowed, she pressed on to the location of the solitary stone dwelling where Laughlan and his kin held their gathering.

She took shelter beneath the twisted boughs of a blossoming willow tree and peered around the ancient trunk. The river burbled softly over rocks and crags nearby, and the evening was calm and peaceful.

Fearing an ambush at the hands of Thomas Mac-Clure, Liza crept forward carefully into the empty main chamber of the cottage. She encountered neither sentry nor salutation. Perhaps Lachlan yet tended his horses at the stables. Perhaps Wallace, Moray, and MacClure had journeyed to Stirling on war's grim errand. Perhaps Grete was tucked safely in her chamber in the castle where she rested peacefully with no strife in her heart.

A sudden rustle and coo in the back chamber of the dwelling met her ear.

At first, she thought some gentle dove had strayed within. She stepped softly to the low opening, then halted.

A woman's voice, tender and fraught with longing, sighed. It was a sound Liza knew well, for she'd made that utterance herself during a faraway occasion in her chamber, under a cover of darkness. She'd made that utterance with Lachlan, and would carry the memory to her dying day.

A man's low timber answered his lover, and Liza's blood ran cold in her veins. Forsy had come to live with her love after all.

Her limbs weighted with dismay, Liza made to depart when another commotion arose beyond the cottage walls—male voices mingled with the neighing of steeds. Liza peered through the open window into the dusky gloaming. She could discern the figures of

William Wallace and Thomas MacClure as they tethered two dust-laden, dappled hobelars to the ancient tree.

The fervent murmurs from the rear of the cottage swelled with ardor, and Liza sought to shield the lovers by stepping forth to converse with Wallace and MacClure, though she possessed no wish to encounter either of the men. Likewise, they looked none too content to encounter her, but they kept their daggers by their sides.

"Aye, the lady herself," said Wallace. "To what do we owe this pleasure?"

Liza noted the wry wit in his tone.

"I've come tae talk with the bailie," she said, "Finding him not inside, I'll now take my leave and bid ye a good eveningtide."

Thomas MacClure inclined his head toward the north. "He remains with the herd. He cares for them as though they were his own bairns." Thomas turned to Wallace. "Those beasts shall no' learn their ways in the wild with that daft one mollycoddling them so."

Liza knew Thomas MacClure was mistaken—Lachlan was within the dwelling. She said not a word.

Wallace ignored Thomas but laid a keen eye on Liza. "Lachlan speaks highly o' ye, he does."

And yet, he lay with another on this eve, Liza thought. She compelled a false but fair expression to grace her countenance. "Aye, well..." she muttered.

"Nightfall is upon us, and I must return to my quarters."

She moved to pass without imparting any of her newfound knowledge when Wallace seized her arm with a firm hold. "What tidings did ye need to impart upon our friend Lachlan?"

Liza paused without speaking. Her gaze shifted from the resolute face of Wallace to the cruel countenance of Thomas MacClure. She'd come to bring Lachlan tidings of the rumors concerning Grete, but she would never share those murmurs with these ruffians.

"I simply came tae say the rumors of an ambush at Stirling grow louder."

Wallace peered into her face as if he might see into her very soul. "Hae ye spotted Andrew?" he inquired, and Liza shook her head firmly.

She yanked her arm free from his grip. "I spotted no one here." That surely be the truth. She had laid her eyes on neither Lachlan nor Forsy, though she'd heard them well enough.

Wallace tilted his head toward the far side of the cottage. "The man's steed lingers close by."

Liza turned her gaze toward the riverbank, where indeed a chestnut horse stood silent and vigilant, its dark coat blending with its surroundings. She had not even taken note of the creature.

"I–I didnae see him," Liza confessed.

Seconds later, Andrew Moray stepped forth from the cottage, with Grete trailing behind.

Andrew cast his eyes upon the men, then settled his gaze upon Liza. "To what do we owe this pleasure?" Unlike Wallace, his tone bore the ring of sincerity.

"Lady Elesbeth was just emergin' from the dwelling," said Wallace, his eyes dark. "She claimed she saw neither ye nor her sister."

Grete's cheeks flushed under Liza's watchful eyes. Aye, it was Grete and Andrew caught in a tender embrace. Liza felt such a surge of relief she could barely summon the will to chastise Grete.

Wallace, who recognized the truth, took it upon himself to speak instead. "If ye must bed the lass, at least do it when yer back is shielded," he barked.

Andrew Moray stepped forth, his face inches from that of Wallace. "Ye shall no' speak of the lady as if she were some field beast."

"Then stop treatin' her as one," Wallace retorted.

"I honor her with the love I bear for her," Andrew declared.

"Love!" Wallace spat the word as if it were poison. "We stand on the brink of war, and ye prattle on about love! Ye're naught but a fool, and ye've rendered her a harlot."

Andrew adjusted his footing and his arms, ready to deliver a blow to Wallace, yet before his arms could rise, Lachlan charged ahead through the forest. Upon witnessing the scene before him, he halted and declared, "Men, the hour for folly hath passed. We must speak of our cause."

Grete stepped forward, inquiring of Lachlan, "What of it?"

This caused Wallace to step back. Andrew grudgingly did the same as Lachlan dismounted and gestured for the others to go inside.

Before he followed, he noted Liza's presence. He looked upon her with renewed alarm. "What is it?" he inquired away from the hearing of the others, who had preceded them into the dwelling.

Liza, still grateful it was not his whispers she'd heard in the back chamber, placed a hand upon his arm. His gaze softened and dropped to her lips, but he made no move to touch her further.

Liza forced her mind back to the task at hand. "I hae overheard talk between the sheriff and his advisors—Donvaldus and Peter," she said. "They whisper o' the Maid o' Norway."

Lachlan's jaw was set firm. "Aye. I've heard the same whispers."

"Do they whisper o' Grete?" she asked with urgency.

"Not yet," he answered. "I fear they will."

Liza swallowed hard. "Hexilde has voiced her suspicions o' the lass. I dinnae trust she won't share those words with the sheriff."

Lachlan nodded. "All the more reason tae act swiftly."

He began to turn away, but then turned back, capturing Liza in his embrace. She barely had time to react before he pressed his lips to hers. She returned his fervent kiss.

He released her and strode into the cottage. "It is time," he declared. "We must depart for Stirling at dawn."

Thomas MacClure let out a hoot of excitement. "I will ride through the night tae spread the word and dispatch the legions," he proclaimed. "Are the hobelars ready?"

Lachlan nodded. "They are gathered near the forest, and my most trusted groomsman awaits."

Wallace gave a nod of approval, and Andrew Moray held Grete's hand tightly. "This is it," he declared. "Tomorrow, we ride to reclaim our realm."

"Fer Scotia," Grete whispered.

Andrew Moray gazed upon her. "Fer ye," he said.

Liza's heart sank. Grete had surely revealed her true identity to Andrew Moray, despite her promise to carry the secret to the grave. If she'd told Moray, others might soon discern the truth, as well. They would not make it out of this alive. Liza felt it deep in her bones. And yet their cause was now her cause. Perhaps it always had been.

"Use me in yer purpose as ye will," she whispered,

though her heart drummed swiftly in her breast.

William Wallace looked upon her approvingly. "My lady, we surely will."

Chapter 27

Liza and Grete trod silently across the grounds, cloaked by the veil of night. Upon reaching the footbridge spanning the dry moat toward the guard-house, Liza lessened her pace.

Grete flashed a grin that shone under the light of the low moon. "Leave this tae me, sister," she murmured. She then emitted a sound akin to the eerie hoot of a night raven.

Liza gazed at Grete with curiosity. "Where did ye learn tae make such a noise?"

"Andrew taught me," Grete replied. "'Tis a cunning trick tae send secret word."

It certainly hadn't been all Andrew had taught Grete, but Liza left that observation for now. "A night raven, though?" Liza whispered. "'Tis a bird of ill omen."

Grete brushed off Liza's worries. "Pure folly. The creature is but a tawny owl that feasts on rats and vermin."

Liza reckoned Andrew must've shared this knowledge with Grete, and she spoke no more on the matter, but asked, "Fer what do we wait?"

Grete pressed a finger to her lips, and soon an answering call echoed back.

"Come. We must make haste," Grete urged, and they scuttled over the footbridge, bodies low to the ground. A solitary watchman loomed in the tower, raising a hand when they passed over the bridge. They quietly slipped into the keep.

"That be an English sentinel?" Liza inquired once they were alone in the stairwell. The moon's silver glow shone like a beacon through the open encasement, lighting their path.

"Aye," Grete confirmed.

"How do ye ken tae trust him?"

Grete pulled Liza along the corridor into her chamber. Only then did she speak again.

"Not all the English are wicked," she said. "Some, like us, have reasons to loathe Longshanks. Ye just hae tae find yer brethren."

Liza didn't ask how one might undertake such a task, pondering the risk of trusting anyone in these tumultuous times, even those who claimed kinship.

When Liza moved to take her leave, Grete said, "Stay with me this night."

Liza nodded. "Aye, sister." This might well be their last night on this earth together. The thought caused her chest to seize painfully. She and Lachlan had risked much to bring Grete to safety at the castle. Now Grete would willingly give that away for her righteous cause.

Though the chamber was already warm, Grete moved to kindle the fire, fetching a small bundle of logs from the hearth. "Fer a bit o' cheer this eve," she explained in response to Liza's questioning look.

When the fire danced brightly, Liza and Grete sat shoulder to shoulder upon the mattress, their eyes fixed upon the flames' entrancing depths.

Liza spoke first. "I shall no' attempt tae dissuade ye from yer mission."

"And I give my thanks fer that restraint," Grete answered.

"I…" Liza began, then halted, pondering her next words with care. "I chanced upon ye in the cottage with Andrew."

Grete remained silent. Liza averted her gaze to spare them both the shame.

"I ken ye believe ye're in love with him—"

"'Tis undeniable," Grete responded with little shame, but with a simmering anger burning through her words. "O'er these past months, he hath shown me what it means to possess conviction. And he hath taught me there are deeds to be done to right the many wrongs in the world."

"Because he is noble does not mean ye must yield yer body unto him."

Grete cast her eyes upon Liza. "Ye're in no position to chide me on this matter, having done likewise yerself with the bailie."

Liza was momentarily without the power of speech. She was finally able to whisper, "Who has spread that tale?"

"'Seems tae be common knowledge. Moreover, the bailie did not refute the claim when William Wallace inquired of it. In truth, 'tis why Wallace has placed his trust in ye."

Liza's countenance burned in the shadowed night, not from shame but from the sanctity and secrecy of her union with Lachlan. It grieved her that their love served as fodder for idle tongues.

But no matter. Her union with Lachlan was not the subject at hand. "Andrew could have well gotten ye with child," she said tae Grete.

"A happy chance if he has," Grete responded, to Liza's surprise. "I would welcome a bairn of the character of Andrew."

"Ye ken naught of the man." Her retort came swift and firm. Liza had known Lachlan since her earliest days. Though they were not of equal standing, she had grown with his trust and the knowledge of his heart. Even so, she could not imagine bearing a bairn with him. Such a scandal would taint the child for all its days, just as a bairn born to Grete and Andrew would suffer the same fate.

"I know Andrew's father is locked in the dungeon of the Tower of London, a ransom placed on his head by Longshanks himself. The English king knows well the might of Andrew and his warrior companion, William Wallace, and runs scared."

Liza knew not if this claim was true, though Longshanks likely had many men imprisoned in the Tower of London. Perhaps King John had met the same fate. She was dubious Longshanks ran scared from two country ruffians, but she had no hunger to debate the worth of Andrew Moray nor the virtue of his cause. "I'm only worried fer ye, Grete, and wish tae see ye hale and hearty fer all yer days. We've both suffered much loss."

Grete seemed to consider this, then nodded. "Ye're right. Let's no' battle each other with words, on this o' all nights," Grete said.

"When ye depart, I shall endeavor to conceal yer whereabouts," said Liza. "The attendants might perceive yer absence from yer chambers. I can fashion it to appear as if yer chamber is still occupied. With such a significant battle close by, ye may go unnoticed by the sheriff fer a time."

Grete gave a firm nod and clasped Liza's hands tightly. "There'll be others within the castle walls who'll lend their aid. Ye may not know them, but the tales shall be carried far and wide."

"Tell me their names so that I might know the trustworthy souls."

Grete shook her head. "'Tis better ye ken less, not more."

Liza wanted to argue, but a fresh dread stirred within her heart. "And what of Lachlan's absence?" She felt sure she could conceal Grete's absence, but Lachlan played a much larger role within the castle walls.

"The hobelars will be missing, as will Lachlan," Grete replied. "His groomsmen shall give word of the theft and Lachlan's chase after the brigands."

Liza nodded, though she knew it would only be a matter of time before tongues would wag and tales would spread. "How long will ye be gone?" Liza asked, though she dreaded the answer. For she knew not if either Grete or Lachlan might return.

Instead of a response, Grete reached beneath the mattress filled with straw and brought forth a small leather pouch. It was a bag Liza recognized; it had accompanied Grete on that fateful night when Lachlan had transported Grete from Watret Abbey. Liza knew not what had become of it, and had forgotten about it entirely.

Grete handed it to Liza. "Can ye keep this safe fer me?"

"What is it?"

Grete motioned for Liza to open the front flap. Inside, she found a number of small white figures carved from ivory. The visages of each of the figures were glum, and they bore bulging eyes.

"What are they?" asked Liza.

"They are game pieces." Grete reached forward and

plucked a small man bearing a shield and riding atop a diminutive and disproportionate horse. "My grandmother Ingeborg carved them for me afore I was even born."

Liza ran her fingers along one of the larger figures—a queen wearing a wimple and veil sitting atop a throne, her right hand cradling her face. She did not look pleased to be in her position. "What kind of game be this?"

Grete shook her head sadly. "My grandmother fell ill before she could pass on its purpose tae me. And some of the pieces are lost, likely on that cursed isle where my body is meant tae be buried." Grete shrugged. "This is all I have left of my kin."

Liza tucked the smooth ivory back into the pouch and held it to her breast. "I shall guard it with my life and keep it safe within the castle walls," Liza vowed.

Grete let out a gentle laugh. "'Tis just a game."

They fell into companionable silence until Grete said, "I may not return, dear Elesbeth." The declaration was uttered as if the weight of her quest had just occurred to Grete.

"Ye dinnae hae tae go."

"I do. 'Tis my destiny."

"Yer destiny is what ye make o' it."

"Yet *this* is what I make." Her tone was resolute, though fear had caused her voice to tremble.

Liza did not argue further. "I expect we'll meet

again," Liza said instead, and she believed the words with her whole heart.

In the moments that followed, the fire transformed from a blaze to a flickering of merry flames. By and by, Grete said, "We should rest now."

Liza nodded. The words were a portent. For rest would not come easy to either of them for days to come.

Chapter 28

Almost two days since Grete and Lachlan had taken their leave with Andrew Moray and William Wallace, Liza had yet to hear any news of their arrival at Sterling. Information of this import was not typically slow in coming, and the lack of tidings troubled her greatly. Perhaps they'd been captured and imprisoned in some dank quarters. Perhaps they'd been slain before a battle could even take place.

Though Liza dared not voice her queries, she listened keenly in both the great hall and in the bailey courtyard as she distractedly performed her chores. But not a word was spoken among the throng of attendants as they toiled in the mild air of mid-September.

Upon the third morn following the departure of her kinsmen, Donvaldus MacTavish made his way to her side as she lingered by the fallen sycamore, the very spot where Liza herself had lain more than a year past.

Amidst the fields, she'd just gathered the final blossoms of the season to bring cheer to her chamber when she spied a sapling rising where the mighty tree had once been rooted.

She marveled at the miracle of its return to life.

Donvaldus appeared to notice neither the sapling nor Liza's blooms. "The chambermaid Mariot hath given word she's scarce seen yer sister of late. Naught in the past few days and nights." His words were a statement, and given no query, Liza stared at the chamberlain with a blank look.

"Are ye mute now, lady?"

Liza drew herself up. She would not argue with the man, but when her father and brother finally returned, she would surely impart the impudence with which she'd been treated.

Perhaps even Donvaldus sensed the rashness of his words because he retreated in both position and tone. "Have ye knowledge of her whereabouts?"

Liza lingered before answering. She'd been careful, entering Grete's chamber each day to rumple the bedclothes, crafting the illusion of occupancy. "I laid eyes upon my sister not two hours past," said Liza in what she hoped was a heedless voice.

Donvaldus narrowed his eyes. "Is that so? Then where be she now? She's not been spied in the great hall for sustenance. I've inquired around."

"Perhaps she's taking her meals elsewhere."

"The kitchen wenches have seen nothing of her."

Liza opened her mouth to respond, but Donvaldus said, "Dinnae insult me by sayin' the lass is ailin'. If illness is upon her, she'd be now in her chamber, which lies empty."

Liza kept her gaze fixed on her blooms, prepared to deliver her next untruth. Her answer was halted by the swift and urgent approach of Peter Syward, who spared Liza a leering glance.

"Longshanks rides this way from England." His announcement was low and urgent. "I've been given orders," he added, though he said not what those orders were.

Liza glanced about her, but there was nowhere to flee.

"Brings he news of the battle?" Donvaldus asked.

The escheator lifted a shoulder. "I know not his purpose, nor does the sheriff." He turned sharply toward Liza and demanded, "What know ye o' the bailie and his quest tae recover his useless herd of ponies?"

"I know nothing except that which I overheard, same as ye," Liza said.

The man looked as if he didn't believe her, and Donvaldus too raised a thick, bristled eyebrow. "Are both the bailie and the wayward lass yet tae be located?"

When Liza did not readily respond, Peter Syward said, "What o' the bailie's betrothed, the girl, Forsy? Has she news of him?"

Donvaldus shook his head. "She's been sent home

tae tend tae her sickly mother, who lies upon her deathbed."

Liza had not known this of the maiden, and a true sympathy filled her heart for the lass, for she wished the girl no ill will.

"I'm sure the bailie shall not tarry long," said Liza with haste in an attempt to divert suspicion. "He has his duties at the barony."

Her words did little to quell the doubts of the men, who exchanged wary glances. "My orders include takin' care of the vermin, and I scent a rat," said Peter. "A wee, quivering hare about to ken the folly of its deceit."

Before Liza could know his intent, the chamberlain's arms slithered around her, clasping her wrists. She let the flowers tumble to the earth at the root of the sapling. She strained fiercely against his hold. "Unhand me this instant," she snarled, teeth gritted with fury.

Peter Syward's face split with a wicked grin, and he thrust his face close to hers. "I've been biding my time to catch ye alone, Lady Elesbeth, and now, bereft of the bailie's safeguard or the company of the lass, ye stand with scant defense."

Liza knew not of his intent, but any prospect was unseemly—be it questioning, ravishment, or death.

"Shall I take her to the sheriff?" Donvaldus asked as Liza struggled against him.

Peter Syward shook his head. "I want her tae ken

the fear of a scared, trapped animal before I do with her what I must. Take her tae the dungeons."

Liza halted in her movements, and she was thrust toward the chamberlain.

Never had she ventured into the castle's dungeons. As far as she knew, the underground vaults had been unused during her father's time as laird. When she'd been but a bairn, her brother Alexander had told her tales of prisoners shackled to the walls until they'd wasted away to nothing but bones, the vermin feeding on their flesh. Liza had giggled nervously, sure his words were but imaginary tales meant to frighten her. While she prayed this was the case, she shuddered at the thought of sharing a dark chamber with ancient bones. Then she shuddered at the thought of becoming another pile of bones upon the cold stone floor.

As Donvaldus hauled her away, Liza pleaded with him. "Ye cannot lock me up. My father will return soon from France where he's been exiled. I hae it on good authority."

"Save yer beggin' fer the sheriff," the man answered.

Liza held little faith she'd ever stand before the sheriff. Her sole hope lay in Lachlan and Grete's return to rescue her. Yet they could not save her if they could not find her. Her heart quivered at the thought that the last place they'd search would be the dungeons.

Must she pray the English king would summon her

upon his arrival? He'd once ordered her protection along with that of Grete. But that had been many months ago.

Now, with the other happenings across the land, and with Lachlan and Grete missing, he'd perhaps burn her at the stake for some imagined deed of sorcery.

She felt the eyes of the castle's attendants upon her as she was hauled to her doom. Despite her pleas and her cries, none came to her aid. Her reckoning was surely near.

She fell to the ground, which made Donvaldus struggle to haul her up into his arms and carry her through the kitchen. He opened a heavy wooden door and carried her down the dark, damp, dank staircase. They traversed a narrow stone passageway, and she scraped her flesh against the walls in an attempt to free herself.

Finally, he thrust her forward, and she tumbled into a deep pit.

In the weak stream of light coming in from a lone encasement high on the wall, she saw the form of Donvaldus hesitate.

"Donvaldus, I beg of ye…"

Her imploring tone fell on deaf ears, and she tried again.

"My captivity be fer nothing but the accursed merriment of Peter Syward, who has always borne ill will toward me. Should ye release me from this cell, I promise I will entreat my father to grant clemency tae ye upon his return."

He nearly turned; she sensed his hesitation.

He didn't meet her eyes, and his footsteps echoed on the damp stone steps as he walked away. In the distance, the heavy wooden door slammed behind him, leaving her alone in the darkness.

Liza cried out again and again, hoping her voice might meet some ear in the castle kitchen. She knew full well she was far below. And even should her plea reach a cook or a servant, no rescue was likely. Attendants were not in the habit of rescuing prisoners, no matter their station or the name of their clan or kin.

Liza thought of Hexilde, the mistress of the kitchens, who had been her one-time protector. She knew not whether the woman had betrayed the Ramsay name by taking allegiance to King Edward through her consorting with the sheriff, Walter Hastings. Liza's trust had been broken. She knew if such treachery had written her fate, then none of her father's ilk nor any who shared his convictions would stand free, either. And perhaps this then was why she now herself languished in a dungeon.

Moreover, she had no idea what doom Peter Syward had ordained for her. She found it strange indeed that her only slender hope for survival was that the man might deliver her into the hands of Longshanks upon his arrival. But such hope was scant as a flame before a swift hoolan.

Liza clutched her limbs. Her bones and flesh ached from her rough treatment, and the blood pounded fiercely in her head. Still, on and on she cried out, for she had no other choice.

Then, at last, she stilled her cries. Her throat was raw and parched, and her whole being wilted as a downtrodden flower. Liza peered around the dank stone chamber. It was not utterly dark, for a thin shaft of daylight slanted through a small hole high in the stone wall. It was scarce the size of a river stone, but it was something. Liza searched her wits to determine the location of the cleft. Surely its placement was beyond the bailey courtyard and closer to the watchtower, where only English sentinels—who would delight in the wails of a captive—might tread. The stream of light was unbroken by any moving form, either man or beast.

Finally, Liza concluded the presence of the illumi-nation was but a false and cruel hope, and it bid her no solace. She turned away.

Though the day had been mild, the dungeon's depth was cold and clammy. A drip of water echoed from some hidden passage. Clad but in her simple léine and slippers, Liza trembled, and her teeth chattered. Time eluded her; the only mark of its passing was the waning glow from the high aperture which she cursed beneath her breath.

She wondered if tidings of battle had reached the castle. If Lachlan and Grete had survived and saw fit to return, would they seek her? Or would Peter Syward fashion some fanciful tale of her undoing?

The last gleam of daylight finally did leave her, and she found herself in utter blackness, unable to see her own hands before her face. She had spied no bones in the cell—some small comfort—yet cared not to explore further. Sinking upon the cold slab, she drew her knees close, laying her brow against them. Hunger and thirst had begun to gnaw within her, but finally weariness prevailed, and she drifted into uneasy slumber.

In her dreams, she wandered strange realms where hundreds of great, gleaming towers reflected the light and stabbed the sky. Folk in unfamiliar garb surrounded her, pointing and uttering kind words in a tongue she only half recognized. Their faces, though foreign, filled her heart with comfort.

A gentle elder man—one who reminded her greatly of Robert Wishart—reached forth to help her, and she held out her hand. But when he opened his lips, the piercing howl of a night raven emerged, instead. Liza shrunk back as the man's visage twisted into that of John Comyn, holding a dagger in hand above her head.

His mouth opened again, and as he brought the dagger toward her, the same caw sounded from his lips.

Liza recoiled, and with a gasp, she awoke, heart hammering. She was still in her cell.

No kindly man nor the evil John Comyn stood before her, yet that uncanny, beastly caw resounded once more from the opening both above her head and beneath the watchtower.

She waited for another call. Silence ruled the darkness. Had madness finally claimed her? But then again, a low, drawn-out note broke the stillness. The call was close, perhaps just outside the chamber's crevice.

Her throat raw, Liza summoned her voice. Only a hoarse rattle answered. She coughed, then strained to utter a stronger cry that might pierce the walls of stone.

Immediately it was answered by that hooting wail—urgent, imploring—and she called again. Then all fell silent and remained so. Though Liza cried until her voice failed, a reply was not issued.

What seemed hours later came the scrape of boots upon stone. The glow from a rush light flared from the high passageway, and finally, a lone figure stood revealed.

Liza didn't know whether this was lad or lass, friend or foe. Though doom might lurk behind the torch, this shadow was her sole hope.

"Help me, I am here!" she managed to audibly croak from her ruined throat.

In the eerie illumination, the figure lifted a finger to its lips and stepped forward, the flame from the torch sputtering. It placed the rush light upon the stones, then something solid fell against her and spilled to the floor. It was a coiled rope.

Liza knew not if her limbs held the strength, yet she clung to the end of the rope as the figure drew the twine tight. After much struggle, the figure—whom she discerned to be a man—at last managed to heave her up the walls of the cell. Her legs faltered beneath her, and he clasped her against his solid frame.

"You must remain sturdy of body and of heart," he whispered with an English lilt. "And we must make haste." He waited until her feet were sure upon the stone, then he flung a heavy mantle about her shoulders to shield her from watchful eyes. He picked up the sputtering flame and said, "Stay close to my side, and if we be halted, hide your face and prepare to flee to the river."

Steadily, they retreated from the dungeon's corridors, emerging into the desolate kitchen. The man's breath flowed rhythmically, and Liza endeavored to match her faltering breaths to his unwavering cadence. They made their way out the rear door, traversing the gardens with cautious tread.

Though Liza asked not their course, her heart knew the path. Under a waning moon, they fled over the grounds, then slipped into the wood, the murmur of the River Creagan close beside. When Liza stumbled over ancient and gnarled roots, the stranger seized her firmly, setting her right and guiding their path anew. Not a soul did they meet.

Presently, they reached the familiar stone dwelling by the water's edge. Holding her behind him, the man peered inside. Once he'd determined the cottage to be empty, he guided her inside. The man lit two candles, their glow feeble in the gloom. He guided her to the blankets in the larger of the chambers and bid her rest. Then he produced a crust of bread and a small flask of venison broth. Liza ate and drank deeply.

She had questions for the stranger—who was he and why was he helping her? But she dared not ask. Instead, she said, "What news of our friends?"

"They make their way homeward, but must keep their march secret," he replied.

Liza noted only his voice—broad and youthful, yet hardened by his tasks.

"Longshanks possesses your stronghold, Lady Elesbeth. Our kinsmen must remain hidden."

He knew her identity. And his voice was grim, hinting at a journey gone awry.

"But they live?"

His strong jaw was set firm in the wan light. "Aye."

Relief coursed through her, lightening her limbs. "And what of the quest?"

"Moray and his men fell upon the English like

wolves upon lambs. Moray's strategy prevailed. The foe was trapped at the river's crook, their banners torn, their men felled, and they did yield. John de Warenne, Earl of Surrey and the surrogate of Longshanks, retreated with his tail between his legs. Stirling Castle is possessed by Scotland again."

A bloom of both astonishment and joy rose in Liza's breast. She let out a laugh. "Surely we should make merry," she said, slightly with question.

The man shook his head. "Now is no time for high spirits," he said.

"Why?" Liza's voice was a whisper.

The man shook his head and seemed prepared to answer. Then the sound of distant voices did meet their ears.

"I must away," he said. "Venture not beyond these walls. Stay hidden and silent, and if any approach, hide yourself well." Before Liza could query again, he'd reached the threshold where he turned back. "Nothing is safe here and there are few you can trust."

With no other words, her unknown savior vanished into the night's embrace.

Chapter 29

Heeding the counsel of the benevolent stranger, Liza doused the candle's glow and nestled herself beneath the woolen blankets bearing the scent of horse and men. And though her nose did quiver, she stifled the urge to sneeze. She quickly fell into another slumber, though this sleep was deep and dark and dreamless.

Yet when a loud commotion did reach her ears, she awakened quickly and used the blankets to hide herself in a darkened corner of the room. There came the sound of horses' hooves, soft nickers, then hushed, urgent whispers.

A group of souls entered the chamber, and they marked not Liza in the shadowed corner. Liza dared not move nor make her presence known. She became as stone, though her heart clattered within her breast.

Then the breathless voice of Grete spoke. "Not here. Bear him to the back chamber…to the straw mattress that shall ease his pain and bring him comfort."

A low murmur answered, and footfalls shuffled as

Liza cast aside her blankets.

"Grete!" she cried, her voice breaking through the hush of night.

Three of the four who stood before her started back, and one drew his broadsword quick as a spark. Thomas MacClure's blade almost struck her breast before Lachlan flung down his burden, sprang forward, and struck the man's wrist, sending the metal to the ground with a thud.

Though Liza stumbled back, she had but time enough to spy the burden, abandoned by Lachlan, yet still partly cradled in Grete's arms. It was Andrew Moray, pale as moonlight, lying rigid and still. Grete's face was a storm of grief, fury, surprise, and resolve. Thomas MacClure's jaw was set in grim silence.

Lachlan bore Liza into his arms. "Ye're safe," he murmured. "We had word ye'd been taken prisoner."

"I had been," Liza answered. Her ordeal seemed of little import now. Her eyes remained fixed on Moray's motionless form. "Is he…dead?"

"Nay," Grete said swiftly. "We shall save him."

Lachlan and Thomas exchanged grave glances, and Liza knew not what more to say. Though her tribulation in the dungeon had been fearsome, she had not been near to meeting her end.

Grete turned to Lachlan. "The weight is too heavy for me alone."

He set Liza down, then, with Grete, bore their fallen friend to the rear chamber. Liza hurried behind while Thomas stood guard at the threshold.

"What has befallen him?" she asked as they laid him upon the straw. Then she saw the dark stain upon his left side. The blood had soaked through his clothing, turning it black.

"Have we ale or mead for him to sip?" Grete entreated.

Liza cursed her greed for imbibing the last draught of broth when she'd entered the cottage. Surely, she could not have known…

"I'll fetch some at once," Thomas said, and before he vanished into the gray dawn, he said to Lachlan, "Ye must keep watch."

Lachlan dismissed Thomas with a gesture of his arm. His focus was torn between Andrew Moray and Liza, whom he clasped close by his side. Liza perceived a shift in the air between them. No longer would they fret over rightful ranks and stations. This war—and the trials they had endured—had altered the course of all things. Though this brought her contentment, she felt the sorrow of Grete's lament as if it were her own.

Her sister's face was caked with mire, her fair hair darkened by earth. Yet it was her look—so cleaved by sorrow and rage—that rendered her nearly unrecognizable as she cradled Moray's head upon her lap.

Liza turned to Lachlan and said quietly, "What of Wallace?"

Lachlan bowed his head. "Wallace yet lives. When victory was ours, he seized Stirling Castle, and will soon ride tae Edinburgh tae vow his allegiance to Robert the Bruce and Scotia. Our triumph turns the tide in our favor, and Wallace shall take his rightful place as leader of this rising and new Guardian of the Realm."

Though Lachlan's tone was gentle, Grete cried, "He takes Andrew's rightful place!"

At her outcry, Moray's lids fluttered open. Liza saw the awakening in him first. Her mouth fell open, prompting Grete to look down and gasp at the sight.

"Grete," Moray whispered hoarsely.

"Oh, Andrew, ye have awakened," Grete wept, her expression at once tilting toward joy. "Conserve yer strength. Thomas will bring ale to slake yer thirst."

He shook his head, but the movement was slight. "I crave neither food nor drink."

"Ye must take strength," she pleaded. "Soon shall ye ride once more upon the field and claim yer place. Stirling was *your* victory, and all of Scotia will hear the tales of yer brilliance and bravery."

A soft smile crossed his lips. He raised a trembling hand to stroke Grete's soiled cheek, wincing with the effort. "Wallace shall take my place."

Grete clasped his hand to her cheek and shook her head. "Nay—you are the rightful leader."

"Nay, *mo ghràdh*," he murmured in Gaelic, "'tis ye

who are the rightful leader of this land."

Grete closed her eyes, and a single tear carved its path through the grime on her face. "I would give it all up tae stand by yer side."

"Ye will always be by mine side," he whispered. "Always."

The gentle sobs of Grete tore at Liza's heart. She guided Lachlan from the chamber so the lovers could share their last moments together, all aware the end was upon them.

The dawn's light seeped through the windows, and Lachlan tenderly caressed Liza's cheek much like Moray had done to Grete.

"Are ye well, my love?"

She smiled and nodded. He'd scarce made his feelings for her known, and her stomach fluttered, though she did bid it still as she spoke. "An Englishman saved me—one of the guards—after Peter Syward commanded the chamberlain to imprison me in the dungeons. I know not what fate awaited me there. Perhaps they meant to deliver me to Longshanks."

"Edward does no' reside alone," Lachlan warned. "John Comyn also makes his presence known in the keep. Both are wrathful and shamed by their defeat at Stirling. Who can say what vengeance they might seek?"

"Do they know if my father still lives?" Liza asked, anxious for their lands to be set right once more.

"If Wallace has such tidings, it is likely Longshanks too holds the knowledge."

As Liza was considering this, Lachlan continued, "Young Edward is to wed King Phillip's sister, and the exile o' yer father and brother in the countryside shall be made perilous."

Liza shook her head. "France holds sympathy for Scotia's cause."

"The marriage is Edward's bid at peace with King Phillip."

With the loss of support and England's strengthened reinforcements, this boded ill for both their country and their kin. Then Lachlan's meaning dawned upon her. She looked up at him sharply. "We cannot return to the castle."

Lachlan nodded. "Aye, which is why ye were brought here tae the cottage—tae await our return to fetch ye away."

"Where will we go?"

"Wallace has secured a spot by the name of Auchinleck above the Lugar Water in a remote eastern shire. We shall be safe and hidden there."

A sob welled in Liza's throat. She was loathe to leave her home, and it grieved her as though a death. And yet, it was not her love who was dying. She steeled herself and swallowed her tears. "What of Moray?" she asked quietly. "Can he survive?"

Liza knew the answer before Lachlan shook his

head. "It was Grete's desire tae bring him here to pass to the heavenly realm in peace. 'Tis a rash idea, but the passing shall not be long."

They shared a moment of solemn silence.

Then Liza asked a question she must have an answer to. "What of Forsy?"

Lachlan averted his gaze. "I've sent word to her I shall away for my safety."

"But not for *me*." She knew she was being petulant, yet her heart ached at his half-truth.

Lachlan caught Liza's hands in his. "Aye, I have told her o' my love fer ye. I will not deny ye, Liza. Ne'er again."

Liza's heart caught in her throat, and just as he leaned in to kiss her, a shadow darkened the doorway and a voice thundered, "Well, is this not just the picture of love and happiness amongst traitors!"

Lachlan and Liza sprang apart, and beheld the looming and foreboding form of John Comyn. Liza shrank back, though her eyes darted around, seeking something she might wield as a weapon against him. Lachlan did likewise, for he bore neither sword nor dagger.

"I couldnae help but overhear yer tender words," said the man to Lachlan. "I must give my thanks to ye for alertin' yer spurned lover, the maiden Forsy, to yer plan." He lowered his tone. "Ye have much to learn about the fairer sex. They seek revenge when cast aside." He gestured toward Liza. "Especially when discarded fer a witch."

Liza's gaze drifted to the window, but the evil Guardian caught her intent. "Nay, ye won't, lassie. Ye're mine now." He advanced toward her. "Though I think I'll chain ye to the dungeon wall, as I bade Peter Syward do." He shook his head. "One can ne'er send a meek lad tae complete a man's task."

"It was ye…" Liza began and backed toward the rear chamber.

John Comyn laughed heartily. "Ye feign surprise." Then he shrugged. "In fairness, I suppose, I've tried to slay ye afore and failed."

Liza blanched as the man continued, "'Tis a pity how much the maiden wench Wyolet resembled ye from behind." He turned to Lachlan. "I reckon ye were also bedding her, too. Ye seem to like the harlot wenches."

A fury swept across Lachlan's expression, and John Comyn marked this response keenly.

He bared his teeth. "I didnae fail in capturing the wee rogue Uilleam, though. The bastard bairn caught wind of my scheming to do away with Margaret, the Maid of Norway, on her voyage to Orkney."

Liza's heart squeezed in her chest as the flood of anger filled her breast.

She caught a movement from the corner of her eye. Grete. She needed to distract John Comyn further if they were to have any chance at all.

"And Claray," she spat. "Did ye kill her, too?"

The man sighed. "Aye, an error. I'd entered yer room tae lay waste tae ye once and fer all, and she followed me in the darkness. I didnae ken until the next morn it was the lady I'd slain instead of ye. Pity, that. I rather enjoyed bedding her."

"Ye've been found wantin' in nearly every matter," Liza declared. "Ye've even failed in standin' with King John and Longshanks. Stirling's fall is a victory fer Robert the Bruce, yer sworn adversary. And William Wallace does ride again."

John Comyn's grin twisted into a snarl; he bared his teeth like a wolf giving warning. "Wallace is naught but a brigand," he declared, "and I find pleasure in knowing the true menace, Andrew Moray, lies slain. The fall of Moray may well have been worth the surrender of Stirling."

Liza opened her mouth to offer a retort, and before she realized what was happening, Grete did fly from the back chamber wielding a *sgian dubh*. As she was about to plunge the blade into the flesh of John Comyn, he moved swiftly and caught the girl's wrist, then wrenched her against him.

Lachlan took this opportunity to pounce, but the Guardian pivoted, and using Grete's blade, he pierced the flesh and sinew of Lachlan's arm. Lachlan cried out, and Liza whirled around, wide-eyed.

All was silent for a moment, save for the labored breath of both Grete and Lachlan. The Guardian began to laugh.

"Do I dare tae believe I hold the Maid of Norway in my arms?" he declared, curling his arm about her neck to hinder her breath. "Walter Hastings told me it be so—the corpulent cook brought him the news. I did no' believe it at first, but curiosity got the better of me, so I sent inquiries tae the Isle of Orkney. A purse full of coin can be a powerful persuasion for many a truth. Imagine my shock when I discovered that Robert Wishart himself—the daft old man—rescued the lass from her destined demise."

He clenched his hold until Grete's face flushed crimson and her breath gurgled in her throat. "I understand why the bailie made his way back—for the sake of his beloved Elesbeth Ramsay. Yet why would a maiden of yer stature tread these perilous lands again?"

He surveyed the trio before him, and a knowing look dawned upon his face. Casting his gaze toward the rear chamber, he whispered, "Ah, 'tis love's folly indeed." Another wicked laugh escaped his lips.

As he turned his back and entered the rear chamber, Liza leapt to Lachlan. She tore a strip of cloth from her léine to tie around his blood-soaked arm.

"Ye must ride swiftly," Liza whispered. "I shall stay with Grete."

"I'll not leave without ye."

Before Liza could answer, John Comyn's laughter echoed from the room. "So Andrew Moray does lie before me," he said. "And he is alive, but barely."

Grete's choked voice responded, "Dare not ye touch him."

"I don' think I hae te. He'll be dead soon enough. Isn't that right, nephew?"

Liza froze. *Nephew.*

"'Tis no true!" yelled Grete. Andrew's weak voice followed. "I shall ne'er claim ye as my kin, just as my mother denounced ye."

Liza stared at Lachlan whose mouth fell agape.

"Think I care of yer mother's judgments? Along with her, ye've brought shame upon the Comyn Clan and kin, and ye've done a great disservice tae our uncle King John Balliol."

"King John was betrayed by none other than the likes of ye," Andrew said.

"It matters not now. Toom Tabard has been exiled, and yer cause shall be extinguished presently, just like yer life. And the life of the lassie here ye love. The Maid o' Norway," said the Guardian grandly, mockingly. "English interest must prevail if we are tae keep our power and our lands."

"A curse on both," Andrew said, and spat weakly.

John Comyn chuckled. "It is most fortunate ye lie yet awake, nephew. Ye can watch me slit the throat o' the Queen o' Scotia. I'll kindly allow ye tae lie together in death."

Liza rushed into the chamber, heeding not Lachlan's warning cry. It was at that moment Thomas MacClure flew into the dwelling wielding a sharpened broadsword.

As they both lunged toward the Guardian, a confusion ensued, and it was Thomas MacClure's weapon that did clamor to the floor. Grete lunged to retrieve it. The Guardian brought Grete's dirk above him, preparing to plunge it into the maiden's neck.

Liza acted on instinct, shoving her sister aside with force, taking her place as the blade descended toward her. It pierced her chest with ease. She felt no pain, only a fierce pressure and a mild surprise.

Turning away from her attacker, she managed to call out to her kinsmen, "Take leave now!"

In what seemed like slow motion, Lachlan rushed toward her, while John Comyn withdrew the *sgian dubh* to confront Liza's would-be protector. The warm flow of her blood escaped her chest. There was a sharp, intense pain that nearly as quickly subsided.

Liza's limbs grew heavy, and her vision narrowed.

It was difficult to speak, but she managed, "Lachlan, ye must save Grete, and ye must fight to save Scotia." She gasped as she collapsed against the inert form of Andrew Moray.

Thomas MacClure gripped his broadsword, and with a savage cry sliced the thigh of John Comyn. The man fell to the ground, wounded. But Liza knew he would again rise.

"Take him away, Thomas," Liza gasped, referring to Lachlan. Then to Lachlan, who was bent over her, futilely attempting to quell the flow of her blood, she said, "I will find ye again."

"No," he cried out. But Thomas grabbed him. "Liza, I will stay with ye forever."

Her eyes closed to the dim image of Thomas and Grete dragging Lachlan from the room as John Comyn struggled to rise. A bellow escaped his lips as his quarry escaped.

She thought she heard the sound of horses as an inky, velvety, beautiful blackness enveloped her.

Next to the resting body of Andrew Moray, Liza smiled. Then she slept.

Chapter 30

"Liza!" The deep and troubled voice reverberated through the shadowy void of her mind.

Liza felt herself being dragged from the comforting embrace of oblivion into the harsh and naked light of some unknown consciousness. She made a humming sound at the back of her throat before she could summon the strength to lift her heavy eyelids.

The urgent, agonized call came again.

"Liza!"

She knew this baritone. She knew this man.

With great effort, she wet her lips and croaked, "Lachlan? Be that ye?"

"Liza…" This time, the urgent tone was tinged with relief. "Can ye hear me?"

She exhaled and blinked her eyes open slowly—first one, then the other. The light was brilliant, and she furrowed her brow as she lifted a heavy arm to block the intensity of the world of the living.

"Oh, my God…*thank you*," Lachlan repeatedly murmured, recognizing an entity she'd never heard him entreat.

Liza was dimly aware of his words, but she was focused on fitting the pieces of her existence together. Her memories were muddled. There had been a cottage and a king. There had been a war. There had been…a sister?

That couldn't be right.

She prodded her temples with her fingers, as if to ensure she were made of flesh and bone.

The last memory she had was of lying on a straw mattress…

She shook the memory free, thinking it might have been an illusion.

There had been lights—thousands of sparkling lights, then a great crack of thunder…

Or had this image been but a dream, too?

Lachlan gently pulled her close against his chest. "What were ye doin' out in the storm, ye silly lass?" He laughed, and the sound bordered on maniacal. "I thought I might've lost ye." He laughed again, but another sound bubbled up into the words.

Liza blinked, struggling to look at him. When his handsome face came into focus, his cheeks were wet.

Was he…crying?

She made another humming sound to clear her throat. "There's no need fer weepin'," she managed. "I'm right here, in yer arms."

Lachlan breathed and stared down at her, his expression transforming from wild-eyed relief to confusion. "Why are ye talkin' that way?"

"Like what?"

"Yer words are liltin' with a brogue..." He shook his head, his tone angry. "This is no time for jokes. I thought I'd lost ye."

Liza wasn't sure of his meaning, and she didn't answer. Instead, she looked around her. She was in a bedchamber. *Bedroom*, she corrected herself silently. This was her bedroom. The one she shared with Lachlan.

Lachlan...

Why did she feel as though she'd lost him? When the next sob came, it was from her own chest. At his alarmed expression, she inhaled sharply, attempting to quell the emotion. His stare was intense, and she remained bewildered. She buried her face into his chest. Again, he pulled her close.

She had come home, she knew. But...from where?

Not only was she dreadfully thirsty, she felt an intense pressure in her chest. She put some space between them and placed a hand to her breast. She seemed well and whole.

When she trusted herself to speak again, she asked, "Could I have some water?" These words, she spoke slowly, forming each syllable with great care.

"O' course." He laid her gently against the soft pillows that felt like resting upon fluffy white clouds themselves.

He rushed into the adjacent washroom, and she heard the forceful rush of water from the tap. "I think ye may hae been struck by lightnin' in the storm," he said over the water's flow. "The poor old tree took a direct hit, it would seem. Dr. Patel is on his way tae check ye out."

Liza conjured the memory of the middle-aged doctor who'd cared for Laird Callum Ramsay, and who'd examined her after she'd been trapped in the castle's secret passageways less than a year prior.

"Dr. Patel," she repeated as Lachlan handed her a glass filled with cloudy tap water.

"I'll call fer Sadie tae bring ye up some tea. I fear yer heart may hae stopped fer a time, but it beats strong now. He may want ye to head to the hospital tae be safe."

Liza took a sip from the glass, and the tepid water washed down her throat. She very nearly could feel the liquid flowing through her limbs, as if she weren't quite solid.

If she'd been struck by a powerful force, wouldn't she feel worse than she did? Instead, she felt as if she'd woken from a long, strange slumber.

When she'd drained the glass, she handed it to Lachlan. "May I have a bit more?" The lilt had returned, but just slightly, and she added, "Please," in her normal American voice.

She was caught between two worlds, teetering on

the edge of each, yet unable to fully grasp the other. She held onto fleeting fragments of a fading dream, trying to remember more, but unsure if she truly wanted to recall the details.

When she'd drunk down the second glass, she felt more herself. She noticed her clothing—a pair of jeans and a plain green blouse—was damp and covered in dirt. She wore no shoes, and her feet felt sodden. Her fingertips tingled.

"I–I don't remember what happened," she said.

Lachlan set the tumbler on the side table and said, "Ye didn't come tae bed last night. When I woke early this mornin', I thought I'd find ye in the library, then the kitchens, or the office. Finally, I glanced out the window, and there ye were—unconscious—under the great sycamore."

"The sycamore," Liza murmured. Something shifted in her mind.

"Ye wouldnae awake, though ye were breathin' just fine. If there was a lightnin' strike…" His words trailed off. "I've heard tales of people bein' struck. The electricity scrambles their insides."

Liza held a hand to her temple. She remembered being under the tree when the strike hit. And then…she remembered something else. She remembered waking up under that tree on her own with Lachlan leaning over her, he taken aback when she'd reached up to embrace him.

She remembered a woman named Claray—her stepmother. And a boy named Uilleam—her brother. Other images began to flood her mind, and the memories must have been broadcast on her face, because Lachlan leaned close and stared at her intently.

"Liza, what's wrong?"

She shook her head. She couldn't possibly express the avalanche of memories and emotions crashing over her.

How could she explain that once upon a time their love had been forbidden? That a Scottish Guardian of the Realm from the first wars of independence had tried and failed to kill her more than once before ultimately succeeding?

How could she explain she'd had a brother who'd been murdered by the same man, and a make-believe sister who'd been born the rightful heir to the Scottish throne? A sister who'd fallen in love with a hero of battle who'd never received his proper due?

"Could you…?" Her words trailed off as she began to weep. Lachlan moved closer, and Liza held up a hand. "I just need… Could you check on the tea?"

He didn't immediately move, and she whispered an urgent, "Please." She needed just a moment to herself.

"I'll be right back," he mumbled.

But before he got to the doorway, Liza thought of something. "Lachlan…"

He turned back.

"What happened to John Comyn?"

He frowned, shaking his head. "I don' ken anyone by that name."

"John Comyn of Badenoch," she clarified. "The Scottish Guardian."

"From the First War of Independence?" A furrow appeared on his forehead.

She nodded, and he looked poised to question her further. She silently begged him not to interrogate her, and perhaps her telepathic plea worked because he finally said, "If I remember my history, he was killed by Robert the Bruce, some say in Greyfriars Kirk in Dumfries, but my gran once told me his murder had taken place no' far from here in the old Watret Abbey."

"The Watret Abbey," Liza exclaimed. She knew that place.

Lachlan nodded. "The place is nothing but ruins now, if even the ruins remain."

At this, Liza laughed, and Lachlan regarded her as if she were mad. "Why would ye ask that?"

Liza overlooked his query. "What about Robert Wishart? Did he live a long life?"

Lachlan raised his hands helplessly. "We really need tae get ye tae the doctor—"

"Please," Liza entreated.

Lachlan sighed again. "Wishart fought for Robert the Bruce and the independence of the nation against King Edward. I think he was captured for a time, but released and lived his final days in peace." His eye-brows again knitted together. "It's odd ye should bring him up. There were always whispers Robert Wishart was the one who sent Robert the Bruce to kill John Comyn at the chapel in the abbey. Did ye read that somewhere?"

Liza smiled, relieved. "I must have. And what about the Maid of Norway?"

He had given up arguing with her, though frustration colored his words. "Ye're testin' my memory of Scotland's history along with my patience," he said. "Margaret, Maid o' Norway, died during passage from Norway to Orkney when she was a girl."

"And there was never any sighting of her again?"

He began to shake his head, then looked at her, mystified. "Actually, there was a story a woman claimin' tae be Margaret returned to Norway at some point. But her identity was proved false, and the imposter was burned at the stake, accused of witchcraft or sorcery."

Liza nodded, mourning the sister she didn't know.

"I know of William Wallace," she said. "But what of Andrew Moray?"

"He died after he fell at the Battle of Stirling Bridge. Some have said it was he who should have been the hero in the fight for independence during those first wars."

Liza rubbed her temples. She could still feel Andrew's body beside hers as they lay dying.

"And William and Alexander Ramsay? Did they return from their exile in France during the First War of Independence?"

Lachlan gave her a strange look. "Aye, tae my knowledge. We can check the family records in the library." He made an impatient gesture with his hand. "How would ye ken tae ask these questions? Hae ye been studyin' yer Scottish heritage in secret?"

Liza nearly told him all of it then. Of Claray, Uilleam, and Grete. Of Hexilde, Wyolet, and Forsy. Of John Comyn, Robert Wishart, Peter Syward, and Donvaldus MacTavish. Of William Wallace and Andrew Moray. But she didn't. She *couldn't*. It was a story for another day.

Before Lachlan could leave, Sadie came into the room tentatively with a breakfast tray of tea. "My lady," she said.

Liza widened her eyes. "Call me Liza!"

She watched as Sadie exchanged a glance with Lachlan. "Well, I won' be doin' that, but okay." She set the tray next to Liza and set about pouring her tea. "I'm glad ye're well," she said. "Ye gave us all a scare, and right before yer weddin'."

"Wedding!" Liza exclaimed. She hadn't forgotten, but her mind had been filled with the whole of another life and death. A whole other existence where a wedding with Lachlan could never be.

In this life, nothing must go wrong. There was no chance she'd lose Lachlan again.

Sadie said, "Mr. McClaren, yer kin, Margaret, is on her way."

And at this, Liza glanced up sharply. "I must meet her." But this was a silly demand. She already knew her.

Lachlan cocked his head. "How about ye see the doctor and rest afore ye meet visitors."

Liza was firm in her resolve, and she argued until Lachlan finally gave in.

Sadie took her leave, and Lachlan sat back down beside her on the mattress. "*Mo ghràdh*," he addressed her in his Scots Gaelic, taking her hand. "We can postpone the ceremony. Ye've had a scare."

Liza blinked at him. "Last night…" Even as she uttered the phrase, she paused, considering the illusion of time. That conversation with Lachlan had in one sense taken place the day before, but in another perception, over seven centuries had cleaved the distance. She took a breath. "You said some things that made me think you might be having second thoughts about the wedding. Do ye now want tae marry me?" she asked, aware the lilt had returned naturally.

This time, he didn't comment upon it, and his silence caused her heart to hammer. Had she lost him for centuries only to lose him once again?

"Elesbeth," he finally whispered, and her breath

caught in her throat. "A thousand deaths couldnae keep me from marryin' ye in this lifetime."

Liza pressed her lips to his, and he returned the kiss deeply.

She had come home. Home was the Ramsay Castle, yes. But it was also Lachlan McClaren.

A movement at the doorway caught her attention, and she looked over to find a tall, regal-looking blonde woman politely averting her eyes. "I'm so sorry to interrupt," she said in a familiar musical lilt. "Sadie directed me to come here straightaway."

"Margaret," Lachlan said, and jumped from Liza's side to greet his cousin. She accepted his embrace, but her eyes were on Liza, and Liza's on her.

If Lachlan noticed, he gave no indication. Instead, he ushered her over to Liza's bedside. "This is my soon-tae-be wife, Liza Ramsay," he said, then added, "She's had a minor incident."

Liza smiled at this depiction of what had befallen her. And she also smiled at this woman. At *Grete*.

"It's good to see you," said Liza.

"And you, as well," said Margaret in her melodic accent. Her voice was thick with meaning.

A spark passed and burned brightly between them, and when they joined hands, the bond was unbreakable. All of their memories merged, including their final, fateful meeting, when Liza had taken a blade to her chest—a dagger intended for the woman before her.

"A light emerges," murmured Grete. "Ye are now that light, Elesbeth."

Liza's eyes filled with tears. "As ye hae always been, Margaret. *We* are the light."

Epilogue

Liza stood alone in the narrow antechamber opposite the chapel, her antique ivory lace gown whispering lightly against the stone floor. Sunlight filtered through a slender stained-glass window, painting ruby and sapphire patches on the worn oak desk where a ledger once lay.

Centuries ago, this had been the chancery of Peter Syward, the very man who'd condemned her to the castle dungeons at the behest of John Comyn. Today, it served as a quiet office. For Liza, the walls still held the faint echo of the footsteps of the seneschal.

She was satisfied these walls would today bear witness to her joy.

Her wedding dress fit her perfectly. Ivory silk overlaid with lace that was threaded with silver strands. The bodice was cinched snug around her slender waist as the skirt billowed in gentle folds. In her hands, she held a simple bouquet of pink and white Juliet roses, and she gazed into their fragrant blooms as 'Scotland the Brave' met her ears from the bellows of a bagpipe as their guests gathered and made their way to their seats.

Shortly, 'Highland Cathedral' would begin to play, indicating Lachlan would have moved to his place at the altar, followed by Detective Chief Inspector Marion Dean, who would officiate the ceremony.

Finally, Liza would walk down the rose-petal-adorned aisle to the music of 'She Moved Through the Fair.' And honestly, Liza had moved through both the fair and the dark alike. But her wedding day was all light. She would allow no darkness this day. Only perfection.

Liza longed only for the ceremony to begin, for the moment when she could step beyond dusty corridors and be truly joined with Lachlan at last. She had waited centuries for it.

Her grandfather, who had originally planned to escort her down the aisle, now sat in the congregation. The long hours of travel had rendered him nearly immobile. Even over the past year, he and her grandmother had aged by what seemed like decades.

He'd insisted he could still do this duty, but Liza's will was stronger, and she'd pressed a kiss to his forehead, promising him the first dance, instead, if he was up for it. Liza had been on her own for so long, and she'd been through so much. Walking herself down the aisle felt fine to her, and she did not fret the change in plans.

As 'Scotland the Brave' played on, a soft rap sounded on the door.

Marion Dean—who'd saved Liza from death on more than one occasion—peered in. The woman wore her short brown hair shorn close to her scalp, and she was clad in a dark suit, tailored and crisp. Unlike her aged grandparents, Dean seemed to have reverse-aged a decade. Her skin was clear, her body was toned and fit, and her eyes were bright. Working private security and investigations for the billionaire Petrus Bothas clearly suited her more than her past role as detective chief inspector for the Specialist Crime Division.

But behind her glasses, her brown eyes brimmed with concern. "Are ye all right?" she asked.

Liza offered her a smile. "I'm fine. Thrilled, even. Why wouldn't I be?"

Dean strode into the room, her sensible dress shoes clicking on the flagstones. Liza embraced her, careful not to rumple either Dean's perfectly pressed suit or her gown. "I'm glad you're here," Liza murmured.

"When I arrived yesterday, ye hadn't mentioned yer…incident under the sycamore. I just heard the talk out there. Rumor has it ye were out cold on the very ground under which we found Brodie Graham hanging."

Liza didn't say anything.

"So, it's true? Not an exaggeration?"

"I'm fine *now*," Liza insisted.

Dean narrowed her eyes. "There's more tae the story, though, isn't there?" In response to Liza's silence, she said, "Ye aren't a good tale-teller, ye ken that, lassie?"

"There may be more to the story, but I'll need a stiff drink or three before I tell it to you."

Dean's lips curved. "I'll take ye up on that after we get ye married off tae that handsome groom. Perhaps some Spirits Rose," she said, referring to the brand of whisky that had flowed so freely between the billionaires who'd been sequestered in the castle the prior winter. Liza made a face at its mention. Rabbie Rose, the proprietor of Spirits Rose, was still in prison, but the company itself had seen renewed interest after his arrest.

Dean waved the memory away. "I have an offer fer ye. A request of sorts, really."

Liza frowned and gestured toward her gown. "I don't think I'm in a position to grant requests at the moment."

Dean lowered her voice. "Ye can grant this one. His Royal Highness would be honored to escort you down the aisle."

Liza's eyes widened. "The Duke of Rothesay wants to give me away?" She was referring to His Royal Highness, the Prince of Wales, by his Scottish title, used while he was on Scottish land.

"Aye. He still feels partially responsible for the scandal last winter." Dean gave her a sheepish look. "So do I, fer that matter."

Liza waved her flowers in front of her, and from them streamed the lovely scent of roses.

Dean cleared her throat and continued, "His Majesty asked me personally. I told him I'd convey yer answer." She paused. "He doesn't want to distract from the day, though," Dean added. "If ye think the action would cause yer guests tae look at him instead of ye…"

Of course that would be the case, Liza thought. But the one person who would be looking at her instead of the Duke of Rothesay was Lachlan McClaren. And he was the only one who mattered to Liza.

In fact, all the better.

"Please tell him I would be honored," said Liza.

"Are ye sure?"

"I am."

Dean nodded. "He's just outside. Shall I send him in?"

"Please." Liza smoothed her skirt, took a steadying breath, and watched Dean slip through the doorway.

A moment later, the heavy door opened again, and the Prince of Wales, the Scottish Duke of Rothesay, entered. Tall and muscular, with fair hair cropped closely to his scalp, he was dressed modestly, though he wore a sash of the deep red tartan of his house.

Liza curtsied deeply, her skirt skimming the floor.

The distinctive notes of 'Highland Cathedral' filled the air, indicating Lachlan was making his way to the altar to wait for his bride.

"Please rise," the prince said in a low voice. "This is your day, my lady." He tipped his head in a courteous bow. "And I'm honored to be the one to accompany you on your journey to your future."

She straightened and looped her arm through his.

As they waited for the cue of 'She Moved Through the Fair' to enter the chapel, Liza hesitated, then said, "Is this not…painful for you given your recent loss?"

A muscle ticked in his jaw. "It is," he admitted. "Seeing you in your elegant costume brings back many happy memories of my own wedding day." He lifted a shoulder in a shrug. "But life waits for no one, and I suspect now is as good a time as any to get on with it."

"It doesn't wait. You're right," Liza murmured. "But it's also no time at all. You'll see her again in the blink of an eye."

He glanced at her curiously. "I wish I could believe that."

Liza smiled. "I expect you'll see soon enough."

Before he could question her further, the sweet notes of her entrance song began to play. "The moment has arrived," she said. The moment she'd been waiting for over 700 long years, which had passed in a flash of light. The space of a dream.

The prince patted her hand as the doors to the chapel were swept open by two men.

On the left stood the round beaming face of Bruce Baxter, once her foe and now a steadfast friend. To her right, Liza's breath caught as she recognized Thomas MacClure, the criminal-turned-warrior who'd fought valiantly for Scotland's freedom and saved Lachlan and Grete from peril centuries earlier. He had not been able to save Liza, but not for want of trying. In this lifetime, he was an American who'd met Lachlan by chance a decade earlier at university.

When their eyes met, his gaze danced with amusement. "It's good to see you again, my lady," he said softly.

She opened her mouth, but no words came out. The haunting notes of the music wound around her and the gazes of the standing congregation felt demanding and invasive in their awe.

Her knees trembled, and the prince's arm steadied her. "Take your time," he whispered. "These few steps can feel heavy."

She nodded, and they moved slowly down the aisle under a kaleidoscope of colors made brilliant by the light of day through the stained glass.

The faces of the guests were bright with smiles and tears, but Liza's gaze sought only one pair of eyes. Lachlan stood at the altar, his expression so tender it made her chest ache. In that moment, centuries of longing and separation melted away.

Beside Lachlan, as witness to the ceremony, stood his cousin, the beautiful Norwegian maid, her fair hair pinned neatly at her nape.

The prince leaned close. "Who is she?" he murmured.

"Margaret," Liza replied softly. "A dear friend. She's been like a sister to me for years."

Liza realized she'd been waiting for Grete, too, though she hadn't known it.

"Will you do me the honor of offering a proper introduction after the ceremony?" he whispered.

Liza smiled. "It would be my pleasure," she answered in a whisper.

When they reached the altar, the prince kissed her cheek, and Liza handed her bouquet to Margaret, who met her with a warm, encouraging smile, though her gaze drifted to the prince, who was staring right back. Perhaps Margaret, Maid of Norway, would take her rightful place upon the throne in *this* lifetime.

Lachlan stepped forward to take Liza's hands in his. The chapel's golden light haloed them both.

"I love you, Elesbeth Ramsay," Lachlan said, using her ancient name as softly pronounced in days long past.

"And I love you, Lachlan McClaren," she whispered back, her voice steady with joy.

Marion Dean spoke the words that wove their new lives together anew, and Liza's vision blurred with tears of happiness as she and Lachlan sealed their vows with a gentle kiss. Around them, the light danced, and a gentle breeze drifted against their cheeks. Liza imagined the soft air was the blessing of ancient friends and ancestors. Those who had not come back in the flesh to meet them once more in this present day.

When, at last, they turned to face their family, friends, and countrymen, Liza felt the weight of ages lift from her shoulders.

Today marked not only the fulfillment of a prophecy, but the beginning of a new life—one she would share, forever, with the man who had waited just as long to love her properly.

THE END

Acknowledgements

Two years ago, I was lucky enough to travel to Scotland for a trip of a lifetime. During that vacation, we spent a night in Dalhousie Castle, once the seat of the Earls of Dalhousie, the chieftains of Clan Ramsay. It was a magical place amid a magical holiday, and I decided to write a novel that paid homage to not only the castle, but the other places we visited over those ten days. That story became Perils Past—the first book in the Ramsay Castle Mystery Series.

The Dalhousie Castle was kind enough to feature Perils Past in its library, and a few months after publication, I received an email from a recent visitor to the castle. That visitor shared a tale of a ghost named Margaret. Though I had been drafting Of Mistress, Friends, and Wealth at the time, the ghost of Margaret was never far from my mind, and that email became the inspiration for A Light Emerges. I'd like to offer my tremendous thanks to the Dalhousie Castle for being willing to share my stories. To Bernt-Andrew Nergård, thank you for reaching out and sharing your own experiences and those of your family members.

As always, my sincere appreciation to my family for reading and sharing my stories; for understanding when I need a writing day; for overlooking my artistic moodiness when my characters go off on a tangent I don't understand; and for sympathizing when distractions foil my passion.

To my Adam, who doesn't read but is proud of my writing nonetheless—thank you for talking about my books and for "introducing" me to the real-life Thomas MacClure, who inexplicably became crucial to the storyline of A Light Emerges. And thanks to Tom for your love of reading.

To my friends—old and new—who read every story, analyze every word, and share with your own families, friends, and connections. I wish I could list you all here and thank you all personally.

To The Plot Twist bookstore in Connellsville, Pennsylvania—I'm so glad you've opened your doors in my beloved hometown, and I am so appreciative of your support of local authors. For my Western Pennsylvania readers, go check out this charming little place!

Finally, and as always, my books would not be what they are without the care and expertise of Paul Carson at Seminal Edits who catches every error, inconsistency, and nuance in my writing, particularly those of Scottish phrases and history. Reach out to him at seminaledits@mail.com if you're in the market for an expeditious, thorough, and thoughtful partner in your writing. Likewise, to my careful proofreader who polishes the manuscript and doublechecks EVERY-THING—thank you, Sarah Michalowski. You make my writing better. Contact Sarah at sarah.editingservices@gmail.com for outstanding service.

It has been my honor to write the story of Liza and Lachlan over the past two years. While this is the final planned book in the Ramsay Castle Mystery series, perhaps we'll meet them again in a new tale at some point in the future.

In the meantime, I have some other stories to tell, and I hope you'll check them all out. Visit my website at www. sjcunningham.net or email me at sarah@sjcunningham.net.